BOOKS BY DAVIS GRUBB

Davis Grubb

THE
BAREFOOT
MAN

SIMON AND SCHUSTER · NEW YORK

First printing

SBN 671–20821–7
Library of Congress Catalog Number: 75–139624
Manufactured in the United States of America
by H. Wolff Book Mfg. Co., Inc., New York

FOR DON CONGDON
FOR NORM SCHKLOVEN
FOR SAUL
AND AGAIN FOR
MY BROTHER LOUIS

Part One

IT was through the north window that they would see the killers when they came, but Cal had long since moved his chair away from that cracked and dusty square of winter sundown and now sat by the hearth staring through the queer light at his mother. He had even put his old rifle back on the two square Wheeling nails driven into the wood above the fireplace and settled restively into the steady oval of lampshine as if the night's vigil were indeed over and the gunmen were not coming after all. Still he could smell it in the room: the fear, the scent that laced unmistakably through the smells of smoke and coal oil. He wondered shamefully if it was his own sweat which made the smell. He knew only that it was not his mother; he could smell her smell —scent of camphor and threadbare taffeta kept sweet by some sachet of wild meadow blossoms and green, secret woodland things she dried each autumn and kept in small muslin bags among her clothes at night. There was something else about Mother Dunne's smell too—perhaps the odor of hot, indomitable outrage itself—and as Cal watched and breathed in the faint whisper of it, there seemed suddenly to be some small wine of courage in the motionless, lamplit air. He was not a brave man and so his mother was a riddle to him. She seemed to move among them all untouched by that night which had brought the rest of them to their knees. She was a small woman, with high, white hair piled into a sort of pale, cold flame round the waxed oval gentility of her neat English face. Cal was proud of her. She neither smoked a pipe nor took snuff like so many of the old women in that besieged mine town. She was clean too—clean as a scrubbed morning hearthstone—and wore her ragged hand-me-down taffeta tight to her throat where it was done together with a small, neat gimcrack of a pin: fake jet and pinchbeck she had found among trash once in the Glory streets and rubbed into something of elegance. On her nose she wore small rimless spectacles, unheard-of extravagance in those parts except that a peddler had come through town one summer day bartering eyeglasses he had gotten from the two Glory undertakers, and she had traded him her dead husband's work shoes for them. Her own high shoes were cracked and dull but the buttons were intact and she kept the poor leather brushed and clean from toe to tops. Cal now marveled at her face which showed nothing of their common hunger and terror, nothing but that stunning radiance of rage and fortitude like the ambience of a hot iron stove. His soul wondered at her now, fed by something which had nothing to do with their poor provender of fried mush and boiled beans that was now their single daily meal. It was not Scripture that sustained her either, like so many of the Bible-ranting elders of that place; she was a paradox with a string of clean, ragged lace round its neck.

Cal glanced at the back of his wife who stood by the stove stirring the black iron skillet of frying mush.

I keep thinking they won't come tonight, he said. Nor tomorrow either. Half the time I'm looking out that window yonder, searching up the holler out there beyond the railroad tracks—half the time it's the organizer I'm hoping to see come whistling down that road.

Hoping, Jessie murmured. It's been six weeks now.

I know that. But I can just fairly see him coming. I wouldn't be surprised to see him now.

He struck the table.

He'll come, he cried softly. Tom Turley was in Glory after rifle

10

ammunition last night. He heard word in the Moon Cafe that they was sending the organizer this week.

Mother Dunne stopped the cadence of her rocker and looked at Cal across the lampshine.

Now listen here to me, she said. Every day you're on strike is a gift of life. No matter how lean it gets. Don't you know that? What if the company sends their sonsabitchin gunmen into town tonight! Or tomorrow, either one. Is that any danger next to what you're facing under that hill in Breedlove Number Twelve? Every shift waiting for what must surely come? That mine's like a powder keg. When the blast comes it'll be worse than Monongah. Don't you know that? I'd rather have you up here than down there no matter who they send in to break the strike!

Cal said nothing.

How long can we last? he pondered silently. Beans and cornmeal is in mighty short ration in this mine town.

He went to the window again and stood staring up the cheerless prospect of soiled earth. The dust of coal lay everywhere. It was like some residue of earth's own dark breath. It clung to tipple and grassblade, to windowpane and leafless branch of winter. It was as if the crackling winter weather had fashioned some strange frost of blackness. And yet the miners lived with it, breathing dust and danger with their air, eating it with their food, as though dust and danger were as odorless as blackdamp, and yet as sweet, oddly, as the breath of a beloved wife.

Now the old woman rocked again, setting the chair crying faintly with a prim thrust of her small, neat shoes. She turned her spare, elegant face, sniffing lightly the sour smell of mush frying in the lard.

For Christ's sake, consider it a spell, she exclaimed. Isn't it better to be facing anything above earth than that fiery hell down there? What can a man do against that? There's no gun to fight that with!

She rose suddenly and crossed the room, her spare, small figure moving like some light-footed antique doll, and fetched the rifle off the wall. With a practiced gesture she threw the safety with one hand and with the other dragged the rickety chair to the un-painted sill, stationing herself where he had been at the window. She sighed as if her hands held the implement of some household chore while Jessie served the meal.

Come on, Mother, Jessie said.

Thank you kindly, she said in a firm, clear voice. But I'm not the least bit hungry.

Again Cal wondered at her strength; she had eaten only a few bare mouthfuls those past few days. He stared, troubled, at the back of her white hair, knowing that she was really hungry, that she was saving food for them.

Getting too fat anyways, she quarreled to the dusk now deepen-ing in the hills. Anything I can't abide it's a fat old woman.

Jessie turned to Cal with the skillet.

There's no blackstrap, she said softly. We used the last drop last night. You'll have to eat your mush plain.

Fat and overfed, said Mother Dunne to the windowed reflec-tion of her face. That's a thing I purely can't abide.

She turned her head in the light the barest inch and breathed in the fear smell. Then she swallowed.

I could do with a swallow of tea, she said. Or did we use up the last of the sassafras?

Come on, Mother, Cal said, staring at her across the room's ragged patch of rug, relic of some ancient town elegance now come to tattered secondhand. Have a bite of mush. You know you're hungry.

Don't tell me what I am! scolded the old woman. Hungry! I'm too mad to be hungry!

She scanned the slope of soiled earth below the hills, the ragged road that ran seeking among them as if in escape.

As Jessie and Cal bent above the table the lamplight caught the gleam of their tin spoons; they seemed like creatures moving in a dream. And so they ate in silence broken suddenly by the faintest of sounds outside the house. Was it the wind? Mother Dunne glanced sharply at the door.

Someone's yonder, she whispered.

Cal turned from his meal and watched her rise and go to the door, the rifle steady in her hands. He knew he should have gone himself but she always seemed so in charge of things. They watched as she flipped the latch and flung the door wide. The winter cold poured among them in that reeking warmth like water round their feet. The ragged child on the stoop stared unconcernedly past the gun in the old woman's hands to the table. He made no sound, merely staring, his nose running a little, and the wind, which seemed to flow from the cold curd of moon above the hillside, blew the dark hair round his vivid, mournful face. The old woman stared an instant, then thrust the rifle against the wall with a cry and flung her arms round the boy, dragging him into the warmth.

Why, it's Bud—Tom Turley's child! she cried, hugging him to her crackling bosom. Poor lad. He's come to share a bite with us. Are they all out of grub at Tom's house, poor darling? Poor babe. Jessie, there's a little extra, isn't there? Lucky thing I wasn't the least bit hungry tonight. There, darling! Is there a smidgen more on the stove, Jessie? Cal, make a place.

Jessie rose sadly and fetched another plate. She stood by the stove an instant, looking down at the small, gray mass of beans at the bottom of the pot. She fetched up half the portion of beans and forked one of the two last bits of mush in beside it. Tom Turley's child scrambled onto the bench and set upon it ravenously.

Mother Dunne fetched up the rifle and went back to the window. She shook her head, listening as the others ate, that meal always so joyless and so brief because there was so little of it. Jessie finished first because her portion had been the least. She rose then and fetched a large lump of coal from the box by the hearth and set it carefully into the coals on the grate. The embers shone like the ghost of summer flowers, summer sunlights, the red and blue and yellow of some lost meadow wildness. Jessie stood a moment feeling that spectral warmth against her eyes and yearned for that winter's end, when she could go out for a little sun and a breath of summer air. The coal kindled quickly among the bright embers, the flames of it rising blue against the furry soot. Coal, Jessie thought. It was the one thing they had enough of in that dark village. It was their sole surfeit and yet it was a plenty that was, at the same time, cursed.

Mother Dunne leaned forward into the window.

Yonder comes Tom Turley! she cried. Now, I just hope he doesn't scold this poor, hungry child for asking.

Cal went to the door this time and stood back as the big gray-faced miner moved into the fireshine to come stand by the hearth, blowing on his cold fingers. Turley looked at his son and the empty plate. He lowered his eyes to his work boots and flushed.

I'm real sorry, Cal, he said. I've never begged. Not once. And I'm ashamed tonight to have one of mine come asking.

It's all right, Tom! cried Mother Dunne. I wasn't hungry tonight. There was extra.

The big man lifted the child from the bench and held him awkwardly a moment before setting him down by the door.

Are they coming tonight, Tom? Cal asked.

Tom Turley shook his head.

God only knows, he said. Bob Maxwell sneaked up the road a ways after sundown. On the hill. He said there was no sign of them anywheres. But that don't mean a thing.

He sighed.

There's only six guns among us in this whole town, he said. And one of them ain't much account with a busted stock. In a ways I wish they'd show themselves and get it over with. A man gets tired of waiting. Worrying.

Cal went to the window and peered out over Mother Dunne's head. The cold moon lit the land. It shone upon the rows of miners' shacks. These stood on either side of the single, dirt street, houses like the scuffed toys of some dirty child who had grown tired of their idiot repetition and left them to be swept away by time or random chance.

At sundown, he said, I seen one or two of them up on the road. There's no one there now.

He cleared a thin veil of steam from the glass with the heel of his hand and looked harder.

I wonder where they are at.

They're getting drunk, cried the old woman beneath his elbow. I know those strikebreaking scum. Is it the first time I've faced them? I've stood face to face with Mister J. P. Shaloo, the man that recruits them, too. And what sort does he hire? Ex-convicts —the scum of the cities! Murderers, bank robbers, brawlers, child molesters. I know where they're at this very minute. They're every man of them up at the scab's bar at Mexico drinking his raw hell-on-the-border and getting primed. Primed for what they wouldn't have the guts for sober.

She glared up at the shadowy, deserted road.

I hope they come tonight, she said. When the last man of you is ready to quit there'll be one old woman at this window who won't let them forget her.

Tom Turley seized his child's hand and moved toward the door. Then some afterthought gripped him and he went to sit on the stool by the crackling fireside.

If I let myself, he said presently, I'd wonder if it was all worth it, Cal. This strike is six weeks old. And no sign of the organizer. No sign of the one man who could bring us the guns and money to stick it out. Then let them call out the state troopers. We've tried hard enough to get this mine in the governor's eye. But no sign of the organizer. Six weeks. That's a long time, Cal.

Hush that talk, Tom! cried Mother Dunne. And listen to me. Sixty years. Does that seem like long enough to you? Sixty years of my eighty-two I've spent in times like these. Sixteen years of them spent here at Breedlove, with letters going out from the miners every day of the year to the governors of four administrations pleading for their lives. Sixteen years of living on top of this

15

powder keg that took the life of my own Ben back in nineteen-fourteen. I tell you the time has come to stand and fight.

Tom Turley's stomach growled and he struck it and chuckled at the folly of the sound.

I know, he said. I know, Mother Dunne. Still, it's getting awful lean. Six weeks of strike. And my boy comes asking at doors. If we hadn't taken over the company store and driven Cheeky Walker into Big Elk Creek we'd have starved long before now. And now we stand a hundred and twenty-three men and six rifles between us to fend off J. P. Shaloo's band of hired gunmen.

Tut! sniffed Mother Dunne. I've been through tighter ones than this.

I know you have, Mother, said the big man, suddenly ashamed of his fears.

She sleeved steam from the window again, peering out, her pale-blue eyes bright behind the glasses.

There's a shadow on the road, she said. Above that big locust beyond the tipple. I thought it moved.

It's only a shadow, Tom said. Bob was up there not an hour ago—just before the sun slid down behind the hill. He said he seen a wagon on the road. But he was wrong.

How do you know?

I looked myself, Turley said. Just before I knocked at your door. The road's bright lit by moon. There was no one.

Maybe it's the organizer, Cal said hopefully. With a wagon full of food and guns.

He'd never get past that army, Turley sighed.

But there's no sign of them on the hill, Cal said. I tell you, it's strange.

Mother Dunne squinted harder at the pane and struck her fingers on the sill.

Come looky, Cal! she cried. I swear my old eyes make out the shape of a horse and wagon a way ways up yonder. Up beyond the locust. Beyond the foreman's house. Come look, Cal.

He went and squatted by her side by the sill and put his eye to the place she had rubbed on the steamy pane. He sighed and shook his head.

I don't see nothing.

She struck the wood again smartly.

Sure, I tell you! she cried. A horse and wagon with two people setting atop it. I'll swear to it!

I see what you see, Cal said. It looks some like that. But it's the moon. It's the shadows under the foreman's house. The wind and shadows. I tell you it's only moonshine, Mother.

Jessie cradled her breasts in her folded arms and stared at them. She laughed cheerlessly.

Maybe it's the barefoot man, she said.

It was like another cloud among them—the mention of that phrase.

The barefoot man, Jessie said again. Though I don't reckon even he'd much want to fill our shoes.

Suddenly Cal, crouched still by the old woman's side at the window, moved closer, rubbing a larger place on the steamy pane and pressing his face to the glass.

Mother, you're right! he cried. It *is* a wagon. With two people atop it.

He stood and turned a worried look at Tom Turley who had come to stand by his side, rubbing the glass and peering out at the hillside.

Do you reckon it could be the organizer, Tom?

The big man grunted and shook his head.

Not likely. There's two of them.

Maybe they sent two, Tom, Cal cried. Two organizers!

Not this pair, Cal.

How can you be sure?

Tom Turley sighed.

Because one of them's a woman, he said.

Farjeon, from the wagon seat beside his wife, stared round at the moonlit valley, the mine town and the ugly upthrust of tipple reared above the blue-shadowed slag heap as if he had come upon some new kind of hell. He reined in the tired brown mare and slipped out of his shabby overcoat, laying it round his wife's shoulders against the chill of the winter's night. She wore a coat of her own but it was thin enough to show the shape of her shoulder blades. Far off among the leafless trees to the north an owl cried softly. It was like some vague warning that the place they had come to had no room for them, even that it held for them some unshaped menace.

It's a mine town, Farjeon said. It don't look like much of a place to beg supper.

We've got the money, said Farjeon's wife. It ain't like we was beggars.

He turned a tired, stern look upon her. Then he patted her fingers with one hand on her knee and pressed the fingers of his other hand against the small lump sewn deep within his clothes.

This money, he said. It's the last of it. I told you about that. It's the last of everything. It's the one thing we held out on them—this and the horse and wagon. They've taken everything else, Jean. If they could have, they'd have taken us from each other and sold us for our old clothes. We can't spend a cent of this here two hundred dollars. Not with him almost here.

The woman Jean touched her big belly lightly under the heavy drape of the two coats. It was a gesture like Farjeon's own when he had touched the feel of the money. She nodded. Her face grew solemn considering these two hidden treasures: the creature in her belly, the money sewn into Farjeon's underwear with careful stitches of the last of her thread. They were miracles alike: something of the future hidden beneath the shabby cloth of both of them.

I ain't really hungry, she said.

He turned his great, level eyes on her again—the smallness of her in the hugeness of his threadbare greatcoat. His eyes seemed almost frightened at the love he felt for her. They had tried so many years to have a baby. He kept thinking he should have carried her back in the wagon, packed in cotton like the frail, yellow cream pitcher she held carefully in her hands, between her knees.

Not hungry? he said softly. Sure you are, honey. It's me that ain't hungry. Besides. What about that small chap in there? What about him being hungry? Don't you reckon folks feels hungry before they're born? Jean, you've not had a bite since two nights past at that woman's house at Hannibal Station. You need food, dear love. Your time is nigh here.

He searched her tired, pretty face like the contours of some beloved landscape. That face was lifted, slightly tilted to the moonshine, shadowed beneath the stiff felt brim of the old man's hat she wore. So that he could not see her eyes. He lifted the hat from her hair and held it a spell to see her whole face plainly lit by moon, her cornflower blue eyes—clear and not opaque like those of most blind people—eyes that had never seen him but that knew him better than if they had. He thought to himself as he leaned his face close in the cold, thin air to kiss her blue lips that if it came to it he would find a knife of some sort and carve off some flesh of his own to feed her.

It's me that ain't hungry, he said again. Not the least small bit. But I'll swear, every time this wagon slowed down for the past five hours I've heard that baby's stomach growl.

She touched his face with her thin fingers; they fluttered like a kind of laughter.

That's your fancy, Jack, she said. How could you hear such a thing through all these here clothes?

His hands tightened on the reins. Again something in the scene below made him hesitate. Farmer bred and born he had an innate mistrust of the very notion of begging. Still it was more than this. As the wagon drew closer down the steep, random road he had the curious sense that he had come upon this desolate scene once before, perhaps in another life, and met with dire misfortune there. Something in him wanted to lift a hand into the moonlight and pull away the veil. It was like a sort of shroud—that everlasting, everywhere presence of coal and smoke. It lay like a thin film upon the picture of the village. It was an obscurement alien to his eyes, so used to the flowering bright plateau of the green Canaan valley where his hands had never taken anything from the earth but its ripe surface provenders. There seemed something obscurely threatening to the veil of smoke, the smell of burning in the air.

We can spare enough of this grubstake for your supper, he said suddenly. If we can find a place in this here town that sells eats.

The horse picked its way down the canyons of the rutted, frozen road, the rickety buckboard jostling along behind. There was nothing in the wagon bed. They had salvaged little from the debacle of foreclosure. In the woman's lap, between her knees, beneath the cloaked heaviness, she held the yellow cream pitcher. In a scratched wood box by her feet she had brought away the bright steel parts of her sewing machine. Even with the machine gone at auction it had seemed important to her to save these useless things. They had seemed to her like bright keys to something, some mystery that lay ahead. This handful of uselessness—these and the mare and the wagon—had been their only survivals of the old life. The wagon had been hidden in the woods below the barn the morning before the auctioneers came. Otherwise they would have been set out to walk the winter roads. Farjeon had seen many on the country roads of those lean, cold times who had fallen into such misfortune. He smiled, setting his jaw against the raw hunger which beset him. He forced his mind to busy itself with those twin miracles: the child within his wife, the wad of bills she had sewn into his underwear which would pay for the child's birth. It frightened Farjeon to think of how much that child's birth meant to him. It was almost as great as his helpless adoration of Jean herself. The twin miracles. Beyond them there seemed to stretch a void, a country vague as the village into which they now moved in the wagon's unsteady progression. The sense of shadow deepened as they passed up from the road by the creek, past the town's common pump, and turned up what seemed to be the sole street between the rows of miners' shacks. These rose in slipshod drabness against the bleak, almost treeless hillside. A lean gray dog ran out barking at them, then stopped suddenly and sniffed the air in slow, thrusting gestures as if sounding the dusty air for some scrap of food. The woman's fingers stole to his hand; it was as if she, too, shared it—the feeling that they were being watched, the unshaped sense of danger.

Farjeon heard the bullet sing by high above his head before he heard the echoing chatter of the shot itself. He turned his face, laying his hand tight on the woman's shoulder, and stared almost unconcernedly up between the houses toward the clump of laurels on the coal-strewn hillside. The blue smoke curled low on the worn, moonlit soil.

Get down slow.

Farjeon almost laughed, because the voice had been a woman's voice and an old woman at that. The voice had echoed in such a way as to seem to come from another direction. Farjeon hesitated, watching the gunsmoke wear slowly away in the motionless, moonlit air. He waited on for the voice again, not feeling surprised somehow at the shot or the voice of warning itself. The only fear he felt was for Jean. It seemed risky to wait for the voice again so he jumped down into the frozen, coal-strewn ruts of the street and reached back for Jean's fingers.

Easy, dear love. It'll be all right, he whispered.

The old woman with the three men behind her came down the sparse grass with the rifle in her hands. Farjeon again had that welling sense of laughter deep within him. The moonlight blazed in her great waves of white hair, it caught glinting on the small, rimless spectacles on her nose. She might have been a loving, fussy grandmother come to ask about Jean's condition.

Who are you?

Farjeon opened his mouth, then closed it. He waited a spell, measuring the spirit and intention of the old woman. Again he sensed that feeling of doom, of something foreplanned, the very spirit and presence of the place, the warning that he had sensed on the road back there.

One of the men—a thin, hatless fellow with sandy hair—came to the old woman's side and tried to take the gun. With a grunt she shook off his hand. The thin man left her and came forward a few paces. He tilted his head, his eyes searching Farjeon hopefully.

You ain't the organizer, are you?

Farjeon shook his head miserably and wondered again how a man begins when he must beg. All the stubborn farmer's pride in him flinched at the approach of that instant. Then he thought again of the child inside his wife and of the tiny pouch sewn into his underwear.

We'd be mighty beholden, he said, if one of your women could spare a little supper.

The words came forced and thick from Farjeon's breast, he seemed to hear himself speaking at a distance; he dreaded this act of asking more, in some curious way, than the threat of the rifle in the hands of the elegant old lady.

Some supper, he said again. For her yonder in the wagon.

One of the men made a humorless chuckle.

It ain't for me, Farjeon went on numbly. It's for her.

The woman in the wagon lifted her face to the moonlight, the big hat brim shadowing her sightless eyes.

I can do without, she said. Honest, Jack. Maybe if I could just have a drink of water.

Aside from a sudden faint light-headedness Farjeon seemed hardly aware of his own hunger. He saw the faces of other miners come to gather behind the old woman and the three. He saw obscurely the faces of women and children at the small windows of the shacks beyond the streetside; they moved like dusty moths against the ruddy stain of lampshine. Some clock inside his belly made Farjeon think that at this hour of winter's evening the air should have come sweetly alive with the smells of bacon frying and coffee in the pot. But there was nothing here but the smell of burning coal, laced with the faint reek of coal oil. And the smell, too, of something else, that Farjeon knew was the smell of fear. He hoped his wife had not smelled it, sensed it too.

How did you get through? said the old woman in a low voice.

Farjeon considered.

We just come—that's all.

Mister, that whole hillside is alive with strikebreakers—hired gunmen of J. P. Shaloo. They've got sworn orders to shoot the organizer on sight.

The thin man searched Farjeon's face again hopefully.

You sure you ain't the organizer? he said in a high voice.

'Course he's not, Cal! cried the old woman. Any fool can see that. He's a wanderer—that's all. No organizer would come toting a woman along with him. Lord, Cal, use your wits.

Farjeon fancied he heard the growl again, faint and sorrowful beneath Jean's heavy coats.

He gestured awkwardly toward the fullness that hung there above the cream pitcher in her hands, between her knees.

Her time, he said, is nigh come. If you could spare a smidgen of something—

Mister, I don't know how you got that woman and horse and wagon down that hillside of gunmen into Breedlove. My hat's off to you, said the thin man. If you're that lucky maybe you're bringing a little of your luck here to share. We could sure as hell use it.

He cocked his head, his face washed in moonlight.

Mister, you sure you don't know where you're at?

Farjeon smiled when he shook his head. The shake of his head was part in reply, part to ward off his light-headedness. He considered to himself how ridiculous, perhaps how dangerous it might be if he should faint just now.

The old woman shouldered past the thin man, gesturing toward the hill, toward the road they had just come down.

You're at Breedlove Number Twelve, she cried. This mine's in the sixth week of a strike. We've been waiting a month for the organizer.

She glared, still gesturing toward the road.

Three organizers have died on that road you just come down. One of them was shot two nights ago—right up there past that big dead locust.

The thin man cocked his head and stared at Farjeon and his woman with gathering amazement.

How *did* you get through?

I'll tell you how! cried the old woman. They're not there is why! I already told you that. They're over the hill at the scab's bar at Mexico right now—every damned bastard one of them—getting drunk for the night's orneriness. That's why this stranger and his woman got through. That's why they ain't up yonder! Shaloo and the whole sonsabitchin, ornery, murdering lot of them. Getting drunk and storing up bloodshed to set upon us once the moon goes down.

Farjeon's big fingers stole to his jacket and pressed the tight cloth, feeling for the faint, small treasure hidden beneath his shirt.

We can pay, he said. It's just for her yonder. I've got a little. We can pay. She ain't had a bite now in nearly two whole days.

Mister, you come to a mighty poor patch for a handout, said the thin man.

Tut now, Cal! cried the old woman. Where's your mercy? Jessie's got more mush in the stone crock. There's a handful of beans left in the pot. Tut, now! It would sour our luck to turn away these two—and her with her time nigh come! Come along! Up to the house with me! Jessie! Jessie!

Farjeon followed her up the ragged path to the porch. He held Jean's hand close, dragging her in his wake, feeling somehow the shame in her fingers, the sense that they had actually come to this, to begging in the roads.

Jessie stood in the doorway and watched them come. She frowned as she searched the shapes of Farjeon and the woman;

24

they were strangers and they looked to have come from too-recent prosperity to be begging from this little she had saved for her family. Farjeon met her gaze on the threshold and smiled wanly.

He led Jean round him, helping her up the stoop with anxious, careful hands.

Her time—he began again.

I know that, Jessie said. She's nigh due. I can see. Come on in. I'll fix something.

Jessie went to the window by the stove, shaking her head and sighing. Farjeon and his woman stood awkwardly by the door.

Go yonder and set, Cal said, motioning to the table. Jessie'll fix you something in a jiffy.

Farjeon went slowly and sat at the table, his eyes lowered, his face faintly colored by his embarrassment at having to ask. Jean had found her way to the far end of the bench, facing a little away to one side, because her greatness would not fit against the table. Farjeon bit his lip, then his hands busied with his buttons; his fingers groped inside the chest of his brushed, frayed jacket, into the blue shirt front, and tugged at last at his underwear, till in the stillness they heard the faint rip of cloth. Jessie, at the gusty window, fetched in the stone jar from the cold box outside the sill and went to the stove with it. She took out the oblong shape of the mush and cut into it thinly with the knife, then sighed, frowning, and moved the knife back, cutting thicker slices. Farjeon at last laid the small muslin tobacco sack on the lamplit tabletop; his fingers undid it and slowly withdrew the wad of green bills tied with a length of Jean's last red yarn. He let his hand fondle it a moment, then laughed.

I told you we could pay, he said.

Mother Dunne snorted from her place at the window once more.

Pay nothing, she said. Money's no good in this cursed place. Besides, we're glad to help out.

Cal came to the table to stand and stare at the money; he shook his head. Presently he stole a glance at Farjeon's face.

25

Can I look at it? he said.

It's good.

I know that, Cal said. It's not that.

He sighed and gave a queer chuckle.

You won't believe this, he said awkwardly. But it's been a long while since I've seen green money. They pay us in scrip here. When they pay. Scrip for everything. Scrip for rent, for food, for carbide. Scrip to birth a baby. They even take scrip to bury you. That is, if you ain't buried already.

He swallowed and searched Farjeon's face again.

Could I see it?

Farjeon handed him the roll.

Can I untie it? I mean, see one of them plain?

Farjeon nodded.

Cal undid the yarn and peeled off one of the bills. He laid it crinkling on the table, pressing it flat with his rough, blackened fingers, spreading it as if it were some fragrant, pressed flower flat on the bare wood, in the quivering circle of lampshine.

'y God, he sighed. Hello there, pretty green thing. It's been a while!

Jean sat smiling faintly, her face tilted in the lampshine. The blue of the cold was gone from her lips, her cheeks shone with the flush of her pregnancy. Jessie set the plate before her, setting a fork into her fingers, guiding her other hand to the edge of the platter. Then she fetched Farjeon his share of the mush and beans.

Cal sat across, watching as they ate.

Jessie she thought you was the organizer, he said after a bit. Jessie was sure.

Jessie found a teacup with no handle and poured Farjeon's woman a little hot sassafras tea.

No, I never, she said. I never thought it was the organizer.

She shook her head angrily.

I've give up looking for him long since, she said.

Her dark lashes glittered suddenly with tears and she hurried to stand with folded arms by the old woman, peering out the steamy window into the cold, smoky moonshine of the night-strewn hill.

The barefoot man, she said to the stillness.

Cal laughed.

That's right, he said. It was me thought you was the organizer. Jessie yonder—she thought you was the barefoot man.

Farjeon had finished; he sat red-faced, ashamed of himself for eating everything so quickly. He cast a sidelong look at Jean who sipped her hot tea, breathing in its fragrance, her food hardly touched. His heart melted at her, knowing how proud she was, knowing that she was holding back because she reckoned he might be ashamed of her.

You ain't eating nothing, dear love, he said.

The woman shook her head quickly above the steam of the tea-cup.

I told you I wasn't real hungry, she said.

That damned barefoot man, said Cal's wife in a choked voice from the window. He'll be here soon enough. He'll be adding his share to all the other troubles we got. Soon enough. That damned barefoot man.

Farjeon felt better, even after the little he had had to eat. He took his gaze from Jean and looked at Cal.

Who is the barefoot man? he said.

Cal laughed and stared at his empty, blackened fingers.

He's a ghost, mister, he said. A haunt, a shadow, a kind of shade that hangs over towns like this.

Farjeon waited. Cal raised his dark eyes to him and shrugged.

Whenever a miner like me tells the company he's gonna strike for more pay, the boss says: "Okay. Go ahead and quit. And when you do, there'll be a barefoot man waiting at the drift mouth to take your place."

Cal thought about it, smiling, and shook his head.

The barefoot man, he said. That damned barefoot man. He's something a miner fears nigh as much as the deputies and strike-breakers. He's a sort of scab, d'ye see? The barefoot man.

He laughed.

That's who Jessie thought you was, he said. That damned bare-foot man. Jessie, the stranger's plate is empty. Is there a speck more in the skillet?

Farjeon flushed and shook his head.

Thank you, kindly, mister, he said. That was more than my share.

Ain't you still hungry? Cal said.

Farjeon shook his head, lying; he could have eaten all night and not filled himself; his mind was busy even now with visions of the tables Jean had used to spread in the old times. He glanced at the roll of money on the table, the greenback still spread out beside it.

I'd be obliged, he said, if you'd take out what you think it was worth.

Cal waved his hand.

It's nothing, he said. I couldn't take your money for a plate of mush and beans and a cup of tea.

I'd feel better if you did, Farjeon said.

Cal sighed.

Besides, money ain't worth much in this town, he said.

He sat down on the bench beside Farjeon and laid his finger on the big man's sleeve.

You're a farmer, ain't that so? he said.

That's so.

And you lost your place, Cal went on. Or maybe you was burned out. With nothing left.

Farjeon nodded and glanced thankfully at his wife who had finished everything on her plate.

Nothing left, he said. But what you see on our backs. And that horse and wagon outside.

In one way, Cal said, you're as bad off as us. In another way you're worse off.

How so?

Because you've ended up in just about the unhealthiest town in

28

West Virginia this cold winter's night. It's bad enough being poor and out of luck—it's something else sitting here waiting for a pack of hired gunmen to come down the road with rifles ablazing. Maybe tonight's the night. We're counting on trouble before the sun comes up tomorrow.

Mother Dunne stirred in her chair by the window.

I'll give them trouble, she murmured, and rapped the gun barrel lightly on the sill.

What I'm getting at is this, Cal went on gently. You come here asking for a meal. The next thing—maybe you haven't even thought of it yet—the next thing you'll be asking is can you spend the night here. It's bitter cold out tonight. I know that. Where else can you go? Your missus being nigh ready and all that. Maybe she'll be having her chap tonight.

In a week, Farjeon said. The doc he said a week.

Here's what I'm getting at, Cal said with a sad smile. As far as my missus and me is concerned you could curl up yonder in your clothes, yonder by the fire. Ain't that so, Jessie?

Jessie glanced at them quickly, then looked away.

Sure, she said.

Farjeon lowered his face. He had been so hungry that the hunger had somehow kept his mind off thoughts of shelter for the night. He had worried about it a good deal before they set out but on the road the hunger had kept coming in between. It was the second of a world of problems, a skyful of threatening miseries. He might as well have stopped the wagon and gone over to sit down by the roadside to figure out where he was going to get work at whatever place they were going toward. Farjeon was a man who could worry about only one thing at a time.

I figured, he said, we'd find a little holler—some place hid between the hills—some shelter from the wind where I could keep a fire going. I figured we could sleep in our coats. Mine's thick enough to keep her warm anyways.

Cal nodded suddenly.

You'd be better off there, he said. You might be cold and lonesome but at least you'd be safe—a lot safer than you are here.

He laid his finger again along Farjeon's sleeve.

Mind me now, he said. It's not that we're trying to get shut of you. You're welcome to the floor by the fireside, like I told you.

He glanced uneasily toward Mother Dunne at the window, he glimpsed the winter night that spread beyond it, moon-bathed and still.

Lord knows what this night holds for us, Cal said.

Farjeon nodded wearily and looked at Jean who sat waiting, listening, ready to go with him wherever he took her. He felt the great tenderness in his heart again, like a burden of sweetness. He would have carried her on his back anywhere, any distance where there was a place in the world for them.

So if I was you, Cal said, I'd gather up that sweet little lady yonder and take her out to the wagon. Then I'd head the horse up that road that goes on through town and up the other side of the valley.

Some sound, faint and obscure as a far flight of birds, broke the stillness among them. In a twinkling Mother Dunne rose, with the gun in her fists, and ran to the table. She cupped her small hand to the smoking lamp chimney and blew out the flame. The darkness sprang among them instantly but so did the moon. The fire of coals on the grate had dwindled to a ruddy glow but the moon-shine poured through the twin windows of that room like soft, blue milk, spilling silently across the rough planks of the floor and lighting the tip of Farjeon's shoe.

It's too late for that! whispered the old woman hoarsely.

What, Mother?

It's too late for that! cried the old woman softly and stole swiftly back to the window. Too late to take that road or any other road out of this damned place!

Cal ran to her side at the window, crouching back against the wall, afraid to look.

What do you mean, Mother?

They're on the road now is what I mean! she cried. See them

yonder. Ten of them if there's a one. See yonder—where we first seen the stranger's wagon! Up yonder above the dead tree, beyond the foreman's house.

Where? whispered Cal, in a perfect nausea of dread, not yet daring to put his head around the corner of the window frame.

There! cried the old woman. There! Yonder on the road and gathering like rats around a crippled bird. There, yonder! Waiting till the moon goes down before they strike us where we sit!

The part of Breedlove called Mexico by the miners lay over the rise of the hill above which the great winter moon now hovered, poised for its disappearance. Mexico was a squalid smattering of makeshift huts and one larger, more solid building even more desolate and dingy than the mine town itself. There was considerable and periodic scab labor at Numbers Ten and Eleven mines, and this was where the scabs themselves dwelt, outcast and even poorer than the miners were. They were Negro mostly, people who lived somehow on the company promise of better times, times when the miners would be driven from their jobs and hovels and they would take over. It was they who worked the pit at Number Ten now, with an occasional casualty at the hands of some bitter striker, and the dim light of hope in the yellow whites of their eyes that fortune would favor them when the strike was done.

In the large, unpainted structure by the edge of the muddy, weed-strewn road was a cramped room with a bar and a scattering of rough chairs and tables. This was a speakeasy run by a big, thick-wristed Negro man named Toby, a darling of the mineowners, who ran the place with a store of cheap, unlicensed liquor stilled in the hills downriver from Glory. Except in these strike times it was a prospering business, bringing many of the Breedlove miners over the hill and down the road to Mexico to find some moment of dreams in the solace of company moonshine.

Toby had been gloomy all the day before but tonight a fake glare of prosperity seemed to shed its light in the place like the smoking, yellow glow of the single, brass-bellied oil lamp which hung from a chain above the crude bar, glinting on the sparse provision of glassware like glowing slag fires. Even in times of poor business Toby was thankful enough, for Mexico had meant a sharp improvement in his fortunes. Toby was a convict—a man serving life for wife murder—from the Glory prison, loaned into trusty status by the offices of a state administration generous to the mine owners. Tonight Toby was host to important men—not the managers themselves but men from downstate hired and deputized under the name of "industrial relations adjusters."

The fat man who seemed in custody of the twenty hangdog riffraff who crowded now around Toby's bar threw down a new ten-dollar bill and slapped it with the flat of his hand.

What's your name, nigger? he cried in a voice pitched high for a big man.

Toby, sir.

Well, there's green money for you, Toby, and not any of your damned mine scrip! Drinks all round!

Toby stared at the diamond that glittered among the creases of the hand's thick, hairless fingers and wondered if it was real. He turned to seek among his dusty shelves for twenty shot glasses, polishing them swiftly one by one as he set them out on the naked, unpolished bar wood.

Drink up, boys! cried the fat man lifting his own glass so that it glistened in the light. There's more where this came from.

The way Mr. J. P. Shaloo was dressed made him seem, in that rundown region, like a visitor from another world. There was an almost unearthly elegance about his tailored, box-backed overcoat, the mouse-colored fedora, the polished shoe tips beneath pearl-gray spats which had caused him to pick his way almost daintily off the running board of the black Studebaker now parked out front between the two tarpaulin-covered trucks in which the men had traveled all the way from South Wheeling, lifting his polished shoes mincingly through the coal-strewn, hard-frozen ruts to the doorway of Toby's bar.

That had been an hour ago and they were still drinking, the fat man still paying, his small, thickset eyes weighing and judging the look and sound and smell of them until he reckoned they were ready for the night's neat business; drinking until the air was thick with the mingled smell of raw liquor and sweating, unwashed poverty till the man in the old army coat could stand it no more, the one man among them who had not drunk, and yet he was suddenly sick and pressing his way through the shoulders and legs of them toward the door to lean at last into the threshold, gulping in the smoky air as if it were cold water to staunch some sickness within him. He stepped out then into the blessing cold and sat on the rough plank of the stoop, swallowing hard against the nausea which strove within him and wondering if he could go through with it. It was an odd, sudden change of emotion. He remembered how fired he had been with opportunity that morning when the man had stopped him at Eighteenth and Chaplaine and told him that Shaloo was hiring and asked him if he wanted the job. Cotter wondered if it was his hunger and misery that had made him sign or the shape of some hatred, deep as a mine, within the brain of him. When the gray-eyed, faceless recruiter had said the job was to settle the trouble at another mine, all that Cotter could think of was that hatred, all he could see was his father's blackened face coming in the doorway from the deadman's shift, facing his quaking family like a man ready to settle all accounts with a mortal enemy. It would seem that such a toilsome life of heartache and sore muscles would have drained all the hatred from a man, but Cotter's father had used to come in the doorway renewed, refreshed as it were by his own wrath and thwarting outrage, his muscles untaxed from thirteen hours under the Benwood hill, his fists unused and newborn it would seem and yearning only to strike out at his wife and eight children. Cotter was the only one among them who had all of his father's temper like a bed of banked coals waiting to be fired into roaring flame by a spill of brandy. He was afraid to drink and yet he had to, he must, somehow, to keep his place in the world, to keep accounts even with

33

people. He had to do that to keep from being like his father, and yet whiskey did that him—made him bestial and hate-possessed, the very image of the man he so despised.

He stared now at the mournful landscape of that place, his eyes searching into that dusk of moonlight for something to break the unrelieved sorrowfulness of that place. He saw the sharp rise of the abused hill and the rough road which dipped across it, feeling deep within him the hated desolation of the mine town beyond it, the place they would soon all be riding toward in the trucks.

Maybe I'd better drink, he thought.

Because he knew that only when he drank could he do the job he had often done for Shaloo before. He was that sort of expert, the kind of man Shaloo chose to lead his masses. If Shaloo was their invisible general, the great, swollen strategist moving bloody pins back and forth across the ragged, ravaged map of those industrial times, Cotter was his trusted sergeant. In three years of depression he had led men to break strikes in a dozen towns—in steel, in mines, in auto parts, at Akron's smoky rubber plants—and always he had somehow rallied and wedded the mismatched, purposeless derelicts behind him into something of an army. They fed somehow, inspired, upon his savagery; he seemed to bespeak something unspoken of their own lives' inchoate outrage. But this regimental magic occurred only when Cotter was sufficiently drunk, drunk enough to be like his father, enough to hate the laboring men so like his father—just drunk enough, never helpless or without the wits to be effectively brutal, just enough liquor, like a splash of coal oil across the ashes of some cold, sad fire, secret and full of radiant embers, some burning child hidden under his breast, deep under the cheap, swap-shop jacket he wore beneath the old army coat which was for him something of a trademark to those who saw him and felt him and sometimes died under him but who in any event would not be allowed to forget, even in death, the awfulness of his passion. Unlike most of the flophouse men Shaloo had recruited for his jobs, Cotter had never served a day in prison. On the contrary, except for the moral lawlessness of

34

his work, he was a paragon of social propriety: a staunch believer in the heavy-browed Mosaic God, disciple of all that was law and the iron order of things treasured most by the corporate management of those times, their hired police and the favor of sold-out federal judges.

Cotter got up from the cold speakeasy stoop, brushing the grit of black dust from his army coat.

Maybe I better drink, he thought. I know what I have to do down there. It's going to be like it always is. Maybe I better get ready for it.

He glimpsed a young Negro woman, some scab's wife, traipsing footsore and limping in huge, broken men's shoes up the rocky road toward the orange gleam of a lantern hung in a broken window of one of the sordid shacks up a piece. Her thin hands upheld the fullness of her incredibly great belly, so pregnant that she seemed to follow her belly's lead as if it were part of her that went ahead to sound the way, holding it as she went as if keeping it away from the soiled, worn earth, as if lifting it away from the earth's ancient tug toward the grave. It made Cotter think of his mother until mad tears sprang to his eyes. He thought how he hated his mother, too, but it was a different side of that spurious coin with which his life had paid him. He hated his mother for her weakness exactly as he hated his father for his strength. Cotter was compelled to become like his father, much as he despised him, lest he be like his equally contemptible mother.

He leaned against the rough oaken frame of the speakeasy door listening to Shaloo's voice back in there, a tone rich with Rotarian joviality droning amid the men at the bar. Cotter tried to stop thinking of his mother; he could never picture her when she was there to be needed, he could not conjure any image of her other than when she was gravid with child, her small eyes red with nausea, her voice a perpetual fountain of complaint. She was eternally full of the child to come: her belly was like some great bill that could never be paid, swelled with the new child who would be another unbidden noise to scar further whatever moments of impoverished stillness were yet left to them. Cotter listened to the men drinking back in the bar. He knew suddenly that if he were drunk just now, just drunk enough, he would have gone deliberately out into the street and struck the Negro woman across the belly, even though she was a scab's wife and therefore not the Enemy. He knew that in a moment he was going to go back to the big nigger's bar and do what he had to do. To be ready. To be sane. He was like a man who is born reeling with the dire drunkenness of soul's disenchantment who must get drunk, just drunk enough, in order to be sober.

Shaloo treated him always with a kind of aloof deference that was not quite fellowship and yet was full of tone and gestures a notch above the way he treated the other men. There was something almost avuncular about the way he now came up behind Cotter, sweating and bright-eyed the way he always got before his final rabble-rousing send-off, and laid the great jeweled hand on Cotter's shoulder. His voice was low and yet not familiar: the general addressing his sergeant.

Cotter, you ain't drinking, said the fat man.

I know, Cotter said. In a minute. It takes me a while. I have to get in the mood for the whole business. First I have to be alone a spell—I've got to think of what has to be done and why it's important to do it. Then I go hang a little one on. That sort of sets everything right in my head.

You're a good man, Cotter, Shaloo said. You've never let me down.

His fat hand fluttered to some inner pocket, his fingers poised on the tips of the fine panatelas hidden there—good smokes, fifty-cent smokes like the one he chewed in his gold-strewn teeth right now. The big hand paused—the familiarity might be dangerous—then chose one and drew it out, proffering it to Cotter.

Thanks, Mister Shaloo. I don't smoke.

Then come have a drink. Have a few drinks, the way you always do before a job.

Cotter stared at the big stogie in Shaloo's teeth; he wondered if

36

the drinks he planned having would make him mind any less the smell of stogie smoke.

My old pap, he said, he used to fill our house with stogie smoke. I never smoke. Maybe that's the reason. I think I will have that drink, Mister Shaloo. It always sets my mind just right.

By God, I know it does, Shaloo said. I've seen you work. I don't have to watch your drinking like I do the rest of those men in there. You notice I'm buying. I never pay them before a job. That's part of my business. Knowing just how much drink improves a man's efficiency. You're different, Cotter. I'd lock you in a room at a table with an open bottle on it. I always know just how much you're gonna drink. To get your mind set right about a job. Ain't that right now, Cotter?

That's right, Mister Shaloo. I don't think I've ever been drunk in my life.

Don't I know it, Cotter, said the fat man. That's why I trust you—made you a noble. This is an important job tonight, Cotter. And a lot more work depends on it.

He shut one wet eye and leaned forward, his breath heavy with drink and cigar and a hint of garlic from his rich supper.

You understand tonight's business, he said. It's strikebreaking and it isn't, Cotter. Do you follow me?

How do you mean, Mister Shaloo?

The fat man grunted and shot his cuffs, the starched, immaculate cloth rustling round his wrists.

Repeat what I'm about to say and I'll deny it, Cotter, he said smiling. I'll deny it on ten Bibles.

All right, Mister Shaloo.

The size of it is this, Cotter, said the fat man. We want to do a job tonight—but not too good. D'ye see? Plenty of bruised heads —maybe a couple of deaths. But we don't want to break the strike. Not yet.

I reckon I understand, Mister Shaloo.

Sure you do, said the fat man, seizing Cotter's sleeve and drawing him back into the crowd round the bar. We don't want to break the strike. Not yet. Not tonight. We want the trouble to last just long enough to get our fair share of business out of it. A while longer. That's enterprise. Well, it's American, ain't it? Some fellers in my line of work end things up too quick. Instead of milking it for all it's worth. That's why I'm top man in this line. When they want to break penny-ante strikes they send for Acme Industrial or that damned Hal Merrill agency. When they want to break steel or coal or auto they send for Jim Shaloo. It's all a matter of instinct. And judgment. And both of them tell me that we can get a coupla more weeks out of this contract if we play it right. Mess 'em up a little. Make it good. A coupla deaths. No more than that. Satisfying to the client. But we don't want to end it. Not yet.

Shaloo nodded on his words, his red, genial face wreathed in stogie smoke, as the two of them pressed through the throng toward the bar. Now he shook a pudgy forefinger under Cotter's nose.

Repeat that, Cotter, he said, and I'll deny it on ten Bibles. But you know from past experience it's the only way I do things. It's enterprise. It's American. There's no sense killing the goose that lays the golden eggs.

I understand, Mister Shaloo.

Then drink to it, cried the fat man, seizing a Mason jar of white liquor and a glass and setting them ringing on the bar by Cotter's hand. Drink up and get your mind right about things.

The whey-faced derelict who pressed between them, seized the fat man's sleeve.

How about me, boss? he said. I drank up them three drinks you stood us and now I'm dry as a bone.

Shaloo shook his sleeve loose, he brushed the cloth where the man's gray fingers had been.

You had enough, he said.

I sure could use me another one, mister.

I said you had plenty. Go wait yonder with the others.

A man gets nervous as a cat before work like this, whined the man, his lips working round his toothless gums.

He put his hand on Shaloo's sleeve again.

Maybe just a little one? he whispered.

I told you no, said the fat man softly, pulling his arm free. I know how much liquor a man needs for a job like this. You were with me at Youngstown last year, weren't you? At the Allied Auto Parts strike?

Yes sir.

Well, you remember then, said Shaloo. I give you boys just enough booze to put a little lead in your pencil. That's my business. That's why I don't pay you a cent of money till the job's done. I don't want any drunken massacres like we had on that East Liverpool railroad shop contract. That wasn't my fault neither. The boys busted into a speakeasy. It broke the strike that same night. Cost me a month—maybe six weeks'—more business.

The gray, dry tongue slipped like a mouse through the glistening, toothless gums and licked dry lips. The old man shrugged and smiled.

Yes sir.

Shaloo slapped his stooped, ragged shoulder and gave him a nudge with his jeweled finger.

First the drinks, he said. Then comes Uncle Jim's pep talk. Remember? Go yonder with the other boys and wait. The party's not over yet.

In the interim Cotter had downed five stiff drinks. The liquor seeped now through the cold ashes of his spirit, drew slowly closer to the flame and the reason. Turning his head, he caught sight of Shaloo's fat paunch. It made him think of the pregnant woman on the road. He seized the glass jar of raw whiskey and poured another level glassful, downed it without breathing. Something flickered and kindled within him and the sound of Shaloo's voice now addressing his troops could not quench his mind's image of his father's face, black and maddened and looming through the stifling doorway of his childhood. He was almost sane now. Almost ready to face that night's righteous business. He thought of the glistening Springfield rifles, stacked in the back of the two

39

trucks now waiting yonder in the night. Cotter felt the sweet, fresh sanity flow from his mind clean to his fingertips; his hands grew warm again, alive again, he curled his forefinger and it dreamed of the trigger's sweet pressure.

An ancient upright piano stood by the doorway. Agile, in the manner of some fat people, Shaloo had clambered to the top of it and stood there now, his figure bent a little, his jovial, sweating face smiling down benevolently at the applauding men, his outspread fingers gesturing to still them. Cotter stared at the clear liquor in the glass and felt again all the strength of his childhood, all its fury, all its muted outrage, none of its helplessness. He hoped suddenly that the pregnant woman had found her way home through the moonlight; he did not want to see her again out there—she was not part of tonight's business. He did not quite trust himself to catch sight of her once his hands had found their way round one of the oiled rifles. Shaloo had hushed the men at last and now cleared his throat stentoriously. Cotter turned his back on him. He never minded Uncle Jim's pep talk but he didn't really need it. Not like most of these other mindless raffraff did. Cotter knew why he was there. The fresh, new thing in him was kindling brightly now, casting a flickering but clear illumination upon certain faces long shadowed in his mind. Shaloo was shouting now.

All right, boys. Now we've had our drinks. Now it's time to settle down to business. Looking over these fine faces I see most of you fellers has worked for me before. That helps, even though I know the rest of you handpicked boys has had experience in some line of work like this somewheres down the line. Hell, you know what to do down there! I don't have to spell it out for you. Let your good American instincts guide you. Some of you boys fought in France—a couple of you are Legionnaires. Well, it's like it was over there. It's a war, boys! Only this is 1933 not 1917! And it's worse than it was then! It's holier too. Because this time we're fighting right on American soil. Fighting for every right that this republic was founded on! Oh, I know, some newspaper people have it in for us. They call us all kinds of names. But we know different, don't we! We know we're in the vanguard of a fight against the Jew communists who agitate strikes like this one down at Breedlove!

Cotter stared at the empty glass. With a sweep of his steady hand he sent it clattering across the bar, into the dust by the big Negro's feet. He turned and began shouldering his way through the tense bodies of the listening men, walking now on sane, steady feet toward the door, toward the trucks, toward the cold, moon-washed air which would sweeten still further the raging reasons in his mind.

We're Americans, that's what we are! Shaloo's voice was shouting. Maybe we're the only hundred-percent Americans in America when it comes to doing a job like this!

The road was empty. Cotter breathed in the smoky air and smelled the hated smell of the coal which was everywhere. His shadow moved slowly across the moon-bathed ruts toward the second truck. Shaloo had stopped shouting now. The ragged men were applauding their appreciation of what he had told them. He was at the piano now, striking up the chords of the "Star Spangled Banner."

Let's all sing it out now! Cotter could hear his high voice cry. Our glorious national anthem!

Cotter clambered over the tailgate and into the darkened truck bed. He walked back and loosened one of the stacked rifles and went to sit with it in the dark, waiting till Shaloo was done. He could hear them all singing. He did not need that. He knew why he was there. Their voices rang like a choir of soiled trumpets.

The land of the free—and the home of the bra-a-ave!

Cotter stared out over the tailgate at the road. She had gone somewhere, the pregnant Negro woman. Cotter was glad of that. He did not know whether or not he would have harmed her had she still been there. And that would have been wrong, unreasonable. She was not part of that night's business. Her face was not among those so clearly lit now in the flaming, roaring reasonable-

41

ness of his head. He would know those faces when he saw them. And he would know what to do. Where a bar of moonlight fell beneath the tarpaulin across his brow there were tears in Cotter's eyes. But he knew at least that they were tears of reasonableness. He hiccupped faintly, but he knew that he was not drunk. He was sober in the only way he was ever sober—when he had had just enough to light the flame, to cast that cold, white light across the faces in his mind, to show his eyes whom they were when he saw them and to make him know what must be done to make them go away.

The moon seemed to them in that small house the last light in all creation. The fire in the grate had burned down to a banked glow of orange coals which shed no light in the room. The moon lay half obscured behind the hill to the north and already the valley shadows were thickening; presently the moon would disappear, leaving only the winter stars which shone brilliantly now, like the lamps in miners' caps at the bottom of some profound pit, distant and sad.

If Farjeon felt fear it was not for himself. And his fear was for more than his woman and the unborn child too; it was strangely for the others in that room. They seemed so hapless in the face of danger and when it came it did not even seem to surprise them. He felt afraid for human beings who seemed to have lived their whole lives with such perils always at hand. And yet despite his fear Farjeon's thoughts kept wandering. He thought of the strange, alien road they had come those past two days, of the solid, comfortable farm they had left, of his three years at Elkins State Normal School. He had tried so hard to make a go of the place; he wondered sometimes if he would have done better at farming without any education at all. It had all vanished somehow under his very eyes. Now they had come at last to this black room, a chamber now dark as a mine itself, a place against whose windows the moonlight now dwindled and failed as if in some terror of its own.

Yonder come their trucks. See, Cal? On the top of the road! cried Mother Dunne. One's leaving. I reckon it's going round to the other hill to pen us up proper.

I'm not scared, whispered Farjeon's woman. Only except for you.

It'll be all right, Farjeon said. You'll see.

But he was really remembering his old shotgun; it had been among all the things they had left behind that morning. Farjeon remembered how he had wondered about it the night before. But no, it hadn't seemed like they were facing anything that might need a gun, he had fancied no roads that would bring them to a place like this, to such a need. Besides, there was something face-less about the danger. The men and the trucks had not come down among them yet and when they did come it would be in the pitch of a moonless dark with nothing to shoot at. Farjeon gave Jean's shoulder a quick, hard squeeze. He chuckled.

What? she murmured, and he could feel her breath against his neck.

Now's a good time to think of names, he said.

If it's a boy? she said, or if it's a girl?

If it's a girl, he said softly. We already decided what to call it if it's a boy.

It was true. They had long since decided to name any boy child of theirs for William G. Hood, the great and good West Virginia senator who had addressed Farjeon's graduating class, the man who had led the fight to save the farms of people like Farjeon and to ease the plight of miners like the one in whose besieged home they cowered that night. Farjeon thought of him now and some-how the image of that great, white-haired head was more comfort to him in that moment than the game they were playing.

I can't think of any girls' names either, Jean whispered pres-ently.

I can, Farjeon said. But I wasn't really trying. I wasn't really thinking about that. I was thinking about him.

About who?

About Mister Hood, Farjeon said. I can picture us reading about this in the Glory papers tomorrow—this and the hell Mister Hood's going to be raising about what's happening here tonight. It's funny. I remember hearing him talk about the mines. Those two times we heard him on the steps of the Glory courthouse. But I never knew what he was talking about till tonight. I guess I never heard anything but what he had to say about the farmers.

I know, she said. I never knew either.

It was a comfort for them to talk about it that way; it made it seem like a danger apart from them, something obscure and impersonal.

These poor people, said Farjeon's woman as if they were not now one of them. These poor souls.

She felt safe in the grip of Farjeon's arm; she felt comforted at the thought of William George Hood who could somehow have canceled out that night with a ringing speech in Washington or maybe with a few scratches of his pen.

Cal crept timorously to the window and laid his fingers round the barrel of the rifle in Mother Dunne's hands.

Give it to me, Mom.

What?

I said give it to me, Cal repeated.

Cal, you know you've got no stomach for this, she said. Let me—

Yes, I do, he went on in a high, strained voice. Give it to me. I'm going out front with it and hide down behind the snowball bush. That way I can cover the house.

No, Cal, she said kindly, struggling with his hand some, though she was full of a sudden, late pride in him.

Yes, I said, his voice went on, flat and automatic. I don't care what happens. I don't want an old woman carrying my share.

They could both see the vague shape of the truck now, the one that had been on the rise of the road, upon the north hill, above Mexico. It was less than a hundred yards off, its headlights half covered, so that only the barest road ahead was visible beneath it.

44

The dark shape, like a creature with hooded eyes, trundled through a dip in the land and rose again, settling, moving again through the now moonless, starlit dark along the low road beneath the tipple.

Still she had to complain some when she gave up the rifle into his hands.

I'm an old woman, she sobbed, but it would give my soul some comfort to use that gun against such devils. Be careful, Cal. Be careful.

Farjeon turned his head quickly as the coal fire blazed up abruptly, lighting the face and hands of the woman beside him on the bench. He could see Cal's face, too, as he went toward the door with the rifle, the pallor of fear around his mouth, but there was anger there, too, now—in his dark eyes—and that seemed to save him. Mother Dunne flung up her hands and clapped them on both knees.

Be careful, Cal, sobbed the old woman in a faint, trumpeting breath.

Farjeon got up and laid his mouth close to Jean's ear, kissing her on the neck.

Wait here, dear love.

Where are you going? she whispered, suddenly afraid.

I've got to go out there too, he said. Don't you see? I've got to find something and go out there with him. Something. Anything I can lay hands on.

He ran his fingers into her pale hair, pressing her head.

Don't you see? he said. I can't let him face it out there alone. It's not right. They've been too kind to us for that.

Be careful, she breathed.

You be careful, dear love, Farjeon said. If there's shooting near the house get down flat on the floor.

Be careful.

The fire had found new life again, like some fresh, wild bloom red-flowering among them, lighting their eyes. Mother Dunne turned from her window.

Jessie, fetch a dipper of water from the pail and quench that fire.

Jessie half rose, hesitating. She paused.

Jessie, do as I tell you! Them trucks is both not fifty feet away, as I'm setting here! Quench that fire. It might give them just the light to shoot us by!

Jessie flung the dipperful of water hissing across the small, blazing embers. Farjeon's eyes in that twinkling had searched the room and seen Cal's bright, sharp miner's pick leaning against the wall beside the battered, tin lunch pail.

That will serve, he thought, and squeezed Jean's hand.

The darkness was back like a palpable, thick thing among them and Farjeon thought strangely that it had never been such a darkness as this within the safe, familiar, unlit world of his woman's eyes.

Be careful, she whispered again, feeling for him.

He wondered if she could feel his fear, maybe smell it, his fear that was for her.

Lie down on the floor now, he said evenly, trying not to let her hear the fear in that evenness. Lie down beside the bench. It'll be safer that way.

She sobbed somewhere deep in her belly, a sound that surely came from near the unborn child, he thought; perhaps it was the creature's own sob, forewarned and fearful. Farjeon felt for her vivid, pale hair in the darkness, feeling its color even in that lightlessness, as she knelt by the bench and stretched out alongside it.

Be careful, she breathed again, and he felt her hand steal up the cuff of his rough denim trousers; he could feel her fingernails digging faintly into the skin of his leg, as if she would hold him that way, until he made himself move off toward the wall and seized up the pick handle from the floor. Outside the house he felt it like a sudden drunkenness—the anger was like that, like the sudden flush after a drink of good whiskey—and the fear was gone, except that part of it which he had left inside the house with her, and he heard Cal whimper somewhere yonder in the faint star-shine. He heard the whimper twice more and a curse, and he knew that it wasn't fear, it was anger like his own, and then he saw the first shot. Saw it before he heard it even—a yellow flash that seemed to linger on his retina like a hole burned in gray paper—where the second truck now stood, moving yet, though seeming to stand still it moved so slowly. The rifle shot sounded toylike, unreal. Farjeon could see the shape of Cal under the mul-berry bush, the black shape of him knotted like something balled-up in anger, with the gun glinting faintly in the starshine like a small, polished stick, and he could hear the sob again and again the muffled curse, a wordless oath that was almost the unsubstan-tialness of outraged breathing.

With the moon gone down behind the hill the stars stood washed and glittering on the sky, with an almost midsummer bril-liance to them, so that everything clear to the hilltop was faintly visible, as if dusted by the moon's own luminous downfall. Cal fired once wildly and stood up, cursing.

Here they come! he cried, and ran down the sloping yard to-ward the ditch, firing as he went.

Farjeon felt so impotent with the pick handle clutched in his hands. There was nothing near to strike at. And yet in that chiarascuro everything gave such a strange illusion of closeness. He yearned for the shotgun which he had let go up with the other things at the farm. He stood, waiting, seeing the faceless shapes of the men tumble from the tailgates of both trucks into the road, yelling like men at a ball game, and firing at the miners' houses on either side. Farjeon heard Cal yell something once and stumble on his side into the berm. He started forward to go to his aid but something checked him. Farjeon heard Jean's cry at the open doorway of the house at the same moment he first laid eyes on the man in the army coat. The minute Farjeon saw him he knew he was something special, something different and more dangerous than the rest of them. The man walked carefully, slowly, with an almost melancholy purposefulness, across the deep, frozen ruts of

47

the road past Cal's motionless body toward the high place in the yard where Farjeon waited. He did not scamper and shout and fire randomly, nor did he seem drunk like the others. Farjeon knew him for their leader of sorts and yet he seemed heedless of their pell-mell rioting; he seemed held and drawn like a magnetized nail by something else, something behind, beyond Farjeon, who now could think of nothing else but getting Jean back into the house, back on the floor by the bench. But suddenly she was there, against him, her hands fluttering for his face, her fingers against his eyes that were wild and staring with panic for her safety. And then there was someone else pounding down the hard ground behind them, and even before the blow behind his ear flared like a rocket in his eyes Farjeon could see the man in the army coat had come closer, inexorably, so close now that he could see the working of his soundless, cursing mouth, and in the moment before Farjeon fell into darkness he saw the man raise the Springfield to his shoulder and commence firing.

When Farjeon's eyes opened he knew he had been down a good while. He felt the hardness of the frozen earth against his mouth before he felt the pressure of the thing across his legs. He half rose, sitting a long moment, staring with disbelief at the shape of his wife until, presently, his strong heart rallied and told him that she had fainted and fallen there—yes, that was it, she had fainted there. He thought about the man who had dared frighten Jean enough to make her faint till he was almost sick with rage. The man who had struck him from behind with the hickory axe handle was gone off again somewhere among the gray, crouched houses now; gone, too, was the man in the army coat, the one who had fired at Jean, the one who had made her faint. Farjeon stared after the trucks into which the men now clambered again, before, once more, with engines whining in high gear, they set off back up the road to Mexico. Farjeon wondered if he would ever be able to tell Jean in the morning how angry he had been at that one man, how his anger had been greater than his fear could ever be. That was when he crawled across to her. That was when he saw among

48

the winter weeds and bits of coal embedded in that benighted earth the still born body of his son. Jean lay like a child who has fallen and lies catching its breath in the breakneck pitch of some children's game. The fresh-born baby lay motionless amid the sprawl of her legs and skirt. Farjeon bent his face closer in the starshine, shaking his head slowly from side to side as if to clear his foolish vision and groaning in a short, choking voice that seemed to come from somewhere else, somewhere outside his body, back maybe among the rioting sounds behind him on the road.

Why, no, Farjeon murmured and stretched out one finger to touch the dead child's hair, still flattened and moist from birth. No, he whispered in a gastric sound like sickness in his stomach.

He could see the child's fingernails, each small and perfectly crescent; its blue eyes were faintly opened, there was something almost bemused in its expression. Farjeon could see too, the small, bloodless bullet hole in the small breast, the hole the bullet had made that had killed Jean and sent her baby twitching out in a spasm of dying. Farjeon bent closer, his mouth almost smiling in disbelief. His head had stopped shaking when he reached Jean's face. In the dusty starshine he could see her mouth. Her lips were barely parted as though she had commenced saying something and thought better of it. Farjeon cocked his head slightly as if he might still catch a word of it. He could not escape the fancy that she would presently utter some word of contradiction of everything else her dead eyes told him.

Jean?

That was in the moment when Farjeon fancied he saw the rise and fall of her breast. Any second now he would hear her laugh and hear the baby's first fat chuckling outcry as Jean lifted it in her arms. Then he knew it was the wind that had stirred the looseness of her old blue dress beneath the open coat. There was no breath there; there was only death there, and ruin and something destroyed that was, in that moment's perfect horror, beyond Farjeon's feeling. There would be time for such thoughts later—

for anguish, for fury, for retribution. First he had to believe it. Because now it was all something perfectly unreal, and even as he gathered up both of them in his arms Farjeon recalled the way Jean always had something to say against any misfortune, maybe not words of courage, maybe only some fool thing that would set them both to laughing at the way things were. Yes, presently that would happen: she would say the right thing softly and it would be all right and they would kiss over it. He looked down, faintly scowling, at her lolling, lifeless face. Farjeon grunted and shook his head again. In the dusty starshine he could see the tears still on her livid, murdered cheeks and knew that they were ones that had sprung there for love of him and in fears for him when she had raced from the open doorway and come faltering blindly down the moonless night, calling his name, hurrying to her death to keep it from him.

Jean?

He said it again, louder now, as if there was the chance that she had not heard it the first time. Jean?

Farjeon started down the yard with his bloody burden. His eyes saw the moving shapes of angry miners and the yellow smear of torches which now fired the darkness with red, dragging shadows. There was fresh gunfire up the road, some few, scattered guns aimed after the black trucks which were already halfway up the hill. A knot of miners had caught hold of some shape that struggled and screamed in a small, hoarse voice, dragging it downhill toward the railroad tracks. Back in the house Farjeon could hear the old woman's high voice shouting some shapeless thing. He looked down absently again at the bloodless face that rolled, staring, against his shoulder.

Jean.

This time it was not the question. This was when it struck him full-face that two things in his life were really over, and there was no wisdom in him yet to recognize the shape of whatever things might lie ahead.

•   •

Even if Farjeon's mind had been yet conscious enough to seek him out, the man in the army coat had long since vanished with the others in the trucks, now on the edge of Mexico. Only one of them had failed to escape and he was now in the hands of Tom Turley and five others.

Tom Turley was a big man, a lumpish, sullen-faced Irishman whose body had been made somehow stooped and misshapen by his work and by some curious turn of spirit. Tom was, in one way, the loneliest man in that lonely place. He was married to a once pretty Protestant girl who had borne him two children, the last of whom had left her suddenly lackluster and aging. It was small enough family for a mine town but it was enough to strain Tom's back to breaking, to keep him awake long after dark, in the lamplight, chewing a stub of pencil and struggling over a paperful of numbers—the endless sum of his debt, his payday "snake" at the company store. There was a certain thwarted eagerness about Tom's face, some stooped, searching solicitude about his round, huge shoulders and his big, swift gestures. It was hard to guess if this was because of the crouched, crippling effort of his stance as he swung his pick under the hill in the mine or if it was, indeed, some inner, searching, thrusting forward of his whole spirit. He had the art of a man who is about to voice, at any moment, some badly phrased plea for forgiveness. His dust-blackened face seemed dark with thought even after he had scrubbed it at the washstand mornings after the deadman's shift. The coal on his face, indeed, seemed never to yield to such washing; the dust of it seemed blown into the skin, like an old tattoo or a powder burn.

His dark, hangdog face was filled with an air of bad conscience, and that was, indeed, the truth, for Tom was a Catholic and his wife, who was not a believer, had little enough left to praise without bothering her wits about God, especially at the end of a long day of trying to make their poor ends meet. And so Tom Turley lived badly with his haunting, constant sense of—of what? Of sin? No, it went deeper than that, for Tom led a sober, almost stoic life; the sense of sin, it seemed, belonged to the others, the Protes-

51

tant miners who sat listening to long Sunday sermons about sin and hellfire in the pews of Breedlove's single Baptist church. For Tom it was the sense of ritual that was missing. It was all like some strange moral bill that had not been paid, that could never, for him in that place, be paid at all. It made him think sometimes of his snake at the store. Because there was no place for Tom in that Baptist church and that church was the only one Breedlove had. On Sundays he used to ache with it, that sense of something missing, the ritual of it, and it was a moral ache worse than the miner's rheumatism that plagued him often in wet weather. He tried to make the best of it. On the wall of his dingy parlor he had hung a small, dime-store crucifix—that and a cheap oleo print in a chipped frame from which the glass was long gone so that the print was foxed and stained—a colored picture of the Crucifixion—and beneath it a Latin motto that none of them could read.

Twice yearly—at Christmastime and Easter—Tom Turley walked his family the rough eight-mile road to Glory, to the Catholic church there, and back along that same cold road that night. But there were the months between, the months under the earth, in the rooms and tunnels, in which he could almost hear the whisper of accusation like the swish of nuns' habits; there were nights under the quilts beside his wife when he would hear the children stir in their sleep with a mumbling restiveness which Tom knew was a hunger after the religion his life denied them. On Sunday mornings Tom's eyes hated to meet the look of his wife; it seemed as though she might be laughing at him. As though she ever bothered herself one way or the other about such things! She had enough on her mind. And yet Tom had the certain sense that he was raising his children on a diet of something as spiritually poor as the food on his table was meager and wanting. All of this gave him that hunched, curious air of guilt, of odd pleading. And it did more to him. It played an odd trick with his fancy. Tom Turley was always seeing in things the Cross. He would see it suddenly in the shape and juncture of timbers in the mine. The massive wood structure of the tipple itself seemed to him a veritable maze of crucifixes. It was around him everywhere, that constant reminder. Where another man would see the branches of a tree in spring-time intersecting in a lace of greening boughs and twigs against the lemon sky of that smoking valley Tom would make out some-how, inevitably, the Cross.

He saw it in dreams too, in the fitful dreams of his rationed daytime sleep, even in the smoky daydreams of waking, when he would fancy that sharp shape somewhere about him in the glitter-ing black room he had helped hew out, sometimes merely in so chance a thing as the way two pick handles happened to fall one upon the other. Tom would cross himself, too, when the timbers above him would creak sometimes when the roof was working and the black dust would sift down onto his cap, there in that bur-ied solace with the trillion-tonned Appalachians piled miles up above him, or sometimes when the rats would pause and rise up on their tiny haunches, sniffing, listening, to sound the earth's working hushed rhythms for some clue to an impending fall. Still, despite his difference from the other miners, Tom was popular enough.

Tom, how come you never bring your woman and kids to the church?

Oh, I don't know. I guess I'm not too religious, Cal.

Well, there's a church supper Monday night. How about that? That ain't services. Besides, there's going to be chicken.

Chicken was an unheard-of scarcity in Breedlove except on such rare occasions as a church social or Christmas day. Still Tom was not tempted; he would nod gratefully and make some excuse, knowing the kindness behind the invitation.

Everybody knows you're a Popist, his chum would say in the light of their cap lamps. But that don't matter. Come to church anyways, Tom.

They would be sitting crouched against a car of the trip in the narrow, warm haulageway, eating their lunch of water sand-wiches and drinking the thin, bitter sassafras tea from the bat-tered tin dinner pails their women had tried to fill that morning.

You're a Popist, Tom, the chum would say. Everybody knows that. You're the only one for miles around. Still, you know that don't make no difference to us, don't you? Because it's the same Lord, Tom. Why don't you come to church next Sunday? The same Lord, d'ye see? Can't you praise Him a little on our good, hard benches?

And still he would smile about it and think up another courteous excuse. And presently something in his hunched, tired shoulders, his twisted, yearning stance, would seem to lean forward a little as if in supplication to Something beyond, above them both in that black, desperate place. Because he never hated them, the alien ones, the Protestants, with whom he lived and worked. And he would happen to glance down at the narrow-gage rails a few feet off, the way the ties intersected, and he would see the shape of it again, and the timber would work and cry faintly above his head and the dust sift down onto his cap and he would cross himself.

He was like a man who was waiting for something, for someone —a meeting long expected. Something in that hunched, bunched stance seemed to express that—the whole mass of him bent slightly forward a little as if listening for a strange, fresh footfall and the glimpse of some half-familiar, half-forgotten face. So that tonight when they caught the last man who had tried to scramble aboard the second truck Tom Turley was the first to shoulder his way through the others with their clubs and torches and picks. Tom searched the ragged man with his eyes; on his face was an expression of savage, almost religious eagerness. Tom nodded and his eyes brightened. It was as if some great burden were about to be lifted from Tom Turley's round, tormented back. It was as if he had found something for which he had long quested.

The man was a Benwood Pole name Tzack. He had had no gun when Steve Bonar and two others had caught him. He had dropped his rifle at the first rattle of gunfire and had wandered among the moving trucks during all the shooting in a perfect daze of terror, an utter thralldom of wonder at how he had ever come to be in such a place, in the midst of so much noise and danger. A more inept gunman Shaloo's recruiter had never come upon. Still, he had been hungry that morning in Glory when the man had offered him the clean five-dollar bill and the promise of fifteen more at the end of the business. And he had agreed—nodded rather—since he had understood no word that had been exchanged between them. So that he had no real idea what the job would entail. For Tzack was a man in almost total lack of communication with any human being.

He had come to Wheeling before the war and found work in the thriving Weirton steel mills. That spring he had been laid off because of frailness and his inability to understand orders. In the face of this direness he could only stare at the world. He could not speak, he could explain nothing to anyone, could understand nothing that was said to him. Nor was this due to any lack of intelligence. It was because he had never been able to learn more than a few words of English; he had meanwhile forgotten all but a few words of Polish. So that he could utter only a handful of words intelligible to any mortal ear. He was quick-witted enough —it was not that. It was simply that he had a bad ear for language, in the way that some men are tone-deaf and cannot carry a tune or even keep time to a drum. He was in a bad way, this fellow—a man without language, impervious to speech; he might as well have lost the very tongue from between his ruined, yellow teeth.

Now Tzack could only stare in bewilderment and terror at the men who had captured him and especially at Tom Turley who had come up on him slowly, almost gently, with something in his face that made it seem as if he could scarcely believe his eyes, some attitude about the hunched, forward-thrusting stance of his huge body that made it seem as if they had both been a long time coming to this meeting place, as if indeed they might have been remotely separate though treasured relatives or, at the very least, long-lost chums.

At the first sound of Tom Turley's orders the mob faltered.

Then a few shouted and the notion kindled quickly among them. Tzack's mind, when he understood what they were about, went a little mad with terror. He searched the torchlit faces of them for some glimpse of mercy, but there was none. His mind rattled like a dice box with the few words of speech he knew. Suddenly his wits recalled one word he had heard shouted on the Wheeling streets the morning of the Armistice fifteen years before. It was a word the newsboys had cried and he knew it meant something good, something glad and urgent, though he knew not what. He fancied that this good, lonely word would touch some heart among the men who now dragged him to the timbers of the mine tipple. Their faces round him were like the torches—flaming with all the bottled hatred and fury of the six weeks behind them and behind that all the thwarted years of terror in the mine itself. Tzack tried to be sure he said the word right; he remembered how all the happy faces of that other mob had lit at the word's very sound, how their glad mouths had echoed it. Tzack's mouth tried to shape the word as the men stretched his arms out to the cross the tipple timbers made. Tom Turley's hands reached for the sledge hammer and the four ten-penny nails Bonar had fetched from his woodshed. Tzack tried the word again but there was no breath in him to make it come out. They had his wrists now and Bonar was holding the first nail against Tzack's sweating palm for the first fall of Tom Turley's sledge.

Farjeon stood now on the road still cradling the two bodies in his arms. He could hear the hammering. He stared down through the torchlight which lit the miners' caps and saw it all as if in a dream. He watched as they held Tzack's arms upright, at angles to his surging chest; lifting him savagely to the cross the tipple timbers made while Bonar and a man named Telligrew tore the broken, muddy shoes from Tzack's dirty, sockless feet. Every man of them yearned forward into the killing while five of them struggled to fix Tzack into the position in which Tom Turley, now almost sleepy-eyed, had dreamed him. They thrust Tzack's writhing body up against the rough, oiled timbers with a knotted, twisting fury that blazed in their faces like the coal-oil torches. They handled the struggling Tzack with a kind of unstoppered ecstasy which was, of course, unlike that special passion in Tom Turley's own slow-heaving chest. As he held the second nail against Tzack's quivering palm and caught up the twelve-pound sledge again, Turley's calm face was not wet like the others, whose faces streamed with sweat, even in that cold night's air. Somewhere among his anguished wits Tzack found breath for the word.

Extra! Extra! his ragged voice sang out amid the hush among the savage miners. Extra!

But the word did not reach them, he knew that then; perhaps he had repeated it wrong, the glad, good word he had heard the newsboy cry in that morning so long ago. He tried it still.

Extra! Extra!

Meanwhile Tom Turley had left them, hurrying off up the cinders, but he was back soon enough, a little short of breath now, and dragging his sleepy child by the hand. He shoved his way through the shoulders again and lifted the boy, who squinted in the guttering torchlight, until his face was only a foot or two away from the bleeding man on the tipple timbers.

Look good, Bud, said Tom Turley. Look real good.

The boy stared a moment and then sucked in his breath; something told him his father would be angry if he cried just then. Tom Turley pressed the boy dangling closer so that he could stare, inches away now, at the transfixed palm of Tzack's right hand.

That's the right hand of a fink, Bud, he said in a trembling voice. Look at it good. See what happens to finks, boy. And don't never forget it.

The child wondered if it was a game, if the man really hung there panting and slobbering and whimpering on his four nails; maybe there was a strap or hooks behind, holding him up by his bunched, cheap suit. He thought maybe the blood was not real; he could not believe his delight that his dad would make his face be so close to real blood. Still, something about it frightened him, the game to which his father had brought him, some smell about them all, some queer, special smell about his father; he hiccupped, stifling a sob, scared that he might cry, might not live up to something, this game to which his father had brought him there to play.

A man named Telligrew laid a hand on Tom Turley's sleeve and pulled till Tom shook it away.

Tom, looky here! Tom, this ain't no business for kids!

I want him to see! the big man shouted. I want him to remember it all his life. What happens to finks!

Bonar and Maxwell and Shreve intervened then between the child's face and Tzack's body. Tom glared at them an instant before he put the boy down in the cinders. Bud was trembling. The blood was real he knew then—blood that would tint the fabric of his memory till he died. Tom Turley patted his child's head and sent him homeward up the cinders, across the tracks, toward the shacks where lamps bloomed once more in windows. Tom had the expression on his face of a man who had just been to a whorehouse—or a church; there was a great placidity in his eyes, he was sweating now, as in the swooning aftermath of love or some soul's confession. He stared at Maxwell's face, then at Bonar.

Sin, he said. I wanted him to know about sin. The wages of it. You Baptist boys is always ranting about it—sin. But there's no place here for a child like my two to learn about sin, real sin. I wanted that boy to learn it now. Here. Tonight. It's been too many years he's had no place to learn about sin.

He sleeved his streaming forehead.

And there's no sinner like a fink like him yonder to learn from.

Farjeon heard their faint voices and saw their clustered heads down by the tipple; he heard the shot when one of the kindlier among them fired a single charge into Tzack's heaving chest. Farjeon heard and saw it all as if somewhere within a secret dream of his own. The wind blew a first, few snowflakes across his coat which Jean's body still wore. Farjeon watched as the mob dispersed and wandered apart, then saw their shapes converge and quicken at the first bright sound of the bell at the church. When they were gone Farjeon, still carrying his dead family in his arms, walked the hundred yards to where Tzack's diminished, hapless body hung, now dripping darkly, obscurely, on the cinders beneath him. Farjeon searched the face lolling against one shoulder; Tzack's dead mouth was still shaped as if it were about to utter some other word, some wiser, better word, some key of magic and mercy he had desperately found among the ragbag of his wordless wits. Farjeon nodded.

So they got You again, he thought silently to himself and nodded again.

Though there was no moral in it for him. He knew there was not when, after a moment more, he turned from Tzack's body and took the road back up toward the yard below the house where the horseless wagon now stood. Farjeon kept shaking his head. There was no lesson in it, no sign, no restraint in the message of that spectacle. Because now, like the whisper of a blowing coal somewhere within his mind, Farjeon could feel a fury waking, one that dwarfed and diminished what he had just witnessed, one that now stretched and yawned somewhere in his stunned spirit.

In the bloody yard where Cal lay tumbled and done for, below the house, Farjeon turned with his burden and glared far off again at the diminished shape on the tipple timbers. For the first time now there were tears in his eyes.

Because I can't do it Your way, Farjeon said softly to the now abstracted body of Tzack. Because I almost know what has to be done now. And it can't be Your way. I've got to square this for myself. I've got to square it for these two here. It can't be Your way.

And he carried the two bodies up toward the empty, horseless wagon, which was all the home left to him on earth, and he was filled suddenly with a strange and awful peace.

At the first outcry of the church bell Mother Dunne had snatched her shawl from its peg and set off out the door. Not a

59

tear, not a sob, hardly a quiver of her mouth. Jessie envied her that—an outrage that was greater than any grief. She had helped Jessie bring in Cal's body from the ditch, moving without any show of sorrow or loss, helping Jessie to tug the big, wet shoes off his cold, stiff feet and arrange him on the bed. It was the only fitting place they could fancy to put the poor, finished thing. And then, since they had no pennies for Cal's eyes, Mother Dunne, still moving in that cold, awful quietude, had fetched two horn buttons from her sewing basket and set them on Cal's lids, so that he lay on his back now, rigid and ruined, like some stained window mannequin, with those two spurious eyes, black as the mine which had been his life and downfall, seeming to stare up, like the sewed-on face of a doll, at the faint shadows on the ceiling. For one moment the old woman had stared at the face before she left. She laid her fingers briefly on his cheek.

At least we can bury him ourselves, she said presently. At least he wasn't buried alive like a hundred other boys I could name. Lord, at least we have that!

Only that moment's emotion and then she was gone, leaving Jessie alone in the empty house with no other sound but the blowing fire on the grate and the faint, fresh whisper of snowflakes against the window. Jessie was glad that the church bell had stopped its small, brassy hammering down the holler. She had no stomach for the meeting that had been called at the church. She could only sit now with her fists clenched on both knees, staring into the fire. Let them settle it now however they wanted; Jessie had had enough of strike, it mattered nothing to her now whether they voted that night to surrender or go on.

Jessie's eyes searched in the shapes and colors of the blowing fire, seeking visions, hunting for some augury of things ahead. Jessie was often having visions, usually of better times ahead—and yet how few of them had ever been realized. Now she let her eyes make out the shape of faces and figures in the flames, fanciful images of people long dead and gone to earth. She strove with all her wit to keep from thinking about the future. For there seemed somehow no future at all, it was all as dead as the clinkers under the grate, and she dared not let her mind play with that. Still, she could not help seeing in her fancy the faces of other women widowed there at Breedlove: the look in their eyes after they had bundled up all they could carry and set off down the road to Glory. Sometimes there was a smile on their gray mouths, the most foolish, the most presumptuous of smiles, since there was nothing ahead for them and their children but begging in the streets or—if they had been fortunate enough to have been widowed in summertime—berries to be picked in the hollers and sold at Glory back doors. Or, if they were still young and personable enough—prettiness was usually by then past its prime—a chance to find a place for themselves in a Baltimore Street brothel.

Jessie bent forward and poked the fire. Her glance chanced to fall then on Cal's fiddle and bow which hung on their hook along the wall. That was when Jessie realized with a sudden pang of surprise—and not much shame about it either—that the tears on her cheeks were not for Cal at all. The tears and the cold lump at the pit of her stomach—they were not grief for him at all; they were fear, and the fear was of that manless, sudden future which now stretched before her. That was when she went to the window and stared out at the stranger.

The wagon was horseless; earlier that night Farjeon had stabled the mare under a lean-to in the yard back of the house. The trace poles of the wagon rested empty on the frozen earth; Farjeon sat atop the narrow seat—a man going nowhere. The bodies of the woman and baby were in the back where he had carefully arranged them and covered them with his overcoat against the snow and wind. He had even tucked the overcoat carefully under the bodies as if he had been tucking in a quilt on a cold night back at the farm. He had climbed back in the seat and sat now, bowed a little, on the wagon seat with the snow already gathering like thin wool on his uncovered back and shoulders. He sat motionless, contemplative, in the small, sharp wind, the blowing, quickening snow, not shivering, not seeming to feel the cold or anything else except some rapt, inner absorption, the whole shape of him bent forward with that black, vivid introspection, impervious to anything outside him. Jessie hesitated before she went out to invite him in to the fireside. It colored her cheeks to think how he might misunderstand; she was a widow too fresh to speak to a man so freshly widowered himself.

Even after she had gone out the door to the wagon side she paused a moment more. She wondered again if he would misunderstand. Let him think what he pleased of her, she thought after a while; she felt she could not bear a moment more in that whispering house, with Cal's body lying in there. She fancied she might go mad in there on the bench by the fire, searching for the sunlight of some safe tomorrow in the flames of the burning coal. Farjeon seemed unaware of her, of anything, while she stood there thinking that at any moment he would turn his head and look at her; she felt the kiss of the thin snow on her flushed face and hoped he would speak first. But he might as well have been something painted there against the sallow winter sky—unmoving, absorbed, impervious to her stare, to coldness, to anything. After a spell she ventured a step closer, reaching up to touch his sleeve.

You'll catch your death, she whispered.

And instantly fancied that maybe that was what he wanted, maybe that was why he was sitting up there in the wind on that wagon seat with the snow gathering on his head and shoulders. Maybe, she thought, he wants to be done with it and freeze himself stiff as them back yonder under his overcoat.

Mister? she said. Won't you come inside by the fire?

For a spell she thought he hadn't heard her, that the wind had covered her words.

Mister?

Leave me alone, he said simply, quietly, without any anger, or surprise, or any emotion at all.

You'll freeze out here, she said simply.

He paused on that a moment, a good while, as if the cold had thickened his understanding.

No, I'll not, he said presently. I'm not cold. Not at all.

No, she knew then, it was not the cold that slowed him, it was that careful, slow, inner absorption she could sense in him, something rapt and secret in this head that had slowed every thought to a careful, reasoned pace.

Now he hesitated and turned his head the barest inch as if to acknowledge her presence briefly, courteously, then nodded as if he reckoned she deserved some further explanation.

Thank you kindly, he said.

And then again that cautious pause as if he were weighing each word before he breathed it into being. He lowered his hand from his knee and patted the wagon seat beside him.

This thing, he said. This here wagon. It's mine. It's the last thing—the last place in the world that is mine. That house yonder —with the fire inside. That's yours. Where you belong tonight with your dead one. Out here in the wagon. With my two. That's where I belong.

He gestured behind him with his hand.

That's why I laid them back there in the wagon bed, he said. Under the coat. It was the only place in the world I could bring them. Home to.

He looked at her then, a full look, and for a moment she saw his face lit faintly by the light from the open door. She felt the wind through her thin dress and shivered, waited, because she could see he had not done explaining.

After tonight, he said to the wind. After this. There's something I've got to do. And I've got to set out here. Alone with them back there. I've got to set out here till I figure out what it is I've got to do. And who I've got to do it to.

He turned his face back to shadow again.

And how to do it.

I thought you was cold, she said lamely, dropping her hand and shivering again, not so much from the cold through her thin dress as from something she had glimpsed for an instant in the color of his golden eyes, in the twinkling when his head had moved, lit for a moment, more by something behind them than from any light from any fire inside the open doorway. She watched him a moment more—his head turned back away from her again, his body hunched a little forward again on the seat, everything in his attitude saying to her that he had explained enough of it for decorum's sake, that he was done with her for now.

When she was back in the house she stole to the bedroom and looked in at Cal's body. A savage, almost uncontrollable hunger then beseiged her. She remembered her childhood back in Pocahontas County when her grandfather had died and the house, as if by magic, had filled with great platters and crocks of food fetched by neighbors. There was magic, too, in the awful hunger that seized everybody in the wake of death: in a day's time they had eaten every dish of food in sight. Even though she had scarcely passed a day since the strike began in which she had not felt some of hunger's empty ache she knew that her hunger now was that special hunger, that savage, almost mental hunger that seizes people in homes in which death has recently come. She thought of the mush in the crock in the window, she remembered a few spoonfuls of beans in a peanut jar she had put aside.

Her sense of the hunger came long before her awareness of the other emotion. She thought at first that it was caused merely by the thought that she would never sleep by her husband again, that he would never again reach for her in one of those rare nights when he was not too tired for her, when he had salvaged enough will and enough want to turn to her body for that scarce interval of passionless immersion in something that had once been sweet and which was, even still, a few moments escape from his mind's fear and monotony at work in his tunnel. Jessie poked the coals till they blew and blazed. She frowned into the flame, ashamed again, this time of her hunger for a man. She thought of how worthless she was, how this shameless letch, with Cal hardly cold in his bed, proved that she deserved nothing better than the empty future that she could see ahead. It was almost unendurable. She thought of the passionless life that lay before her—the sexlessness of life in a Baltimore Street brothel, the manless void of streets where she might beg for nothing more loving than a spare coin or a Christian word. She leaned closer to the heat from the fire, pressing her thighs together in a perfect welter of blushing, lip-biting shame.

She tried to remember the last time that Cal had wanted her. She could remember nothing but the years of nights when he had merely rolled over upon her as if the gesture were no more than some accident of sleep, some whim he was dreaming, and acted out upon her limbs the ghost of something that had once been fresh and full of honest want—but she could not remember when. She could not remember the last time Cal had made love to her; she could only remember the times that he had lain with her, fleeing into her body as if it were a refuge from his daily wage of fear and frustration. Her body was like a mine into which he fled as if to escape the other one, smothering womb of earth that daily engulfed him. Again she felt the sting of passion in her limbs, in her legs, it ran to her toes and out the ends of them and seemed to marry itself with the hotness of the fire. It shamed her, more than her stomach's hunger, but she could not help it; her mind was spared no detail of the manless, passionless life that stretched now before her: nights of loveless sex in some long-porched Baltimore Street brothel, or days with nothing between her feet but the stones of some street where she had come wandering to beg.

When she heard the knock at the door she forgot everything and hurried to answer it. Farjeon stood hatless in the thickening snow. There was snow on his hair, on this shoulders.

I just want a minute, he said.

Come in and get warm, she said shyly.

No, he said. I'm not cold. It's not that.

When she looked at his face again the passion strangely drained from her; she felt suddenly aged and tired. It was a thing she could see in his face and it curiously frightened her, so that for a moment she half wished she hadn't asked him in. It was a smell too—some hot, furious odor like an overheated wall above a coal stove, something that already smoked.

I'm not cold, he said again in that strange voice. It's not that.

And he sat down on the chair by the door, glancing toward it from time to time as if he had no business really being there, as if he had left his real home out there yonder in the snow, the place he really belonged. Then when she recognized the look, the smell, it made her lustful again. When she smelled the danger in him it made her itch with it, the wanting for him, for any man. He was looking at her. He still had the look of not feeling right in that place, as if he had recklessly left his home out there in the cold to come into this home of hers for a reason he was about to explain. She stared hard into the fire, feeling ashamed of her lust, with Cal hardly cold in the next room, hoping Farjeon would not see the burn of it amid her blushes, hoping he would think it was the fire that colored her cheeks. He stared at her back for a long spell as if still rapt in some abstraction that he had brought indoors from the wagon, and then he cleared his throat.

I won't stay, he said. You're here in your house with him. With your dead one. I belong out there with my two. I won't keep you. But like told you, I have to figure something out.

What? she whispered.

And he went on as if she had said nothing, speaking like some dark-red ribbon unwinding from the abstraction he had brought indoors from the wagon.

I have to know who they are?

She said nothing, not understanding him, keeping her red face away from him, keeping her gaze fixed in the fire as if her senses had become part of it. And he went on as though she had answered him and he was explaining it all again.

I have to know their names, he said. I have to know where I can find them.

You mean the men out there tonight? she said.

He nodded, as if she would hear that, as if she would see his

66

nod with some sense at the back of her. She shrugged.

Some hired men, she said. Hired gunmen.

Who hired them?

Jessie shivered. Her limbs rubbed together, scorching between the two fires. She did not want to look at him. She knew if she looked at his face she would see the other woman in it and that scared her, chilled her; she wanted only to hear his voice and smell the sense of scorched fury in the room and feel the lust that was like hope between her limbs. And she did not want him to see either feeling in her face.

I want to know them, Farjeon's voice went on quietly. I want to know the name of every one of them. In their order. I want to give them numbers. So that I can do what I have to do in a proper order. One by one. Who bosses the gunman?

His voice excited her almost uncontrollably. And yet the thought of the woman in his eyes made her shiver. Between these twin sensations she thrilled and stirred faintly in her shoes.

Shaloo, she said. A man named Jim Shaloo.

Who hired him?

The company, I reckon, she said in a low voice.

I know that, he said brightly, a little irritably. But who's the company? For example, who's the foreman?

A man named Kitto, Bob Kitto, she said.

That's three, he said.

Who's the first? she said. That's only two—Kitto and Shaloo.

I don't know the name of her killer, he said. He wears an army coat. I'll know him by that. Or his face. I won't ever forget that face. Who hires the foreman?

She felt a thrill of fear again and it was part of her shaming lust; she hoped he would not come round by the fire and see her face. Or smell the smell in the room and know it was her.

The manager of the mine, she said. A man named Paul.

Paul what?

That's his last name. Paul. George W. Paul. He lives in Glory.

That's four, he said in a voice that made her half fancy he had a pad out on his knee and was writing it all down. Does he own this mine?

No, she said.

What's the name of the man who owns the mine?

She cast him a look then, briefly, then hurried her gaze back to the fire. She had seen the woman in his eyes and it chilled her to the bone; she wanted only to hear the danger in his voice and smell the hot smell of his anger in the room.

What's the name of the man who owns this mine? he said again.

Nobody knows, she said. It's not a man. It's them.

Them?

A company of men, she said. Owned by one man.

Never mind the company, he said. Who's the one man?

Nobody knows that, she said. Nobody ever did know. I heard them talk about that. I never heard them once say. I don't think any of them know. Never did know.

He pondered that and she could almost hear his brain ticking off the numbers.

Never mind, he said presently. Never mind that. I'll find that out. That may take some hunting but I'll find that out.

She heard the chair scrape as he stood up. She felt him standing there behind her, staring at her with his eyes full of the woman, his hand on the door.

Thank you kindly, he said. That's all I wanted.

She stirred her limbs, still smelling the danger smell he made, still letting it rouse her.

It's warm in here, she heard her voice say. Are you sure you don't want to stay in here where it's warm? You'll catch your death out there—

But he was gone again, gone like some shadow the fire had made, closing the door gently behind him, and she heard presently the cry of the wagon springs as he climbed back up into his place and settled again into his dream.

Jessie felt suddenly empty, spent. She felt her lax thighs fall open to the warmth of the now blazing fire. She was glad he was gone, glad she would not have to see his face with the woman in his eyes. Yet his being there had made her remember suddenly some half-forgotten night in a spring apple orchard with Cal, ages gone by, in a good time before the mines, before fear had come like a chill, unbidden guest to share their feather bed. She got up and went to the window directly and saw him again, on the wagon seat, half obscured now by the quickening snow. She felt again that lust, and suddenly wept for shame of it.

There had been blood on the ground outside that place but the night's snowfall had covered it. Jessie woke early by the side of Cal's body and stared at the light thrown up by the fresh-fallen snow—a bar of brilliance on the sill beneath the drawn window blind. That was when she first heard Farjeon's voice and footsteps outside the house. Jessie had not undressed for bed that night; it had seemed somehow an indecency, with the dead man beside her. She rose now and went to stoop at the sill, easing the window blind up an inch. Farjeon was a few yards off, walking through the fresh snow with Cal's coal shovel in his hand, stopping every few paces to put it to the hard, ermined earth and try it with a stab of his foot. She fancied at first that he had gone mad, but then she could sense the fever in his movements even before she threw a shawl round her shoulders and ran out to look at him. His face was flushed and dry and his eyes glittered with it. He coughed a little, a thick, deep bubble breaking deep inside him somewhere, and stared at her, striking the shovel with his shoe again.

Come inside, Mister Farjeon.

He shook his head again in fierce obsession.

I can't do that now, he said with dreamy courtesy. I have to do this first.

Do what? she whispered, though she knew well what he was about.

Why, I have to dig two graves, he said, coughing again that deep, hidden bubble and leaning wearily into the shovel.

He raised his eyes to her.

Two graves, he explained again. A big one and a little one.

She laid her fingers on his icy hand.

You're mighty sick, Mister Farjeon, she said. You've got to get inside where it's warm. You're half dead with the cold.

Mother Dunne raised the window and stared out at them across the snowy sill.

Get him in here, Jessie, she cried. He's burning up with the pneumonia.

If I had a spade, Farjeon said. This here's a coal shovel. It's no good for digging. If I had a spade.

The shovel had bitten an inch into the hard ground now, he leaned into the handle, straining, then hit it again with his heel. He paused and ranged his gaze round him.

This is my ground, ain't it? he whispered. That's my land yonder, ain't it? This place I'm digging—it's mine, ain't it?

She grabbed his big arm gently; she could feel the throb of fever under the thin coat.

No, she said. This ain't your land, Mister Farjeon.

He glared at her, his eyes like a child's.

Then whose is it? he said. Is it you'ns?

He shook his head, his flushed face not sweating, no tear in his eyes.

Is it your land? he said. I can see by your face that it is. Then looky here. All I want is space for two graves—

It ain't my land, she said gently. Listen, Mister Farjeon—

No, you listen now, he said, his voice full of sudden, quiet reasonableness. It's your land. I can see that. Sure. I know this ain't my part of the country. What was I thinking? It's your land. So looky here. I'll pay you. As soon as I get work I'll give you whatever you ask out of my first pay.

It's company land, she said softly. It's nobody's on earth.

He frowned on that, mulling it over a spell behind his fevered

70

face. He shook his head and stared round him at the white, frozen yard.

But I've got to bury them, he said dreamily. What's left? Don't you know what's left? The county will come directly with the dead-wagon, that's what's left. What if I don't bury them myself? The county, it'll bury them in Potter's Field.

He shook his head again. He stared at the shovel.

If I had a spade, he said, striking the earth again. I can't let them be buried in Potter's Field.

Jessie's eyes blurred with sudden tears. She thought of that place, common end of them all. She glanced upward at the low fleece of gray winter clouds and bit her lip over the fancy that a man might as well reckon to dig a hole in that hard, cold sky as bury a body in company land.

Farjeon mumbled something; he was half delirious, she knew that. She followed him after he had dropped the shovel as if in some sudden, frightening afterthought and went on round the corner of the house. He hurried to the edge of the wagon bed and stared in at the shape the bodies made beneath three inches of fresh-fallen snow.

They're still there, he said softly.

He sighed.

I thought maybe the county had taken them away while my back was turned.

He seemed to have forgotten about the shovel now. He stopped staring at the shapes in the wagon bed and looked down at his trembling outstretched hands.

You're mighty sick, Mister Farjeon, Jessie whispered. Please come indoors where it's warm.

He stared at her, then glanced round at the house, the barren, stricken land.

This ain't my home, he said. I don't know where this is.

Down the white hill Jessie could see a county truck and a sheriff's car and some deputies and state troopers clustered round the tipple. They had pried loose some slumped shape from the struc-

71

ture and heaped it onto a stretcher which two of them shoved in the back of the truck. Presently the truck, with siren wailing and led by two troopers on motorcycles, led the way up the rough road. Jessie reached out for Farjeon's arm, turning him toward the house, hoping he would not hear the county wagon on its way among the houses to pick up the five other dead of last night's raid. Farjeon shook free of Jessie's hand and stared about him again; he seemed oblivious of her, of the nearing siren. On the threshold he looked up at the house and shook his head.

This ain't home, he argued weakly. We don't live here. Where's Jean gotten to?

Jessie remembered how she had felt about him the night before: the smell of violence in him that had roused her so. Now it was only the woman in his face; he was like a shaking child as she led him into the house. Mother Dunne stared him up and down when the door closed behind them.

Get him over to the hearth, she said. Look at him. Just burning up with fever!

They got Farjeon into the chair before the fire while Jessie knelt and rubbed his cold hands. When the siren stopped in front of the house they listened till the boots came crunching up the snowy path. A moment later came the heavy knock at the door. Jessie opened it and stared at the big sheriff who stood there with two troopers behind him. The big man walked in and stared coldly around him.

Who's dead here?

Jessie trembled and her eyes blurred in the first, brief grief she had really felt for Cal. She pointed wearily to the bedroom door.

He's in there, she whispered. On the bed.

One button fell from Cal's eye as they carried him through the room; his left eye, black as the eye of a spoiled doll stared reflectively at the ceiling; on the tip of his nose, upturned to the gray, heavy sky, there glistened, like the bead on the nose of a slaughtered hare, a single drop of dried blood. Mother Dunne rocked in her chair, fresh wrath in her face; she seemed tensed as if awaiting some further, expected outrage. Jessie followed the men into the yard to the truck.

And them, she said, pointing to Farjeon's wagon. Them two in there.

Farjeon seemed to hear nothing that was going on about him. He crouched, huddled as close as he could get to the heat of the fire; it seemed as though no flame in the world could ever warm him again. When the bodies were in the wagon the sheriff and the two troopers came back. The big man looked up and down at the old woman.

Now we want you, he said.

And for what? she snapped, not ceasing a pace of her rocking.

It's known that you're the chief agitator of this place, he said. You and the man named Turley.

Mother Dunne snorted.

Tom Turley? she cried. Why, he was one who voted last night to settle it and go back to work!

Nevertheless, Roseanna Dunne, said the sheriff quietly, you're under arrest.

Mother Dunne scoured him with a look and rocked faster.

What's the charge, mister? she cried. Standing up to those murderers last night?

The sheriff snapped the handcuffs from his belt and opened them.

There was murder done here last night, said the sheriff. An atrocity I've never yet seen the like of. Murder against a deputy of mine named Joseph Tzack. And you and Turley are being charged with it. Mother Dunne thrust out her wrists for the handcuffs and flung her face up at him.

And what of the murder of my son last night by your so-called deputies? she cried as he led her out the doorway. What of the bodies that lie out yonder stacked like cold stovewood in your County dead-wagon? What of the murdered wife and child of that poor stranger who sets back yonder in there, half dead by the fire? You charge me with the murder of one of your fake deputies.

73

That's praise, Jim Kelso! I only wish to God it was the truth!

The wind blew against the house and flakes of fresh snow hurried earthward.

I only wish to God it was so! I'd be proud! Jessie could hear the old woman shout as they packed her into the sheriff's car.

Proud! She shouted the word again, half drowned in the wail of the siren as the cortege headed back down the hill and up the long road to Glory jail. Now Farjeon seemed to remember something undone, a business outside the house, in the yard, in the wagon. When he got halfway to the door and fell, Jessie half caught him and eased him to the floor. Then she dragged him in and put him in the bed, under quilts and comforters, and settled on a chair by the door to watch.

By sundown Farjeon seemed verging on the full glare of delirium. Jessie had stripped him down to his underwear and heaped a whole chestful of quilts and comforters over him but nothing seemed to warm him. She made him drink a whole hot saucepanful of sheep-nanny tea but the sweat would not come. Now he strained and twitched under the covers, from time to time tossing his head on the bolster and glaring about him into the half-light behind the drawn window blind.

Jean? he would say in a clear voice. Where's she gone to? She's got to be careful, you know. It's nigh her time.

After nightfall Telligrew and Bonar came to the house. Telligrew sat at the table in the lamplight, a small, awkward man still stained from the mines after six weeks' strike. He looked at Jessie while Sears stood staring moodily out the window.

Will they be coming down the hill from Mexico again tonight? Jessie asked.

Telligrew shrugged.

I don't suppose so, he said. What need of strikebreakers now? I reckon you know that.

You mean with Mother Dunne in Glory jail, she said. And Tom Turley.

To hell with Tom, said Telligrew. He voted to go back anyway last night. Besides, that killing down on the tipple—that was his notion. She had no part of it. You know that. She was up here all along. I reckon they know that too. That's not why they taken her.

He shook his head.

We should have put up a fight when they come for her, he said.

He looked at Jessie and smiled.

Somehow the fight was clean gone out of everybody when the sun come up today.

Jessie sighed.

Did they vote to go back?

Last night it was a tie vote, Telligrew said. They're meeting again tonight. I think they'll vote to go back.

Jessie was still a moment.

Maybe it's better, she said. Another night like last night would have done us in.

I know that, Telligrew said. It's been deep waters to wade through.

He colored up then and stared at his wreathed fingers in the lamplight.

My woman, he said, she told me to tell you how awful sorry we was about Cal.

Sears turned from the window briefly.

That goes for us too, Jessie.

Jessie's eyes filled up. She glanced toward the shut bedroom door and bit her lip.

Thanks, Mister Telligrew, she said. It's hard.

He saw her blush; he could hear Farjeon's heavy breathing in the other room.

How's that poor stranger? he said. The one everybody's calling the barefoot man?

Awful sick, she said. He sat out on his wagon all night in the freezing weather.

I know, Telligrew said. We could see him. He was there when

we put the lamps out. We seen him again this morning at sunrise.

He's got the pneumonia, Jessie said.

She shook her head.

There's no money for the doctor. I'm nursing him the best way I know how.

Jean? Where'd you go to, Jean? Farjeon's voice rose in the other room. Come back, dear love!

He's mad with the fever, Jessie said.

How do you mean?

He thinks I'm her, she said.

You mean his poor dead lady?

She nodded quickly and shot Telligrew a quick look, coloring again.

I'll sleep in here tonight, she said. In a blanket on the floor yonder by the fire.

She could feel them thinking of her alone there in the house that night with Farjeon; she could sense them measuring her as a widow on the lookout for a man. She was glad when they had gone. She had not been hungry so she ate nothing; she sat on the straight-backed chair in the bedroom staring at Farjeon's red, straining face in the lamplight.

Jean? he whispered, his eyes fixing upon her. Jean, is that you, Jean?

She was glad he was full of the woman again. It eased her somehow; the violence she had smelled in him that had roused her so last night—he seemed drained of it now. She folded her fingers in her lap, watching him, seeing his eyes and face all full of the woman again, watching him yonder on the bed, weak as a baby. It made her feel like his mother for he seemed to her as helpless and woebegone as some child of her own. He mumbled on into the evening, tossing and straining in the quilts; his heavy breath to Jessie was like some strange, hypnotic rhythm. So that, after a spell, she dozed and slept dreamlessly and when she opened her eyes she saw him up now, out of the bed now and sitting on a split-bottom chair by the window, staring at the blank blind with his

76

lamplit eyes quiet and yellow and wholly mad. He was speaking, too, in a soft, crazy voice that was at the same time quiet and easy—almost a whisper—so that she could barely make out the words, the names he was saying over and over, like some sort of soul-restoring litany.

First the man in the army coat. Then Shaloo, Farjeon was saying. Then Kitto. Then Paul.

He paused, breathing sharp and slow.

But who's Number One?

He said the names over in that soft, almost loving voice, over and over again, his mad eyes fixed throughout on the window blind as if he were looking through it and out the black, cold window beyond it into some vision of redemption. Jessie shivered and dismissed any notion of trying to get him back into bed; something in the set of his back and shoulders told her that the fever had made him suddenly strong as he had been weak before.

Jessie rose slowly, never taking her rapt gaze from him, and closed and latched the door into Mother Dunne's little room. Farjeon must have heard her light footsteps for his gaze swung swift as light and his great yellow eyes fixed her.

Jean, he whispered, after a thick, heavy breath. Jean, do you know what has happened?

Jessie nodded, watching his face in fascination and terror of something in her own feelings.

No, he said. You nod yes, but you don't know.

She shook her head, rapt, waiting.

Last night, Farjeon said, five men came here and killed my child.

He shook his head, scowling, his eyes squinting at her as if try-ing to make out something familiar that he had seen there moments before.

Who *did* they kill? he whispered. I disremember. It comes and goes—in patches. I could see it all so clear two minutes ago. Who did they kill? Yes. I remember now. It was my child they killed and that child's name was Jean. They shot and killed my blind

77

child-wife Jean, that's who it was! Oh my God. My God. And who else was it? Who else did they murder last night? Was it my mother?

He lifted his fevered stare from the floor and looked at her again.

Jean?

He glared now, shaking his head.

No. You're not Jean!

She watched him, mad there before her, she stared at him, helpless, thinking to herself that she should somehow go lay hands on him and coax him back to the bed. And that chilled her more, when she knew that she wanted him in the bed not because he was sick but for that other thing that scorched her wet thighs now. But she could not make herself go near him yet; the smell of it was back again in the room—the burned scent, the hot smell like a wall scorching above an overheated stove—and the woman in his eyes, that was gone. Without taking her eyes from him Jessie backed slowly away across the creaking floorboards and sat again weakly in the straight-backed chair, swaying as if in a swoon. Farjeon had forgotten her now; he was reckoning on the fingers of his outstretched hands.

Five, he whispered. Him in the army coat. He'll be easy. Then comes four and three—that's Shaloo and Kitto. Then two—that's Paul. Why, that's easy enough, ain't it?

He could have chuckled, or it could have been that thick catch in his slow, labored breathing.

Easy, I tell you, he said again. But Number One. That's the tricky one. Oh yes, that's the one that takes a little time.

He turned the chair, scraping round now, and sat with his back to the window, staring at her again. His eyes focused, then lost it, then found what he sought again.

Jean?

He nodded slowly, glaring at her.

Yes, it's Jean. Oh my God, Jean, for a while here I thought they'd hurt you too!

He knuckled a quick tear away from the corner of his mad face and beckoned to her softly.

Come here, child-wife Jean, he said softly, tilting his head, his face soft with love. Jean?

He shook his head gently, wisely.

No, he said. I don't want you for that. We won't go near the bed. I know we never do that unless you let me.

He buried his face quickly in his fists.

We won't do that, he murmured. Though God knows there are times when I lay in the bed feeling you there, hearing you breathe and stir, and the wanting almost drives me crazy.

He kept his face bowed a spell before his hands fell away to his knees again.

Do you want me now, Jean?

He shook his head.

I know I'm powerful sick, he said. I have this hotness all around me—this fever. But I'm not weak, Jean. And it's queer, Jean—it makes me want that with you all the more. Lord, I could love you till sunrise, Jean. It's like the fever was all a great, hot wanting inside me. Do you want me now, Jean? Is it time? Or is it wrong for me even to ask? Have you got one of your awful sick head-aches, my poor, dear child-wife Jean?

Jessie shut her eyes suddenly—she could feel the red lids quivering as she clenched them tighter against the sight of him; she pressed her hot thighs closer together till her hips ached. The fancy crossed her thoughts that after she had fainted and fallen beside the chair he would carry her to the bed and take her.

No, Lord, Jessie prayed silently, her lips moving in the lamp-shine. Don't let it happen. For it would be a sin. Don't let it happen, Lord. Because it would be a stain and a shame on both their memories!

His gaze was back on her again, searching her tall, slender shape on the chair, in the lampshine.

Are you *really* all right, Jean? Are you *sure* they didn't hurt you too? he whispered anxiously, tensing as if he meant to rise and

79

come to her. Come here, Jean, he said, beckoning again with his hand. Show me yourself, child-wife Jean. Show me they didn't hurt you there.

Jessie stood up, some remnant of reason left in her that she should somehow get him back to the bed and quiet him, then leave him and go still her own feelings somehow by the fireside in the kitchen. He beckoned her to hurry.

I had this mad nightmare, Jean, he was whispering. That they shot my child and then they shot you too. They did shoot my child, didn't they, Jean? That's so, ain't it? But they didn't hurt you. Did they? Why, no. Look at you standing there—all bright-eyed and pretty and alive. What's tonight? Yes, I remember. It's our honeymoon night, that's what it is. We're here in our pretty little room in the Mound Hotel in Glory and it's our honeymoon night. You're all right, child-wife Jean. Oh, my child-bride, you're as sound as I am. Ain't that so?

He squinted his feverish eyes, focusing on her face.

Show me, Jean.

She had come to stand by his side now, her hand on his shoulder, but it was all wrong because the touch of her fingers was gentle and pressing and she had meant it to be firm and urgent, to get him back in the bed, alone, and then be shut of him for a spell. She made her mouth shape the words.

Mister Farjeon—

She strove suddenly then to remember his first name—Jack, that was it—Jack, the woman had called him; she fancied he would obey her if she called him that.

Show me, Jean, he whispered, tilting his head at her, his face a wreath of worries.

Jack, you better—

She could hear her voice striving numbly over the words; her breath seemed to come stumbling in her throat.

Jack, you must get back in the bed. Then I'll cover you up again and—

No, wait, he was saying, laying his hands gently, shyly on her hips now. I had this mad dream that men came tonight. What is tonight? Is it—? Yes, it's our honeymoon night. I had this dream they came and shot you through the body. Oh, my darling child-bride, it's not so, is it? Jean, show me.

She rested her fingers lightly on his big hands where they rested on her hips and felt the faintness vanish and nothing now but the slow, burning pressure of his hands there and the ragged drum of her pulses, while the ghost of the dead woman and Cal's accusing face, these slowly withdrew from the lamplit stillness around them.

Let me see, Jean, he said gently, in that worried voice and fetched up the hem of her skirt. No. No, I won't touch you. I know you never let me touch you there unless you want me to. I promise, child-bride Jean. I just want to see. Can I see, Jean?

Yes, she heard her voice whisper, somewhere far beyond her mouth.

She stood still at first, letting him lift her clothes high round her small breasts and felt him search anxiously with his hot fingers across the shuddering bare flesh of her belly. He sighed at last and groaned an utterance of love and relief, pressing his cheek close against the place.

No. Why, no. No one hurt you there, he breathed and she could feel the breath the words made and the slight stir of his lips against the bare skin. It was all a dream. No one shot my child-bride, no one hurt my dearest love. Did they, Jean?

No, Jack, she lied softly, but it was all right because the ghost of those two had gone away from between them and she knew what was going to happen and it was all right and she flung her fingers down to his hands, snatching the dress from his grip and pulling it quickly over her head. She could hear in her own throat the whimper of desire and she was not feeling Cal's presence anymore nor the woman's but hearing only the wind against the house and Farjeon's own thick, feverish breath and the rustle her clothes made as she flung them to the floor and the sound, the sense, of the thick drumming of her heart as she drew him up and across

81

the boards to the bedside and down at last on top of her.

Jean! Oh my God, Jean, and I dreamed you were dead!

And she lay back while he sought her body out in the passion of his delirium and fever; she lay round and beneath him slimly, falling open softly, limply at first, then rocking him savagely in the pale, twined cradle of her legs. And suddenly she began whispering savagely the coarse, good love word of urging that had always so shocked and shamed poor Cal's weak, Calvinist sensibility, saying it over and over again in a thick, hot rush of whispering made sibilant by the sudden rich wetness of her mouth.

And afterward when he was out of her and lay beside her by himself again, whispering the names over and over again to the darkness, she thought, And when he's well again he won't call me by her name anymore, when he's over the fever and its madness he won't ever want me like this again, because the grief will be back and his face will be full of her again. And it was like a knife in her heart, that thought. Because she knew, with a sudden clear, singing wisdom, that the night before, after Cal's death in the ditch, she had seen Farjeon only as a provident stranger, a man, any man, to keep her and her child from begging in the streets of Glory or from the latticed porch of some Baltimore Street brothel. Now she remembered only moments before when she had first called him Jack, and she knew that in that instant when she had first felt the word on her tongue it had come easy to her mouth, and she knew that in that moment she had loved him as she had not ever loved any man on earth.

Even with the fever gone, long after the delirium had lifted, the thing still burned in his face, lighting his eyes to a queer, stunned brilliance that held Jessie still in a kind of tingling thralldom. The first morning after the first day he had been able to walk he was up and dressed long before Jessie had awakened. When she opened her eyes she saw him sitting in the big overcoat on the straight-backed chair by the door. On his head he wore the old man's hat the woman had worn the night they had come there. In his hands, between his knees, he held the pale yellow cream pitcher the woman had carried in her hands, staring down at it now in the half-light of the first rays of morning which paled now coldly behind the drawn window blind.

Where are you going? she whispered.

But he had seemed not to hear; his whole face and eyes and mind seemed brooding, deep in the fragile thing he held in his hands. Jessie flung back the quilts and swung her feet to the cold floor.

Jack, where are you going?

He lifted his eyes then, not moving his face at all, scarcely acknowledging her presence, blinking three times slowly before he spoke.

To Glory, he said quietly.

Jessie stared hard at the fingers she curled in the lap of her plain muslin nightdress.

Are you coming back?

He blinked again twice, aware of her now, studying her question gravely. He reached over and put the cream pitcher carefully on the dusty bureau and raised his face full to her now, fixing her with a solemn, thoughtful look.

It don't seem fair, he said. It don't seem right someways. Me staying here at your place. Not with all the things I've got to do.

You're welcome, she said foolishly, and turned her face a little so that he would not see her color.

I know that, he said. You proved that. I reckon I would have died if you hadn't looked after me. And I thank you for that. Still and all—

He shook his head.

I was out of my mind with the fever, he said. For a while there I thought you were her—thought you were Jean. Lord knows the things I must have said to you. Out of my head things. I hope you can understand that.

She nodded quickly.

Oh, I do. I do.

He flushed and looked away to the cream pitcher on the bureau top.

It don't seem right, he said. Me staying here. You with your grief so fresh and all. And me with all the things I've got to do. There's no sense me dragging you into things like that.

Maybe I don't mind that, she said. Maybe I could be some help.

You've already helped, he said. I told you that. You saved my life. I can't ever repay you for that. That's not it.

She could not lift her face to look at him; her gaze seemed woven into the lace of her writhing fingers. She could not bear to look at him and have him see the things she felt to be naked in her face. He coughed and cleared his throat.

Think about it, he said. Me staying here with you. It don't seem right. Sleeping in the same bed with you at night.

He shook his head.

You don't understand, he said. You can't understand how it was between her and me.

I know, she said. You loved her.

It was more than love, he said. She was like a child to me—my child. She was as much a child as the one she carried inside her the night she died.

She was your woman, Jessie said softly.

No, he said. More than that. She was my child. It was like that. She was my child to me. And now that she's gone—

He shrugged his big shoulders and shook his head with a queer smile. He fixed her again with that gaze.

It couldn't never be like that with you and me, he said. So it don't seem fair—

I don't mind, she said with a soft, faint break in her voice.

I know, he said, You're good. You're grownup and not a bit like her. You saved my life and I'm beholden to you for that.

He cocked his head and studied her.

If I stayed, he said, you might misunderstand it. You might take it into your fancy that I felt about you the way it was with her.

He shook his face and smiled sadly.

I couldn't never love anyone again, he said. Not that way. And you might be expecting that—hoping for it. So it don't seem fair.

He squirmed on the chair, suddenly restless and made uncomfortable by the things he was trying to tell her. She felt some vague, strong stir of triumph at something, this thing uneasy in his aspect. She sat on the bed edge in her plain muslin nightdress, rubbing her foot against her ankle, her straight sloe-black hair lying in twin silk ropes down over the faint push of her small, round breasts beneath the shabby cloth.

Looky here, Jack, she said suddenly, fixing upon his face the level stare of her violet eyes. I'm not counting on anything from you—I don't have the right. And least of all I don't figure on you loving me. I know what your woman meant to you. I wouldn't ever hope to fill that place.

She was like my child, he said pitifully. My child-bride Jean.

Well, I know that, Jack, the woman went on, gesturing faintly with her fingers. So that proves it. I couldn't ever be that. Child-bride. Child-anything. I'm twenty-three years old, Jack.

Jean was twenty-five, he said suddenly. So I don't reckon it's a matter of age at all.

I don't reckon it is, she said. And I guess I know what you mean. I saw her in the lamplight for a little while that night. I didn't know her. But I watched her. I can see what you mean. The way she ate. Moved around.

Innocence, he said suddenly. That was it. Sometimes I'd look at her—child there before me—and I couldn't quite believe she was fixing to give birth to one. Another child. It didn't seem somehow that we could have made a child together. And—

He colored up and stared at his hands, smiling a little.

And what?

It's a strange thing to say, he went on heavily. Maybe you wouldn't understand it.

What?

It's this, he said. I couldn't never imagine her going to the bathroom. Now don't that sound like the damndest fool thing to say?

Jessie smiled.

No.

He lifted his gaze to her again and shifted once more in his chair as if the sight of her there uneased him.

I—like you, he said. Not like her. Not that. Understand me. Not that way.

She nodded.

I understand, she said. I like you too, Jack.

I'd like to repay you, he said, gesturing awkwardly. Because you saved my life this past two weeks.

She waved her hand.

It wasn't nothing. I'd have done that much for anyone. You don't owe me a thing.

Yes, I do, he said gravely. And I don't quite know how to go about repaying you. I'm a man who pays his debts. Whatever. Debts of darkness, debts of light. I always pay up in the end. That's the way I am.

I know, she said.

How do you know?

She shrugged.

What did I tell you? he said abruptly. What did I say I was going to do—while I was raving with the fever?

You talked some about five men.

What five men?

The five you figure caused her death.

Did I say anything else? Did I say, for instance, what I will do about them?

She studied a moment, then shook her head, the dark ropes of hair swaying back and forth across the rise of her breasts.

What are you going to do? she whispered.

Can you guess? he said quietly. Can't you figure what a man like me has to do to men who killed his child?

She could scarcely endure the sudden, thick wave of excitement his look just now caused in her.

Yes, she said.

Are you sure I didn't speak it out? he said. Are you sure I didn't say what I have to do while I was raving?

No, she said. But I know.

How do you know?

She flushed and cast a quick look at the coiled fingers in the rounded simplicity of her lap.

I got to know you, Jack, she said. I got to know you pretty good this past two weeks. Not from things you said either. I got to know you by—by studying you while you was lying there all sweating and sleeping like a kid after the fever broke.

He glared faintly at her, then shook his head smiling.

I like you, he said. I wish I knowed what it was. You're not like anybody I ever met before. I wish I could lay my finger on what it is about you. I do like you, Jessie.

She blushed and shot him a swift, lowered stare through her black lashes.

You're just thankful to me, that's all, she said.

No, he said. It's more than that. But I can't place it. I've never had many friends in my life. Nor gals either. Jean was my first gal. The only one. The only one that will ever be. I know that. I don't mind it either—the thought of it—the prospect of always being alone.

He glanced toward the window.

Besides, he said, I may not have too much farther to go.

What do you mean?

He shrugged.

When I do what I have to do, he said, they'll probably catch me. Afterwards. Not before. Not even during. I've thought it all out too careful for that.

She shivered suddenly at something in his voice.

I'd sure hate to see anything happen to you, Jack.

Why, Jessie?

Because I—like you, she said. You don't take care of a person raving sick for two weeks and not get to like them a lot. I'd hate to see anything happen to you, that's all.

Well, maybe it won't, he said, and then cast her a slow, careful look.

What about you, Jessie? he said.

How do you mean?

Well, what will you do? he said. With your man dead and gone. And the old woman—they'll not keep her in Glory jail forever.

She flung her fingers limply from her lap and let them settle again. She smiled at him, a foolish, helpless smile.

I don't know.

Farjeon turned his gaze to the bright bar of snowy light that lay below the window blind along the cracked, dusty sill.

I was thinking, he said. Maybe I could stay on a spell. Here. Until you get back on your feet.

You don't have to—

I know I don't, he said. But I can't just walk away. Not after all you done for me. It's only fair for me to help you get back on your feet.

She blinked away tears and hoped he had not seen their glitter.

Have you got folks you could go live with?

Dead, she whispered. All dead.

Ain't there no one?

She shook her head in a hard, flinging gesture, biting her full underlip, furious with herself.

He stared at her and nodded.

I could, he said again. I could stay on a spell.

She stared at him in a blur of yellow light.

What about money? she said simply then.

He sighed and groped in the pocket of the overcoat, fetching out the small, tight, cloth Bull Durham bag. He studied it in the faint light.

Two hundred dollars, he said.

He cast her a forlorn look.

That was to be for her laying-in, he said. The doctor. Maybe a hospital bed for a day or two.

He put the bag back in his pocket.

Now I have to buy something else with it, he said. I have to go in to Glory this morning and buy it. It won't cost all of two hundred dollars. But it won't leave much out. Maybe a hundred and fifty.

He smiled at her.

That might be enough for a few weeks, he said. Long enough for me to do what I have to do. Long enough for you to get back on your feet.

She lifted her fist to her teeth then, biting the knuckle.

Back on my feet, she cried softly. So I can walk the streets of Glory begging. Back on my feet! So maybe I can walk up to the porch of Rosie Harper's whorehouse and ask for a cot.

The passion of her words touched him and he watched then as her face contorted in a welter of grief and she flung her hands over her face, bowing into her knees, her shoulders quaking with sobs. He sat watching a moment helplessly then rose and came to her side slowly to stand by the bed, his hand resting awkwardly on her back.

You're pretty, Jessie, he said gently. Shouldn't be no problem for you to find another man.

She sobbed something indistinguishable into her fingers and flung her head from side to side.

Lost! Lost! she cried presently in a soft, drowning voice. Jack. Oh, Jack, I'm lost. There's no one. There's nowhere!

He sat clumsily on the edge of the bed by her side, his hand still resting stiffly on her shoulder.

Jessie, listen, he said then. I reckon we're both lost.

He paused, measuring his words, thinking how he could say this thing without her finding a wrong meaning in it.

It's true, he said presently. We're both lost. But that don't mean two lost people can't help each other.

She seemed not to hear him, her shoulders heaving still in the tough grip of her grief.

I have to find a job anyways, he said. Somewheres. Somehow. This money won't last us very long. So maybe—

She quieted some and presently her fingers, still wet with tears, reached out and felt for his hand.

I never worked in a mine, Farjeon said. Maybe there's a job open with five men dead the other night.

He felt an old, strange fear at the presence of her fingers twined among his own. There was a danger of some newness in the scent of her so close beside him and the warmth of her pressure against his shoulder. But his mind seized the idea more firmly.

Maybe the mine would be a good place to be, he said. Maybe they wouldn't notice me there. Maybe nobody would think to look for me down there after I do what I have to do. I'm nothing but a farmer. But maybe I could learn mining.

He shook her shoulder gently.

Jessie, take hold of yourself.

She stopped crying then and turned her tear-stained face to him. He stared honestly into her eyes.

Jessie, I'm still in love with her. Jean. I want you to know that. But I like you. I want to stay and help you. Understand me when I say there couldn't ever be anything betwixt you and me like it was with her.

I don't care, she whispered. I'll be whatever you want me to.

I like being near you, he said, in a shaken, new voice. I don't know what it is. You always smell good. And clean. The way she always did. I don't mean you're like her. You're as different as night and day. Jean was fair. You're black as a gypsy, Jessie. But your smell puts me in mind of her. Like fresh-baked bread.

That's the nicest thing anybody ever said to me, she murmured, knuckling away a tear from her cheek.

She could feel the stir of it in him again and wondered if he remembered the nights he had striven among her limbs, crying the woman's name. Farjeon was trembling now, faintly; she could feel the faint quiver of his flesh through the cloth of the coat on which her fingers rested.

The nicest thing, she said again. Nobody never said such a nice thing like that about me.

It's true, he said, staring at her eyes with that puzzled look on his face. I feel, well, close to you, Jessie. I wish I could put my finger on it.

He looked away toward the chair where he had been sitting when she awoke.

She pressed his arm with her fingers.

Jack, I don't want to lose nobody else to the mine.

He stiffened a little at that.

I'm not yours to lose, he said. I want to make that clear. I don't own you. You don't own me. We will live here together for a spell. But there mustn't be any love in it. There's no more of that left in me to give.

I understand.

Do you? How can you?

I do, that's all.

How can you, Jessie? When you remember what I did to you that first night of my raving?

She searched his eyes and shook her head, disbelieving.

But you thought I was her, she said.

Part of the time I did, he said. Part of the time I knew well and good it wasn't Jean. I didn't know who it was, but I knew it wasn't her. It was all too fierce and full of want for it to be Jean.

You do remember then? she asked, tracing a vein in his hand with her long, pale finger.

Yes, he said. God forgive me, I do. Sometimes I was sure it was Jean. And then I'd see the face beneath me plain. Your face, Jessie. Eyes the color of violets and hair black as any gypsy on the roads. It was like seeing faces by lightning flashes. Now Jean, now you. I was raving. And the fever and the raving—they only seemed to make me want that more. I couldn't get used to it.

She stroked the small hairs on his wrist.

91

Why? she said. Didn't you always want that with her?

He pondered it carefully.

If you want the God's truth of it, he said, she never did favor it much—me doing that to her.

But if she loved you?

I tell you she was more like my child, he said carefully. I only did it to her when she let me. When she asked me. When she said it was all right. She used to have headaches a lot. When she had them she couldn't bear me to touch her.

He sought her eyes then quickly, his brow creased with worry.

Tell me one thing, Jessie, he said.

What, Jack?

I didn't—what I mean to say is, I didn't rape you, did I?

No.

How did it happen?

Her hand settled on his arm again; the trembling had stopped, she could feel only the stiffening of his flesh in tension.

It just happened, she said.

Did I ask you if I could do it to you?

No. You didn't have to. I let you know.

How? he said, his eyes fixed on her face in a drugged fascination.

I done this, she said, and rose boldly and drew her nightdress over her head and dropped it on the bed behind her. She stood before him now, in slender, dimpled simplicity and looked down into his thoughtful, unblinking eyes.

It's a pure wonder, he said, his eyes searching up and down her nakedness with frank joy. Much as I loved Jean, I never wanted to do that to her the way I want to do it to you.

I know, she said.

How do you know?

Because you told me, she said. She was your child.

He drew her down to him then and fell back across the bed with her, staring down still with that childlike incredulity at the splendors of her flesh. She bit her lip and clenched her lashes shut across her cheek as his fingers gently brushed her small breasts; touching them shyly as if he feared he might hurt them. She reached her hands up then and laced her fingers behind his head, dragging his head down to her mouth. The old man's hat fell off on the quilt as she breathed again the old word, the coarse, good word of love's urging into his neck. He stared at her curiously while her hands were fumbling with his clothes. He kissed her shyly and smiled, pulling his face up from her.

Jean would have run off from me for good, he said, if I'd ever so much as breathed that word in her presence.

I know that, she said. But I'm not your Jean. I'm just Jessie.

And she drew his head down again with the fingers of her free hand across her mouth and said the word again over and over, fast, in a pulsing litany of whispering breath against his ear. He kissed her again passionately and when he felt the probe of her small, quick tongue against his own he stiffened and drew up from her. She looked at him through her dark, thick lashes and smiled with a faint, fine irony.

Don't you want to?

He studied her with that plain, unblinking gaze of curiosity. He was like a child who had never had a toy and now this splendid, pale, black-haired thing beneath him was his toy.

You can tell me with your mouth that you don't want to, she whispered, but where I've got my hand tells me that's a lie.

But it's wrong, he said. Jean hardly in her grave and—

It's not wrong! she whispered and gripped him savagely. It's *life!*

Jessie, what is it about you? Lord, I wisht I knew, he cried softly, and rolled gently into the crux of her slender, open limbs. This time was more savage than the first: they rocked and tumbled in a hurried frenzy on the quilts and the things she whispered savagely in his ear inflamed him quickly to a new fierce hunger. Toward the end of it Jessie reached quickly for the bolster and stuffed a corner of it into her wild, open teeth to quench her screams. She lay spent and sprawled then, her long legs falling from around him and smiled up at him, feeling the glow of the hot wetness against her womb where he had been.

Now I've got to go to town, he said after a while, his hat back on his head, his overcoat buttoned up, sitting and watching her curiously from the chair again.

She watched him drowsily and smiled while his eyes searched her body again with that puzzled, devouring curiosity.

I know you do, she said.

She smiled.

But you'll be back, she said.

You know that, don't you? he said simply. You don't even have to ask me. You just tell me because you know I will.

She shrugged.

I like doing it to you, he said. I can't hide that.

He studied a moment in silence.

I like it even more than the times when I did it with her, he said. But I loved her. That's the difference.

I don't mind, she said simply.

He searched her face with that careful gaze.

Do you know what I have to do?

Yes.

And you don't mind living with a man who has such deeds in his mind?

No.

There may be danger, he said.

I've always lived in the shadow of that, she said.

He was silent a minute. Then he felt in his coat pocket for the small bag of money.

Then you know what I'm going in to Glory to buy this morning?

Yes, she cried, with the sudden gaiety of a child.

What? he asked, puzzled.

A flower for me! she cried in a soft whisper.

What?

Not a whole bouquet! she cried. Just one flower. One flower for me to pin on my dress. That won't cost too much.

94

He smiled and stood up.

All right, he said, I'll buy that too.

And he was gone out the door, and she lay back smiling in the quilts, her naked skin suddenly quick with gooseflesh in the chill of the room that he had warmed, and lay listening, smiling, with her lips against the pillow, as his heavy shoes went striding down the frozen snow toward the road that led to Glory.

Jessie was obsessively clean about herself: sometimes she bathed as often as three times a day in the iron washtub in the kitchen. Still there was a natural sexual fragrance about her flesh which still clung to Farjeon's clothes, teasing his mind as he wandered down the bright morning light of Lafayette Avenue. It was a mild torment to him—the thought of his grief for Jean, which was still so fresh, mixed with the wanton vision of Jessie's dark, striving nakedness beneath him in the quilts.

Forgive me, honey, he whispered to the ghost of the dead woman somewhere around him in the pale morning. Forgive me. I purely don't understand it. It's a wonder that I just can't ponder to its depths. The smell of her—

And he quivered in his clothes. For the thought of Jean's blonde, passive body lying frightened before him in the old bed at the farm seemed so obscure and remote now. Jessie was a newness, a strangeness, that frightened him.

But I don't love her, he thought, reconciling it as best he knew how. So it ain't faithlessness. It's a new thing. It's a strange thing. It's a wonder. But it ain't what I felt for Jean. So I reckon in time I'll go away from her and never even remember what it was. And it won't stop me from what I have to do.

Even in the bright, cold wind that blew from the river he could smell the scent drifting up from his clothes, the faint, sharp aroma of laundry soap and the soft, acrid sweetness of Jessie's passion which had left his clothes still rumpled and damp, that compost of pleasant odors which conjured now in his mind's vision—even sharper than his image of the dead Jean—a picture of Jessie's body sprawled loose before him in the quilts, open and beckoning, her pale cheeks flushed, her dark, violet eyes squinting through her thick lashes in a sharp, puckered grimace of desire. It haunted him. Still, it did not shake him loose from the quiet, violent purpose of his morning's quest. During the long, cold walk along the rocky road to town he had decided that it would be senselessly risky to try to buy the gun in Glory. So he waited a half hour on the windy corner of Seventh and Lafayette and caught the street car to Wheeling. On the ride through the farms and mill-town slums he thought how easy it had been years before to walk into the hardware store in Glory and buy his shotgun. So long ago. And for such a different purpose. And a handgun was different—they would want identification.

In Wheeling he walked the streets for a time pondering the matter of how to go about it, his eyes fixed on the pavements as if he half fancied he would find the gun lying there. It was cold but he felt warm, feeling as if everyone he passed had gone away with the memory of something that they had seen in his face, something printed upon him somehow that announced his dark plan. He tarried a quarter of an hour before a hardware store and then sought out another, in a darker part of town, and lingered before it a while, deciding at last not to go in at all, fancying that now he must spend the better part of the morning learning how he might buy a gun in secret. As a man raised around farms, Farjeon had little knowledge of towns and their underworld. Still, it seemed to him that it shouldn't be too hard in times like these to find almost anything for sale, if a man had the money. Yes, it was all a matter of chance, of time and place. He knew he had to be careful about it, to go slow about it; he wanted no one remembering his face to tell about it afterward. It baffled him a little, how to go about it in a safe, intelligent way. Maybe he should just go to a hardware store and buy the thing outright. No—he pondered that a moment and some sense told him that this was the better way. He wandered the littered, cold streets for a spell until he seemed to have come into a section shabbier and poorer than the

96

rest. He saw a breadline which extended a block and a half from the entrance of a Salvation Army soup kitchen and joined the end of the ragged line. Among these faces—some of them fresh and unused to poverty but most of them gray and hardened—it seemed that he might find the clue to what he was searching for. He stood there an instant, shivering a little in the brisk wind that blew from the river, until he felt a sudden touch at his elbow. He turned and saw the short, ragged, unshaven man who had jostled him. The man smiled, lonely, a little ashamed, wanting to talk to help keep the cold off.

Howdy. Been out of work long?

Farjeon shook his head.

Not long.

The grizzled face scowled; the man bit his tongue and grunted.

You won't believe this, he said, but I turned down a job not half an hour ago.

That so?

It is, snapped the other. I'd rather stand here and freeze to death before I get my soup than take that kind of work.

What kind is that? Farjeon asked idly.

The man laid a grimy finger on Farjeon's sleeve and fixed him with a watery stare.

I'd rather starve where I'm standing, he said, than take a job like that.

Like what?

Finking, said the other. That's what they're hiring over there today. Finks to break the strike.

Farjeon breathed in slowly, carefully, then breathed out before he spoke.

Who's doing the hiring?

The short man shook his head.

One of them outfits, he said. One of them organizations of hired goons.

You don't know the name?

No. I never waited round to find out. I was spending my last nickle on a cup of hot coffee in this here diner. Feller sort of sidles up to me and put it to me straight: Did I want to go to work? I asked him what doing and he told me. Coffee was all gone by then or I swear I'd have throwed it plumb in his face.

Farjeon shut his eyes a moment, feeling within him the strong flow of the hunch that chance was guiding him true.

What sort of looking man was he?

Mean-faced. A morning drinker. I could smell it on his breath. Never did trust no morning drinker. Not worth a damn.

How was he dressed?

Hat. Shoes in good shape. Looked like he had a buck in his pocket.

What kind of coat?

Sorty tan-colored.

Army coat?

That's it! Say, did he ask you too? Was you in that diner this morning?

Where is it? Farjeon said quietly.

Across from the Benwood Mill main building. Corner of Twenty-third and Chaplaine. Say, you don't look like the kind of feller who'd take a job like that.

I know, Farjeon breathed quickly, I'm not. But I have to.

He slipped quickly out of the line then and ran across the bricks toward the Glory street car which had stopped at the corner. He caught it and rode it south two miles to Benwood and got off and stood in the wind, his eyes searching for the diner. When he found it he went into it slowly, thinking to himself, but it's all happening too fast. I have to get the gun first. I can't kill him with my hands. He searched the backs of the men at the counter for the color of the familiar army coat. It wasn't there. He sat for nearly an hour, sipping cup after cup of black coffee and staring out at the pickets carrying signs across the street. He finished a coffee and called for another one, and while the counterman was pouring Farjeon saw, from the corner of his eye, the entrance of the man he was looking for. Farjeon kept his eyes on the steaming cup in his hands, feeling the vapor in his nostrils as he lifted the cup slowly and squinted at the image of his eyes, reflected. He sipped the liquid slowly, hoping he looked poor enough, desperate enough, badly in need of work, any work. He tried to make his big shoulders look rounder, more slumped in despair. At the touch of the hand on his sleeve Farjeon looked slowly round.

You ain't a striker, are you? Cotter said.

He was on the stool beside him now. Farjeon stared at the space of throat above the blue shirt collar, fancying how easy it would be to reach out and throttle the man where he sat.

No, he said.

The man nodded.

I didn't reckon you was.

He hunched forward, as if warming to his business.

Hunting work?

Farjeon weighed that and glanced into his coffee again.

What kind of work?

Easy job. Short, though. Just an afternoon's work.

He glanced around him furtively and squeezed Farjeon's arm.

Good pay, he whispered. If you work out it could mean other jobs later. I think you would. Work out. I figure you for a man who'd rise in this job.

What doing?

Cotter gestured with his head toward the pickets beyond the windows and bent his face closer to Farjeon's shoulder. Farjeon could smell the drink on his breath.

Settling that little business across the street yonder, Cotter whispered.

Farjeon moved slightly, trying to ease the stiffness, the tension that had come over him. He tried to look only mildly interested. Cotter cleared his throat and wiped his nose with a knuckle.

Shaloo's hiring, he said.

Farjeon turned his gaze back to the face again.

Who?

Shaloo.

Farjeon shook his head.

Well now, I never heard tell of him.

Never heard tell of Shaloo? Cotter cried softly. Biggest industrial-relations man in seven states. You're kidding.

Farjeon shook his head again, his eyes fixed carefully on the cup in his hands. He breathed twice—a measuring, thoughtful silence.

If Shaloo's hiring, Farjeon said quietly, how come Shaloo ain't here?

Cotter drew back with an expression of mock dismay. Him? Here? Dirtying his shoes in this part of town? Not Mister Shaloo. He don't hardly ever step out of the suite of rooms up at a certain local hotel. Not till the job is finished. Mister Shaloo? In a dump like this? Mister, you're kidding.

He shook his head and stared at Farjeon.

He leaves the hiring to guys like me, he whispered.

He reached over and felt Farjeon's arm through the cloth of the coat.

You'd do just fine, he said. You're a good, stout boy. You ain't a bum neither—not like most of the ones I hire. I can tell that. You ain't no bum. We could sure use you. I got a hunch you'd work up in the job in no time. Most of them bums we hire we never see again. Never have no chance to work up. You'd work up though. I can see that.

That so?

Sure, Cotter said. Like me. Six months ago I was just a plain, ordinary fink. I worked on a couple of big jobs real good for Mister Shaloo and after a while he made me a noble. East Liverpool —another steel strike. Cleveland—auto parts. Then there was that coal strike a few weeks back. Down near Glory. You read about them places, didn't you?

No, Farjeon said softly. I didn't read about them.

Cotter felt Farjeon's arm again and searched him with appraising approval.

I can tell, he said. You're the kind of man Mister Shaloo likes to use over and over again. You're the kind who'd work up fast.

Farjeon felt more quiet inside than he had felt in all the days since that black night. Still, somehow events were not happening to him in their logical order. He ordered his thoughts quickly and faced the man's eyes again with a bold, straightforward look.

I don't need a job, Farjeon said slowly, and patted the small wad of money in his pocket. I've got a little stake.

Cotter considered that.

Stakes run out, he said. A man needs a job. I reckon you'd have a future in this one. A good, stout boy like you. Not no bum like most of them. Stakes run out quick in times like these.

Farjeon shook his head.

I don't need a job.

Cotter stared a spell, then shrugged.

Sure am sorry, he said. We could use a good, stout boy like you. With class and brains to boot.

He lifted his shoes from the counter rail and swung them round on the stool. Farjeon stayed his arm with his hand.

Maybe you could help me, though, he said.

He held the man's eyes in his own steady gaze.

A man like you, he said. He likely knows how to go about certain things.

What certain things? Cotter said.

Farjeon did not blink.

I'm looking to buy something, he said.

He considered what he had said and nodded on it.

I could make it worth your while, he added.

The pale-blue eyes in Cotter's thin, raddled face glinted faintly and the mouth took on a pucker of calculation.

Have you got the money for it?

Farjeon patted his coat pocket again and nodded. Cotter looked away, considering.

A man wants to buy something, he said. He goes into a store and buys it.

No, Farjeon said. Not always he doesn't.

When don't he?

When the something he wants to buy, Farjeon said, is something he don't want it known about.

He patted Cotter's sleeve.

I figured a man in your line of work could steer me right, he said.

Cotter's eyes flicked back to him again.

Dope?

Farjeon shook his head.

I want to buy a gun, he whispered, and waited a spell while the cold blue eyes blinked thoughtfully.

A gun, Cotter said.

Farjeon nodded.

I've been having some family trouble, he said. It's got to be settled. Soon.

A gun, Cotter repeated.

Farjeon waited.

Well now, Cotter said presently. What'd it be worth to you to find out where you could buy such a thing?

Farjeon's hand was in his pocket; his fingers unpeeled a five-dollar bill from the roll and laid it on the counter.

Cotter stared.

Ten, he said.

He sniffed and knuckled his nose again.

It's worth it, he said, and chuckled humorlessly. You look like a man with real family trouble. Like a man who really wants that gun.

I am, Farjeon said. Oh, I am.

Cotter stared at the five-dollar bill beside his coffee cup.

Ten, he said again.

I'll tell you what, said Farjeon. You come with me. Wait outside. I'll give you this five when I go in. When I get what I'm after I'll come out and give you the other five.

And stick me up for the first five, you mean, Cotter said.

Farjeon stared, blinked twice.

No, he said. I'd not do that.

Maybe you wouldn't, Cotter said. Maybe you would. I don't trust nobody. Not in times like these.

Not even Mister Shaloo?

Him. Maybe, said Cotter. He pays me. Pays me good too. If it wasn't for having to stay here on the job I'd take your money and go buy the gun for you. And charge you double what I paid for it. No, I wouldn't. I'm straight. I'm just telling you what some guys would do. I'm straight. I'm just taking ten from you to tell you where you can go buy a gun and no questions asked.

Farjeon stared.

How do I know I can trust you? he said.

Cotter shrugged.

I'll be here all afternoon, he said. Till I get enough men. Then we move.

He stared at Farjeon.

I'll be here, he said again. You can come back if I steer you wrong.

Farjeon looked at him a moment more. Then he reached out another five and watched both disappear into the pocket of the army coat.

Where? he said softly.

At the Polack woman's speakeasy. Northwest corner of Eighteenth and Market. Top floor back.

What's her name?

Sophie. Sophie Worcik.

She'll sell me the gun?

Cotter chuckled.

She's a queer one, he said. Sure. She'll sell it to you. She sells anything. Still and all—

Still what?

She's a queer one, Cotter said again. She's a gambler. Most likely she won't want to take your money as pay. Most likely she'll want you to draw cards for it. Or shoot craps for it. Your roll of

103

dough against the merchandise. She's shrewd, though. She won't let you have it at all if you don't look just right to her.

How do I look to you?

Cotter smiled.

You look right, he said. You look like a man with family trouble. You look like a man who wants a gun real bad.

He nodded.

There'll not be no trouble, he said. You'll get your merchandise. Can I use your name?

Cotter's blue eyes flashed; he shook his head.

Name's Cotter, he said. But don't tell her I sent you.

Why not?

She'll know me is why, Cotter said. She knows I work for Mister Shaloo.

He closed his eyes against Farjeon and turned away.

Never mind what that's got to do with it, he said. Mention Mister Shaloo and maybe she'll tell you. Never mind why.

He fumbled a dollar watch out of his pants pocket and stared at it, scowling. He looked at Farjeon.

I ain't done too well this morning, he said. There's need of thirty men for this job tonight. I ain't signed but twenty-three since sunup.

He stuffed the watch back under the army coat.

Got to get up to the hotel before lunch, he said. Report to Mister Shaloo.

He slid off the counter stool and stared at Farjeon a moment more.

Tell you what, he said. Maybe she'll want to gamble you for it. I tell you she's a gambler. Maybe she will. Maybe she'll stake you the merchandise against your whole stake. So maybe you'll lose.

He nodded and patted Farjeon's shoulder.

If you walk out of her place broke—come on back here. I'll be here. All afternoon, most likely. If you come back broke maybe you'll want that job.

Maybe I will, Farjeon said softly.

Cotter stared at him, up and down.

There's something about you, he said. Like somewheres I'd seen you before.

Farjeon's face did not stir a muscle; he waited.

Whenever I get that feeling about a man, Cotter said, I know he's not just another bum for the job. The kind of a feller who'll work up fast. I figure you for that.

He shook his head.

It's a shame about you, he said.

How's that?

It's a shame you got this family trouble to settle, Cotter said. You look like just the kind of man Mister Shaloo likes to meet.

Farjeon did not smile.

You never know, he said solemnly. Maybe someday it'll happen.

He had the feeling as he watched the man in the army coat walk off down the snowy pavement that it would happen and that the day it would happen on was not yet ended.

Farjeon felt a fresh, quiet peace within himself as he stood in the hallway before the heavy door of the speakeasy and waited after his first knock. He knocked again and waited, feeling even more strongly the new sense of easiness about it all.

The door was unbolted presently, opened, and Farjeon stood staring at a thin, blonde-haired woman with a white scar on her face that ran from her cheek on the left to the corner of her right jaw. She took the dangling cigarette slowly from her mouth and gave Farjeon a practiced, measuring once-over.

Come on in, she said presently.

Farjeon followed her in, glancing round the small, poorly lighted room with its short, unvarnished bar and five empty tables. In the corner stood a darkened jukebox to which the woman now walked and flicked on the lights. Farjeon could see another machine at the other end of the room but its purpose was

105

obscure to him. The woman went behind the bar and stood, leaning into her elbows. Her shrewd, appraising stare was once more upon him.

We got three drinks here, she said. We got whiskey straight, whiskey with ginger ale, whiskey with water.

Farjeon stood still, meeting her stare, thinking how to begin.

You don't look like an early-morning drinker, she said presently.

The cold, blue eyes flickered.

You don't look like no drinking man at all.

Farjeon nodded.

I'm not, he said.

Then what do you want here? Who sent you?

Farjeon hesitated.

Who was it?

A man named Cotter.

The blue eyes flashed.

That son of a bitch, she said. I know him.

She glared at Farjeon now.

Cotter, eh? she snapped. I ought to kick your ass out of my joint.

He's not my friend, Farjeon said.

He's nobody's friend, she said. That son of a bitch.

She drummed her fingers twice on the bar.

I heard he was working for a strike-busting outfit, she said presently.

Farjeon kept still.

And if he's a friend of yours—, she began.

He's not my friend, Farjeon said again.

Still, you say he sent you. You know him. Maybe you're working with him.

She came round to the front of the bar and leaned back against it, studying him above her folded arms.

In which case, she said, you're not welcome here. It was one of them bastards killed my husband Frank in the Weirton strike three years ago.

Farjeon shook his head.

I don't work with Cotter, he said simply and waited.

She glared a moment more and smiled.

I believe you, she said. I know the look. You don't have the look.

She moved to the edge of the table nearest her.

Then what do you want here? she said. You say Cotter sent you?

That's right.

What do you want?

Cotter said you sell certain things, Farjeon said.

The cold, scarred eyes stared again, carefully at him now. The woman pulled back a chair and motioned Farjeon to sit opposite her. He sat slowly and thought to himself how wondrously quiet he felt inside now, now that the thing was begun. He felt there was nothing in his face that could betray what he was going to do, because there was no guilt there, there was nothing but that quiet, peaceful sense that what he had set out now to do was a thing of total and inarguable justice. He met the woman's gaze, liking her suddenly. She had suffered a loss somehow like his own. He felt almost as if he could begin, recklessly, to tell her what he wanted and why he wanted it and she would understand, sympathize and help him. She kept him still in that blue, unblinking study.

You don't want to buy dope neither, she said presently.

She folded her fingers on the table top and stared a moment more.

What *do* you want?

A gun, he said quietly.

She stared back at him thoughtfully, blinking twice, before she got up and went to the door, bolting it.

I don't want no cops coming in, she said. That might embarrass the both of us.

She went to the jukebox and put a nickle in, pushed a button. She stood waiting while the Bing Crosby record began to play.

Then she came back over and sat once more at the table. She searched him again with her eyes, that scarred face weighing the measure of him, ounce by ounce.

You're not a cop, she said. You're not a fink.

She paused.

I can smell a cop, she said. I can smell a strikebreaking fink sonofabitch too. I hate them both.

She smiled a bitter twist of her lips.

I'd give you a gun free, she said, if I thought you was going to kill a cop with it. Or a sonofabitching fink.

She squinted a little at him, tilting her head.

You're not a thief, she said. You're no stick-up man neither.

How do you know all this about me?

It's my business to know, she said quickly. I'd look like some sort of real damned fool if I was to sell you a piece and then have you stick me up for what you paid for it. And maybe the few dollars of my own yonder in the till.

Farjeon waited.

It's family trouble, ain't it? she said, smiling queerly.

She waited then, studying him still, smiling still.

Another man?

Farjeon said nothing. He breathed in slowly, smelling again the sweetness Jessie had left on him but he pushed her now from his thoughts. He knew his thoughts must be of Jean now, his child-wife now; his mind must fix itself upon nothing else but the thing he had to do.

Another man? she said again.

Something like that.

She nodded quickly and rapped the table.

All right, she said, you won't tell me. I'd not expect you to.

She nodded again. The small room was filled now with the music of the jukebox. The woman got up and went to a door behind the bar, unlocked it with one of a ringful of keys from her pocket, and disappeared. She was gone a moment and came back presently with a small cardboard box in her hand. She laid it on the table between them and sat again. She lifted the top from the box and took out the new, shining revolver and laid it on the table in front of him.

Is that what you had in mind?

Farjeon stared at the gun; it looked so small when he thought of the largeness of the things he wanted it to do.

Is it loaded? he said.

She nodded, staring at him with that queer, scarred smile on her mouth.

How many bullets?

Five.

Farjeon's eyelids fluttered slightly.

Just enough, he murmured, half to himself.

What?

I said that would be fine, he said, and touched the gun with his fingertips.

How much? he said.

She had not taken her eyes from his face.

It's worth seventy-five, she said. Maybe a hundred.

She hesitated.

It would cost you fifty if you bought it legal at a hardware store, she said. But then you'd have to leave a record.

She laughed.

You don't want no record, do you?

No.

She searched him some more with her cold blue stare.

How much money have you got?

A little.

How much have you got?

He stared at the gun again, his eyes almost hungry for it.

Enough, he said.

He raised his look to her again.

Did you say seventy-five?

I said maybe seventy-five. Maybe less. Maybe more.

Her blue eyes were dancing with something now. Farjeon watched her, a little more cautiously.

How much have you got on you? she said.

Farjeon kept still. She pushed the revolver closer to his fingers.

What's the matter? Are you afraid I might grab that thing and stick *you* up with it?

No.

Then tell me how much cash you got on you?

Farjeon did not smile, suddenly uneasy.

Two hundred dollars.

Good. That's all I wanted to know. That's all I asked. No harm in asking,

Farjeon shook his head.

It's all I've got. Every penny on earth. And I'm out of work.

He paused.

Still, he said, I've got to have it. I've got to have that gun.

The woman nodded, that odd glitter still in her eyes. She showed a face that seemed almost drugged with some thought behind it.

I know that, she said. That's why I'm going to give you a break.

How do you mean?

Just what I said.

Farjeon still did not smile; he studied her face.

Well, how much do you want for it?

Maybe nothing, she said.

She laughed and lighted a cigarette slowly.

Maybe all you've got.

She stared at him now through the blue curl of smoke.

Didn't Cotter tell you about me? she said.

He shook his head.

I'm a gambler, mister. Didn't Cotter tell you that?

Well, he said—, Farjeon began.

A gambler, she said again. You must understand what it means to be a gambler.

Farjeon wondered what game she might be playing with him.

You're a gambler yourself, she said.

Not much of one, he said. I never bet on anything in my life.

Sure you have, she said quickly. Or you soon will. You're a gambler, stranger.

She chuckled.

When a man takes a gun in his hand he's faced with one of the biggest gambles of all.

It was her turn to keep silent now and she sat staring at him through the cigarette smoke for a long, silent spell. At last Farjeon leaned forward.

You mean you won't sell me the gun outright?

She shrugged and paused again, still thoughtful.

I don't sell guns real often, she said, and when I do sell a gun I read a man real careful first—like weather signs—before I put it in his hands. Maybe that's why I'm still alive. Or not in jail.

She smiled again.

Sometimes then I don't *sell* it to him, she said. Depends on my mood.

She shrugged again.

I told you, stranger, I'm a gambler. I'd rather bet for something than sell it. It's in my blood.

She rose then with the gun in her hand, held by the barrel. She looked down at him.

Will you play? she said.

Farjeon raised his eyebrows and sighed.

I want that gun, he said. I have to have it.

She waited.

So it looks like I've got no choice.

He watched as she went with the gun to the monstrous glass machine that stood against the wall opposite the jukebox. She fetched her ring of keys out with her free hand and turned to Farjeon as she switched on the light inside the machine with a flick of her elbow.

Ever see one of these things?

Farjeon stared at the strange piece of equipment and shook his head.

It's a claw machine, said the woman. It costs a dime to play. See that claw inside yonder? You operate that with these two handles. You try to make the claw pick up whatever it is you want from that pile of junk inside.

Farjeon came to her side and stared through the glass front at the hovering claw, the small mound of cheap wristwatches, flashlights, necklaces, kewpie dolls and mouth harps beneath it. He watched as the woman unlocked the glass door in front and laid the gun inside atop the glittering mound beneath the claw. She closed the door again and locked it. Then she fished in her pocket for a coin.

The first play is free, she said. I'll put the dime in for you each time. The second play will cost you ten dollars. Each time you try to pick up that revolver with the claw. You can tell when your time is up when the motor that runs the claw stops humming. Each time you try I'll put the dime in for you. Each time you fail you pay me ten dollars.

Farjeon smiled ruefully.

It could cost me every cent I've got.

That's right. Or it could cost you nothing. You may pick it up the first try. That's free.

Farjeon paused, fondling the roll in his coat pocket. His hand was sweating lightly.

Don't you want it? she said.

Farjeon nodded, biting his lip.

You could have bought it at a hardware store, the woman said softly, and left a record. There'll be no record with me. I don't care who you use that gun on. I hate cops. There's only one thing lower than a cop and that's a strikebreaking fink. The cops will never get a description of you from me. That's part of what you're buying here, mister. That's part of what you're trying to win.

She searched his face.

Okay?

He nodded and watched as she thrust a dime in the slot and stood beside him listening to the faint whir of the motor within.

He seized the handles hard, suddenly a little angered at her game. He began manipulating the claw till it seemed to swing directly over the gun. He scowled, trying to maneuver it more accurately, trying to get the hang of it quickly. When the humming of the motor grew still the claw stood empty. The woman held out her hand, smiling. Farjeon unpeeled a ten-dollar bill from the roll in his pocket and laid it into her fingers. She took it a moment, then pressed it back into his hand.

You forgot, she said. That one was free.

She chuckled.

Don't get nervous, she said. Show me how steady your nerve is.

She pushed another dime in the slot.

I don't like seeing a gun in the hand of a man without steady nerve.

Farjeon seized the handles again. This time he picked the gun up gingerly by the barrel, held it, lifted it toward the chute, held it until almost the last minute when it dropped and clattered back again. The humming stopped. The woman took the ten dollars from his fingers, pressed in another dime. With desperation his skill increased. By the time he had paid the woman forty dollars his face was sweating lightly. By the time he had given her the fifth bill he was calmer because he knew he could do it. On the seventh try he grasped the gun firmly by the grip and dropped it into the chute.

Fair enough, she said, folding the last bill into her pocket.

Farjeon stood staring at the gun in his hand a moment before he slipped it somewhere into the clothes beneath his coat. He felt her eyes searching his face.

Sure you won't have that drink?

He shook his head.

Sure? You're sweating.

No thanks.

One thing more, she said. I nearly forgot.

Sure. What is it?

Give the gun back to me again, she said. Just for a minute.

Farjeon reached in and brought it out, held it to her by the barrel. He watched as she fetched a man's handkerchief from her skirts and rubbed the gun carefully with it, then held it back to him.

I reckon, she said, they'll be dusting this for prints real soon, mister.

She smiled, unbolted the door, held it open for him.

And when they do I don't want nobody's prints on it but yours.

Farjeon didn't return to the diner right away. He wandered the streets for an hour, luxuriating in the feel of the weight of the thing stuck in his belt. Feeling its cold hardness so close to his skin, he thought carefully of the thing he had to do, he pondered thoughtfully, over and over, the way it must be done. He was on his way back to the diner then, walking along Market Street through the snowy pavements, when a flowered spring bonnet in a store window caught his eye. He stood a moment, staring at it through the steamy glass, and remembering Jessie's childlike request that he bring her a flower back, something pretty to pin on her dress. He studied the price tag beneath the hat. Three ninety-five. It wasn't too much for such a pretty thing. He made a mental note of the store address and moved on. When it was over, when he had done what he had to do, he might come back and buy the hat for her. If there was time. If they were not too close behind him by then.

In the diner there was no sign of the man in the army coat. Farjeon sat anxiously for a half hour, drinking coffee, his head bowed, his shoulders hunched over the steaming cup while customers came and went. He fancied he must make himself look as discouraged and dejected as possible when Cotter saw him again. If he saw him again; if he came back at all. Farjeon knew there was always the chance that Cotter had filled his quota of men for

114

the job. He wondered for one crazy instant if he had not lost his chance back there two hours before; if he should not have taken care of Cotter while he had him so near his fingertips. Still, some hunch was playing games in his wits just now, a hunch that he was going about things in the right way. He had the feeling that somehow Cotter would yet bring him face to face with Shaloo—a confrontation that he might not be able to manage just now, on his own. He was so deep in his thoughts a few moments later that the touch on his elbow startled him. He turned and saw Cotter on the stool beside him.

What happened, buddy?

Farjeon put on his glummest expression.

Did you get it? Cotter said.

Farjeon shook his head and turned his stare back to the empty coffee cup.

We gambled, he said. It was the way you said it would be.

What happened?

Farjeon shrugged.

I lost, he said.

Cotter bent forward, eager.

Cleaned out? he whispered.

Everything, Farjeon said. My last buck.

Cotter nodded, his eyes glistening.

I told you, he said. She's a gambler, that Sophie. I told you how it might be.

He cocked his face and searched the back of Farjeon's head.

No hard feelings?

Farjeon shrugged again.

It wasn't your fault, he said. You gave me a perfectly straight steer. I could have as easily won.

That's tough, buddy, Cotter said. Real tough.

He paused a tactful moment before he laid his hand on Farjeon's arm again.

Here, he said, let me stake you to a hamburg and a cup of mud.

No thanks. I'm not hungry, Farjeon said.

Cotter sighed and sat back on his stool, folding his arms.

Maybe, he said, maybe you'll be interested in that job now.

Farjeon kept very carefully still for a spell.

What do you say, big boy?

Farjeon shrugged ever so slightly.

What's it pay? he said.

Cotter cleared his throat.

Look at it this way, he said. It don't pay one helluva lot when you start. But that's not the point. I figure you for a regular. I figure you as a feller who'll climb up fast in the business.

He paused; Farjeon kept a faintly interested silence. Cotter waved his hand.

Bums, he said. The streets is full of them these days. Bums who'll take a job like this for a one-time deal. That's why it don't pay more at the start. But you—?

How much.

Cotter cleared his throat again.

Two-fifty.

He spread his hands on the counter top.

A day, he added.

Farjeon did not move.

Like I said, Cotter went on hurriedly, that's chicken feed. That's for the bums we hire to scab on a job like this. Still, if you're broke, it's something. It's carfare home. Where do you live?

Pittsburgh, Farjeon said quickly.

Well, then it's bus fare home, Cotter said. But I don't figure you to go home. Not at all. I figure you're going to be a real regular. I figure in a few weeks time you'll work up from fink. You won't be a fink like the rest of them bums. I'm a real judge of character. I figure you to work up to be a noble in no time. Like me. You're the kind of feller Mister Shaloo likes to get hold of. And hang on to.

He paused and scrabbled in his clothes for a cigarette. He found one, lit it, and blew smoke over Farjeon's head.

This Benwood Steel job ain't nothing, he said. By tonight it'll be all over but the weeping. There's plenty of work coming along. This Depression ain't but just begun. Times is getting worse. There'll be plenty more strikes to bust—all over the seaboard. I figure a feller like you has got a real good future with an outfit like Mister Shaloo runs.

He studied Farjeon's profile through the blue smoke.

What do you say, big boy?

Farjeon looked at him.

What do I do?

Cotter chuckled and glanced toward the line of pickets through the window, across the dingy street.

You bust open a few Hunkie heads, that's all, he said.

No shooting, Farjeon said.

Not this time, Cotter said. We're not using guns on this job. Just good old Cahn-Walter hickory clubs. Sticks about as big as a pick handle. Big enough to knock some sense into them dumb Hunkie heads over yonder.

He studied Farjeon then with a faint frown.

Why did you ask that? he said.

Farjeon met his stare.

I wouldn't want to be involved in any killing, he said. I sure wouldn't want that.

Cotter still scowled, though grinning a little, quizzically.

You're a funny one, he said. Not wanting to be involved in any killing.

He paused.

An hour or so ago you wanted to buy a gun.

Farjeon nodded, carefully spacing his silences.

That was different, he said.

Cotter still looked puzzled.

Farjeon laughed.

I just wanted that gun, he said, to scare a couple of people. That's all.

He could feel Cotter's eyes on the back of his head.

I was sore, Farjeon said. I'll get over it.

He laughed bitterly.

Maybe if I get out there and swing one of them clubs a little I'll work it out of my system.

Cotter lowered his eyes to the counter. Farjeon's question seemed to have sent him into a cold revery.

Don't worry about killing anybody, he said presently, strangely. If the time comes when you have to—you'll do it. I can tell that by the look of you, big boy. You'll do all right.

He pondered it a while more.

Killing ain't nothing, he said. Not in this job. It's legal, see? It ain't like ordinary *murder*. Boys that works for Mister Shaloo is doing a good thing. We're protecting property. That's what this country's all about, ain't it?

He reflected further.

A bunch of Reds, he said. That's who we're fighting. It's like Mister Shaloo says: It's a war. Just as much of a war as 'nineteen and 'eighteen was. If you have to kill a man, why you do it, that's all.

What about a woman? Farjeon said, incautiously, but despite himself.

Cotter did not bat an eye.

Same thing, he said. You do it.

A child, Farjeon whispered.

Kids don't get in the way, Cotter said. This is a man's war, buddy.

Is it?

Sure it is.

He studied Farjeon a moment more.

Ain't you killed your man yet? he whispered.

Farjeon kept still.

Ever pulled time in the pen?

He kept silent still. Cotter laughed and poked him a friendly jab on the shoulder.

Okay, he said. None of my beeswax—neither one of them questions. Still, it don't matter. You have the look. The look I like. You'll do. What do you say, big boy? Will you go to work for me and Mister Shaloo?

Yes, Farjeon said. When do I start?

This afternoon, Cotter said. We want to get it all over before sundown. I've got twenty-eight men signed up already. You'll be twenty-nine. We'll move in about an hour.

Where do we meet?

In that carbarn down yonder about two blocks away. In the middle of the block. The boys is gathering there.

Farjeon hesitated, then plunged ahead.

Will Mister Shaloo be there?

Cotter shook his head.

Not this time, he said. He's staying up at the hotel. He's got a suite of rooms up there and he's staying till it's done.

Farjeon felt the weight of the gun, under his belt, against his body beneath the shirt, beneath the underwear.

Go on up the carbarn, Cotter said. Wait for me there. We'll hit them in about an hour.

He studied Farjeon amiably.

Tell you what, he said suddenly. I'm so sure you're going to work out I'm going to pay you three dollars instead of two fifty. How's that?

That's fine, Farjeon said. Thanks. I think it's going to work out too. I think it's going to work out fine.

He studied Cotter from the corner of his eye; it would be so easy from where he sat. It would be so simple to reach inside the overcoat, pull the gun out and fire the single shot. But the hunch still played games in Farjeon's head, the feeling that he must go along with things for a while, that he must wait. He had the hovering vision somewhere in the back of his wits of Cotter's leading him to Shaloo, of having the two men together, alone, so that he could do it all at once and be gone out of town before anyone really knew what happened.

In the carbarn, where the more than two dozen men waited

119

round for Cotter to come and lead them out, Farjeon kept to himself. The air was thick with smells of fear, of unwashed flesh: the scent of poverty and the flushed, angry spirit of the times. The men stood lounging about, leaning against the empty trolley cars which stood on three rails across the floor from the main gate. Farjeon glanced about the men, thinking he might recognize some of the faces of that night when his child-wife had died. But they were as gray and featureless now as they had been then. In an hour Cotter came through the office door with a paper bag under his arm. He strode up to Farjeon.

Hi, big boy. Phew. Stinks in here, don't it? Them bums. I bet ain't one of them had a bath in a month.

He put the bag down and Farjeon saw the four quarts of whiskey inside. Cotter pulled one out, uncorked it and handed it to Farjeon.

Better have a drink, big boy.

Farjeon took the bottle, studied it a moment, lifted it to his mouth and pretended to take a swig. He handed the bottle back to Cotter.

Aw, that ain't no drink. Take a good jolt.

Farjeon shook his head. I want to keep my head straight, Farjeon said, looking away from Cotter's eyes. Good and straight. You see, I've got to do something today I ain't used to doing.

Sure! Cotter cried then, lifting out the other three bottles and passing them to the grimy men who gathered round now, like flies round a honeypot, at the scent of liquor. Sure! Cotter cried again. It scares ye a little at first. But you'll get used to it. I can tell you've got sand.

No, Farjeon said. I'm not afraid.

Cotter studied him, smiling.

You know I don't believe y'are, he said. You've got a certain look around the mouth. Determined. I'd say you know right what you're about. You don't look like a feller who'll lose no sleep over it neither.

He drank again.

When the sun sets tonight I reckon you'll look back on a day well spent. I don't reckon you'll regret a thing you've done.

Farjeon did not smile.

I won't, he said. That's a fact, Mister Cotter.

Cotter was not drunk. He was not sober either. He had attained that liquored level which was his usual prerequisite for violence. Shaloo had learned him well enough to know he could trust him never to go beyond it. His eyes were lightly glazed when Farjeon glanced at him again but the glassiness was not drunkenness—it was the look Farjeon had glimpsed in that face once before, in a shutter-quick vision of winter moonshine, by a roadside, on another night. Cotter moved among the men, striking them on the shoulders, working them up. Two deputies had already unwrapped the bale of hickory clubs and moved among the men, passing them out. Cotter was on a box now, in a frail imitation of Shaloo, warming up to his send-off speech.

Listen! Listen! All of you. Cork them bottles back up and listen.

Farjeon turned his eyes, suddenly saddened, toward the glum light of afternoon which shone down through the dusty carbarn windows. He was moving closer now. Soon he would pass a border that would leave a whole meaning of his life behind it. Soon he would leave innocence and move into a world where he would be a killer, a man little better than Cotter himself, and yet he knew that the tug toward that world was irresistible. He knew that he could no more turn back now than if he had already pulled the trigger twice. It was a debt that he must pay. The image of the child-wife's blind, beseeching eyes filled his mind just then until the vision of the dusty window blurred in tears.

Cotter was stomping his foot on the box now.

Bust every Hunkie head that comes in your way! These here two armed deputies of the Ohio County sheriff's office will be standing by to make sure there ain't no gunplay. And there won't be! We know what they've got. They got nothing we're afraid of. Ain't that so, boys?

Some of the men answered glumly, though most were silent,

staring bemusedly at the heavy sticks in their hands, the fresh wood gleaming like ice. Cotter could see they needed more sand in their craws.

Listen! he shouted. Maybe you birds don't know what this is all about. Maybe you think this is some kind of a church picnic. Well, it ain't. Do you know who them Hunkies out there really is? They're the enemy, that's who. The enemies of everything this country stands for.

By God, that's so! one of them shouted.

Sure, it's so, brother! Reds. Wobblies! Dirty sonsabitching Communists—that's who's out there.

Reds and wobblies, by God! another muttered.

Sure they are! Enemies of you and me and this God-given land! Enemies of every good thing this big God-given land stands for.

Now let's all join in singing our beloved national anthem!

They were with him now, every dispossessed, chafing soul of them rallying to the defense of that thing which had lost meaning to them for a spell—the land, the nation. Now they knew and they sang it out, most of them stumbling over the words. Cotter's glazed glare held them in a trance, his writhing, raddled face lifted above them. Farjeon moved with them to the doors of the carbarn which the deputies slid suddenly open now like twin guillotine blades which sliced the shadows and cast them all spilling out suddenly into the glare and surprise of the street. Farjeon stumbled in their midst into the throng of the pickets who lined the pavement fronting the mill's main building.

Get 'em! Get the Hunkies! shouted Cotter, leading.

Here they come! screamed a woman picket, standing with her feet apart on the snowy pavement, the sign stick clutched in her fists.

Get the Hunkie bastards!

There was no hate in Farjeon's heart toward the haggard, ragged men he confronted. And yet he swung his stick against them, not so much because he fancied he might want to be proving himself to Cotter, but through the sudden throb of something violent inside him against the whole situation in which he found himself. He struck out at the hard, set faces of the two men before him and caught one of them on the shoulder, sending him spinning to the pavement. Someone struck him a blow from behind, between the shoulders, and he staggered. Cotter was not watching him. Farjeon could see the shape of him, the tan length of the army coat, where he seemed to be entangled in a group of five or six of the strikers. The two deputies, armed with rifles, moved along the fringes of the fight, keeping a lookout for any guns among the enemy. But there were none.

Scab bastard! a voice shouted in Farjeon's ear and he went to his knees from a blow across the legs from behind.

That was when, in one instant—kneeling there on the caked snow—he saw Cotter and knew he was in trouble. Six men had him up against the corrugated iron wall of the mill and were raining him with blows of sticks and fists. Farjeon staggered to his feet, wading through the flailing mob, on his way toward Cotter. Farjeon stood a moment, staring over the shoulders of the attackers, and seeing in that instant the image of Cotter's face, streaming blood, as he went down. That was when Farjeon went a little mad. He thought of the gun in his belt and it was all he could do to keep from using it. He waded in then, powerful with fury, almost blind with outrage, seizing the attackers from behind and flinging them aside as he struggled toward the place where Cotter lay. The men fell back before Farjeon's insane and savage assault. Farjeon flung aside the last of them and stood staring down at Cotter who lay on the pavement, against the wall, his face streaming blood.

He's had it! one of the men shouted. Leave the sonofabitch there to die! Come on!

No, by God! shouted another. Let's finish him. He's the scab herder. That's the scab-herding bastard himself!

Right, by God. Let's finish him. All the way!

Farjeon went down by Cotter's side under a rain of blows. And all he could think was, No. It mustn't be this way. No, by God. It's going all wrong. He mustn't go this way. And the fury of his fear was the pulse that gave him all that added strength and he was up again—he had flung aside the hickory club by now—and was dealing with them only with his fists. Two men stumbled and fell under his blows.

Get him too! shouted a woman.

He's the scab herder's buddy! Get the sonofabitch!

Farjeon fought like a man possessed. For a moment they fell back before the fury of his sheer outrage. That was the instant when Farjeon turned and slid his hands under Cotter's legs and arms, scooping him up in his cradling grip and carrying him through the mob, carrying him like a hurt child. Somewhere above the shouting and the din Farjeon could hear his own voice, a pleading chant:

Don't die! Oh my God, don't die!

Once they half tore Cotter loose from his arms and in that moment Farjeon kicked one man in the groin, half falling. The mob faltered.

Don't die! Oh, for Christ's sake, don't die!

And when they were in the carbarn again and the din and hubbub were somewhere lost in the cold light behind them, Farjeon laid Cotter's legs on the rails and cradled the head and torso in his arms, rocking to and fro with him as if he were a child, wiping at the blood with his free hand, and chanting that half-mad, weeping cry.

No. No, by God. I won't let you die. It's not time yet. No. This ain't the way! God damn you, not yet!

There was something savagely tender in Farjeon's crouched figure above the shape of the wounded man in his arms. Cotter's body was held so close against him that it pressed the gun harder into his flesh; he could feel the cold, hard weight of it.

Don't die. Oh, my God, don't die. Not yet.

Cotter revived presently. The cut on his head was a superficial one. Farjeon had staunched the bleeding with a strip of clean cotton waste from a box nearby. Cotter sat up, leaning back on his arms, staring at Farjeon with stunned amazement.

I knowed you had sand, big boy.

Farjeon searched his face anxiously.

Are you all right?

I'll be fine, Cotter said, getting shakily to his legs.

He searched Farjeon's face admiringly.

I reckon you saved my life out there, he said.

Farjeon said nothing. He could feel the slow ebbing away of the emotions of the fight and escape.

Cotter turned as the two deputies came in the carbarn door and stood staring at him. The hubbub in the street had quieted.

Are you all right? one of them said.

Shook up some, Cotter said. Scraped off a little hair, that's all. How's it going out there?

It's all wrapped up, said the other deputy. They'll talk turkey tonight with the management. You boys gave them a helluva working over out there. I figure it's all over. You sure you're all right?

I'm all right, Cotter said.

He turned to Farjeon who, at the appearance of the two, had moved back so that his face was obscured in shadow.

That man there, Cotter said, he saved my life, I reckon.

Farjeon turned away a little so that they could see nothing but the back of his head above the turned-up collar.

Looky there how bashful he is! Cotter cried. Saved my life, I tell you! Looky how bashful.

Farjeon listened as Cotter gave the deputies the money and told them to pay off the mob of finks. When the two were gone Cotter came over and laid his hand on Farjeon's shoulder. Farjeon turned then and looked over Cotter's shoulder, seeing that they were alone. Alone, he could feel the cold weight of it under his belt. But it was not time yet. Cotter was telling him something now.

—Mister Shaloo.

What?

I tell you I'm gonna take you with me up to McClure House right now to meet Mister Shaloo.

Farjeon waited.

I know he'll hire you in as a noble right now, tonight, Cotter was saying as they moved out of the carbarn into the cold light of midafternoon. I knowed you'd work out. Saved my life back there, you did. Say, what's the matter? You look a little pale.

I'm fine, Farjeon said.

Sure you ain't nervous about meeting Mister Shaloo?

No, Farjeon said. The nervousness is all over.

And he walked along by the side of the man in the army coat, feeling that the moment was almost there, sure now that he was right in his hunch to have waited. When they stood under the marquee of the hotel Farjeon's thoughts seized hold of something. He turned and saw the store window across the street.

Come on, Cotter said. Mister Shaloo will want to know how we made out. Mister Shaloo don't like to be kept waiting. Say. You sure you ain't nervous?

No, Farjeon said. That part's all over.

Mister Shaloo, Cotter said, he's rich and big but underneath he's just as common as you or me.

He squeezed Farjeon's elbow.

When you meet him, he said, you'll know how to handle yourself.

I'll know, Farjeon said. Yes, I'll know.

And he followed Cotter across the almost deserted lobby toward the stairs, thinking to himself that as soon as it was all over he would go quietly out of the hotel and cross Market Street to the department store and buy the pretty flowered hat in the window. Jessie had only asked him for one flower, something pretty to pin on her shabby dress, but he knew how crazy she would be about that hat. It just suited her blue eyes and her coal-black hair someway. It was not that he loved her, Farjeon told

126

himself. No, it was not that, not like Jean, not like his child; still, he had promised Jessie something. He felt very calm as he climbed the marble steps behind Cotter and he felt that the calmness would last him until it was over. And even if it didn't afterward, even if they were looking for him then, he knew he had to try to buy the hat; he couldn't disappoint Jessie.

It'll be just me and you and Mister Shaloo together, Cotter said. We can talk better like that.

What?

I said we'll be alone with him, Cotter said.

Farjeon nodded, his eyes gleaming faintly.

Yeah, Cotter said. I seen them three bodyguards of his shooting pool when we passed the billiard room in the lobby.

Farjeon kept thinking about the hat, that pretty flowered hat. He kept telling himself that he mustn't let the pressure of things, the violence, whatever, make him forget. Cotter led the way, whistling, down the narrow, dark, carpeted hallway.

Things work out funny, Cotter said suddenly.

He paused, his eyes searching for the brass door number in the shadows.

Yes, they do, he said. First you and me meeting up in the Star Diner. Now Mister Shaloo. Makes a feller think there's something to fate. It does now.

Yes, it does, Farjeon said softly, his hand already inside the overcoat, his finger round the trigger, as Cotter found the door and knocked three times.

Part Two

COTTER went through the door first. Farjeon paused on the threshold behind him, moving now as if in some sharply etched dream, putting one foot before the other with careful, dreamy lightness, and, in the moment of his hesitation, transferred the gun from inside his clothes to the overcoat pocket. The gun itself felt unreal in his cold, careful grasp, amazingly light, like a toy. Farjeon caught a glimpse of Shaloo over Cotter's shoulder. He was in his shirt sleeves, collarless, lying on his back on the big brass double bed, his hands behind his head, a cold, thin stogie clenched in his glittering teeth. Farjeon stepped round by Cotter's side, yet stayed a little to the rear, in the shadows, in an attitude of proper respect. He thought to himself that he might have begun shooting the moment the two men were before him, but some sensibility held him back. The moment was not yet nigh. It seemed curiously indecent to kill a man to whom he had not yet been introduced. And he felt an artist's preoccupation with the way he wanted them both facing him, both knowing him; he wanted one extravagant instant of explanation, of preface to his deed. Cotter was now at the foot of the bed describing Farjeon's magnificence in the streets outside the mill, but Shaloo's plump jeweled hand twinkled in the light as he held up his fingers in a gesture to silence Cotter's voice.

Listen. I want to hear this, Shaloo growled sharply, and motioned with his other hand toward the big radio which stood against the wall beyond the bed. Listen a minute, will yuh.

That was when, as if in a dream, Farjeon became aware of the third voice in the room, the voice from the radio—the new President addressing his nation. Shaloo was enthralled, his small eyes bright with excitement, the pink flesh of his moon face sweating lightly. He motioned for Cotter and Farjeon to sit and be still. The vibrant voice racketed small and sharp from the radio speaker. Farjeon sat quietly, feeling the fingers and palm of his hand against and round the gun, warm and steady. Shaloo giggled and struck fist against palm and jiggled a little, setting the springs of the bed to crying faintly.

Listen to the son of a bitch talk, will you! Listen to that bastard!

He tittered again and groped on the bedside table for his silver cigar lighter and struck a flame against the cold stogie tip. Cotter stared a spell, listening to the radio voice. Presently he shook his head and muttered a curse under his breath.

I don't trust him, he said. Not one little bit. I just don't, Mister Shaloo.

Shaloo waved his hand and sat up, his fat legs dangling over the edge of the big bed, the tips of his polished shoes barely touching the rug.

He'll do just fine, Shaloo said. You wait and see. He'll be true to his class. And that's one class I know inside and out, backwards and forwards. I'm talking about the class of man that feeds you and me with every job strikebreaking we've ever had and will have for the next ten wonderful years.

Cotter pondered, scowling yet.

I heard, Cotter said, that he's a Jew.

Shaloo grumbled.

I heard, Cotter said, that his real name was Rosenvelt. I heard his real name wasn't Roosevelt at all. That's what I heard, Mister Shaloo.

That's bullshit, Shaloo said.

He reflected, studying the ash of his stogie.

I know a Jew when I hear one, Shaloo said. Or see one either. I can smell 'em by the sound of their voice.

He flicked the ash thoughtfully onto the carpet.

This boy ain't no Jew, he said.

He held his stogie in front of him now, staring at the blue, curling string of smoke that wove itself into the shadows above the bed light.

He'll do just fine, Mister Roosevelt will, he said. Him and his class will keep outfits like ours up to a hunnert percent of capacity for the next ten years. Maybe twenty. Relax, Cotter. We got nothing to worry about. Business is about to boom. The rich men is taking over.

The voice on the radio was gone now and a fresh voice had begun, higher, less resonant. Shaloo waved his hand, scowling.

Now there's the bleeding heart that makes my guts sick, he said.

He leaned his face out, spitting carefully into the brass spittoon on the rug beside the bed table.

Hood, he said. Almighty God U.S. Senator William G. Hood. He's the one that's for turning this country over to the communists lock, stock and barrel.

Farjeon waited still, the gun warm and now somehow heavy in his grasp, hearing the voice again, the voice that he and Jean had heard so many times, the voice they had listened to together in joy and hope on the courthouse steps in Glory so long ago, the day they had decided that if ever they had a boy child he would bear the senator's Christian name.

Cotter rose and walked to the radio. He put his hand on the switch and turned his head, waiting.

Can I turn this thing off now, Mister Shaloo?

Turn it off.

Shaloo glanced toward Farjeon's shape, obscure and small in the shadows.

Who's this you brought me? Shaloo said.

Cotter's face moved back into the bar of light from the bed lamp, his mouth bent in a ragged smile.

Mister Shaloo, meet Jack Farjeon, he said. A born noble if ever I laid eyes on one.

What can he do?

What can he do! cried Cotter. It's what he did I'm talking about. He saved my life down there at Benwood Steel this afternoon.

Shaloo grunted and fished in the cabinet under the bedside for a quart bottle of whiskey and three glasses.

I got word that it went all right this afternoon, he said, pulling the cork off with a smart pop. I heard the bastards have called the strike off. They'll sign in the morning. How's that for Shaloo efficiency?

Cotter clapped his hands together smartly and crowed softly.

I knowed we had 'em! he cried.

Farjeon, invisibly, had the gun out of his overcoat pocket now and rested it beside him on the worn velour of the chair.

I knowed we had 'em, Cotter said again.

He rested his palms on the brass rail at the foot of the bed, leaning forward.

Still, I'll guarantee you one thing, Mister Shaloo, he went on, if it hadn't been for Jack Farjeon here Yours Truly would be lying down there in a Benwood gutter at this very minute.

Shaloo had poured two drinks. He held the lip of the bottle neck over the third glass, peering into the shadows with a bemused look on his face.

I can't see him, Cotter, he said, still smiling, scowling a little.

He's bashful, that's why, Mister Shaloo. Bashful a boy as ever I did see. But he's all right, I tell you. He's all right.

Shaloo poured the third glass half full, again the bottle poised, hesitating, the brown glass twinkling in the poor light. Shaloo grunted.

How do we know, he said evenly, that he ain't some embittered striker whose buddy or dad got killed in any one of two dozen places between here and Steubenville in the last two years? Somebody, I mean, who's come here to—

Shucks, Mister Shaloo, what kind of fool do you take me for!

Shaloo's hand moved, he poured the third shot glass full.

Well, you never know, he said. Them two guards of mine is down yonder in the hotel billiard room. It'd be real easy for somebody—

Come on, Mister Shaloo. I'm just about to introduce you to the best kind of material for a first-class noble you've laid eyes on since you first met up with Yours Truly.

He moved across the worn rug toward Farjeon's shadow in the chair and held out the little glass of yellowish liquor. Farjeon saw the glint of the glass in Cotter's hand, wondering if either man had seen the duller glint of the gun he pressed now, carefully, thoughtfully, against his thigh.

Jack Farjeon, say hello to Mister J. P. Shaloo.

Farjeon stood up, watching their faces.

Hello, he said.

He did not move any closer, his finger tight against the trigger. He could tell that neither man had seen the gun yet; he watched their faces that he was about to quench and end forever and wondered that neither had seen the glint of the gun in his fist. He decided that Cotter would be the first to go. He wondered then sharply why some instinct had not told these two old hired hands what he had come there to do. Cotter moved suddenly into the shadow, his arm round Farjeon's shoulder, his body pressing him, dragging him out into the light.

In years to come Farjeon could not remember which had crossed his consciousness first, the look of terror on Shaloo's face as he flung himself backward across the bed, his fat hands grappling for the big revolver in the bedside table—that or the sudden crash of glass yonder in the shadows behind the silent radio. Cotter, unarmed, seemed frozen, even as the two men came over the sill from the black lattice shape of the fire escape beyond it. The broken glass beneath their feet crackled like ice as Farjeon glimpsed the oily shine of the thirty-thirty rifles in their hands. Shaloo screamed once, a thin, high skirl of sound that silenced the laughter and talk in the billiard room far below. The first shot was Shaloo's, poorly aimed in the bad light—Farjeon heard the bullet smack into the wall above the window. A door slammed somewhere in the hush of rooms below. Farjeon saw the shape of the two men now as if in the texture and unreality of a dream.

This is for scab herders and finks, one of them said in a clear, steady voice like a cattle auctioneer's chant.

The crash of rifle shots filled the room in a sharp, thunderous chatter. Farjeon watched, unbelieving, as Shaloo's body went jolting backward across the bed as the bullets struck him, jerking under the impact as if snapped on puppet strings. Cotter was down behind the big chair now, cursing softly as the bed light shattered and darkness drank up the shadows in a soft, swift wave. Farjeon stood, stunned and amazed, watching as Cotter's shape crept across the rug toward the place where Shaloo's revolver had gone spinning out of his dead fingers.

Get him. Yonder. By the chair.

Cotter had locked the door when he had come in with Farjeon. Beyond it now Farjeon could hear the swift, distant thud of footfalls on the carpeted stairs.

Yonder.

The rifle blazed again and Cotter soundlessly bucked and rose, his body arcing like a black rag in the dimness, and fell heavily in the pools of blackness beyond the chair. Some instinct stinging his wits to waking, Farjeon moved now behind the men toward the shattered window. He could feel the cold thrust of air across the sill, he could smell the sharp smell of smokeless powder.

Yonder. Get him. The third one. He's getting away!

And then, and not for the first time, Farjeon dully sensed that he had heard the voice before, that he knew the timbre of that voice as some thread in the whole tapestry of that winter's fear-someness. He heard the splintering of the heavy oaken door as the bodyguards set their weight against it.

He's out the window. Get him, Tom!

And he scarcely knew then whether the shot that came stinging past his shoulder was theirs or that of Shaloo's belated sentries.

He's making it down the fire 'scape. Get him, Steve.

And now he could hear their feet on the iron above him as he strove and felt his way through darkness toward the alley below. And all the while the dull, unused, senseless weight of the gun in his hand; and all the while the waking sense of loss, the knowl-edge that although Shaloo and Cotter were both dead it was not his hand that had slain them. On the packed snow of the alley cobbles his feet struck and caught as he swung down from the rusty iron.

Get the scab son of a bitch!

He thought numbly that he must face them, show them his eyes, make them believe. His wits strove for a way to let them know that they had done the thing that he had failed to do.

And yet, because he could hear them alight in the alley behind him, he hurried on, and as he moved he heard their voices again and knew that the voices were part of memory. He thought of foolish things, he thought of the pretty flowered hat for Jessie and how he might somehow go swiftly and fetch it and show it to the men and somehow win them away from the faith that he was one with the men they had killed. He would show them his gun, he would tell them how he had spent the day getting it and what for and how he had failed because they had succeeded. He would show them his eyes, he would show them his hate. Yet he ran, hearing them still behind him. He had crossed Chaplaine Street, passed before the eyes of a half dozen people, before he realized that he still clutched the gun in his fist. On the sidewalk in front of an abandoned cafe a small Salvation Army band thumped and blared in the icy night air. Farjeon paused a moment, glancing swiftly over his shoulder, and saw the two men walking stiffly with the rifles now held tight against their bodies under the shabby overcoats. He leaned against the door frame of the blackened, empty cafe and shut his eyes hard against the mind's image of what he had seen. No, it was unreal; it could not be so; the fate he had pondered with dead Cotter an hour before in the doorway of Shaloo's hotel room—it could not be so bizarre as this.

He glanced again quickly at the men; they had paused in the middle of the street, they had seen him. The band clamored like some fevered brass machine and the street light glinted like an imprisoned flame in the vast brass bell of the tuba. Farjeon shook his head, opened his eyes again, pressed on the cafe door. The lock had been broken and the door swung stiffly inward and Farjeon's nose was filled with the ghost of grease and hash and poor fare long ago dispensed and vanished and forgotten. He felt his way along the dim row of empty, dusty stools, past a shattered, silent jukebox toward the gray, distant shape of the kitchen door. As he took the last step behind the counter he trod on something soft and heard a muffled curse. The band was so loud that Farjeon could barely hear them—the words from the toothless mouth of the specter that rose up before him in that checkering of shadows.

You Salvation Army guys! Damn you. First you make so much noise a man can't even sleep! Then you come in and try to drag a man out to a salvation he don't even want, don't even need, something he's long past and never—

The colorless eyes in the gray face of the derelict saw something then in Farjeon's face—perhaps a fear rich with contagion; perhaps he saw or sensed the oiled blue gun fisted in Farjeon's grip. He sucked in breath so sharp that it drew in his lips across the gawp of his toothlessness; he shrank back.

I never meant nothing wrong, mister.

Farjeon watched as the wretch scuttled off toward the front, shouldering his way through the still open door through which the rich cold air flowed in like the shock of cold water, staring now with refreshed horror at two newcomers who stood before him, searching him with swift stares as they drew the rifles out from the concealment of their unbuttoned overcoats, did not even trouble to curse him, flung him sharply aside as if he were some insensible human gate and made their way into the checkerboard of darknesses in whose deeps Farjecn now strove to hide himself. Against the soiled light of the street beyond the cafe windows Farjeon could now see, sharp cut, the shapes of them, and still his wits strove to deny that it was them, that it could be them, and yet his mind was already a little mad with certainty that it was indeed them. He hunkered low behind the frame of the end of the counter beyond the kitchen door. He cowered lower, not so much in fear of them, not so much in reflex against what they wanted to do to him as from the sudden, sickening horror that he might have to do something to one of them, if only in simple preservation of his own survival. And he thought to himself even now, still, I could have been wrong. It might be two other men. It might not have been those two from Breedlove Mine at all. But he knew better. His skittering wits tried to comfort him but some wisdom of his flesh that still clutched the steel thing in its fist told him that it was them. Yes, it was really them.

Farjeon?

He fancied foolishly that somehow if he kept still they would go away and that in a place so dark as this he might play hide and seek with them until they wearied of the game and went away. But it was no game. He thought of his resolve of all those weeks gone by, the resolve so anguishedly come by—the purpose to kill the men who had so unequivocally earned their death. He thought of this and his wits sorrowed now to ponder how two of them had already died, and not even by his hand, and now he was faced with the prospect of killing two other men, innocent of everything save their own ignorance. He could not see over the counter now; he could hear their stealthy tread down the dusty, shadow-checkered way past the empty stools.

Farjeon!

He lifted his face above the sharp angle of the counter and saw the shape of them.

Listen, Turley. You too, Telligrew. I—

In the flash of the rifle shots he saw senselessly, as in the flash of a camera shot, the large blue NRA eagle on the cracked, dusty mirror. He hunkered back into the blue-gray ocean of shadows again, counting his thick pulses and fingering the oiled pistol in his fingers. He could hear Tom Turley's heavy, smoker's breathing in the brief interim of silence as the Army band paused, reset its music sheets and gathered in fresh breath.

You scab sonofabitch. I suspicioned you from the first night you set foot in Breedlove's street.

Farjeon fought back the sudden, foolish impulse to laugh.

You don't understand, he said quietly, in the voice one reserves for misled children. I wasn't one of them.

We follered you all day, Turley said.

You don't understand, Farjeon said again.

You was one of Shaloo's spies. All along. That woman they kilt —she was too. I bet she wasn't even your woman.

Farjeon grew grave and still in the presence of this; his mouth and mind stood humbled before the affliction of such madness.

You're about to die, Farjeon, you scab bastard.

I was—, he began again in that careful, reasoning voice, but the laughter strove like sickness again in his throat—he choked.

I was about to kill them both, he said. I spent the day planning it. I spent weeks planning it. I—

You're a goddamned liar.

She was my woman, she was my *child,* you fools!

Turley cleared his throat, he spat among the darknesses.

We follered you all day, Farjeon. We was at Benwood on the sidewalks. We seen you. We watched you working. We seen you beating up them Polack working stiffs with him and them other low-down, bastard, murdering scabs. Stand up, Farjeon.

And the laughter in him was gone now and nothing but the

140

rage and hatred of Shaloo and Cotter so sharp in his mind that he wished they were alive again so they might die again and this time by his hand and by his mind the way he had planned it and dreamed it all those aching days and nights.

My *child!* he cried again in a tight, furious voice. She was my *child!*

Your child, Turley spat softly. Your child, was she? When every man and woman in Breedlove seen how quick you was to take up with Cal Dunne's widow Jessie.

He could see now, incredibly, the toe of Telligrew's shoe around the edge of the counter, he could fairly smell the sweat of them both, and the drifting stink of the smokeless powder was there in the stifled air again. Farjeon was remotely frightened at his own rage in that moment. He could hear above the dim murmur of the silent street outside the clamor of fresh voices.

Listen to me, Tom Turley, he began again, struggling to keep the outrage from his voice, striving to make them understand him in this last split second left to any of them.

Stand up and take it!

That was when Turley stepped round the counter into the checker of shadows and kicked high, missing Farjeon who was to the left of him and who rose and fired once, twice, point-blank into the clear-cut shapes of them against the distant, soiled light. The din of the Salvation Army band beyond them in the cold, sad street sounded like an uproar of other weapons in some different conflict. In the flash of Turley's rifle Farjeon's mind shuttered a swift, dreadful image of Telligrew's face: surprised emptiness across his fallen mouth and the small hole in the middle of his forehead like a third eye. Farjeon fired again, sobbing in a swift intake of breath and heard the bullet crash in the mirror above Turley's shoulder. The rifle flashed and roared again and Farjeon felt the swift cut of the bullet through the cloth of his overcoat, above the shoulder. That was when he flung himself against the kitchen door and strove, stumbling backward, into the blackness of the deserted pantry. He leaned a moment against the hooks

141

where pans had once hung, feeling the cut of them through the cloth of his coat into his flesh and felt then, too, the flow of cold night air from somewhere behind him. He saw the blue crack of the forced door into the vacant lot behind and flung himself against it, staggering out into the night. He felt the sudden melt of a snowflake, cold and wet upon his mouth, and walked, unhurrying, unfeeling, across the shadow shapes of buildings a dozen yards away.

Farjeon!

He shut his eyes, walking on, feeling the cold kiss of fresh snow.

Farjeon, you scab bastard!

The yard was dark—still he could not be sure that Turley, who came lumbering in his wake, had not seen him. He little cared just then. His mind was like a photographic plate, fresh-etched with the image of Telligrew's dying face. He heard the sharp metallic cry as Turley cocked the rifle and heard the breathy noise he made somewhere behind him in the night's sad wreckage. Farjeon stared at the dim shape of the pistol he held up close to his face. He could smell the smell it had made. Two bullets gone. Yes, two of them gone—as he had planned.

Farjeon!

The voice remote and faint now as Farjeon found his way out of another alley into another street. He felt the weight of the gun striking against his leg from inside the coat pocket as he strode aimlessly on. Tinny, childish and remote, he could hear the clamor of the Army band, and weaving amid its clashing din, the thin skirl somewhere of a police siren. Farjeon walked on into the thickening snow. It seemed to him at last that he had walked for hours. He paused then for breath, eyes closed, something cold and smooth pressed against his forehead. He wondered in his lidded darkness what place his feet had brought him to. Perhaps when he opened his eyes and shut them again he would not see it anymore—the image etched in lightning, Telligrew's ruined face. He pressed his forehead harder against the smooth, cold place and opened his eyes and saw it beyond the plate-glass window on

142

which he had been leaning in his wearied anguish; saw it as he had seen it for the first time that day—the flowered hat he had meant to have for Jessie. But the lights behind it were out; the store was closed.

Mother Dunne grimaced slowly at herself in the small piece of mirror nailed to the bare wall above the basin where Cal used to shave himself. She stuck out a tip of tongue at herself and giggled in a soft, crowing breath.

Hello there, purty thing, she said. Nine days in Glory jail and you're not the least bit peak-ed.

She pinched her plump cheek till it glowed pink, and backed off, her gaze enthralled by her own gay image.

Nice skin, she said softly. Cal's daddy always used to say I had the nicest skin. He said I was the fairest gal in nine counties.

She turned her back on the mirror and folded her arms, staring out the dark window toward the road and wondering what kept Jessie so long at the company store. It was long hours past the early sundown of winter and a keen wind honed against the sharp eaves of the shack and there was the dry hiss of fresh snowfall against the windows. Mother Dunne went to the fumed oak Victrola, cranked it and fetched a record from the skimpy pile on the shelf beside it. Soon the room was alive with sharp, small music. Mother Dunne spread her black-clad arms and danced in a circle round the naked floor.

Barney Google and his goo-goo-googley eyes—

I wish it was a waltz! Cal's daddy was the best dancer I ever knowed, she said aloud. When we danced it was like two vaudeville actors. On a stage.

She whirled silently for a moment more and then fell breathless into her rocker.

I wish I knew why I feel so gay tonight, she thought. Things couldn't look much worse. Hardly a spoonful of food in the house. The strike busted. Jessie gone to the store with our last handful of scrip tokens to buy coal oil. And yet—and yet—

143

She stood up again suddenly, as if in a gesture of defiance against the way things were, and pirouetted again slowly, with her slender arms uplifted, like the girl she could scarcely remember.

It's like I was tipsy, she thought. Like I'd had a couple of jelly glasses full of that good old elderberry wine Dave Turner used to give us every Christmas. I wish it was a waltz.

She turned her face to the cracked, bitter window of winter, feeling even as she faced it the thin trickle of cold air through its insufficiency. She snapped her fingers in the chill and thrust out her lower lip.

I feel good tonight, she said aloud. And for no good reason under God's gray heaven!

She glowered then suddenly, remembering Kitto's man Harbert who had been there that morning. That was another reason for not feeling good. Harbert had said they owed rent on the shack from the night of Cal's funeral, and that was nearly a month. He said there was a job in Breedlove Number Twelve for Jessie's new man if he wanted it and how he ought to be thankful for the chance with things the way they were and if he didn't report for work at five next morning they'd have to be out of the place by noon that day. Mother Dunne didn't know how Farjeon would take to the notion of being a miner. She considered the prospect that he might not take to it at all. And yet somehow she could not fancy herself and Jessie set out on the winter roads—likely as that might chance to be. She snapped her fingers against the silence again, a silence broken only by the wind and the snow and the rasp of the ended record like the sound of heavy, struggling breath. Then she laughed aloud.

Lord, she said softly, it's going to be all right. I know it will. Lord, I wouldn't feel like this if it wasn't going to be all right. It's a sign. For sure. It wouldn't make no sense me feeling this good if things wasn't going to be all right. The Lord would forewarn me!

144

That was when she heard Jessie's running steps in the blackened snow outside the door and stopped rocking, her bright eyes burning behind the small lenses of her spectacles. Jessie flung the door open, slipped swiftly in and put the heavy stone jug of coal oil on the floor.

Jessie, what's wrong?

Jessie flung off her gray cotton shawl and went to the fireside to still her chattering teeth.

Lord, child, you're half frozen!

It's not that, Mom, Jessie said.

She caught her breath and her dark gaze swept the room.

Jack's not back yet, is he?

No. Where's he at?

Jessie shook her head.

I don't know.

How long's he been gone?

Since sunup. Mom, I'm worried.

Shoot! cried the old woman. You're worried because Harbert was here this morning.

No. It's not that. Mom, I'm worried about Jack.

Mother Dunne rocked again, twice, and watched Jessie shrewdly.

You think he's deserted us, don't you, Jess?

Jessie flung her head violently from side to side.

It's not that, she said. He'd not do that.

She sat suddenly on the bench before the fire, her legs apart, her fingers outstretched—like a man—toward the warmth.

It's not that, Mom. There's been murder done.

Murder?

Jessie nodded quickly, her eyes still on the blazing fire.

In Wheeling.

Murder in Wheeling. Well, who got murdered?

Jessie was silent, her violet eyes fixed on the yellow flames.

Who, Jessie?

145

Lord, you'd never guess, Mom.

Well, tell me, Jess. I'm no good at guessing. Not on this poor, old half-empty stomach!

A big man, Mom, Jessie said. A bad man, too.

Well, for Lord's sake, girl, who was it?

Shaloo.

Who?

Mister Shaloo. Mister J. P. Shaloo.

That murderer? No!

Mother Dunne was out of her rocker now and had scurried to Jessie's side. She clapped the girl on her shoulder and sat on the bench beside her. She crowed softly and saw the blaze blur in her eyes.

It *was* a sign! she whispered sharply.

What was?

The feeling I've had since sundown! cried the old woman in a sharp whisper as if the wind itself might be listening. Tipsy. Like I was tipsy. Lord, Jessie, not ten minutes ago I was out yonder in the middle of the floor dancing like it was forty years ago. Dancing all by myself, Jessie. Like I was tipsy. But I wasn't. It was this feeling. This good feeling like things was all going to turn out right. I tell you it was a sign.

Jessie shook her head.

How'd you get word? whispered the old woman.

On the radio, Jessie said. On WWVA. The radio down at the company store.

Hah! cried the old woman in a thrust of breath and clapped her palms sharply to the flames. Then she put her face closer to Jessie's.

Was it him that done it?

Jessie shook her head, her gaze fixed wild on the flame.

Did they get the one that done it?

Jessie nodded.

Who, then?

Jim Telligrew.

Mother Dunne reared back and gasped.

No. Why, I'd never guessed he had the sand!

She searched the flames again as if for answers in its summer colors.

Was it him single-handed?

That's what the cops say, Mom.

Did they catch him?

He was killed.

By the cops, you mean.

I reckon. I didn't hear that part. Mom, oh, Mom! I'm worried about Jack.

Pshaw! Maybe he went to Wheeling for a toot!

No. No, Mom. Jack wouldn't do that.

Maybe he did! cried the old woman. Maybe he saw the handwriting on the wall. Maybe he knew he was going to have to go to work in Breedlove Mine to keep head above water. So today he went to town for a toot.

He still has a little money.

That won't last. Harbert said we'd have to be out of here by noon tomorrow if we didn't pay the rent since Cal's funeral.

That's not Jack's worry.

Sure it is, Jess.

Why is it?

Because he loves you.

Did he say that to you?

He didn't have to. You told me, Jess.

I did? When?

Not with words, Jess. I seen it in your face this morning. I seen it the minute I walked in that door fresh out of Glory jail.

Maybe not, Mom.

Jess, I seen it in your face. A woman don't get that color in her cheeks by withering on the vine. I knowed the minute I laid eyes on you that him and you had been loving it up every night since I been away.

Jessie's face grew solemn.

147

Ain't you mad, Mom?

Mad? Why should I be?

Jessie shrugged.

Your son, she whispered, your Cal—my husband—hardly cold in his grave—

Mother Dunne smacked Jessie on the shoulder and leaned again on her elbows toward the fire's brief radius of warmth.

I hold with the living, Jess, she said. Cal's dead. That Farjeon feller—he's alive. I hold with the living, Jess.

Jessie shut her eyes suddenly against quick tears which brimmed there, glistening in the fireshine. Mother Dunne sighed.

Jessie, you never loved my Cal.

Mom, I did!

No, you didn't. You couldn't. Poor Cal. Child of my womb and yet I knowed him. You couldn't have loved my poor Cal.

I did, Mom, Jessie sobbed amid her upflung fingers.

Pitied him maybe, said the old woman gravely. We all did that. Poor Cal.

She shook her head angrily.

He never had a chance, she said. He never had the food—by God, I mean just the simple food it takes to make a man out of a child. It wasn't his fault. It wasn't his daddy's fault neither. And it wasn't mine. And God only knows it wasn't your fault, Jess.

She glared into the flame and stroked her pale, bright knuckles.

That's why news of the death of a man like him—that scab herder, she said, 't's a sound like the singing of angels, Jess.

But Jack—

Jack will be back, said the old woman. Your Jack will be back, Jess. As for Cal—he'd be glad to see you— Jessie, what is it?

She turned then and followed Jessie's swift passage to the window.

Someone's coming, Mom.

Jack Farjeon, I'll bet ye!

No.

Who, then?

Someone with a rifle.

Who, Jessie?

I can't make out. It's snowing.

Is it a cop?

It couldn't be. He's got a child with him.

A child?

It's Tom Turley. It's Tom and his boy Bud, Jessie said and ran swiftly to the door.

She flung it open and stood aside as Turley made his way in, pushing the weeping child ahead of him.

Is Farjeon here?

No.

Turley's hot gaze swept the room. He left the sobbing child and went to the doorway to the bedroom, thrusting the door open with the gun barrel. He returned to the child and motioned him toward the bench.

But, Pap, I—Pap, listen, I—

Turley went over carefully and struck the child across the face with the flat of his hand.

Stop your sniveling, Bud, Turley said in his hot, careful voice. I've brought you here to watch something.

Pap, I don't want to see nobody die. Pap, I done already seen somebody die.

Not somebody, Turley said. A scab. You seen a scab die. Remember that. Not a man—a scab. Tonight you're going to see another scab die. That's what I brought you here to watch, Bud.

Pap, I don't want to watch!

Not now maybe, Turley said. Not tonight. But someday you'll remember what you're going to see here tonight. And on that day you'll thank me. I'll be dead and gone then but you'll thank me, Bud.

Pap, I want to go home.

Would you like another smack across the mouth?

No, Pap.

Then shut it, Bud. Shut your mouth and sit there and watch

149

what's going to happen in this house of traitors. Sit there and wait for the sight of a scab getting what's due him.

He looked then at the two women who throughout all this had watched him in stunned stillness.

My boy Bud, he said carefully, ladies, he don't have every opportunity. I mean he don't have the chance for real proper Christian upbringing in this mine camp. I know that. I do the best I can. That's why I try to fill his childhood with proper object lessons. That's why I try to fill in the breach left by his being deprived of proper training.

You're crazy, Tom Turley! cried Mother Dunne in a soft, thick whisper.

No, he said, I'm not crazy. You don't know the facts. You don't know what me and Jake Telligrew seen with our own eyes this day.

He blinked slowly and looked at Jessie, then back to the old woman.

You're all right, Mom, he went on. I'm not blaming you. You ain't mixed up in this. No. You was duped like everybody else the very night he first showed up here in Breedlove. The night they called him the barefoot man. The night of the raid.

His burning gaze swung to Jessie.

As for you, he said, you knowed from the first. Didn't you, whore?

Jessie shook her head slowly.

I don't know what you seen in Wheeling, Tom Turley, she said. I only know Jack hated Shaloo more than you ever could.

Hah! cried the old woman, clapping her hands. Hah! *You* was in Wheeling, Tom Turley!

She folded her arms and fixed him with a smile.

Maybe, she said, you helped Jim Telligrew kill Shaloo.

There was only one man, Turley said quietly. The cops will swear to that.

Maybe they only *seen* one man, said the old woman.

Turley shrugged.

150

What's the difference? That's all they know.

You could have been there!

There's fifteen men, said Tom Turley, who know about this. Fifteen men who'll swear I was working at the foot of Number Three tunnel all the day shift.

He wiped his hand across his mouth, his gaze shuttling back and forth between the two women.

I haven't had the chance yet, he said, to spread the news of what we seen today throughout the rest of Breedlove. If I had there'd have been a hundred men up here tonight to kill that scab bastard.

Tom Turley, get out of here! cried Mother Dunne.

She sprang up from her chair, scurrying across the room, her hand uplifted toward Cal's old rifle where it hung on the wall.

Stop, Mom, Turley said softly, putting his rifle on the table.

He crossed the room, hardly hurrying at all, and wrested the rifle from the old woman's hands, then flung it through the bedroom door. He stared down at her furious face.

You don't know what's been going on here in this house, he said, betwixt the two of them whilst you was in Glory jail.

I know Mister Farjeon's all right—that's what I know!

Turley went back to sit on the bench, swept up the rifle in his hands, resting it on his knee again, pointing toward the door. Beside him the child gasped and choked, struggling to quench his sobs.

Shut your crying up, Bud.

I can't, Pap.

I said be still, Bud.

He did not turn his gaze, did not bother to look at his hunched and whimpering child.

Now, said Tom Turley, we'll wait.

Maybe he'll not come, Jessie said in a hushed, scared voice.

He'll come.

How do you know? said the old woman.

Because, said Tom Turley, I seen him in South Wheeling. I

chased him a spell, then lost him. Then I seen him again. Getting on the streetcar for Glory.

You could have killed him then.

Turley smiled.

But I wanted him to come here.

Why, you devil?

Why, so's I could bring Bud. So's Bud could watch it. I want Bud to see what happens to scabs. Firsthand. Bud, he'll be a workingman someday. Like me. I want him to grow up remembering what's going to happen here tonight. Like what happened to that other scab we nailed to the tipple. I know my boy Bud he don't have the best chance for a real Christian education in a place like this. That's why I have to make up for it.

He paused, blinked twice, nodded.

Now be still. I think I hear someone on the road.

Pshaw. You heard the wind.

Maybe, Turley said. And then again maybe not. Be still. You too, Bud. We'll see.

And then throughout the slow inch of ticking minutes the cold wind was murmurous in a sighing ebb and flow like the rush and retreat of some vast, invisible winter sea. The snowflakes laid swift touch upon the glass in a rhythmless hiss. And yet soon the sound beyond these sounds grew like the burden of some heavy, laboring song. Then suddenly a ruddy light flushed the cold window like a stain of blood. Turley rose, scowling, and went toward the door. Mother Dunne sprang lightly to the window and peered out.

Lord save us! she whispered.

She and Jessie followed Turley out the open door onto the porch and watched the mob of miners that stormed up the frozen road. Few of them had guns, which were scarce in that poor place, but all had picks in their fists and some brandished torches of cotton waste and blazing coal oil. Steve Bonar, a haggard,

152

wild-eyed man, led them. When he spied Turley he strode up to the steps.

Where's Farjeon?

Not here, Turley said glumly. What do you think I'm here for!

Bonar glanced back toward the black, fathomless road to Glory. Turley shook his head angrily and struck his fist into his thigh.

You damn fools! he cried.

Why? You aimed to kill him yourself. That's what you said, Tom.

And I would have too, Turley cried, if you hadn't come like this to warn him off! Them torches can be seen for three miles.

Jessie seized the old woman's dry, warm hand and squeezed it.

Tom's lie—it's spread fast, Mom.

Yes. Like every lie, Jess. It's got a life all its own.

Jessie's dark eyes searched the shadows and shapes beyond the luminous swarm of miners.

Mom, where's Jack? she breathed. What will happen to him?

Mother Dunne shoved the girl ahead of her back into the room and shut the door behind them.

Throngs of men, she said. Lord save throngs of men. They're such fools.

Jessie searched the old woman's face in the lampshine.

What will happen to him, Mom?

Happen to him! snapped the old woman. Well, at least he's warned off. At least he'll not be shot down on yonder threshold by that murdering, crazy Tom Turley!

She went quickly and gathered into her arms Turley's stunned and whimpering child and pressed his head against her bosom.

Stop your crying, honey, she whispered. You'll not have to watch nothing bad tonight. Hush, child, hush.

She went and fetched him a tin cup of cold tea from the saucepan under the window and held it to his lips, stroking his damp, tousled hair.

Nothing worse than you've seen already, poor little lamb.

Outside they could hear Turley shouting and cursing at Bonar and the others.

I had a perfect trap laid! he cried. He was headed here. I know he was. It would have been all right, damn you! I could have picked him off the minute he crossed that threshold. And now you damn fools come herding up here with your torches—

This is our business too, Tom! Bonar shouted.

I could have handled it for all of us, Turley cried. I was all set to. I was the one he shot at. I was the one who seen him shoot Jake Telligrew in cold blood. I could have handled it. And now you fools come herding up here to warn him off!

Bonar cast a hangdog look backward up the bleakness of the black road to Glory, snow now gathering in its frozen, windswept wagon ruts.

We wouldn't have come, he said, if we hadn't figured he was yonder in the house.

How could he be? I told you he boarded the Glory streetcar in South Wheeling. I beat him home by hopping an eastbound freight. The walk out here from Glory would take him better than an hour. I thumbed a ride on a coal truck. That means he was out yonder on the Glory road a mile or two when he seen your torches. You damn fools! If you'd have left it to me—!

You don't reckon he'll come, then? Bonar asked weakly.

Of course not! Not tonight! Not tomorrow. Not if he's got good sense. And he does. We've lost our prime chance. Maybe day after tomorrow. Or the day after that.

The mob faltered as if the taut, invisibles ropes that had held it together had been severed; the swarm of angry, coal-blackened faces broke into small, hoarse knots of whispering, thwarted men. Turley went back into the house and slammed the door till the kitchen pans chattered on their nails. He gestured brusquely with one hand toward the child whose great eyes watched him in fierce terror from above the poised tin cup.

Come on, Bud. We'll go home now.

He glanced toward the window and struck the gun stock with the heel of his hand.

Them fools. Damn them. He's sure to have seen their torches. And now we have to wait!

Wait! cried Mother Dunne. You're not going to spend the night in this house!

Turley sneered.

No, he said. But I'll bet that whore of a widow yonder by the fire would as soon take me to her bed as anyone.

To hell with you, Tom Turley. Get out and stay out.

No. We'll be back, Mom. We'll get him. He'll show his face here sooner or later.

He glanced wrathfully at Jessie and sneered again.

He'll be back, he said. Drawn by her yonder. Like a butterfly drawn by privy filth. There's time.

You've said enough, Tom!

Sure. We're going. Bud and me. There's time. Time for Bud's good, Christian lesson.

He was gone then and the ruddy stain faded as if washed from the frosted windows and the dragging sea-sound of mob voices was washed back and away and obscured at last by the grieving of winter wind against the claptrap eaves and the endless hiss of snow upon the shack's poor panes.

Fools! murmured Mother Dunne from her rocker. Throngs of men. Such fools.

Jessie sat on the bench before the fire. She kept her bloodless face covered for a long spell in the basket of her laced fingers.

Jessie did not take her fingers away from her eyes, even though her gaze had been fixed for a long spell on Farjeon framed in the bedroom door. For a moment she thought it might be his ghost, fresh from some catastrophe out yonder on the Glory road. But then he came out of the shadow into the fireshine. He looked tired, he looked older. But Jessie could smell it in the air, the thing

155

in him that had not changed, that had not grown faint in him.

I've been back yonder in the bedroom an hour or better, he said.

Mother Dunne ceased rocking, sat staring, smiling faintly.

Farjeon sat wearily on the bench.

I figured Turley might have beat me back here, he said with a tired gesture. I came up to the window yonder when I crossed the yard. I saw him with his gun. I saw his kid. I figured he'd be here. I hid in the yard beneath the puzzle bush. Then I saw the mob with their torches.

How did you—?

I snuck in the back door, he said. I've been lying in the bedroom. Under the window.

You was eavesdropping on us! scolded the old woman gently, rocking again.

I had to be sure, he said to the old woman. I didn't know if maybe you'd be on the side of Turley and that mob of miners out there tonight.

Jack!

Farjeon shrugged wearily.

I didn't know, he said. Strange things has been happening today. I couldn't be sure that you too—

Jack, we'd never believe bad about you! Jessie cried.

He shrugged again.

I wasn't sure I should even come back here, he said. Bringing danger and trouble with me like a shadow.

This is your home, Mister Farjeon, said the old woman in a high, sure voice.

No, he said, it's not.

It is as long as you want it! As long as you need it! the old woman said.

Farjeon leaned toward the fire.

Thank you, he said. Thank you both for that, at least.

He pondered a bit, then nodded to himself.

Yes, I'm thankful to you for that, he said presently. Because I'll need a place to be for a spell more. One place to be—to sleep in, at least—to be with two good friends, at least—

He cracked his knuckles, then reached for Jessie's hand again.

Things went wrong today, Jess.

I know that, Jack.

You heard what Tom claims—what Bonar and the others are all saying?

Yes.

That I was one of Shaloo's men.

Yes.

And do you believe it?

No.

Are you sure you don't?

Sure.

He bowed his head, ran his fingers through his hair, still wet from the snow.

Thanks, Jessie. Thanks, Missus Dunne.

The old woman rose from her rocker and stood straight, facing Farjeon's back across the room.

I'd never believe such of a thing! she said in a firm, high voice. Never! Why, it was Shaloo and his killers who slaughtered your wife and baby, Mister Farjeon. I seen the agony in your eyes that night. I've lived with grief enough years to know its look. Lord, how could those fools believe such of a thing. Men in throngs! Lord save us!

It's Turley, Farjeon said. He saw me with Shaloo's noble in Benwood today. He saw me beating up men with the other scabs. He followed Shaloo's man and me to the hotel. Jess, don't you see? I was pretending so's I could—

Jack, you don't need to explain it.

No, he said, it wants explaining. I was pretending to be on their side so's I could get at them both. That man I was with—the one who hired me—he was the one who killed Jean and the baby. And Shaloo was the boss of it. Don't you see? I was making believe so's I could have them both in a room together. I had a gun—

Yes, Jack. I understand. And Turley saw you.

Yes, he said. Turley saw me throughout all of it. Followed me. Saw me with the man Cotter in the streets outside Benwood mill. Saw me save his life. Save it so's I could take it! Don't you see? I had to pretend so's I could get them both in a room together!

He fell silent, a little breathless, staring into the flames that broke and blew from the coal.

Turley and the man Telligrew, he said, they cheated me.

How?

They killed them is how, he said. And they were mine. They weren't theirs to kill. I'd worked so hard. Planned it all. Waited so long! They were mine—they didn't belong to Turley and that poor fool Telligrew.

Jessie put her hand on his shoulder, pressed with her fingers.

Jack, we'll go away. Tonight. We'll pack up—Mother Dunne and you and me—

No, he said.

Jack, we can't stay here.

Yes, we can. We have to.

Jack, why?

Because I'm going to work in the morning.

Jack, what do you mean?

I mean I'm going to work in the morning. That's plain enough.

Where, Jack?

Why, in the mine. In Breedlove Mine.

Jessie's fingers fell from his shoulder then and rested on her knee, the pale knuckles shining in the fire glow.

Jack, no.

He nodded.

Yes, he said. I signed up this evening. Before I come up here to the house.

Signed up where?

Down at the office, he said.

He shook his head.

Kitto, he said, he wasn't there. Neither was Paul. If they'd have been there maybe Turley and the others would know different about me. Things would have happened if they'd been there.

He paused, breathing slowly.

It was a man named Harbert signed me, he said, and reached in his coat pocket. He held out a circular brass check, like a soiled, battered coin.

Here's my number, he said. One-four-three.

Jessie sat a spell in stricken silence, then pressed against him, her fingers flying up to pull his face round to see her eyes.

Jack, no.

Yes.

Jack, why?

Because I've got to stay here, he said.

Jack, why? We'll go into Glory. We'll leave West Virginia. We'll both look for work. There's jobs somewhere, Jack. I used to be a waitress once, Jack. I can do it again. There's jobs!

I've got to stay here, he said. I've got things to do here, Jess.

He drew away from her and stared darkly into the shadows of the bedroom, as if remembering vows he had made in that darkness once.

Kitto, he said, Paul. And then there's Number One. They cheated me out of the first two. But that leaves three, Jess.

Jack, even without *them,* that mine—Breedlove Mine—it's a deathtrap!

I made a vow, Jessie.

I know you did, honey. I know. But Turley and Bonar and them others! Jack, you can't go into that mine with them. Even if it don't blow up and kill you before they can—even if it don't kill all of you—! Jack, that mine is like a powder keg. And there's the miners, Jack. Jack, Jack, they'll kill you, Jack.

Mother Dunne stopped rocking, rose and came briskly to the fireside to stand and stare down at both of them.

Listen to me, Jessie, she said. Maybe you'll misunderstand me when I say this thing I've got to say. Maybe you'll think I only want your man yonder to work in Breedlove Mine to keep a roof over my own tired, old head. That's not so. If it made good sense I'd as soon say leave me on the winter roads and go off wandering into that black, jobless land together. I'd make do! I'd hold soul and body together, I swear to you! Why, I'd peddle shoestrings and gum or go begging in the streets of Glory to give you both that freedom—if it was freedom, if it made sense! But Mister Farjeon's made a vow, Jessie. And when he shows up at the pit mouth for the morning shift tomorrow there'll be some among those poor, bewitched fools who'll know by the fearlessness of his being there that he has nothing to hide! *Some,* I say—a few friends. And what's a man ever have but a few friends to stand betwixt him and the rest of the world?

Mom, you don't understand! Jessie cried in a lost, sorrowing voice.

Yes, I do, Jess. Mister Farjeon has made a vow. Part of that vow has been denied him. But there's the rest of it. A vow, Jessie. You don't know what that means to a man, I reckon. A vow. Even the smallest, meanest vow. And this one's neither small nor mean. It's from his soul, Jess.

She faltered beneath the unchecked passion of her words and caught her breath with a little shiver. Her blue eyes wandered to the winter window.

God knows, she said, God knows I dread to see any man go into the pit beneath that deathly hill. I buried two husbands in mines like Breedlove and never even saw their graves to lay flowers on. And there was never a stone to their memories—nothing but the tipple to mark where they lay hidden and smashed and gone in a blackness beyond even the decency of worms.

She shivered again, her worn, slender hands twisting against her black skirts.

And there's Tom Turley and a throng of men, she said. Men. Throngs of men. Poor, mistaken fools who fight in a war where

160

they don't even see the real enemy. No, Jess. Let him go to work in the cold, gray morning. And get used to it. And know he'll come through it somehow. And if he doesn't come through, know it's something he had to do because he made a vow.

She faltered and finished and touched each of their faces with her hand before she turned and crept into the chill, dark of the bedroom and her little room and cot beyond it.

Jessie was still a while, her cold fingers touching the back of Farjeon's hand on the bench. At last she felt his hand draw away from her touch. He struck his fist into his palm and murmured something under his breath.

Cheated! he whispered.

She watched him in sorrowing love and helplessness.

And yet, he said, there's Kitto left. And Paul. And the one whose name I don't even know yet. In a way it's bigger now, Jessie. Don't you know that?

I think I know, Jack. Maybe—

No. No maybes, he said. It's bigger.

I think I understand, Jack, she said. You have to get even for her, Jack. For your child. For your baby.

No, he said. Bigger even than that. Now it's bigger. Don't you see?

She waited, still, her eyes yearning toward him.

It's bigger now, he said. Because it's not just for them now. Don't you see?

She was silent still, searching his face.

I've got to get even for someone else too now, he said.

Who, Jack?

He covered his face and sobbed once, a thick, clotted sound that broke in his breast like a bubble. Then he uncovered his dry eyes and looked at the gun he had withdrawn from his coat pocket and now held gleaming dully in the fireshine by Jessie's knee.

I've got to get even for him now too, he said.

For who, Jack?

161

He did not look at her, stared at the blue gun in his hand.

For that man Telligrew, he whispered in a stricken, dry breath. For him—for the man they made me kill today!

He chuckled and broke the gun, plucked out the two spent cartridges, stared at them an instant and then threw them in the fire. He chuckled again and covered his face with his fingers.

Where does it end, Jessie?

She waited, not touching him yet.

Yes. Where does it end? Because it's bigger even than that.

What do you mean?

I mean it's like Mom said, he went on apace, his words in the sibilance of a dry, rushing whisper. It's more than three men to be killed. It's a system. And that means—

She waited, wanting to touch him, her outstretched fingers poised above his cheek.

—that means there's more to avenge than just Jean and the baby. More than them and the man Telligrew. It doesn't even end there. There's more to avenge than that.

He put the gun back carefully in his coat pocket and looked at her.

It means there's another murder to get even for, Jessie.

Whose, Jack?

Turley, he said. For Turley. Maybe even for him.

Why for him, Jack?

Why, for the murder of his mind—for the killing of his soul! Don't you see, Jess, don't you see? Tom Turley! In a way they've killed him too!

She watched him from the pillow. He sat in his underwear by the black window, the shape of him pale against it. He sat on the straight-backed chair that he had fetched from beside the door.

Come to bed, Jack.

He did not answer.

Jack?

Not yet, Jess.

162

She felt drained of desire for him that night; the fears for him that whispered now among her wits chilled that. But she wanted him near just the same.

Aren't you cold?

She saw his head turn, the pale wedge of his face toward her, his eyes burning dark against the paleness.

Is it cold? he whispered.

You know it is, Jack. It's freezing in here.

He studied that a moment.

That's funny, he said, I don't feel it. Not a bit. I feel hot.

She was silent, her eyes under heavy lids watching the livid, lonely shape of him cut out of the shadows like a white shape of scissored paper.

She waited, puzzling.

I've just got to set here by myself by the window, he said, till I cool off. I've got to stay here till I get over it. Till I figure out why I can't let myself come touch you.

She kept her eyes on the white, forlorn shape, saw his face turn away from her toward the blankness of the drawn window blind.

Is it about tomorrow, Jack?

What about tomorrow?

I mean about going into the mine?

No. No, Jess, it's not anything like that.

She listened to the faint drum of her pulses in her head.

Jack, I'm scared for you, she said softly.

He breathed thoughtfully but did not stir.

I'll be all right, Jess.

I prayed for you, Jack, she said. Whilst you was getting undressed I said a fast little prayer for you.

Thanks, Jess.

A freight train sounded its grieving cry somewhere behind the dark.

I'll be all right, he said again.

She shut her eyes, shuttered out the vision of him over by the window, so far, so very far from her.

Jess, I hope you'll understand, he said after a while. I can't let myself touch you tonight.

Why, Jack? she whispered, though she well knew why.

Because I'm too scared, Jess.

Scared of what, Jack. The mine?

No.

Scared of Turley?

Not him neither.

Then scared of what, Jack?

Scared of the way things keep changing round, he said. Like things moving round in a blackness. So's a man don't know where he's aiming. So's he can't be sure who's the enemy.

He might have groaned, she thought, and yet it could have been the sound of the wind.

I killed a man today, Jess.

You knew you'd kill someone, she said. You meant to.

Five, he said. I meant to kill five.

Yes.

Someone else killed two of them, he said. That leaves three. I mean to kill them too. That's not the same, Jess.

If you had been the one who pulled the trigger on Shaloo and his man in Wheeling today, Jack, would you still be scared?

Now I'm not sure. The way I feel now. I don't think so.

He thought about it a little longer.

No, he said presently. No, I wouldn't, Jess.

Yes, she said. Yes. I reckon I know the difference, Jack.

Sure you do. Sure. Things went wrong, that's the difference. I seen it so plain, Jess. It was all lined up. Then it's just like God went and moved things around on me. It's like God switched out the light on me and I shot in the dark. At anyone. Jessie, I killed an innocent man today. Jessie, a man who's suffered maybe every bit as much as me.

You killed him so's he'd not kill you, she said softly.

That don't matter, Jess. What matters is that things went wrong. It's like everything is suddenly shifting round on me.

He made a sound that was half a bitter chuckle, half the groan she thought she had heard.

Before today, he said, I saw it all so plain. It was cut-and-dried, Jess. The enemy. The evilest men my mind ever thought it could conceive of. The ones who murdered the creatures dearest to me on earth. Five men, Jess. And that was hard enough, because for one of the five I don't even know the shape nor look nor name of him. So part of that even was shrouded in a kind of shadow, a sort of unknowingness. Yet I knew I'd hunt him down and know the name of him and the look and shape of him. And kill it. Like it deserves to be killed. But now I can't even be sure that—

He bit off his sentence and sat motionless in the dark, pondering it.

That what, Jack?

I can't be sure it even ends there, Jess. The blame. The guilt for the deaths my whole mind and soul and body tell me want evening-up.

He was quiet again then. Then he stirred and she heard him strike his knee.

When Mom said that word "system" tonight it just plain throwed a cold chill over me, Jess.

She lay motionless, silent, striving to fathom what he was trying to say and knew he was trying as hard as she.

At first, he went on after a bit, at first it was only them—Jean and the baby. You see, they were all I'd ever had. Nothing else could be taken away from me. Nothing else was personal.

There's nothing personal to you about the system Mom meant, she said.

There is, when it makes me kill someone like Telligrew, he said. There is, when it drags me into a coal mine that's like living in the guts of a bomb. It's personal when some poor, half-crazy man like Turley twists a town into thinking I'm its enemy.

He struck his knee again.

I tell you, Jess, it's like I had everything all lined up real good in my sights and then God moved it all around. Moved it all around and turned out the lights. I feel like a blind man—a blind man with a gun. Who'll be next, Jess? Who do I kill next? Turley? I've got no score to settle with Tom Turley! It's Kitto next—then Paul —then the nameless, shapeless one I've got to find the name and shape for. They're the ones I'm after. And they're just as much Turley's enemies as they are mine. Who do I kill next, then? Turley? Or maybe some crazy fool he sends after me? It's all moving round, I tell you. Maybe that's all we are on this earth, Jess— things moved round in the dark. Is that how God works it? It's all moving around, Jess. All wrong. In the dark. I'm aiming that lonely little gun of mine into a blackness. Maybe Mom was right —the blackness of a system. Who do I shoot next, Jess? Kitto? Paul? That would be a justice. Do I kill them? Maybe not. I can't see the faces in the blackness. Maybe I kill Tom Turley. Just like I shot his friend. That man Telligrew. The innocent one whose blood is on me tonight so's I can't touch you, Jessie, because I'd feel the smear of it on your white skin. Who do I kill after Turley? That poor crazy Bonar or one of the others who believe his tale—poor, crazy Bonar with his scaredness and his torch? I can hardly bear to face it, Jess. I tell you it scares me fierce.

He stopped then and the wind fell silent, as if a breath were being held, and both listened then to the thin, sad, far sound—so close and yet so distant, so sad—beyond the window, beyond the hushed dark, a sound far and yet close by in the harsh, frozen yard beneath the very sill—the whimper of Turley's child Bud in the bitter night just outside.

He's back, she whispered in a husky dread.

Hush, Jess.

His fingers stole up and pressed across her lips lightly. She flung her face free, whispering.

Jack, fetch the rifle.

Hush, Jess. Wait a spell.

Jack, I'm scared for you.

No need to be. He's gambling. He can't be sure I'm here.

Nobody seen you come in?

No. I'm sure of that.

And then both were still again, hearing the child's sobbing, muffled complaint.

Hush, boy! they heard Turley say. Be still, I tell you! This is a moral. This is all of it a moral you'll thank me for someday! Hush your whimpering, boy, 'gainst I fetch you a smack!

And then the crisp, faint press of his footfall on the frosted earth and the bandaged, muffled creak as he leaned into the snowy windowsill and pressed his mouth close to the crack.

Can you hear me, woman?

Jessie trembled and flung herself free from Farjeon's comforting clasp.

Are you alone, woman?

Farjeon stared at the white shape of Jessie in the darkness. He marveled at how little he was afraid. He found it hard to think of mad Turley out yonder as an enemy; he could think just then of nothing but the invisible pressure of an enemy that had shaped them all into that moment.

Jess, come back to bed, he whispered, turning his back to her.

The wind was still at the ebb, that wind like a breath held in shock of something, so that they could hear the child's smothered whine and the breath of Turley against the window crack.

He could be in there with you now, woman. Well, I know that.

They heard then the soft, wet sound as his fingers struck the child's face. Then his mouth was back to the crack again and they heard him chuckle, a dry sound that was almost a whimper.

I'll chance it, he said. I'll chance that maybe he's there with you, woman. Then again maybe he ain't. It don't matter. Because there's tomorrow. In the mine.

He paused then; they could hear his breathing.

I been down to Kitto's shack. I got the news. Your man's been took on at Breedlove. He'll be checking in on the deadman's shift. So there's time. There's tomorrow.

Jessie stood erect in the cold dark, hugging her arms round herself. She moaned softly. They could hear Turley's breathing; they could hear his silence as he measured his words like soft, fierce blows.

Maybe you've fetched the rifle, he said. Maybe it's aimed square through that windowpane, fixing to blow me to kingdom come. But I don't reckon so. You ain't a cold-blooded killer like him. No. You're just a poor weak whore. Woman, I feel sorry for you.

The snow creaked faintly as he shifted his weight.

Hush, Bud. Hush, I say. There's a moral in this. You'll thank me some day.

The voice of him—disembodied, unreal somehow, as if it were some tongue the wind had found and used against them now, pressing them to a terror beyond madness.

Sure. He might be in there. In the bed. In your arms. I'd be in there with Bud now if it wasn't for that. There's some things I don't want Bud's young eyes to see yet. Vengeance. Justice. Them's the things I want Bud to see. Early. While he's still young. But I don't want him to see whoring and filth. He'll see enough of that later.

That mad fool! Mother Dunne whispered sharply from the little doorway to her room. Farjeon turned and watched the small, gray muslin shape of her in the dusk of the dark. She stood a moment and then went barefoot to the window and stooped to the sill.

And it would serve you right, Tom Turley! she cried in a high, proud voice. If Jack Farjeon was in this bedroom with Cal's rifle aimed at this window. A sinful, crazy sonofabitch of a fool who'd drag his child into the snow on such of an insane mission. Go home, you mad bastard. Go home, I say, and leave decent folks to their rest.

They could hear him breathing, the slow, measured breath against the crack like his wits' turgid, crippled striving toward truth. When he spoke again his voice was lower, somehow puzzled.

I'm real sorry, Mom, he said. Sorry you're dragged down into all this.

He paused.

I can't figure you in this, Mother Dunne. I purely can't. Shielding a murdering fink. You was always our friend, Mom.

And I still would be if you had any sense! she cried. And he's not a fink. He never was, you twisted, mad bastard. He's as innocent of any crime against us here at Breedlove as that poor, crying child you've dragged out tonight into this bitterness of cold.

Turley hesitated.

The miners know the truth, he said. There's not a man of them—

Listen to me! cried the old woman. I'll stack my good sense against yours any day, Tom Turley. I've lived sixty of my seventy-nine years in the midst of mines and miners! Longer than you've been on earth. Long enough to know who's the miners' enemy and who ain't!

She leaned her wrathy face into the stirring rag of curtains, her small knuckles white on the sill. They could hear Turley move faintly, meditating.

He was with them, with Shaloo, the scab herder, he cried bitterly. With him and one of his killers!

He was not, Tom Turley!

Mom, he was! Me and Telligrew seen him. He was setting there with Shaloo and his killer in that Wheeling hotel room, drinking their whiskey and smoking their big Cuban see-gars. I tell you we seen him, Mother Dunne.

Maybe he was there for a reason! Some good reason!

What reason! What other reason could there be?

I don't know. I only know I trust him!

You're wrong, Mother Dunne!

You're a fool, Tom Turley! Listen to me, will you? You was in Breedlove the night Shaloo and his men struck us all. You remember the dead that was laid out like stovewood next morning. And who lay amongst them? Jack Farjeon's wife and unborn child! Now, will you tell me how could a man—

Scab killers ain't like other men! Scab killers don't love their own the way other men do! I never trusted him from the first minute her and him showed up in Breedlove atop that wagon! And everyone laughed and said he was the barefoot man. Not me! I suspicioned him from the outset, I did! I suspicioned him as a spy sent here to muddle our wits somehow in the hour before Shaloo's army struck.

Mother Dunne's eyes darkened with a sudden glitter.

And tell me, Tom Turley, what was you and Jake Telligrew doing in that hotel room to be seeing Jack Farjeon there?

They could hear his big shoes shift on the hoary earth.

Well? Answer that, Tom Turley!

Never mind what, he said.

Aha! Never mind what, says he! You had come there with a purpose, I'll judge!

We did.

As he might have come for the same! she cried, striking the sill. And which of you was it that slew Shaloo and his man? Was it Jack Farjeon or was it you and Jake?

Again he was still, and the wind was down yet, so they could hear the measured, sobbing breath of the child Bud.

Who killed the murderers, Tom Turley? Are you confessing that to me?

I'll say no more on that, Mom. It was done—I know that.

So do I. That's fact. It was done. But who was it done it? Was it Jack Farjeon? God knows he had reason! Was it him who done it, Tom Turley?

He was one of *them!* the big man cried. He was one of Shaloo's men. We seen him—Jake and me! That afternoon! We watched while him and the rest of them beat up steel puddlers in the Benwood gutter!

Who killed Shaloo and his man, Tom Turley? the old woman cried again.

He waited.

If you knowed I was one of them that did it, he said presently

170

in a heavy voice. Would you go to the law against me, Mother Dunne?

She snorted.

I wouldn't go to the law, she said, if it would bring back the dead, Tom Turley. You know that.

Then why you keep asking me if me and Jake—?

Because I'm thinking somehow it was Mister Farjeon's plan to worm his way amongst them. I'm thinking it was his purpose to do what was done by someone else!

He's one of *them,* Turley said again.

And I'd stake whatever days of life are left to me that he ain't! she cried. I'd stake it against the hottest pit in hell, Tom Turley!

Mom, he shot Jake!

Prove that.

I was standing beside him when the bullet hit him.

Did you or Jake shoot first?

What's that got to do with it? What's that prove?

A man defends himself.

Defends himself! I tell you, Mom, we seen him strong-arming steel puddlers in the Benwood gutter. Is that defense?

Tom, you're a fool. I've knowed you for years and I've always known that. I'm sorry for you.

Mom, Mom, it ain't like you to shelter a man like him. I tell you it ain't.

Sorry, she said again. I mean that. I'm sorry for you that's had your wits crippled. It's this life that's done it to you. I know that. A life not fit for animals. Maybe I'm sorry for all of us for that.

He's one of *them,* I tell you, Mom!

Go home, Tom Turley. For that poor child's sake if for no other!

A train blew faintly somewhere within the dark, unbeating heart of the winter hills.

Is he in there now, Mom? came the big man's voice, his lips close to the crack.

I'd not tell you if he was, Tom Turley.

He is, Turley said. Yes. I'll wager so. He's in there. Quilted up snug with his whore. He's there, ain't he?

Shame to talk such filth before a child! cried the old woman.

Never mind that, Turley said. I do all right by Bud. I'm raising him right. To grow up knowing justice by the sight of it. Christian justice, Mom.

He sighed, thoughtful amid the coils of his madness.

I'm just real sorry Bud won't be with me in the dark hours 'fore sunrise. I'm just purely sorry Bud won't be there to see it—in the black, deep tunnel of Breedlove Number Twelve six hours from now when Mister Farjeon meets his justice.

There'll be two sides to that matter, Tom Turley!

What do you mean?

I mean there'll be them that holds by your beliefs and them that thinks like me.

He snorted.

You seen that mob of men that followed me and Bonar up here tonight!

Mobs go to bed, Tom Turley. When mobs get up in the morning they sometimes reasons differently.

What could change their minds?

I could! she cried, suddenly striking both numb, angry palms on the peeling windowsill. I'll knock on every door! I'll go amongst them!

It's only six hours till the deadman's shift, Mother Dunne.

Six hours to shape up sides! she cried. There's fair-minded, sane-headed men amongst us here at Breedlove, Tom Turley! They're not all as cripple-witted as you and Steve Bonar!

Fifty men, he said evenly, fifty out of a hundred and fifty miners. No. I'll wager there's seventy-five who'll believe me, Mom!

They listened to the far, hacking smallness of the child Bud's croupy cough.

God help you, Tom Turley.

He is my Savior, said the big man in a strong, emotional voice. Though it's hard to see His face in this heathen place.

172

And would you know the devil's face if you seen that, Tom Turley?

I seen it yesterday in the gutter in Benwood outside the mills, he said in a broken, passionate voice. I seen it setting there in that Wheeling hotel room drinking good whiskey with Shaloo and his other scab killer! Oh, I know the devil's face good, Mother Dunne. And I aim to kill it wherever! You can rest your faith on that! Whatever faith that may be!

My faith is men, she said. And there's always some men who won't swallow lies. Not even if you try to cram it down their throats with a silver-plated shoe horn. There may not be a church for it, Tom Turley, nor any book of prophecies, but my faith is men!

She leaned her old face closer to the ragged, stirring curtain, her eyes dark with glittering.

Did you hear me, Tom Turley? Or is your poor mind shut to reason?

The curtain stirred faintly in the stillness. Jessie crept barefoot to the old woman's side.

He's gone, Mom, she said.

Mother Dunne turned her face wearily and looked at the girl beside her. Then she looked at the motionless shape of Farjeon beneath the quilt. Jessie smiled.

Thank God, she said. The day clean spent him out, I reckon.

Did he hear?

No, Jessie said. He slept throughout. Thank the Lord for that. If he'd heard Turley's words he'd likely have been out in the yard to face him.

The two women looked at Farjeon's hunched, exhausted shape in the bed.

Let him sleep, poor, dear man, said the old woman. Let him sleep well.

She turned her eyes again to the blankness of the drawn blind.

Let him sleep well, she said again. God knows he'll need all his quickest wits about him in that black hole tomorrow!

The lamp on the single bedroom table had been turned low so that the light in that strange little room was faint gold-amber as of deeps below water in some soundless, somnolent sea. Jessie went, bent her mouth to her hand cupped above the faintly smoking chimney and blew back the dark. Then she followed the old woman who beckoned her into the kitchen. The old woman smiled and went to the cupboard. She turned her face, still smiling, and winked at Jessie.

With such of a night as we've got facing us, she said, what us two women need is a good, strong cup of black coffee.

Jessie shrugged and smiled weakly back.

Some chance, she said. Sassafras tea is more like it.

No, cried Mother Dunne, I said coffee and coffee it will be.

Jessie stared at her.

The last time we had coffee in this house, she said, was Christmas five years ago. That time we found it in the Charities basket.

And long enough it's been! cried the old woman merrily, fetching a small brown-paper poke out of her shadow beneath the cupboard. She held it up to Jessie's nose.

Sniff, Jess.

Jessie sniffed and stared, marveling.

Where'd you get it at, Mom? Wherever?

I sold my brooch in Glory this morning, said the old woman. Got fifty cents for it too, though I'll swear it was worth every bit of seventy-five. Still, it was enough.

Ah, Mom, you loved that brooch!

Stuff and nonsense! cried Mother Dunne. That ugly thing. I never did like it. It wasn't nothing but a gimcrack of glass and fake gold. Such of a thing as you'd see on a dressed-up corpse. Besides, all I could think about was coffee! Coffee, Jess!

Why, Mom?

Why, I reckon, because they give us coffee in the jail, said the

174

old woman. Coffee rank as stump water! I swore when I got home
I'd have me a cup of *real* coffee, Jess!

She stared at the small, tight poke.

It's only a half pound, she said. It won't go far. But it's what
you and me need tonight, Jess!

She fetched an old, cracked enamel saucepan, filled it at the
pump, and set it on the coal stove.

Strong coffee, she said with a nod, and dumped a third of the
poke's fresh grounds into the water, then came to sit by Jessie's
side on the bench before the fire.

Let it come to a good boil so's it'll be strong as lye, she said.
Meanwhile we'll talk, Jess.

What's to talk about now, Mom? I reckon it's all in God's hands.

Partly, said the old woman. Even so—sometimes God's hand
needs another hand to help it. Sometimes it's a woman's hand.

What do you mean?

I mean there's things I've got to do before I sleep tonight, girl.

What things?

Doors to knock at, said Mother Dunne. Words to be said.

Words? To who?

To the ears of sane, reasonable men here in Breedlove.

Tonight?

Tonight.

Everybody's sleeping, Mom.

I'll wake them. I'll wake them to sense—to justice.

Jessie shrugged, her elbows on her knees, her shoulders bowed.

You saw their eyes out there tonight, Mom.

That's so! cried the old woman. And I saw those same eyes the
night they looked at Jack Farjeon holding the bodies of his murdered family. Some of those eyes haven't forgotten that dreadful
sight!

Do you reckon so, Mom?

It has to be so, said the old woman. He won't have a chance
tomorrow morning unless he has a few friends amongst them—a

few against the ones that believe Turley's tale. If I can wake a few of the miners to sense, he'll maybe have a chance.

Mom, they come to kill him tonight!

Mobs simmer down. Men go home. They sleep. Sometimes in their dreams comes reason. They can be woken up. They can be changed.

Jessie flushed and looked at her hands.

You don't want me to come with you, I reckon?

The old woman's hand came to rest on her knee; she pressed the faded cloth of Jessie's skirt.

Better not, said the old woman. They believe me, Jess. They've always believed me for some queer reason. Maybe it's because I've never lied to them. I know miners, Jess. They suspicion everybody. That's why what I have to do needs such careful handling.

They wouldn't believe me, you mean?

Maybe. Maybe not. They know you've got something to lie for.

What thing, Mom?

They know you love him.

Jessie's face colored again and she looked at her broken nails.

I don't love him, she said. Not a bit, I don't.

Mother Dunne smiled, her eyes darkling and bright in the fire-shine.

I don't, the girl said again.

She smoothed the cloth on her thighs.

We just need each other is all, she said. That's all it is, Mom.

She frowned and shook her eyes at the flame.

I don't know what it is, she said. Maybe the Bible would call it lust of the flesh. I don't love him though. We—we just need each other. That's what it is.

I know, said the old woman, I remember.

Remember what, Mom?

I remember life.

She reached her fingers up and drew the girl's gaze round to her own.

Tell me about Mister Farjeon, Jess.

176

What do you mean, Mom?

Tell me first what *he* means, Jess.

You mean what he aims to do?

That's part of it, Jess.

How come you ask me that, Mom?

Lord, girl, because I don't know anything about the man except what my blood tells me. I trust him. I know that. My blood is old and it never lies to me about people. But think, Jess girl. I've been away in Glory jail all these weeks. I haven't traded a dozen words with him.

Jessie looked at her pale hands again. Then she went back to the old woman's stare.

Do you suspicion him of being with *them*, Mom?

Never.

Are you sure?

Sure as I'm sure of sunrise, Jess. I've seen enough scab killers in sixty years not to know one by smell.

Then what else is there to know?

Mother Dunne went to the stove, fetched a ragged strainer and poured two cups of coffee. She brought one back to the girl who sat with it, staring into the steamy darks of the tin cup.

What does he *mean?* she asked again.

Jessie shrugged.

How can I tell you, Mom? He just—

He didn't kill Shaloo yesterday—him and the scab that was with him in the hotel room in Wheeling? He didn't, did he, Jess?

No.

But he went there meaning to kill them?

Jessie sipped her coffee, shivering a little.

Well, he did, didn't he?

Yes.

He went through all of it, said the old woman. Hiring on as a scab, being a scab in the Benwood streets, just so he could get them both together. In that Wheeling hotel room.

Yes.

To kill them.

Yes.

But Turley and Jake Telligrew got them first.

Yes. I reckon, Mom, he—

And that fool Turley and poor Jake had followed him the live-long day and seen it all and believed it all and thought—

Thought he was one of Shaloo's scabs.

Mother Dunne cradled the tin cup in her fingers.

Lord, this coffee is elegant. Elegant! After that slop in Glory jail!

The girl said nothing. The old woman lowered the cup an inch and stared across the tin rim at her.

He had a gun.

Yes.

With which he shot poor Jake.

I— I guess—yes.

In common, ordinary self-defense.

Oh, yes, Mom! Jack didn't mean—!

I know that, Jess. I know that. That fool Turley was the plain cause of it. Jake Telligrew would follow anyone. Never had the good sense of a chicken!

Jessie, dry-eyed, sobbed.

Now tell me this then, Jess, said the old woman. Mister Farjeon, he still has the gun?

Yes. I reckon he—

Why, Jess?

Jessie covered her face with her fingers; she shook her head swiftly, her dark hair flying round her wrists. Mother Dunne laid her fingers across the girl's shoulders.

He's not done with the gun yet?

Jessie nodded, sobbing faintly again.

How many more, Jess?

Jessie was silent; the house settled more deeply into the stillness of the fallen wind.

Are there others he means to kill, Jess?

Jessie was still a breath longer, then she turned and flung her face around to the old woman.

Mom, I'm so scared for him.

I know that, girl.

Mom, what will happen to him?

It seems to me, said Mother Dunne, that what we must worry about tonight is what a few, wild-witted miners may do to him in the morning. As for the law—

Mom, he means to get every man that was in back of the murders that night.

The murders of his wife and babe.

Yes.

And whose names are on that list?

Shaloo and the man in the Wheeling hotel room. Jack said that man was the one who pulled the trigger.

Dead already. And not by his hand. Who else?

Jessie's eyes flooded with fearful tears.

Mom, you'd not tell on him?

Shame on you, Jess! You know I'd not do such of a thing! Whatever I think, whatever I feel is right or wrong, I'd not betray him.

Jessie searched the old woman's squinting, thoughtful face.

Mister Kitto, she said. Mister Paul.

The mine foreman, said Mother Dunne. And the manager. And does it end there, Jess?

No.

Who else, then?

Jessie shook her head.

One other, she whispered.

Who?

Jessie shook her head again.

He—he doesn't know, Mom.

Hah! Would it be the man who owns Breedlove mine?

Yes.

Hah! The guiltiest one of all—maybe the *only* guilty one of all in the long run of things! And he doesn't know even the name of him!

Jessie searched her face again.

Do *you* know, Mom?

Mother Dunne smiled and shook her head.

The only guilty one, she said again. The *only* one in the long run of things.

Do you know, Mom?

No.

She chuckled and twisted the hem of her blue skirt.

Ain't it something? she said. To feel the life being crushed slowly out of you and not know who's doing it? No, Jess. I don't know who owns Breedlove.

She sighed.

There's not a man in this camp, she said, who wouldn't be backing Mister Farjeon to the hilt if they knowed his dream. And yet I can't go out there tonight and tell them that.

I know.

You never know who to trust. Not even among ourselves.

You'll not tell them then, Mom?

I told you I wouldn't. Of course I wouldn't. I'd as soon go to the law. I'll not tell—whatever I think.

Jessie stared hard.

That's twice you've said that, Mom.

Said what?

"Whatever I think." What *do* you think?

Mother Dunne smiled.

I think Mister Farjeon is wrong—that's what I think.

Jessie shook her head and pressed the old woman's hand.

Mom, how come you think Jack's wrong?

Mother Dunne's eyes narrowed, thoughtful. Her fingers stole to the ragged neck of her dark dress, remembering where the pretty brooch had been.

180

Jess, I don't just know how to put it, she said. I don't know how to tell you what I do think—not without seeming the biggest hypocrite in the world.

Jessie bided, watching the old woman's face.

Jack Farjeon wants vengeance, said Mother Dunne.

Can you blame him?

No. No, I don't blame him. That's not what I'm getting at.

What then?

Jessie, I'm a violent old woman. I've lived a violent, troubled life.

Then you understand.

Yes, that's how I *do* understand. That's how I know.

Know what, Mom?

That it never works, said the old woman. Because it never ends.

Vengeance?

Violence, Mother Dunne said. It mates and breeds upon itself. It's like some weed of hell. It's never done.

Jessie bided longer, studying this, then she frowned.

Mom, you of all people—

I know! I said that, didn't I? cried the old woman, striking her knees. I've lived by violence. Sixty years of it. Isn't that long enough to get to know the real nature of it?

Mom, I purely can't figure you, Jessie said with a troubled smile.

I know! I know! cried the old woman, rising impatiently and walking round the bench to stand glaring again into the glowing coal in the grate. God knows I've lived a violent life. The Lord knows my heart is full of it. But it's all in my mind, Jess. For my blood tells me it's wrong. And still—as you say—God knows I've lived it, preached it. Even when my blood told me it was wrong.

She flung her gaze on the girl.

Jess, I've buried two husbands in the mines—and a son. I've seen their lives crushed out like rats in a slate fall. I've organized —I've rallied miners to violence. Sixty years, Jess. Sixty years of

181

that. And all I've ever learned, all I've ever come up with is something small as a handful of coal dust. Small, Jess, but precious—more precious than coal, Jess.

Jessie waited.

It's the knowing that violence never works. It never ends. It only multiplies itself like some evil, hellish weed.

But, Mom! The night Shaloo's killers came down the road shooting. You tried to get the rifle away from Cal. To kill them yourself, Mom! You—

I know! I know! In self-defense. Lord, I'm not even sure that kind of violence is right. Not any more! Lord, I don't know. Not any more. I recollect it, Jess—I wanted the gun that night. I wanted to kill the bastards. My whole life's been that—wanting to kill the bastards. Even when I knowed it wouldn't fix anything, change anything. Maybe I thought it was right that night!

She struck her knee with her fist.

No! I didn't even think it was right then. It was my mind, Jess—that old, violent mind of mine. It said shoot the sonsabitches. Even while the blood in me kept on awhispering it was wrong!

Why is it wrong, Mom?

Because—God, how can I tell it! Because the twisted sonsabitches who come down that black night road to shoot us—Jess, they was poor like us!

Scum of the earth, Mom.

Sure, I know. Scum of the earth. Ragtag drunkards and crazy hoboes from the slums of Wheeling. But poor. Maybe poorer than us.

Too lazy to hold a job, Mom.

Or too dumb. Or too crazy. Too crippled and lamed by things as they are. Too smashed down and busted by some—some—system!

What about Shaloo himself?

Crippled even worse than them! cried the old woman. Only God Almighty would claim such of a man as human! But human he is, Jess. Human as you and me. Only some *system*—some Goddamned, Lord-forsaken, twisting, laming thing above us all has shaped and made him.

God, Mom?

Jess, don't lay this on God. Lord, he bears enough.

She smiled a bitter smile, she laughed a bitter laugh.

Poor God Almighty, she said. He sure must get blue sometimes. The things men lay on Him. He sure must get blue sometimes. It's a marvel He don't get blue enough sometimes to pray to *us* for help!

What about Mister Number One, Mom?

Who?

The man that owns the mine?

Mother Dunne snorted and flung her fingers high.

Lord, crippled worst of all! she cried. Sorriest of the lot, Jess! I can't hardly fancy a man more lamed and twisted by it all. It's got *him* trapped worse than the others!

"It," Mom? What is "it"?

The old woman shut her eyes and made a crooning, meditative sound.

Jess, I don't know it by name.

What do you reckon it is?

Something, said the old woman. Something that was real pretty once, real good. Something that was true and tall among us that growed to be—crouched and ugly. Something that's crippled us here, Jess. Crippled us from top to bottom!

Mom, you sound like that communist organizer that was hanging around the company store last spring, Jessie whispered.

That poor fool! cried the old woman scornfully. With his poor little packet of grimy leaflets! As if his system wasn't just as bad. That poor idiot boy! As if his lameness wasn't even worse than ours! No, Jess—

She rose briskly and went to the stove, lifting the saucepan to stare at the little coffee that was left among the heaped grounds.

There's a mouthful left, Jess. You drink it.

I don't want no more. Thanks, Mom. You.

Mother Dunne stared into the saucepan.

Funny, she said, I don't neither. You'd think doing without coffee for five years, a body couldn't get enough of it.

She flung the saucepan back.

Funny, she said. Somehow I'm too full of my thoughts tonight to have any taste for anything good. Or maybe being poor so long, your mouth disremembers anything good at all.

She glanced toward the bedroom.

What time is it, Jess?

Jess stole to the bedroom and looked in at the Big Ben beside the door.

It's five hours till Jack goes to work.

Five hours. Five hours to rouse them idiot miners from their sleep and try to talk some sense into them. And here we sit chatting like two housewives. Still—there's things wants talking about tonight, Jess. Between you and me. I've got to tell you what's in my mind tonight or lose it. I'm so full of fool feelings. About him in there. About what them poor fools may do to him tomorrow. About what he might go and do himself. And I've got to clear my mind of things that's long wanted saying. Things about him in yonder. About why I think he's wrong. I've got to tell you, Jess— so's maybe you can tell him.

She went and sat in her old rocker by the window, away from the fire glow. She did not look at Jessie.

You never knew I done housework in Glory once, did you, Jess?

You never told me, Mom.

Well, I did. After my first man was killed in a rockfall down on the Big Sandy. I wandered north again. Home to Glory. I was nigh penniless and Cal was a baby. I carried him on my back like an Injun papoose. I went to work for a man in Glory—an educated, rich gentleman, name of Hood. It was just him and his boy. His woman was dead ten years. Diphtheria. It was only him and the boy. And, Lord, the sun rose and set on that boy!

Jessie went to the stove, stood a moment biting her lip, then poured the last of the coffee in her cup. Mother Dunne rocked slowly back and forth, her head back, her eyes shut, her small mouth smiling as she remembered.

I can just remember one thing, she said. I can remember how much I hated that rich man when I first saw him. You see, I was still bitter. Bitter about my husband Viney's death. I hated all rich people. That was before I got to know Mister Hood. Oh, he was rich all right, rich as Solomon. But after a spell I come to know that it was a kind of richness that didn't seem to hurt anybody. He didn't seem to own anything—he just had money. And his mind. Lord, what a grand mind he had! Harvard College, I think it was. And somewhere in England too. Books along the wall like canned goods in a store! Paintings that was hand-painted in every room. He was rich, he was! But it seemed like the kind of richness that didn't hurt anybody, didn't push anybody down. It was a revelation to me. He didn't own any factories or mills or mines. Nobody seemed to know where his money came from. But it always came. Or maybe it was just always there.

He used to take off and go on short trips to Europe and Asia and France and Lord knows where-all. Every month or so. And I'd be there in the big house in Glory, cooking and keeping house for the boy. Lord, how he loved that boy! And I tell you, he was rich, Jess. But it was the kind of rich that didn't seem to get that way from hurting people. There was a goodness about him, something fine and gentle. I tell you, Jess, it taught me a lesson. Because I'd come there to Glory so bitter. Lord, I was so bitter over Viney's death in that mine down at Logan. Mister Hood—he was a revelation to me. He was rich but he was good. I couldn't quite swallow that at first. It's taken me a spell of thinking. And reading. All them books. Thick as trees in a woodland. Oh, I used to read, Jess. When the work was done and Cal was asleep. I used to creep down to that big room and read. Lord, I used to read. I'll bet you never knowed I'd ever read books, Jess.

What sort of books, Mom?

Poems mostly, said the old woman, quickening the pace of her rocking. I wasn't never much on stories. Nor history. Poems mostly.

What kind of poems, Mom?

Blake, said Mother Dunne abruptly. I'll bet you never did hear tell of him. Now, did you, Jess?

No.

Blake, said the old woman again. I don't mind his first name right now. Robert. Walter. No. William. Yes, William! That was it—William Blake! Lord, what a fine, wrathy kind of man he must have been! Prophecies and visions to beat the Scriptures! Lord, he was *like* a kind of Bible writer in his way! I was raised, titted and weaned on Bible, Jess, so I had a fair taste for this Mister William Blake. Oh, I did! Lord, he seemed to pick up where the Bible left off! In some ways he was better! Because the Bible—specially the old part—it's so full of wrath and vengeance and meanness! The very things that I was so full of when I come to work for Mister Hood. And then I read these poems by Mister Blake. Wrathy they was—and violent too! But there was a great, strong gentle thing—a something green and strong as trees in them! Things like I'd come to learn from Mister Hood himself! D'you see, Jess? A kind of mercy that leaned down over all poor, weak human things and pitied them and tried to raise them up.

She sighed, smiling, shaking her head from side to side.

I mind one line, she said. My most favorite of all—

The wind that had lain still for so long a spell now rose and tried itself faintly against the house; the dusty panes chattered once and were still again.

"For everything that lives," said Mother Dunne, "is holy."

Jessie's eyes dreamed in the fire, and in the bedroom Farjeon muttered thinly and turned in his quilt. Mother Dunne sighed, and her head, thrust back against the dusty rocker's headrest, weaved from side to side.

Lord, Jess! she said. When I first come across that line my mind

186

pulled back its fingers like they'd been burned on a hot stove lid. It fair shook my soul. Because, you see, I'd left the Big Sandy so full of hate for almost everything that walked upright on earth. I hated Viney because he'd been poor and dumb and misbegotten so's he'd had to work in the mines in the first place. And I hated the rich because I knowed some of them ran the mines. And the rest owned stock. Or ran something else in the land to lame and crush men down. And then I come across that line of the poem one winter afternoon—"For everything that lives is holy." Jess, it was like a pail of ice water throwed in the face of some deep sleeper. I tell you, it wokened me. Lord, it was that winter afternoon that I commenced to know things in my blood. Sure!— things my mind didn't yet have the good sense to know yet! Things you know in the blood, Jess, they're the deepest knowing God ever meant for you. And that's when I stopped hating Mister Hood for being rich. Because he was the kind of rich that didn't hurt nobody. No. It was more than that. In my blood I knowed suddenly that we was all something that matters—that keeps on. Even the mineowners. Even poor, dumb, unschooled fools like my poor Viney.

Jessie smiled and turned.

But you still hate, Mom, she said gently.

Yes! cried the old woman, thrusting the rocker angrily with her toes. And that's why I never amounted to more than the poor old fool you see here tonight, Jess. My mind—it always got the better of my blood. Don't you see, Jess? My blood always told me it wasn't men that was wrong, it was some damned-fool system men had made—some system men will always make. Till they learn better. And I've almost give up hope of that! Whether it's us or England or Rooshia! Whatever! Human beings is holy beings— but they've made unholy things! The systems, Jess! Lord God save us from the systems! My blood told me that! But my poor mind— it wouldn't never listen to the things my blood kept on awhispering. Don't you see, Jess? That's why it don't matter a hill of beans

187

to anything if Jack Farjeon kills Mister Kitto or Mister Paul or Mister Number One—whoever he may be. Because then someone —the law or God knows who—will kill Mister Farjeon. And then maybe you or me will try to kill them. And where does it end? Tell me, where does *that* end, my girl? *Where,* I ask you that!

She stopped rocking, cursed faintly under her breath and suddenly stood up straight, staring at the door. She sighed.

Mister Hood, she said, Mister William G. Hood. Lord, how talking tonight brings him back to me, Jess.

Jessie watched her in silence.

That year with him—in his home—cooking, keeping house, said the old woman. That year changed me, Jess. Maybe not enough to make any difference in the way I turned out. But it changed me. It put whispers in my blood, Jess. It did!

She shook her head.

That good man, she said. That rich, good, wise man.

Why did you leave the job, Mom? Jessie asked. Why? If you was so happy?

Lord, things change so quick, smiled the old woman. A year later and I was married to another miner. A year later and I was back in the same old life.

What happened, Mom?

Mother Dunne closed her eyes, searching back into the way it was.

One sweet spring night, she said, his son died. Rheumatic fever. Died in his sleep. Lord, I mind what a fair, sweet April night it was.

She shook her head.

Lord, how he loved that son. It was like he'd died himself that night.

Did he take it that hard, Mom?

Hard! It was like he'd died instead. I could see it in his eyes that morning. Something perishing in him. Lord, the sun rose and set on that boy.

Then you left him, Mom?

I never seen his face after the day of that funeral. He gave me three months wages that night and bade me goodbye. Nailed up the big house like a coffin next day—books and pictures and all. I hardly had time to throw the food out of the icebox. Nailed it up. Like a box of dreams he was done with.

What happened to him, Mom?

He went away. To Europe or France or China or somewheres. He said it was business but I knowed better. He was nailing up something of himself that was dead. That boy! Lord! How he loved him. So he nailed up all that past and left it. Went away. I never saw him again.

She smiled.

Well, I wonder if he's changed much, she said.

Jessie frowned.

I don't reckon you'll ever know, Mom.

Oh yes, I will, said Mother Dunne. Yes, I'll know.

Is he alive still, Mom?

Oh yes, he's alive.

Where?

Jess, you've seen his name in the Glory *Argus* a thousand times.

Mom, I don't remember.

Sure you do, Jess. Mister William G. Hood is a U. S. senator now. From West Virginia.

Jessie tilted her head, remembering vaguely.

Yes, she said. He's the one Jack's always praising. Yes, I mind the name now, Mom.

She smiled faintly.

Jack, he said they'd aimed to name the baby after him if it was a boy.

Yes, said Mother Dunne. And I hear tell he's a friend of workingmen.

She pursed her lips.

He was, back then, she said. Maybe he still is.

189

She nodded thoughtfully, cautiously.

I'll know when I see him. Yes, my blood will tell me like it did back then.

See him, Mom? Where?

Why, here, Jess, said the old woman. I heard them talking about it at the store in Glory when I bought the coffee.

What's he doing in a place like this?

He's coming from Washington tomorrow, said the old woman—here, to Breedlove Mine.

What for, Mom?

To investigate conditions. To look into the mine.

At the thought of that night she frowned again. Then she turned her gaze on Jessie, her strong, small face imploring.

Jessie.

What, Mom?

Jessie, maybe Mister Hood will bring peace amongst us.

Jessie turned her face back to the fire, feeling the heat of it against her eyes, her mouth.

Maybe, she said listlessly.

Jessie.

What?

Jessie, try to talk Mister Farjeon out of it.

Out of what, Mom? Jessie whispered.

You know what, Jessie. Out of more killing. Jessie, maybe Mister Hood is going to bring us peace. Jessie, I remember him. He was such a good friend of the poor. I hear tell he still is. Jess, try.

Jessie kept her gaze in the flame—the heat of it made her eyes tear.

Jessie, please. Let the killings end. Good new times may be acoming, Jess. Betwixt John L. and Mister Roosevelt and Mister William G. Hood we may get good new times, Jess.

Jessie bit her lip and knuckled the wetness from her eyes. Her nose smarted from the fragrance of the burning coal.

Jess, try.

I don't know if I could, Mom.

Jess, please. I know what vengeance feels like. I've spent my poor foolish life wanting it. But it's a fool's quest, Jess. Don't you see? It won't help. It will just keep on till it crushes us all! Won't you try, Jess?

Jessie could not answer; she could not meet the old woman's shadowed, passionate stare. Jessie could think only of the revolver under Farjeon's end of the pillow—the cold steel thing under his dreaming head which whispered to itself now of a vengeance even greater than he had begun. And what if Mother Dunne's quest among the sleeping miners failed to gain him any friends? What would he have but that small steel fact to save his life in the dark of the deadman's shift? Yet it was more. The violence in him—it was the very smell of that which had drawn Jessie to his manhood from the beginning. She could not fancy any whole sense of Farjeon at all without that—the turbulence and anger, the scent of it. It was like some queerly transmuted smell of life itself, some integer of his being that she had breathed in on first glimpse of him and made part of her whole sensibility of him.

Mother Dunne stood now by the door in Cal's old coat. It fell nearly to her shoe tips. She looked like some sage, strange, ancient child—an odd, violent doll created out of winter's wildest fantasy, her pale, shrewd, passionate face peering out from beneath Cal's old army hat. Jessie's eyes fell to the strange, pale, round thing in the old woman's hands.

What's that you've got, Mom?

Mother Dunne lifted Jean's pale relic of survival into the lamp-light, staring at it now gently.

This? she said. Don't you mind, Jess? She was carrying it in her lap the night they come in the wagon—the barefoot man and his woman. Don't you mind? She was holding it in her hands.

The cream pitcher, Jessie said. Yes.

I'll show them this, said the old woman. Maybe it'll help them remember how it all was. Her carrying it in her hands under the fullness of her belly that night. All she had left of her world.

Maybe it'll help them remember the sight of that. And maybe it'll help them remember the sight of him holding her murdered in his arms a scarce hour later. All he had left of his.

She opened the door and stared out at the ragged, dim shapes of lanternless shacks racked along the dark hill beneath the black, starless night. A small wind stirred the straggle of snowy hair along her cheek beneath the absurd old hat.

Maybe it will help them remember who he really is, she said. No scab killer nor scab spy. Not even the barefoot man. No. Only a man amongst them here. Only another miner like themselves.

Then, swiftly, she was gone.

Jessie sat alone by the fire for a good long spell, troubled by things the old woman had said. The fire in the grate had diminished to a few glowing coals and the room had grown cold. Jessie stole, frowning, into the bedroom and undressed slowly in the dark. When she had dropped the coarse cotton nightgown over her pale nakedness she crept under the quilt beside Farjeon. He slept as soundly still as he had during Turley's last visit outside the window. Jessie lay scowling into the dark, biting her lip and yearning to wake him. After a spell she turned her face, and in the dusky light between them, saw Farjeon's eyes open wide, watching her silently.

I wokened you.

It's all right, he said. I slept good. What time is it?

I'll look.

Is it time to go, Jess?

Jessie held the face of the old alarm clock close to her eyes, then put it back on the chair.

No.

How long?

Four hours yet.

He said nothing, pondering something in the darkness.

Are you scared, Jack?

192

He shrugged.

I ain't got much of a choice, Jess.

She was silent, counting the alternatives. She envisioned crudely the stretching vastness of the great American night—the jobless, haunted towns, the ruined, bankrupt farms. In her fancy she could see all of this only in the state; her imagination was not rich enough to fancy a whole nation of such desolation. There was nowhere. She knew only that. Still she knew it was more than this choicelessness which made her want him to stay there. It was that thing in him she loved, it was the smell of danger that quickened her heart even now as she thought of it—the scent of violence on his skin, in his hair, in this wake when she followed him by day or thought of him absent. And now she wanted to hear him speak of it to her—there, now, in the fragrant darkness of their bed. She swept the memory of the old woman's preachments from her mind as she breathed in the presence of Farjeon's flesh beside her, searching that smell for the scent of violence that excited her so. The face of the old woman kept coming between her mind and its object.

She's old that's all, she said. She's forgotten how life is.

What?

Nothing, she said. I was just thinking out loud.

Thinking what, Jess?

About why you're going to work in the mine tomorrow, she said.

You know why.

Why? she said foolishly, childishly, wanting to hear him say it, reassure her.

He studied it.

A man don't exactly take his pick of jobs in times like these, Jess. Even if there was nothing else.

It was the wrong answer somehow; she urged him on.

What else is there?

You know, Jess.

Maybe, she said, childishly, foolishly, her heart honing to hear him talk of it to her again. Tell me, Jack. Tell me what else there is.

He studied it, silent again.

Why? she said again, in a child's voice.

Well, you know why, Jess.

Yes, she said. But I want to hear you say it. I want to hear you talk about it.

She breathed slowly three times.

I want to know you haven't changed, she said.

Changed? How come you say that, Jess?

She traced the profile of his nose with her fingertip, the finger coming to rest on his lower lip.

No reason. No special reason, Jack.

I ain't changed, Jess. There's nothing changed. Nothing but them fool miners out there tonight.

That, she said. That will be all right, Jack.

What makes you think so?

I know, she said. Sure, there'll be some of them against you.

All of them, he said. The whole mob against me.

No.

You seen them tonight, Jess. Turley and his mob.

I know. But there'll be friends among them. You wait till morning. There'll be friends, Jack.

How do you know?

She sighed, smiling on her secret.

I just know, that's all.

She bided again, breathing slowly, heavily, wanting him to talk about what he was going to do again, wanting him to waken in her the thing that had been sleeping uneasily all that long night, a sleep somehow tormented by the words of the old woman. She breathed in deeply, searching the smells he made for the smell of violence which would waken the thing in her which slept.

You and me, she teased, we could take Mom and run away tomorrow.

194

Where to?

Lots of places.

She waited, dreading that he might agree.

Lots of places, she said again. Mom's got kin down at Logan. Down on the Big Sandy.

Jess, there's a depression in the land. I'm lucky to have that job in the mine to go to in the morning. Jess, we can't go nowheres.

She was still a moment.

Is that the only reason?

For what?

The only reason you're staying.

Well, now, you know it ain't, Jess.

What other reason?

You know, Jess.

Tell me though.

To find out, he said.

Find out?

Find out who *he* is.

Number One?

Yes.

She shut her eyes, shivering faintly, the secret in herself stirring restively in its sleep, not yet wakened.

What will you do to him when you find him, Jack?

He was silent.

Well, now, you know that as well as I do, Jess.

He searched her face in the dusk between them.

How come you ask me that, Jess?

She was still, then she shivered again.

Did you figure I'd give up, Jess?

No, she whispered.

Then how come you asked?

I like it, she said, shyly. I like it when you talk about it, Jack.

He was still at that, faintly shocked.

It ain't nothing to like, he said. It's a bad thing to have to face— to have to do. It's nothing *I* like, I'll tell you that, Jess.

She was still an instant.

But you made a vow, she said.

I did.

He breathed slowly; she could feel the stir of his breath against her hair, along the high bone of her cheek.

What's the matter with you, Jess? he said with a queer laugh. Did you think what happened in Wheeling yesterday—did you figure that had made me give it all up?

She shrugged her shoulder under the timid touch of his fingers.

I don't know, she said. Back a while there earlier tonight you was talking so funny, Jack.

What do you mean?

Oh, about how God had changed it all round in the dark.

Well, He did, Jess. He moved things round on me. He sure did that.

She searched for the dim shape of his face beside her.

But you know what wants doing? she whispered. That ain't changed?

No. It ain't.

And you're going to do it?

Yes.

He chuckled and squeezed her shoulder with his fingers.

Jess, what's got into you tonight?

Nothing, she said quickly, her eyes suddenly closed.

Then how come you keep on asking me that? If I aim to go on with it?

She half buried her face in the pillow.

I don't know, she said slowly. Mom she said some funny things out there tonight whilst you was sleeping.

What things?

Jessie measured her thoughts carefully.

Oh, she said it wouldn't do no good. She said that, for one thing.

That what wouldn't?

Getting even. She said it wouldn't change anything.

He was still, thinking about that.

Well, what's it supposed to change? he said presently.

He thought about it again.

Changing anything, he said, that's not what matters. I don't figure it to change anything. Except there'll be five less murderers alive to prey on innocent folks. That's all. What's it supposed to change? It's just something I have to do, that's all. It's how I'm made, that's all. It's a justice.

She stared into the dark; she was still for the count of three long breaths.

Mom said I should talk you out of it, Jack, she said presently.

He studied that.

No, he said. No, Jess, you shouldn't. In fact, you couldn't.

You're set on it, then.

Yes, I am. More so than ever.

Why more than before?

Because today has opened my eyes to things, he said. Today has opened my eyes to a thing or two these men have done besides kill my wife and baby. I've seen what they've done to a few others here. Men like me. Maybe things worse than murder, Jess. It's more of a justice than ever.

So you're more set than ever, she whispered, smiling.

I reckon. Yes. Yes, I am.

He cupped her chin in the cradle of his hand and searched out the dim shapes of her dark eyes against the dark frame of her wild hair.

Are you doing that, Jess?

Doing what?

Trying to talk me out of it?

She clung to him suddenly.

I don't want you to die, Jack!

But are you trying to talk me out of it? he whispered into her hair.

No.

Do you want me to kill those men?

She was silent, her heart beating thickly, her breath flowing heavy between their faces.

Do you, Jess?

Yes, she whispered.

Why?

She flung her head twice from side to side.

I don't know! she cried faintly.

He touched her fine-boned cheek with his finger.

I only know one thing, she said.

What's that, hon?

I just know, she said softly, that it wouldn't be the same thing between us if you was to back down now.

He measured that judgment thoughtfully, then nodded.

Yes. Why, yes, I reckon I understand that feeling, Jess.

She sobbed suddenly then, seized in panic as if she had thrust him across some unretraceable threshold. She thrust her bare arm across him.

Oh, but, Jack, Jack, I don't want nothing to happen to you!

She trembled.

I don't know what I want! she whispered. I don't want nothing to happen to you—but if you didn't do it, it wouldn't be the same.

It'll be all right, Jess, he said, comforting her with his hand.

She sobbed again, faintly, behind the edge of quilt.

You'll see, Jess, he said. When it's done—we'll go away. I'll find a good job somewheres else.

Yet now, somehow, she seemed inconsolable. She trembled under his hand.

I don't want you getting killed too, she whispered in a child's whisper.

Nothing says I've got to.

Mom said it. She said you would.

That don't make it so.

Mom—she said—, she faltered on.

Never mind that, Jess. God's on the side of justice. Mom should know that.

Jessie pulled free from him, staring at his dim face in the dusk between them.

Mom, she said God hates vengeance, Jack.

He pondered.

Mom better read her Scriptures some more, Jess.

She trembled, frightened almost speechless now at the vision of him in danger—hating herself for urging him on to that danger, yet already melting and helpless in the presence of that danger's radiant heat.

I'd never turn back now, he said, his fingers at her breast, his fingers prying back the tight hem of her bodice to cup her breast's tight, heavy fullness.

At first, he went on in a rush, at first it was just Jean and the baby. That's all I could think of, all I could see. At first it was just my own ones that wanted vengeance. Then yesterday in Wheeling I learned even more reasons why them five men ain't fit to live.

He breathed twice and she felt him nod in the darkness.

I saw what they done to a few more, he said. It suddenly seemed like that was part of the score that wanted settling. That too. A larger thing than just Jean and the baby.

He laughed and snuggled down lower beneath the quilt.

But I'm scared, he said. I'm even more scared than I was.

I'll bet, Jack, she whispered. I'll bet you're scared.

He laughed again.

I'm scared like I was when I was a kid, Jess.

Why, what scared you then, Jack?

When I was a kid?

Yes.

He sighed.

I don't know, he said. I guess I was always scared of something up till I met her.

Jean?

Yes.

What happened then?

199

I stopped being scared, I reckon.

How come?

I don't know, he said simply.

He pondered it.

It was like I'd stopped being a kid, he said. And now she—now Jean, she was the kid. Like we'd switched places somehow.

He thought of it more.

It was like some kind of mothering thing between us, he said.

Jessie lifted herself so that the strap of her nightgown slid over her shoulder, freeing her breast's fullness to his fingers. He stared, his eyes close to the pink aureole of her nipple in the quilt's dim dusk.

Funny thing, Jess.

What? she murmured huskily.

I can't say it, Jess, he laughed.

Why? she whispered.

You'd laugh at me is why. You're laughing at me now, Jess.

No, I ain't! I ain't laughing, Jack! What funny thing?

He was still until he'd found the courage to tell her.

I feel like you're my mom now, Jess, he said. That night before my first day in school.

She lay back, still, letting his fingers knead her breast. When he put his lips round the small nipple she shut her eyes and breathed a soft hissing sigh, as if in some strange pain. He took his mouth away presently, searching her face.

Jess?

What?

How come you kept on asking me if I aimed to go on with it?

What?

With the killing, he whispered.

She was silent, staring, her head strained back into the feather bolster, the dark shadow of her black hair spilling like a stain against its whiteness.

Why, Jess?

Do you want to know? she said in a soft, harsh voice, then laughed strangely, nervously.

Yes. Tell me why.

Because it makes me hot.

She waited throughout his stillness, hearing the thick heavy rhythm of her pulses.

Is that queer, Jack? she whispered. Do you think that's all wrong?

I reckon not.

She thought about it more.

Cal, she said, he never got mad about anything. No matter what they done to him. He took it. He never seemed to care. Nothing mattered to Cal. Nothing got him mad.

She shut her eyes and moaned faintly.

Cal, she said, he never smelled like a man somehow. He just smelled scared. Not the way you smell, Jack—the way you smell when you talk about it. The way you smell when you're mad—it makes me hot, that's all. I reckon you think I'm a fool.

No, he said. I don't.

He weighed the measure of it a while longer in his mind.

Is that all, Jess? he asked presently.

All what?

All you care about in me, Jess?

No.

But that—it makes you feel—

It makes me feel hot, she said. From the first. And for the first time in my life. I never felt hot with Cal. Not like I get with you, Jack. And it was that way from the first night.

She breathed in and out twice, slowly.

I could smell it, she said directly. I could smell it in the good smell you make. The madness. The vengeance. The thing you had to do, Jack. I could smell it. From the first night after you come indoors—after they was dead.

He shook his head. Presently he rose, fetched a candle from the

201

other room, lit it, then set it on the trunk by the window. He stared down at her then through that shadowy twilight of candleshine.

And if it wasn't in me—that madness, you call it—that thing in my smell, you call it—then I'd be just another man.

No.

You sure, Jess?

I never said such of a thing, Jack.

Did you mean that though?

What does it matter, Jack?

She stretched her arms and strained her body against him and her fingers touched the cold steel thing that was beneath his end of the pillow and at the touch of it she jerked as if her hand had touched a live wire. He was up on one elbow, staring down at her strangely now.

Have you got two nightgowns, Jess?

What?

I mean have you got another one, another nightgown?

What? she murmured drunkenly again, her wits stumbling, her thoughts like crooked, melting steps.

Is this your only one? I don't want to spoil it.

Yes, she said. What? Jack, what?

He gripped the bodice of her nightdress then and with a swift, downward sweep of his arm ripped it clean to her knees. He knelt above her, between her knees, staring down at her through tears.

Lord, he whispered, I'm scared, Jess. I'm scared. Worse than that kid was the night before school. I'm scared half crazy. And I'm mad, Jess. Mad half crazy! I'm so anxious to kill the rest of them that I'm half out of my mind. And the scaredness—the being mad—it all seems to make me want you worse than ever. Ain't that crazy, Jess?

Oh, my God, no, Jack. I know! I know!

She whimpered and danced in a slow, twisting grace beneath his eyes on the tousled quilt, the ragged tatter of the rent nightdress clinging to her ankles. And she was whispering again thickly

202

the rough word of love's urging while he stared down at her, kneeling between her trembling knees.

No, he said. No, not this time.

My God, Jack, please! Please!

No, he said again softly, heavily. No, Jess. This time I want to do something I never done before. Not even with Jean.

She twisted, weeping, imploring him, whispering the word over and over.

Jess, maybe you'll get mad, he said gently. Maybe you'll mind! I won't mind! Only hurry!

Jess, it's a thing I never done before. Not to no woman. Not even Jean.

She watched the dim, kneeling shape of him drunkenly, her mouth gone slack and crazed.

You might get mad, Jess, he murmured. You might think I was dirty—or some sort of fairy.

No! It's all right. Anything! Only hurry! I'm burning up!

Do you know what it is I want to do?

No, she whispered, choking. I don't think so. But it's all right, honey!

Jess, it's the wild feeling in me tonight that makes it! he cried softly. It's the being mad. It's thinking about tomorrow and maybe dying! Lord, it's thinking about what I have to do that works me up this way!

It's all right, she wailed, now weeping. Anything. It's all right, hon! Anything you want! Please!

I want to kiss you down there, he said, touching with his fingers the parted, secret redness of her sex beneath the small neat whorl of curls.

For a moment they looked at each other in the dimness. She saw him as if through a veil of blood, believing, disbelieving, sure of what he meant to do to her, yet not sure at all—this thing so alien to her life's wildest fantasies.

Can I, Jess?

She made a fainting, choking sound—no assent, no denial; he

saw her pale, oval face nod drunkenly, disbelieving against the dark patchwork of the quilt.

He seemed then to bow down to her, almost disappearing from sight beneath her glazed, astonished eyes, nuzzling his face into her deeps as if he were setting his lips to a portal where he might call forth some undiscovered goddess in herself. In one quick, passing flash of thought she could think only of one thing and that was her pride, her thankfulness for her cleanness, for her obsessive cleanness, and then that thought was dashed away, high on waves of hectic, surging passion. Her heels locked above him, her fine white thighs rode his face like a steed as she stared down drunkenly at his dark head burrowing between them, seeing this in vague glimpses between the tossing hither and yon of her proud, high breasts, across the flat, dimpled roundness of her heaving abdomen. And yet it did not seem as if he fed upon something of her there, it was more as if he struggled to merge his whole self into the very catacombs of her flesh, to hide himself safely in the warm womb of her—as if that red, sacred room were surrogate to the dark reality of the mine he must enter in the black, cold morning which beckoned now, so imminent. She was transported—in flames, then stretched on some soothing glacier, tossed between worlds of cool peace and fire. She could not make her tongue shape any word, she could not even make any human sound with her throat now save a high, keening whimper as her white, strong teeth bit blood from the pale, hard apple of her fist. He strove his mouth there as if to enter her entire, as if to hide himself in her flesh's warm haven, tasting as he did so the faint, country sting of laundry soap from her afternoon bath and tasting as well the musky attar of her femaleness whose fragrance he had scented on his clothes that morning in the streets of Wheeling, and he breathed in as he kissed her there the ancient savor of fathomless seas, the salt of deep, menmonic oceans: Mother of us all. She believed it was happening to her, she did not dare believe it was happening to her; she knew feelings she had never known, nor ever dared to fancy—this act of union so unimaginable to women of her stark, literal upbringing. Her heart, once pounding in her throat, now seemed to have risen into her brain itself; she thought that she might die before he was finished with her, and she did not fear that death. And then suddenly her eyes flooded with tears at the abrupt, shameful thought that she was doing nothing back, that she was not giving him such wonder too, such disbelieving belief, such unearthly and unutterable pleasure. She whimpered for him, she reproached herself, she scorned her own heartlessness, she felt a sudden burn of hate against herself who had thought till now only of her own pleasure. He rose up from her then, puzzled, thinking he had displeased her, as she struggled loose from him, flinging herself free, scrambling herself round upon the quilt, her white legs flying, her dark, silken hair spilling out loose across his belly.

Hon, hon! she crooned in tearful whispers. Oh, hon, I'm sorry, hon. You too, hon! Oh, Christ, you too!

And she whimpered penance and shame for thinking only of herself, of her own pleasure, as her long fingers sought his sex, her breath cool and quick against him, her mouth at last devouring him. They locked again then and strove, their dumb, wordless cries muffled and stifled within each other's flesh, tossing and striving into one another upon the poor, faded glory of the old country quilt. And when she knew that she could endure it no more, when her ecstasy at last was cousined to pain, when she grew even more certain that she would die of her joy and was not afraid of that death, her throat's last, rich, woman's cry was drowned and hushed in the quick, drumming gush of his glory. And he lay long after with her soft, strong thighs pressed close against his ears so that in that vast, small world of her embrace he could hear no other sound save the strong, subsiding thunder of her heart.

She lay soon later with her cheek upon his flank. She did not raise her eyes to him, she wanted for a while to see nothing save the rosy, warm mist of contentment before her dark, drowsing eyes. Then presently she rose on one elbow and looked down at his sex, once so proud, now the limp, defeated warrior. For a moment she rejoiced in her female power over him, her soft, woman's strength over that high, butting pride of his maleness. With a pitying, crooning sound she touched gently with her fingertips the fallen creature; for a moment more she was smiling and proud in that soft, small arrogance of her woman's moment. She lifted it gently and smiled down on it in small, mock sorrow.

Poor little thing, she whispered.

He stirred faintly beneath her touch.

Poor little thing, she said. It's like he was forever dead.

He laughed softly.

Like Lazarus, he said, he will rise again.

She lowered her mouth then, grateful, unspeakably thankful, and with slow, ineffable tenderness she kissed the pale, fallen creature whose flesh bore yet the faint, red bruises of her teeth. When she saw these she pulled back with a soft cry.

Oh, hon, hon, I hurt you!

No, he said softly.

But, hon, there's red marks! Oh, Lord, hon, I'm sorry—sorry!

He looked.

It's lipstick, he said.

No. I didn't have no lipstick on! Oh, hon, hon, I'm sorry—sorry! Christ, I'm so sorry!

If you hurt me, he whispered, I never felt it.

She lowered her lips again, crooning, whispering, cradling him in her fingers, showering his sex with small, swift kisses. She pressed her cheek against it.

I'll learn how, she said. Next time I'll know how.

She lay thus a long while, her breath slow and contented against his flank. After a while she raised her face, staring up at him, watching his face through her dark, rich lashes.

While we was doing it, she said, I thought sure I'd die. And I didn't care if I did.

He touched her cheek with his fingers, pressing her face against him, staring down at her in wonder.

It was never like that before, Jess, he whispered. Never in my life.

I know. Me too, hon. Me too!

Do you know? he said.

He lifted her face in his gentle hand.

Do you know? he said again. Jess, I never done that with no other woman but you. Never in my life.

He paused.

Not even with Jean, he whispered. And I loved Jean. God knows I loved her. But I never dreamed of doing that to her.

Me neither, she whispered, sharing his wonder. I never even thought about it, hon. Not with Cal. Not with nobody.

She pondered it, her breath against him again.

There was a couple of boys before Cal and me, she said. In the country. Before me and Cal was married. But I never thought of such a thing with them.

She sighed, breathing her breath now against the fine, dark hairs of his chest.

I heard about it once, she said. In a joke.

She sighed, her heart still clasped within the dream of it.

It was no joke, she said.

She raised her face again, staring up at him with the dark, candid eyes of a child whose mind is brimming with some rich, recent adventure of which it must still speak. She yawned, stretching her nakedness sensuously beside him, her slim fingers cupped round the fullness of her small-nippled breasts. She squeezed them, stretching again, arching her small back on the quilt, smiling as she remembered how it had been, roiling her senses in the rich, hot reminiscence of it.

Did you like it? he said.

She blinked thoughtfully, considering remembering.

It scared me, she said. At first I got scared. When it commenced in my mouth.

He looked down at her, his eyes faintly dismayed.

Was it awful, hon?

She glared up at him softly, smiling with fierce devotion.

No! she whispered hotly, in a kind of reverence. No, hon! It was beautiful! Beautiful!

She shut her eyes gently, smiling into herself.

But it was strange at first, she said. It scared me at first. I thought I'd choke. So powerful. So busting wide with power.

She thought of it some more, fixing upon him still that frank, remembering gaze, her voice lilting with simple, childlike candor.

It was like egg, she said. Like hot egg

She liked telling him how it had been, this lovely new thing he had done to her.

So much, she whispered. I kept swallowing. It kept coming. I dreamt it would last forever. So much when it began—so little when it was over.

Her dark eyes were lashed in half shadow, her cheeks burning at the memory.

Then it was like—like cherry brandy, she went on, roiling her mind and senses in the fresh, scalding memory of how it had been. It was something wonderful and hot in my throat, in my breasts, in my stomach. And then it commenced to spread clean through me. To my toes. To my fingertips. And pretty soon I could feel it all over. Just lying there afterwards. Making me glow all over. The way cherry brandy does.

She turned her face, smiling faintly, and touched with the tip of one finger his spent limpness.

Poor little thing, she breathed.

Then she glanced at him, smiling, her eyes wide in mock alarm.

Will he ever have any more for me? she laughed softly. Ever ever again?

Soon again, he said.

Are you sure? she said, pouting in spurious solemnity. Poor thing. Poor, little, wrinkled thing.

Soon, hon, he said. Soon again.

She smiled at him with her eyes then, and with her small tongue tip she licked her lips once quickly, savoring his taste still upon them. She lay back then, her cheek against his hip, her thick lashes closed over her eyes, and her fingers presently sought out her own sex, fondling its close, dark ringlets gently, almost sadly, while with the left hand she found him again, rolling the small thing lightly in her fingers, rejoicing in the remembered beauty, pitying the small thing now, yet faintly high with some small, strong, feminine arrogance at her soft body's victory over his hard maleness, and lightly rekindling her senses afresh in that moment's sensuous nostalgia. After a spell she opened her dark, glowing eyes and flung him a gay, sidelong look. He stared at her in the candlelight.

Am I glowing, hon? she cried softly. Am I glowing all over?

Yes, he said. You're pink as a wild, swamp rose, Jess! And your cheeks—they are red like they was fresh-rouged, Jess!

Aha! she laughed in her rich, yolky voice. See what you done to me, hon? See how pretty you made me be! Jack, you fed me so good! You loved me so good! Ah, Christ, hon!

She nuzzled her face into the light hair of his chest, biting him till he winced, then laughing in soft, joyful gasps against his flesh. Suddenly she raised her gaze to him again, troubled.

Was I—all right? she whispered.

You were wonderful, Jess.

No, she said. No. I don't mean that. I mean did I taste good?

He blushed and twisted her dark, straight hair in his fingers.

Tell me, hon, she went on. Was I sweet and clean? Lord, I bathe myself three times every day. I can't bear the thought of not being sweet and clean.

You were sweet as cinnamon, he said. But you did taste like soap.

She laughed, bowing her face against him.

Can't help that! she cried softly. Wash myself three times every single living day. Morning noon and night. Can't abide dirty women!

You were beautiful, Jess, he said. It was beautiful, hon.

She frowned, still watching him with that thoughtful, frank child's stare.

Still, she said thoughtfully, I wouldn't want to do it like that real often.

She thought some more, then shook her head.

No, she said. It's too wild. Too scary.

She thought on, then shook her head with grave finality.

No, she said simply. Fucking is best.

He meditated silently for a spell, his fingers combing her wild, silken hair which lay loose across his breast.

For two people, he said after a while, who ain't in love—we sure do have a good time, Jess.

She flushed, then bit him lightly on the chest. Then she raised her eyes, studying his face.

You love me, Jack, she said. You do. In your way.

Yes, he said. Yes, I reckon I do, Jess. But what I mean is, with Jean it was—it was—Lord, I don't know how to say it. We had such a different life, her and me. We done it all so different. Yes, though. I do love you, Jess.

Say it then.

I done said it, hon.

You said it with a lot of other things, she said. Now say it by itself.

He pressed his fingers against her dark, full mouth, his gaze searching her great, liquid eyes.

I love you, Jessie, he said.

Her eyes brimmed then till the lashes glittered yellow; she flung her face against his breast.

Ah, Christ, Jack—Christ, I love you so!

She lay thus, in stillness, for a long quiet spell. Then she lifted her face to him again, her eyes again full of the wonder of the thing they had done to one another there upon the faded squares of the old country quilt. She smiled. Then she planted her small elbows on his chest, tucked her fine, round chin into the cradle of her long fingers and smiled up at him mischievously.

Eleven times, she said.

What, hon?

Eleven times, she said. And one little one. One almost. You made me come eleven times, Jack.

Lord, now, did I? he marveled.

He thought about it longer, still amazed.

I guess girls is purely lucky that way, he said, wondering at such physical wealth. Jean, she never did.

Come?

No.

She worked her fingers under his shoulders, hugging him hard.

How could she help it? she said.

She never, though, he said.

How could she help it? With someone like you, hon.

He thought about it a while more.

My Lord, now, he said. Eleven times?

Yep.

He pulled her face round to look at him.

Did you count them?

She nodded.

I don't know how I done it, she said, but I counted them. I don't know how. I thought I was going crazy. Or dying. But somehow I could still count.

He touched her lower lip with his finger, pressing it, releasing it, pressing it, till she seized it in her hands and bit it lightly.

I reckon I must be something special, he said then. Something real special. My Lord. Eleven times. I must be pretty good for a man who—

His voice dwindled off; he stared down at her thoughtfully.

For a man who what? she whispered.

For a man who may be dead this time tomorrow night, he said.

211

She flung her face aside as if he had slapped her. After a moment she looked at him again, smiling, a crooked, grieving twist of anguish to her lips.

Don't say that, Jack, she whispered.

He pondered it, her gaze still fixed on him in agony.

Jess, maybe that's why we done what we done tonight, he said presently. More than anything we'd ever done before. Something —something *closer*. Maybe we both knew. Maybe something in us knowing—

Stop it, Jack! she moaned, trying to stop his mouth with her fingers.

No, wait! No, hon. Maybe something in us knowing more than our minds know, Jess. Something inside us knowing something that the rest of us ain't found out yet.

Christ, please! Christ, don't talk that way, Jack. Please! she implored him in that voice of simple agony, the dark, silken scarf of her hair bowed upon his breast.

Well, Jess, what else would possess me to do such a thing to you, Jess?

I done it too. To you! she cried softly. Remember that! Christ, and I loved it, hon!

To do such a thing to you, he went on, as if he had not heard her. Who wasn't raised to such things. Nor you neither, Jess. A practice that's maybe against nature—against God.

She pressed her cheek hard against his chest, she struck him lightly with her fist.

I don't care about nature! she whispered in a fierce breath. Nor about God. I loved it. I loved it, hon!

No, wait, he said, heedless. Listen to me. Maybe we had to do it like we done tonight. Closer. Maybe we had to get deeper inside each other than we ever done before. As if some thing in us knowed a wisdom beyond our minds to know. Of things to come, Jess. D'you see?

She pressed her mouth hard into his breast, pressing her bared teeth into the flesh above his strong, slow heart. He could feel the

212

wetness of her grieving mouth against him, her measured, thoughtful breath cool against his skin.

Jack, let's run away, she whispered suddenly.

He was silent a moment.

No, he said.

Yes, Jack. Oh, Jack, yes!

No, he said again, gently.

Jack, yes! We'll take Mom and run. Away from the damned mines. We'll find somewheres, Jack!

He smiled down at her, his eyes questioning.

Well, Jess, I reckoned you was the one who was so bound and determined for me to go through with it all.

She glared a moment, then shook her head violently; she seized his chin in her hands, pulling his gaze round to her eyes.

I've changed my mind, Jack!

He still smiled, his face almost teasing.

Why, Jess, you said you liked it.

Well, I didn't! she cried savagely. I lied, Jack. It wasn't that at all. I never cared about your killing those men!

He shook his head.

You said when I talked about it, he said, it made you all hot and bothered, Jess.

No, no! she cried softly. I was lying. It wasn't true. It was you that made me hot, Jack!

The smell of violence, he whispered, still smiling. You said it yourself, hon.

I lied! she cried in a soft, gasping voice. It was you that made me hot. You always did, Jack. From the very first. When I first seen you in the wagon on the road. With her even. Back when she was still alive. With her even! I didn't care if you was already hers! I didn't care! When I first caught sight of you by the light of the fire in the kitchen that night—before she was killed—before you even dreamed about vengeance—I knowed it, Jack! I seen you and right away—you made me hot!

Her dark, rich eyes brimmed gold with tears; she shook her face

213

angrily, scattering the tears across her shadowed cheek. Her face wrinkled like a child's in sorrow.

The smell of violence, she whispered, her lip trembling. It's gone now, Jack. Now I can smell something else.

What, hon?

Nothing. No, I won't say its name!

The smell of death, hon?

I won't say it's name. Oh, I can't bear it, Jack. Don't you see, Jack? Look at me! I've changed! You changed me tonight. The thing you done to me tonight—it's made me all different. All new. Jack, I don't want you to kill anybody now!

He smiled sadly down at her; he shook his head slowly.

But I have to, Jess.

No, you don't! she cried passionately. Don't you see? You really don't have to now, Jack. You love *me* now, Jack!

I loved her too.

She flung her face to his breast again, weeping silently.

And I don't want you getting killed in that black mine neither, she sobbed in a lost, forlorn wail. If it ain't one it'll be the other. Christ, Jack. I can feel it.

You can't feel it. You can't know, hon, he said.

You said it yourself! she cried. Something in us that knows what our minds ain't found out yet. You said it yourself.

You can't know, Jess.

I know! she moaned, disconsolate. I feel it inside. Strong, Jack. Like a warning from the Lord. It's like what you done to me tonight—it opened me up to hear the Lord's whispers. Jack, I can feel things now I couldn't feel before.

It'll be all right, Jess.

Jack, Jack—Christ, you even smell different tonight. It's not the good old furious smell that used to make me hot.

We can't run away, Jess.

Jack, Jack, I can smell death now!

It'll be all right, Jess, he said.

She flung her face back, glaring at him an instant.

I won't let you die! she whispered in a breath of sharp insistence.

She struggled up across him then, seizing his face in her hands and setting her mouth hard against his, her strong, small tongue struggling between his teeth, tasting even as she breathed the scent and salt of herself still upon his face. Then suddenly she stopped sobbing, slowed, grew stilled and gentle as if some sudden, fresh, desperate, feminine mood had seized her to take whatever life, whatever now was there between them in the moment. She shut her eyes, she bit her lip, wincing as his fingers sought her out. She pressed her teeth against his mouth, moaning.

You're wet again, he said. You're wet clean to your knees, hon.

I know, she whispered. You make me wet. You make me hot like no man who ever lived.

She swung her eyes round to him, close to his, smiling down at him, the pale, soft oval of her face halved in ruddy shadow. Her fingers found him. She shut her eyes, bowing till her nose touched the tip of his.

And you, she said softly, you were right. Like Lazarus.

No wonder.

Do I excite you that much, Jack? she whispered, pleased almost beyond words. And so soon after?

Yes.

She raised herself, staring down at his belly.

So soon after, she said again. It's a marvel. Like Lazarus, he has risen.

She squeezed his sex gently.

He's hard again, she marveled, hard as the horn of a steer.

And you, he said, you're wet again. And all opened up. Like the petals of some kind of pretty wild flower. Ah, Christ, Jess—like a rose. Like a wild rose!

How lovely, she moaned. Lord, how beautiful we are!

She lifted herself again, staring down at his belly again, still marveling.

Did I do that, Jack? Was it me? Now how could I do that, Jack?

So soon after! Lord, he was so little—so played out and little before! That poor little thing. Now look at him, hon. Does he want me again, Jack? Jack, did I do that?

There was never a woman like you, Jess.

She hesitated a moment, then swung her gaze back to him.

Not even her?

Who?

Jean?

She fondled him, waking him with her hands. He smiled up at her.

Not even Jean, he said.

She paused a breath, then plunged hopefully on.

Then maybe, she said softly, maybe you'll take me and Mom and we'll run away from here.

No, he said.

Why not, Jack?

No, Jess.

But you love *me* now, Jack. You said that.

I know that.

Better than her?

I never said that. I said there was never a woman like you, Jess.

Not even her?

Not even her.

So you love *me* now, Jack. So there's nothing to avenge.

He shook his head, smiling up at her.

We'll talk about it after, he said.

After what? she whispered thickly, the manhood of him now risen proud and living again in the gentle ring of her fingers. She looked down and made a chiding sound with her lips.

The great, huge, butting creature, she whispered. Not ever satisfied. And after all I done to quiet him before!

There was never a woman on earth like you, Jess.

Ah, Christ, Jack—you swear it?

Yes.

Then, she began, you'll take me and Mom and we'll go—

He did not answer her now, he rose beside her, pushing her back beside him on the quilt. He stared down at the small, pale nipples of her round, full breasts, touching one gently in the cup of his hand. He looked down at her great, dark eyes beneath the veiled, thick lashes, watching him now, warm and heavy in her regard as if with a great, sweet somnolence.

Like we done before? he whispered.

No.

What then?

You know, she whispered.

He put his mouth into the dark scarf of hair that fell beside her pale, small ear.

You know, she said again. The regular way.

I know, he said, but I want to hear you say it. The word.

She stiffened, breathing evenly.

She wouldn't never say that word, would she? she whispered. The word I always say.

No.

She thought about it.

And you like it, hon? It pleases you for me to say it whilst we're doing it?

Yes.

She was still a moment, thoughtfully.

Why? she whispered then in a small voice.

He considered it.

I don't know why, he said. I don't, Jess.

She breathed slowly beneath him, her breasts rising and falling slowly against his chest. She looked up at him presently, her big eyes faintly troubled.

What's wrong, Jess?

Nothing, she said.

Yes, there is. What is it, hon?

Nothing, she said again. Only you make me feel like it was something dirty—me saying that word.

Why?

Because she never said it.

She never knew, he said gently, the word for it. How to do it. Nothing about it, Jess.

Yet she still seemed shy, troubled, silent beneath him.

All right, she whispered after a spell, I'll say it. In a minute. Only don't look at me.

Still she was silent, waiting on, then quickly put her mouth close against his ear, behind the secret cloak of her dark, fragrant hair, almost as if she was shy of his seeing her face when she said the word, almost as though she had never said the word before.

Say it, Jess, he urged softly.

And still she waited.

Fuck me, she breathed then suddenly, abruptly in his ear, in a child's shy voice. Ah, Christ, Jack—do!

And they wrought upon each other an act of love that was as slow and sad and fiercely thoughtful as it had been careless and rich and violent before. He could not fathom her mind in this new mood. She seemed to take the same hot joy in his loving, rocking him staunchly in the slim, pale cradle of her limbs, kissing his face, crooning small sounds, caressing his face with her fingers, but she did not say the brazen, good word again the way she always did, so fast, so fiercely, in such quick, savage urging in his ear. And he knew when he was done that she had come to no climax although she had, indeed, pretended one. And when he lay beside her again on the quilt at last she lay speechless and silent and grave, staring up solemnly at the shadowed ceiling, pleased only that she had pleased him as she felt the hot, fresh abundance of his seed spill slowly out onto the country quilt from beneath the warmth of her gentle, opened thighs.

There was never a woman like you, Jess, he said then.

She still seemed quieter than before, even sad, as he searched her profile, trying to fathom her mood. Presently she pulled free of his embrace and sighed profoundly, laying her face back on his

218

chest. He felt her slow breath, her strong, distant heart, felt her heavy, silent meditation for a long, still while.

Jack? she whispered after a bit.

What, hon?

She paused for a few breaths, silent, thinking.

Jack, are we holy? she asked presently.

What?

Us, she said. Are we holy? You and me?

What, hon?

She turned her great, grave regard on him slowly.

Something tonight, she said, something Mom said in there. A poem she said.

He waited.

A poem, Jessie went on. One she remembered from a long time ago.

How did it go, hon?

Not a poem really, she said, just one line.

How does it go, Jess?

She buried her face in the hollow of his arm before she answered and he could sense in her still that great, slowed shyness.

For everything, she began presently, for everything that lives is holy.

He chuckled.

Is that funny, Jack? she said.

No.

Then how come you laughed at it?

He sighed.

I just had to think, he said, after all the sinning we done tonight, Jess—you reckon God would call us holy?

She considered it carefully.

Yes, she said. Yes, He would. I do believe that.

How do you figure, Jess?

Because, she cried softly into his armpit, because we was alive tonight. Like we was creatures on fire. It was like God was in the bed with us—on the quilt—telling us what to do. Like He was telling us how to love each other. Like loving each other was the only important thing. The only thing in life! God in the bed with us, hon! Showing us how to make each other feel good. Showing us how to be almost like Him! Yes. Yes, I do believe that, hon.

Maybe, he said.

It's true, she cried softly, her thoughts mounting to conviction. It was just you and me, hon. And God in the bed with us. On the quilt. Making it all work. And nothing else was real. Not Jean. Not killing anybody. Not the mine. Not tomorrow morning. Not death, Jack. No—nothing real but you and me and God in the bed with us here.

She nodded her head hard, affirming it.

We were living, she whispered, living. You and me and God. And nothing else was real.

He was silent a while.

Then maybe, he said presently, maybe we are holy. Like Mom said, hon.

Yes, she said passionately. Yes, Jack. I do believe it. I do believe we are!

He lay a moment more, then caught his breath, sitting up on the quilt, swinging his legs to the floor. He glanced anxiously toward the old woman's little door.

Mom, he said. I just remembered.

What about her?

She's in there, he whispered fiercely, gesturing nervously toward the door. Lord, she heard every bit of it. The things we said, Jess. All the racket we must have made.

Jessie bided, silent a moment.

She's gone out, she said presently.

Gone? Where to?

Gone out to the miners. Jessie sighed. To wake them up.

Wake them up? Whatever for?

Jessie rolled over, she sat up on her haunches staring down at the great dark stain they had made throughout that hour or two.

Lord! she scolded. Did all that come out of us?

She made a face.

This poor quilt, she cried softly. It goes to the washtub in the morning!

Farjeon stared at her.

What's she out there waking up the miners for?

Jessie looked at him.

To try to talk some sense into them, she said. To try to talk up some friends for you. Before the morning.

He lay back, groaning; he glared at the shadowed ceiling.

What's wrong, hon?

Nothing, he said. Only it makes me feel like a poor sight of a man.

What does?

A poor spectacle of manhood, he went on, when an old, old woman has to go out on a winter's night like this and fight his battles for him.

She flung herself by his side, pulling his face round with her fingers. She shook her head.

She's not fighting your battles, she said. It ain't that at all, hon.

Yes, it is.

No, Jack, it ain't. She's only trying to talk some sense. She's only trying to make it so's you'll have some chance to fight your own battle.

He was still, staring upward, not looking at her at all.

I don't like it, he said. An old, old woman.

She kissed his cheek, her long fingers stroking his hair. She smiled ruefully.

Maybe, she said, something good will happen tomorrow.

He was silent.

Maybe, she said, you won't have to kill those—

He sighed.

Now, Jess. Don't start up again.

He squeezed her hand.

You know what I feel, he said. You know what I have to do.

I know, she said, with a flicker of faint hope in her voice. But someone's coming here tomorrow, Jack. Maybe he'll change your mind.

Who's coming? he asked after a little bit.

Senator Hood.

Our Senator Hood?

Yes.

Senator William G. Hood? Of West Virginia?

That's what Mom told me.

Coming here? To this mine? Him?

Yes, she said. Him and John L.

What for? He sighed despondently. Even a man like him. A great man. What's he coming here for?

To look into the violence, Jessie said. That's what Mom told me.

She felt her mind quicken, her thoughts suddenly racing with fresh hope.

Maybe, she said, maybe there's a law.

What do you mean?

I mean maybe they'll punish those men, Jack, she said in a voice small with child's hope. Maybe the law—

Are you serious, Jess?

Jack, maybe the law—

He cleared his throat.

I'm the law in this, he said. I'm all the law there is. Because there ain't no other law. Not for things like this. You know that, Jess. There's no law for the poor but ones they make.

She sighed, her face punished and pinched by her fear. She laid her cheek against his mouth, her eyes clenched close and quivering.

Jack, Jack, I love you so! she breathed.

I know that, Jessie. I love you too. God knows I do!

She lay silent in his clasp, listening to his slow, thoughtful breath.

Still, I'm glad he's coming, he said after a while.

222

Who? John L.?

No, Senator Hood, he said.

Why, Jack? she whispered, still fearful.

Because maybe I'll get to talk to him.

Yes! she cried, sitting up and staring down at him. Oh, yes, hon! They say he's such a good man.

She waited.

Maybe he'll make you see things different, she added presently.

No, he said, he couldn't do that, Jess.

He measured his breaths thoughtfully.

No, he said again presently. But maybe he might do something else for me.

What?

He might give me a clue.

A clue to what, Jack?

He waited.

A clue to who Number One is.

Jessie sighed again, pulling the wet quilt over them both; she shivered her nakedness against him.

Mom, she knows him, Jessie whispered.

Mother Dunne?

Yes.

Knows Senator William Hood?

Yes.

How come?

She worked for him once. Years back.

Doing what?

She was his housekeeper, Jessie said. You ought to hear Mom praise him. She said he's the best old man in the world.

Yes, Farjeon said, that's true.

He remembered back.

Me and Jean, he said, if she'd lived—if our boy had lived—we was going to name him Bill. After him.

He thought about the man whose name was legend in that land.

I reckon he's about the only friend we have.

He gave Jessie's shoulder a squeeze.

And maybe, he said, he'll give me that clue.

Jessie shivered again, her breasts against him, her nipples hard with cold.

Give it up, hon, she whispered. Christ, Jack, give it up.

But he said nothing. And she knew he would give up nothing—not even for her. And they lay long then in stillness. And when they both slept at last beneath the old quilt, spent by a mingling of mystery, love and fear, wound in each other's arms and legs like lost, forlorn children in some alien land, the old woman came upon them so and stood a moment staring down at them fondly.

Lord, she whispered to the blackness, wringing her numb fingers. Lord, I done my damndest out yonder! Them fools! Did I talk any reason into their poor, beaten heads? Did I, Lord?

She lay down on the narrow pallet in her small, cold room, fully clothed, too tired even to unlace her high black shoes. She pulled a twist of ragged blankets over her shivering body and stared at one faint winter star which shone from the room's one poor, cracked, small window.

Lord! she whispered, let there be friends amongst them. Lord, let him have at least one friend amongst them when he goes to the pit in the morning!

Long before the clock was due to sound its shrill awakening Jessie was up and dressed. She stilled the alarm button long before it could ring and sat now in the straight-backed chair by the door, her eyes on Farjeon for a while, then across to the inching black hands of the Big Ben, then back again to his huddled, soundless shape. She had been sitting there a long while in the chill of the room before she realized that Mother Dunne had been up before her; the door to her small room stood open. She heard then the faint scrape of shoes in the front room. At first the sound frightened Jessie, then she stole to the door and saw the old

224

woman sitting straight and wide-awake in her rocker by the window.

Hello, Mom.

Mother Dunne did not stir, did not even turn her head.

Did you try to talk him out of it, Jess? she asked after a while.

Yes.

Did you try to talk him out of all of it—not just the killing?

Yes.

I mean did you try to talk him out of even trying to go to work down there today?

I did, Mom.

Mother Dunne rocked twice angrily, then stared at the girl through the small steel spectacles.

No good, eh?

Jessie shrugged, smiling foolishly.

No, she said. No good, Mom.

The old woman struck the arm of her chair.

In some ways, she said, they're all cut from the same bolt. Fools. Lord save us—men!

She rocked angrily.

In some ways, she said, Jack Farjeon's as big a fool as them!

Jessie went to the older woman's side, laid her hand on the back of the chair.

I done everything, she said, I said everything, Mom. He's set on it.

The old woman glanced toward the bedroom door.

How long is it till it's time, Jess?

Fifteen minutes till I have to wake him, Mom.

Did he sleep?

I reckon so.

Did you?

Not good. Not good. Ah, Christ, Mom, I'm so scared for him.

There was the faintest of sounds out yonder in the blackness but she fancied it was the wind or the falling of a snowdrift.

There's no more time, Jessie whispered.

The old woman sniffed disdainfully.

Last night, she said, that was the time. You and him, Jess—you should have left me and fled last night. Lord, you should both be miles from here by now.

We'd never leave you, Mom.

Did you try to talk him into it, at least? cried the old woman in soft anger. Or did you spend the livelong night just rolling in his arms?

Jessie flushed.

I tried to talk him into running, Mom.

The old woman set her firm chin toward the window.

It would be bad enough, she said, if it was only the mine he had to face out there.

She shook her face, furious, tears standing bright on her old, pale cheeks.

How many mornings—black and cold as this—I've risen to set waiting to see some man off to that, she said. And nothing but that kind of death waiting for him. As if that weren't enough!

She laced her fingers, writhing them together for a moment.

As if it was only the mine, she said then. Not like this. Not with a pack of armed fools out there waiting.

Jessie looked quickly at the old woman's face.

Are they out there?

Yes.

Now? Jessie whispered.

Well, didn't you fancy they would be, child?

Jessie went to the window, pulled the blind up an inch, peered out. She could see nothing but the morning star, low on the hills, and the pale, stained stretch of snow to the road and, upon it, a few shapeless darknesses that could have been only shadows.

I can't see no one, Mom.

They're there.

Mom, how—?

I heard them is how, said the old woman. A good half hour ago. Afore you got up and dressed, Jess.

Talking?

Whispering, the old woman said. And their shoes scuffling in the snow. And a clink now and then.

The clink of guns, Mom?

It could have been their dinner buckets, Jess.

Is Turley out there?

I don't know. Most likely. Him and that fool Bonar!

Jessie's fist flung up to her mouth, she stifled a sob.

Mom, ain't there no friends out there? Not even one friend for my Jack?

Mother Dunne shook her head.

If my words won anything last night, she said, there'd be a dozen. But, Jess, I don't know.

Jessie knelt to sit suddenly on the bare floor by the rocker. Her fingers stole up and felt for Mother Dunne's hand.

Mom?

Yes, child?

Mom, last night we done every kind of sin. Every kind there is. If there's a sin we didn't do—I never heard tell of it.

The old woman squeezed Jessie's cold, small hand.

Nonsense, child. You loved each other is all.

Jessie shook her head, suddenly aghast at invisible, threatening dreads.

God—He may just purely despise us now, Mom, she said.

Jess, said the old woman, there's nothing about love that God despises. Remember that. Nothing love could ever be nor do nor say. It's only hate He hates.

Jessie was still a spell; then she smiled shyly, her eyes faintly cheerful.

One all-right thing happened though, she said presently.

What's that, child?

Last night was the first time he said he loved me.

The old woman squeezed the girl's cold hand again.

Sure he does, she cried softly. I could have told you that, Jess.

Jessie smiled, thinking about that, the moment when he had said it—it was the shining part of it all.

It's a fool thing to be talking about now, she said, glancing toward the cupboard. When I ought to be busy over there fixing things to put in his dinner pail.

She rose silently and went to the shelf, fetching down the old pail that had been Cal's, dusting it thoughtfully with a rag of old bandana.

It's a fool thing to be talking about, she said, at a time like this, Mom. But I like to talk about it now. It makes me brave.

Sure it does, child, said the old woman. Sure.

He never said it before, Jessie said after a while, still staring at the dinner pail. In fact he was always telling me how he never loved me at all—not like her, not like his dead woman.

Well, I knowed he did! cried the old woman. I bet I knowed it before either of you did.

Jessie fetched the can of lard from the shelf. She spooned it out, spreading it between two layers of hard, stale bread. Still, there was a treat for him: she reached into the cupboard's deepest shadows and fetched it out—an egg that she had bought at the company store the day before, a miracle made possible because of a nickel she had found that afternoon in an old jelly glass. She had boiled it and hid it in the cupboard that evening. She stared down now at the egg in her fingers, the tears falling slowly off her face, splattering on the simple oval thing in her hand.

Mom, I can't lose him now, she breathed. Christ, Mom, he's the only one I ever had!

The knock at the door was a small enough sound, almost timid, but it broke the room's stillness like a pistol shot. Mother Dunne stopped rocking and stood up. She went to Cal's rifle on the wall, then she stared at Jessie.

You heard my fancy words last night about killing, Jess, said the old woman. But the first man—

She fetched the rifle down.

The first man that comes through that door will face this. In my hands, she said softly.

Again they both stared dumbly at the door, as though neither of them could move, as if neither of them could believe in it till they should hear it again. Then it came again, a little louder this time, more urgent, and yet withal a small—an almost timid—sound.

It don't sound like Turley, said the old woman. Not him. That coarse brute—he'd just come charging in.

Again for a spell both of them seemed frozen, transfixed by speculation, their wits and senses straining to fathom who it might be who stood now yonder in the black air beyond the door.

Open it, Jess. I'll hold the gun, said the old woman presently.

Jessie flung the door wide and stared out; a moment passed.

Well, who is it, Jess?

Jessie bowed her head.

Who, Jess? cried the old woman.

It's Missus Telligrew, Jessie whispered, stepping back.

Nan Telligrew crossed the threshold like a woman walking in her sleep. She came two steps in and stood, her black, bursting shoes pressed close together in a small space of melting snow and mud. She stood thus a spell, staring at the floor, frowning faintly as if trying to remember where she was; she did not look at Jessie, or at the gun in the old woman's hands. She was a small, lean woman with fair, washed-out hair and her face was raddled and blotched as if not only by the fresh tears of the night just past but by tears of years long past. She stood there straight, her head bowed, her shoulders tight, as if she was already braced for some further mischance of her fortunes in that alien, rumored household from which misfortune seemed somehow, recently, to be the touchstone. After a spell she glanced at Mother Dunne.

Can I set? she whispered.

Jessie swept the straight-backed chair from the bedroom and put it behind the woman. Nan Telligrew stood a moment, absently, as if she did not know the chair was there, then she felt for it, groping behind her, and sat down. Her deep, forlorn gaze was fixed on the floor again for a while, then she looked first at Jessie then at the old woman.

They're waiting for him out there, she said. But I reckon you know that.

Turley? asked the old woman.

Yes. Him. And a passel of others.

Jessie breathed deeply; she felt somehow steady and calm.

Is there any friends amongst them? Jessie asked.

Friends?

Nan Telligrew shrugged.

Who has any friends in this black place? she said.

I mean, are there any against killing him?

Nan looked at Jessie evenly.

I am, she said. Me for one. I'm against killing him.

Lord, murmured Mother Dunne presently. Then I touched your heart with the truth of it last night, Nan. You believed what I told you!

I don't know what I believe, said Nan Telligrew, but I'm against killing Mister Farjeon.

Why? whispered the old woman, smiling faintly.

I don't know why, said Nan Telligrew. They claim he shot my Jake in Wheeling yesterday.

She shrugged.

I reckon, if that's so, I ought to be out yonder with them—panting to spill his blood. But I'm not. I should be. I know that. Because now there's nowhere. I'm left with six small children and there's nowhere. There's nothing. Nothing at all on this earth for a woman whose looks is all spent in the bearing of babies and working and waiting—of being used up—of living always in the shadow of some breed of death or other.

She looked at Jessie.

I'm only thirty-seven, she said plainly.

She raised her arms so that the faint traces of her limp, flat breasts showed faintly beneath the blue, worn dress under her tatterdemalion, hand-me-down coat.

I'm thirty-seven, she said, and I'm done for. I know that. I'm not complaining. I'm just telling the truth of it. My kids, they'll go to the kids' home in Cameron. That's all right. I reckon they're lucky. But me—I'm done for. There's nowhere. I'm clean played out.

She stared hard at Jessie again.

But I'm a fair woman, she said. I may not be much but I'm fair. I'd sooner be dead than not be. And I seen that man Farjeon the night they shot his woman. And he looked finished too—finished as I am now. I seen his face. I seen it by the light of an oil torch held by that same man Turley who's out yonder tonight with his gun waiting to kill him. I seen him the night he led them others up the hill after they'd crucified the Polack scab on the tipple timbers. I seen his face by the light of Tom Turley's torch. And I knew then what I know now—I know it as purely as I know I'm done for. I know—

She gulped and swallowed and smoothed the cloth over the bulge of her spare, hard knees with trembling fingers.

I know, she went on apace, I know that a face that full of grief could not be the face of a goddamned killer scab. That's all I know.

Where are they? asked the old woman.

The miners?

Yes.

There's six or seven right outside in the yard, said Nan Telligrew.

Is that all?

No. Turley and his mob—they're down on the road. Betwixt here and the tipple.

Have they got guns?

I only seen one, Nan Telligrew said.

Who's carrying it?

Him. Tom Turley. The rifle he had the night Shaloo's men come.

Do the others have guns?

I never seen any.

She shivered.

The rest of them, she said, they're not like Turley. Yet they seem drawed to him.

She stared forlornly at Jessie.

I lost my man, she said. I know what you're going through.

She lowered her eyes to the puddle her great, cracked shoes had made.

I don't want your man to die, she said. Maybe I should. Maybe it's unnatural not to want him to. Still—still there's thick mystery in this. And I've only Tom Turley's word that it was your man Jack that shot my Jake. Only that—that's all. I can't be sure. I don't know. I only know one thing, and I know it clean to my bones: I know that your man wasn't one of Shaloo's scab-killers. I seen the look on his face that night. I know. And whatever else I am, I'm fair. I want fairness to prevail in this.

Did you tell Turley that? asked the old woman.

Nan Telligrew nodded.

He said I was mad with grief. He said I didn't know right from wrong anymore.

The room fell silent then as their eyes turned. He had been standing there for some little while, in the bedroom door, watching and listening on the threshold—Farjeon, wearing Cal Dunne's miner's hat and the old, worn boots he had had on the night he died. Nan Telligrew stared at him a spell, her face pursed and furrowed with speculation. Farjeon met her gaze without blinking. Then Nan Telligrew turned her face away.

No, she said, I'll not believe it. Turley's mad or a liar. Or maybe both.

Are you sure? Farjeon whispered.

Sure as I'm sure I'm finished, said Nan Telligrew, staring at her fingers a while; then she flung a tearful look at Jessie.

There's been enough killing, she said. Christ knows there has. And I don't want you to face what faces me, Jess Dunne.

Missus Telligrew, Farjeon said softly.

Yes?

Part of what Turley claims is true, he said.

Nan Telligrew did not look at him; her eyes were fixed still on the wetness her shoes had made, her shoulders slumped, almost cringing, her face filled with a forlorn look that seemed to say no further blows could hurt her.

I shot your husband, Missus Telligrew, Farjeon said.

Yet, still she did not move; nothing in her aspect changed, she seemed beyond anything more. Then she looked at him.

Why, mister? she whispered.

Farjeon met her eyes gently with a sorrow almost as desperate as her own.

He was trying to kill me, he said.

The woman nodded, pondering it, thoughtful, silent for a breath.

Him and Turley, she said. I figured that. Jake had no mind of his own. He followed that fool Turley like a dog.

But I was there, Farjeon went on, as if he must rid himself of secrets to this woman. I was with Shaloo and the man Cotter.

Cotter, murmured Nan Telligrew in a faint, stunned echo, the name meaningless to her.

Cotter was the man who killed my wife and baby, Missus Telligrew, Farjeon said.

She nodded at that, looking up at him presently.

Then you had come there after them yourself, she said.

Farjeon was still a moment. Then he stared at the floor.

If I told you why I was there, he said, it might be worth my life.

Nan Telligrew smiled wearily, shrugging.

It's worth your life, she whispered, to go through yonder door into the black of this cold morning.

Jessie sighed and came from the pump with the dinner pail in her fingers. She slipped the steel ring of the handle into Farjeon's hand. She stood a moment, staring at his chin, her eyes somehow unable to look at his.

Nothing can change you? she whispered.

Jess, it'll work out somehow, he said.

You're going out there, then?

He nodded, staring down at the dinner pail in his fingers. Jessie waited a moment, then went and stood behind the old woman in her rocker, her face a pale, calm mask of suffering resignation. None of them moved in the hushed stillness that followed the sudden knock at the door. Mother Dunne stopped rocking and stared at Nan Telligrew.

You said Turley was down yonder with his mob by the tipple?

Yes. When I come in. I passed amongst them. But there was six or eight others. Right out yonder in the yard.

The knock came again—no timid woman's knock as before. Mother Dunne looked at the revolver now in Farjeon's hand. She shook her head.

Hold on, she said. It mightn't not be Turley at all. Put that thing away, Mister Farjeon.

She sniffed and stared hard at the door.

This may want wit more than guns, she said. So keep that thing in your pocket. Let us see who's yonder.

But, Mom! Jessie cried, racing to the old woman's side, it might be Turley—coming for him!

And it may not be, said the old woman with a wave of her hand. I'll believe in one great mob of fools—yes, I'll believe in that—but not a whole town full. Hush a spell more, Jess. Wait yonder, Mister Farjeon. I've a hunch—a hunch that maybe all this wants more wit than guns. Don't ask me why—it's something my blood tells me! Wait!

When the knock came again she went quietly and put her mouth to the crack.

Who's yonder?

234

Friends, came back the whisper.

Hah! cried the old woman, clapping her dry palms smartly. What did I tell you, now!

Again she put her lips to the doorjamb.

How many? she said softly.

There's six of us, Mother.

Hah, she cried again, that's Bill Soames's voice! A fine man of a miner—somebody whose wits hasn't been scrambled by all this. And if he's there, then I'll wager Bob Tar's with him. And who else, now? Let us see!

She flung the door wide and stood a moment beckoning quickly, then stepped aside as the six men with picks and helmets filed into the room.

Here's Jim Link! cried the old woman. And Bill Weathers! And Sam and Joe! Lord, it's good to know there's men left with sense in this cursed place!

Soames was a big-boned, full-faced man who stood a moment staring first at Farjeon, then at the old woman.

Mother, he said, there's more to all this than clearly shows. I'll not deny that. There's not a man of us here that knows for sure why him yonder was in Wheeling yesterday.

Then he smiled at Farjeon.

Though there's some of us, he said, who have our own notions of what he come to be doing there. No proof, mind you—just a notion.

His gaze dropped suddenly to the puddles of snow and yellow streaks of mud he and the others had tracked in.

Lord, Mother, he whispered, I'm sorry now at all this on your clean floors.

Never mind that! cried the old woman. Floors can be scrubbed clean. And it's better mud than blood!

Soames sighed. He stared at the old woman.

Mom, what you told us last night— he said. To some of us it made sense.

He looked at Farjeon again.

Besides, he added, he don't smell like a scab, somehow. And the good Lord knows I've smelled me a few.

He thought a moment more, then nodded.

Besides, he said, you was right, Mother. We all six of us seen him that night—holding his dead woman and baby in his arms.

He kept his careful, thoughtful gaze on Farjeon's face, then shook his head slowly.

No, he said, it ain't fair. We all six agreed on that.

He studied a moment more.

It ain't fair, he said. Christ knows it's hard enough to be a miner. Just that. Without your own kind ganging up to lynch you.

How many are down there by the tipple? asked Mother Dunne.

The whole of the deadman's shift, Soames said. Saving us six.

Forty men?

Close to it, Mom.

Mother Dunne stared at the men alertly. She searched their faces, still stained with the coal dust of many morning shifts.

There's none of you got guns, she said.

Soames nodded.

None of us had any, he said.

That's good, she said. That may befuddle him. He may not know how to face six unarmed men. No. That's so. Mad as he is, it may throw him off guard.

She looked at Soames again, her blue eyes hard and measuring.

How do you aim to go down the road? she asked softly. The six of you around him?

Yes, Mom.

And if he tries a shot?

He'd have to hit one of us, Soames said. None of us figures he'll do that.

No, said the old woman. That's a safe wager. That would turn the rest of the mob against him. Still, there's something wanting here—some extry thing—some one thing that wants more wit than force.

She shot Soames a swift, anxious look.

And when you get through to the mine face, she said, clean past Turley—what if the others rush you?

Soames sat down carefully on the bench and stared into the fresh, bright morning fire. He was still a long while.

I don't know, Mom, he said presently.

Hah! cried the old woman. Don't you see? It still wants something else to make it work—some trick of wit and wile!

Soames shook his head.

I only know one thing, he said, and that's to hell with them.

He shook his head.

A man has a right to go to work, he said. That's plain fairness.

He stared at Farjeon, who had stood without speaking so far, watching them all, listening, weighing in his mind the chances of it all.

God knows, Soames said, it's bad enough to have to work in such a mine as Breedlove. There's death awaiting—awaiting at every turn. Yes, there's plenty of that—without all this. God knows there is. And Mom yonder—she's never led us wrong. Never lied. So if she swears by you, then I say to hell with them down yonder and to hell with Tom Turley!

Mother Dunne flung herself into her rocker and set it pacing and stared hard at the dark window.

No, she said presently, no, Bill Soames, you're wrong. To hell with Turley—yes. But not so fast with your to hell with the rest of them down there! There's not a boy amongst them that I don't know as well as I know you, Bill Soames—you and these other five fine lads. And I know that there's many a boy amongst that mob that Turley has whipped up to such madness—many, I say, who knows and trusts me as much as all you'ns do.

Soames shrugged.

That may be so, Mother, he said, but still they're standing fast with Turley.

I know that! cried the old woman. And that's why I'm wracking my mind right now for the thing that will make them remember that they trust me, for the one trick of wit and wile that will make them remember who I really am!

Then, as if it were a voice among them, the whistle blew from afar, down in the black, cold shadow of the drift mouth. Soames sighed and caught up his dinner pail in one hand, his pick in the other. He glanced at the other five and then he stared at Farjeon.

There's the second whistle, he said. It's time to go down.

Wait, said Mother Dunne suddenly.

They turned their eyes then and saw her standing in the doorway, the ragged collar of Cal's old army coat up around her vivid white hair. In her hand she carried again the cream pitcher that Farjeon's woman had brought that night.

What are you doing, Mom? cried Jessie suddenly.

Just what I've done a lot of times before, said the old woman softly. I'm going to lead the way.

Now Farjeon who, till this moment, had stood throughout, watching and listening in a spell of impotent resignation, roused as if from a sleep and moved out of the bedroom doorway.

No, he said, that won't do. None of this will do. I'll go alone.

That's madness, Jack! cried the old woman. You'd not get three steps past that threshold!

Farjeon shut his eyes and shook his hand.

Then that's the way it will be, he said. I'm tired of it now. Whichever way it's going to be—I want to get it over.

His eyes ranged the men.

Thank you, he said. I appreciate it. But it won't do. None of it. So all of you go down there your separate ways. And I'll go mine.

He stared down at the revolver in his hand once more. He shook his head.

There's three left, he said. Three bullets. I know. I meant them for something else. Still and all—

Mother Dunne crossed the room and laid her hand on the pistol, pressing it back toward Farjeon's pocket. He shook it loose from her grasp and for a moment struggled softly with her for it.

Then you're a fool! cried the old woman, standing back, her fists on her hips. Don't you know that's what men like Turley reckon on!—the one thing he has an answer for!

Farjeon shook his head, his face fixed in a kind of numb daze.

I don't care about that, he said. I'll not have a woman facing gunfire for my sake. Nor even six strange men who have nothing at stake in this game with me.

Soames stirred. He looked timidly at Mother Dunne.

He's right about one thing, Mom, he said. It ain't fair for you to risk your life in this.

The old woman whirled on him, her eyes ablaze.

And would it be the first time? she cried. Did you tell me not to risk my life, Bill Soames, the morning I led you and a hundred others like you up Parr's Run against the convict-scabs the state had hired against you?

Soames stared at the worn pick handle beneath his fingers.

It ain't the same, Mother, he said.

And how is it different? she cried.

Mom, that was our first strike.

And how is this different? You said yourself there was fairness involved in this. Is it fair only when it threatens your own hides? Is that it?

Soames stared at her a moment, then looked at Farjeon.

Mom, he said softly, his eyes still on Farjeon's face, Mom, you say that him yonder—he's all right. You tell us he's hired on to go to work this morning. Turley, he's roiled up most of the dead-man's shift to stop him. And so me and these boys here—we're willing to see him down to the drift mouth. And into the mine. And stand by throughout the morning to lend him help if he needs it.

He swung his tormented, heavy gaze back to the old woman.

But, Mom, he whispered, for you to risk your life—No, I say. And I know these here boys'll agree.

But it's no risk! cried the old woman. Don't you know me yet, Bill Soames! Don't you know how well I read the mindless soul of a man like Tom Turley. Lord, I've lived amongst more than one like him in half a dozen mine towns between here and Welch! If I lead the way down yonder this morning—if Tom Turley sees me in the fore—he'll not dare fire. Because amongst that mob down there—there's most of them still my boys—most of them, I tell you, who know Mother Dunne and who'll swear she's never deceived them. Lord, I know those boys down there—all of them—good men whose minds have been turned and tricked for the moment by the madness of Tom Turley! Don't you see, Bill Soames, that for him to see me in the fore—Lord, it will be the one thing he'll not be able to answer—a thing he'll not even understand.

What thing, Mom? whispered Soames, not looking at her.

Innocence, she said sharply. He's no answer for that. For he'll simply not understand it. Innocence!

Soames swung his gaze to Cal's old rifle on its hooks near the door.

Maybe if you was carrying that—, he began.

No! cried the old woman. No, I tell you! Because he'd understand that. Don't you see? He's got the answer to that already in his hands!

She turned her imploring gaze to Farjeon.

And it's more than that! she cried. When them boys down yonder—that poor mob of men as helpless as us all—when they see me there, there'll be fresh friends amongst them! Don't you see? There's many a miner down yonder in that black cold by the drift mouth who's not sure about Mister Farjeon.

Soames lowered his eyes to the fire again, he smiled wryly.

There's some here, he said, some amongst us six here now, Mom, who ain't so sure about Mister Farjeon.

Then why are you here? snapped the old woman.

Mom, you never lied to us, Soames said.

He stared at the figure of Nan Telligrew, bolt upright and pale-faced in the straight-backed chair.

Farjeon stirred softly and stared at the revolver in his hand. Then he looked at Soames.

Then it's time, he said. Time for me to explain.

He shut his eyes.

You all know what happened the night I came here, he said. Even back then there was some of you—a lot, I reckon—who wondered what I was, who I was. Me and my Jean. Some of you called me the barefoot man—a stranger come to take a job away from one of you. Or a spy for the company. Or some other such breed of scab.

He looked at the pistol in his hand.

You all know what happened that night, he went on. You know how—they killed the only two things in my life I ever held dear. You remember that?

Soames and the others stirred faintly, listening carefully, watching his face.

I had no notion of what goes on in places like this town, Farjeon said. I'm a farmer—or was. I've never known a miner—till you. I don't know how miners feel or how they act when things happen to them such as happened here that night.

He paused.

Maybe I'm different, he said. Maybe I'm the only man in the world who figured as I figured what had to be done. And if none of you who lost dear ones—well, if none of you figured the same as me—I'm not blaming you.

He held up the revolver.

I went to Wheeling yesterday, he said. I bought this gun. Then I found the man who shot my family. I hired on with him—so's I could get to the boss. The next thing, I had both of them in that hotel room. Then Turley and—the husband of that lady yonder—they come through the window shooting. They killed Shaloo, shot him and the man who killed my family. Before I could move. Then they seen me.

He paused.

241

It was natural, I reckon, he went on. They figured, me being there—they never knew why I had come there—they figured I was *with* them, was one of the killers. I ran. They cornered me. They tried to kill me.

He stared wearily at Nan Telligrew who wept now silently into her hands.

I shot that woman's husband, Farjeon said softly.

He stared at her a moment longer.

I reckon you'd call it self-defense, he said.

He turned his gaze to Soames.

In some ways, he said, in some ways I wisht it had been me.

He shook his head.

In some ways I wisht it had. It might have been better. For me—for Jessie yonder—for everybody.

Then he gazed with a burning, wistful silence toward the door.

Still, he said, still, in a more important way I'm glad I'm still alive. Because—the thing I have to do—it's not done yet.

What thing? whispered Soames after a moment.

Farjeon stared at the gun in his hand.

There's three bullets still in this thing, he said. And they're meant for the other three men I reckon were responsible for my family's death.

He sighed.

No, he said, it's not done yet. When it's done—then maybe I can die.

He looked at Soames with a long, thoughtful gaze.

And that's the truth of it, he said. And you can believe it or not—as it pleases you, mister.

He shivered faintly, putting the pistol back into his coat. Soames stirred after a spell, then looked at the old woman.

Is that the truth, Mom?

It is, said Mother Dunne, staring hard at him.

She kept her unblinking regard on him for a breath.

The truth, she said, the secret truth. And if any man of you in this room ever so much as breathes a word of it to the law—or to

242

anyone who might go to the law with it—well, I'm done with you all forever.

Soames looked at Farjeon.

Well, we'd not do that, Mother, he said. I reckon you know that.

Mother Dunne put her hand on the latch and pushed the door open a foot. She stared at Farjeon, then at them, smiling faintly.

If you want to know, she said, I think he's wrong. Wrong to have gone gunning after them two in Wheeling. Wrong to want to shoot down three more like them. No—I don't blame him. I just think he's wrong.

She shook herself and stared out at the bar of dark morning the half-open door disclosed.

But that's not what's at stake here this morning, she snapped. Mister Farjeon—he has a right to go down to that mine this morning—to work. For whatever reason. The right of miners to work—I've always fought for that. And when there was death in that fight, I've forever loathed it. I've ever loathed and detested it—the death. That's why there's not a man amongst you who can ever remember me taking up a gun when I led you—not even when we faced them. Because I've always loathed it so when there was death in it. That's because the death—it always cancels out something good, even when it seems only to be killing something bad. It's a failure even when we win—when death happens—no matter what else succeeds. Still, I've fought and marched and shouted my lungs empty for that one thing—that right to work—and prayed there'd be no death in it. Yes, I've always fought for the right of miners to work. And to draw a decent wage.

She smiled at Soames.

You know that, Bill, she said. And so do the rest of you. And so, for that matter, do most of them poor boys down there now in the black cold behind Tom Turley.

She snatched Cal's old army hat off the peg on the wall and tugged it over her hair. She stood there, watching them through the small lenses of her spectacles a moment.

243

Come on, boys, she murmured, pushing the door wide.

Soames hesitated.

Come on, she said again softly. It ain't the first time you've follered me.

Don't do this, Mother Dunne, Farjeon said.

He shook Soames's hand off his sleeve.

I'll not go out there if you go, he said. I won't go, Mom!

Hurry! cried the old woman. It's four minutes past the second whistle! Miners have been fired for half that much tardiness!

Farjeon shook his head, as if in a dream, and stared bewilderedly at the six men who flanked him now in the doorway. Mother Dunne stepped briskly out into the morning, which was black and cold as some deep place in the sea. Farjeon shook his head again. Then Soames laid his big hand along his shoulder.

She's right, Soames said. Come on, man.

No.

Come on, man, Soames said again. She's right. The way she always is.

No.

But I tell you it'll be all right, Soames said. Turley, he won't know what to make of it when he sees Mom in the lead.

He'll kill her.

No, he'll not.

Why wouldn't he?

Soames snorted.

Because if he did, he knows he'd have every shift—every living miner in this town—out of their houses to nail him to the tipple the way he had us do to that Polack scab—that's why!

Farjeon stood a moment in the midst of the six men. Before they began to move he turned his gaze to seize one last glimpse of Jessie's face but he could not see past the shoulders of Tar and Link. Beyond the doorway the black air was like a thick, tremulous wave of icy water. A dozen feet from the shack—almost on the very spot where Jean and the baby had gone down—Farjeon stared over Soames's shoulder into the bleak, ragged distances they had to go. It seemed a very long time since he had ever in his life felt fear for that life; he could think now only of the old woman who moved in small, frail fury just ahead of them: Mother Dunne, whose hair beneath Cal's old hat was a faint ring of whiteness in the vague, vast dark beyond Soames's shoulder. Far down the slope, beyond the bitter road, beyond the scissored tipple shape against the slaty sky, by the very hunch and slide of the black drift mouth, someone struck a kitchen match and set it to a coal-oil torch. From thence it moved, zigzagging like a slow, ragged moon, to light another oil torch yards away, and then another, and more, until at last a dozen torches flamed in dirty yellow magnitude, lighting the big, furious silhouette of Turley and the black heads and shoulders of the forty men around him.

Farjeon moved amid them, the pistol once more heavy and living in his pocket; he could feel it strike against his leg like some blow of memory as he strode down the snowy land. And now he could think only that if Turley commenced firing he must break through that hollow crown of shoulders and legs and run out ahead of them, ahead of the old woman, with only those three bullets to answer him with. He felt the strike of the gun through his clothes and prayed that that would not happen, not because he feared Turley but because he knew now more than ever how his soul and flesh yearned to put those three bright bullets into the targets it had dreamed of. And again, and more than ever before, the scorch of vengeance burned in his belly, and now he knew, and more than ever before, the truth of what he had said that night to Jessie: that it was more than the murder of his dear ones that wanted evening up: it was the murder of a town, the slaughter of the minds and wills—the souls—not only of the miners ringing round him but of the forty down yonder in the shadow of the drift mouth, even of Turley himself. At that moment he saw something new and strange in the fire-tinged air above Mother Dunne's hat and his breath caught sharply at the recognition of it, the thing she held up for their eyes to see—the cream pitcher Jean had carried in her hands the night they came there. At the first chattering echo of the shot from Turley's rifle Farjeon sprang and strove against Soames's and Tar's arms, linked to hold him.

Let me loose!

No, man! That shot was high and wide!

Let me loose! He'll kill her!

Christ, he knows better! Soames bellowed.

Let me—loose, I tell you! Farjeon cried again, striving against the wall of them. It's only me he wants, boys! Let me run ahead.

Hold it back, man.

But it's only me they want! Farjeon shouted. This—all this—it ain't your fight!

It is if Mom says it is! And she said it is! Soames said.

Farjeon strove a moment more, his feet skidding and slipping for purchase on the hardened snow. At the second shot he heard the bullet go winging by with a sigh above him, a soft sound, an almost gentle sound, like a dark, wet finger skidding down the wet gray slate of the torch-tinted sky. And then ahead of him, some-how above him, he heard it—the thin, high skirl of the old woman's voice, something clarion in it and yet, withal, a chanting child's voice, full of an almost infant sweetness and fury and somehow shy defiance.

Hark to Mom! Soames cried out, gripping Farjeon's arm. Hark, man! She's saying her psalm!—the way she said it the morning she led us up Parr's Run against the convict-scabs—only that time we was facing a machine gun! Hark, man—listen to Mom saying her psalm.

Psalm, murmured Farjeon, stumbling on amid them. Psalm?

And then he heard again the bright explosion of Turley's Win-chester and the bullet sighed closer now. The dark finger wet down the slate above them and Farjeon strove to break through and again the arms of Soames and Tar restrained him and he could hear his voice shouting something to them, furious and impotent.

But he won't! Soames cried, in a voice already edged with fear.

He won't I tell you! His shots is high and wide! He'd never dare, I tell you!

Tar flung his square, dusky face round to Farjeon.

Listen! he cried. Listen to Mom, man! Christ, ain't she the wonder of the ages!

Her psalm! Soames cried. Lord, hark to it! Hark to Mom asaying her psalm! Lord, it's like old times!

It was as though fear made their grip round him firmer now, it was as if love for her who led them made them hold closer round the one she had said was honest, and they moved stumbling down the slippery, frozen waste—that clumped crown of men with Farjeon in their midst, moving now like one single, dark, humped beast with fourteen striving legs. Farjeon half fell and rose, feeling the wind against his face now like the soft thongs of a wet, cold whip, and he heard again, believing, disbelieving, the old woman's high, clear monotone—child's voice and chanting, clear as nursery song, above the murmurous, male hubbub of the mob below.

"But as for me, my feet were almost gone"—Remember, boys?— "My steps had well-nigh slipped. For there are no bands in their death: but their strength is firm." Remember Parr's Run, boys? "Therefore pride compasseth them about as a chain—Violence covereth them as a garment."

And again Turley's shot, and even before he heard it Farjeon saw the cream pitcher vanish into pale, thin smoke like a cloud of apple blossoms between the old woman's thin, upheld fingers, and he could see where one sharp chip had cut her hand—a thin, glistening darkness snaked down her bright, gnarled wrist. But the voice, in child monotone, did not waver, persisting still like a dream among, above them.

"Surely thou didst set them in slippery places—thou castest them down to destruction." Remember, boys? Have you forgotten 1928? "So foolish was I—and ignorant—I was as a beast before thee."

Yet all Farjeon could remember now was the sight of blood on the old woman's wrist, and in that moment he fancied that one of Turley's bullets had struck her, and as he strove again, his feet sliding and snatching for purchase on the icy earth, he caught sight—between the shoulders of Soames and Tar—of Jessie running down the slope beside them, her face twisted with grief, her wild hair flying like a banner in the torch-stained light. At that moment Turley was not ten feet ahead of them, and as he lifted the rifle again, aiming now from a kneeling position, the clot of miners round Farjeon paused, faltered and stopped. There was no sound for a moment save the whine of quickening wind in the high-tension wire that stretched down earthward from the tipple to a high pole to the left. Farjeon stared between the shoulders of Soames and Tar at the figure of Turley. Beside him, in the fluttering light, he could see the shape of the child Bud, not held by hand now but held as if more firmly in sheer, soundless dread, his large, bushy head thrown back, staring at his father, and his tearless eyes wide in horror, while across his lower face, like a carved mustache of jade, lay the unchecked runnings of his nose. Turley did not move. Mother Dunne, straight as a die and unfaltering, took three steps down the crackling snow toward him.

Let Farjeon through, Tom, she said softly.

Turley, in answer, ejected the spent cartridge and sent a fresh bullet into the chamber.

You let him through, Mom, he said, so's he can get what he deserves.

Behind Turley ranked the troubled faces of the men he had led to the tipple, their faces stained in a sanguine wash of scarlet by the guttering torches. Mother Dunne lifted her gaze from Turley and her eyes ranged the faces of the men behind him. She spat on the snow like a man, glaring at them all.

So this is what we've all come to! she cried suddenly. Us poor who have to cower and fall beneath the guns of company hirelings! This is what we've fallen to! Is this it? Are we now turning guns on each other? Have the bosses driven us to this?

Farjeon's a scab killer! spoke up a voice behind Turley, but the outcry was halfhearted, already rotted with disbelief brought on by the old woman's presence there before them. The miners stirred their great, broken boots on the hard, frozen earth, their eyes wandering and restive in the weltering light, their black hands nervously gripping pick and pail handle.

And is this what you think of me? cried Mother Dunne, her hands on her hips, her face turning back and forth in a semicircle, her burning gaze ranging their faces. After all the shit we've been through together! You follered me through all that—and now you think I'd shield a scab-killer!

She tossed her head, her white hair beneath the absurd hat brim streaming pale in the black wind.

You make me ashamed I ever knowed you! she shouted.

Turley's eye squinted close to the left of the gunsight.

Just let him come through, Mother, he said softly. Let him take his punishment.

Mother Dunne's high-topped shoes strode four feet closer down the snow, her steps mincing, her skirt held high in one hand. She stared down at Turley through her spectacles, her face furrowed with sorrow.

Why, you poor thing, she said. God have mercy on you, Tom Turley.

She raised her eyes, glaring up at the black timbers of the tipple against the pale glow of the morning star.

And God have mercy on the men that have twisted your soul into this sad shape!

My soul is in fine shape, Mother.

You're mad, Tom Turley.

Let the scab-killer through, Turley said softly then, and fired one more quick, winging shot into the air, close above the old woman's hat. He cocked the rifle again, aiming again as she strode again, in that fine, mincing pace, so close now that the muzzle of the rifle was no more than a yard from her.

Shoot me, Tom Turley, she said softly.

Turley's face shifted behind the gunsight.

Pull that trigger, Tom, said Mother Dunne. Aim that gun at my heart and pull the trigger.

No, Mom, Turley murmured.

Why not? cried the old woman. Are you afraid to? Well, why should you be? Don't I deserve to die if I've really betrayed you?

No, Mother Dunne. All we want—

All you want is a death, snapped the old woman. Well, murder's murder. So why not make it two deaths, Tom Turley? They can't hang you but oncet!

We got nothing against you, Mother, Turley said.

No, said the old woman, and nothing much *for* me neither. Despite the long, bloody road we've come together. Since long before John L. ever come to you—since way back in the days of Mitchell!

She stretched out her bleeding hand toward the rifle muzzle, pointing.

Shoot me too, Tom Turley! she cried. Then I'll be out of the way! Then you can shoot the man you call the scab-killer, the one I'm protecting the way I used to protect every one of you'ns!

I'd not hurt you, Mom, Turley murmured uneasily. Not unless—

Unless what? cried Mother Dunne. Unless I got in the way, protecting him? Is that it? Protecting him here in the black of this cold, shameful morning the same way I strode ahead up Parr's Run —protecting you and shouting out the Seventy-third Psalm so's the bosses and their convict-scabs would know we had God on our side!

Mom, we're after him, Turley said. It's him, Mom—

But don't you see, Tom Turley, said the old woman softly, I'm between you and him, Tom Turley. And whichever way you point that gun at him I'll still be in the way.

Farjeon struggled, cursing, in the knot of Soames and Tar and the other four. Jessie stood apart, watching, her hand across her open mouth, the thin blue dress whipping round her pale, bare legs.

Yes, said Mother Dunne again, in a voice as cozening and gentle as if she were speaking to a child, yes, but don't you see, Tom Turley?—I'm between you and him. And I aim to keep on being.

She picked her way through the frozen clots of snow and mud, holding up her gray muslin skirts with one delicate hand, the other poised a bare foot above the foreshortened rifle barrel.

So, you see, Tom Turley, she said in a clear, high voice, you see—you'll have to shoot me first. That's the way it is!

Turley's eyes behind the V of the gunsight swam and blazed in a sudden spill of fury.

Mother Dunne, God forgive me, but if I have to—

She knelt suddenly in the snow directly before him, her face not a foot from the rifle muzzle.

Mom, don't make me! Turley sobbed, his finger whitening on the trigger.

The old woman did not stir, she knelt on the hard snow, her head upright and unquavering, nothing about her stirring save some tendrils of white hair that blew brightly beneath the old hat's brim. She hesitated a barest moment more, as if thinking very careful thoughts, then smiled softly, her hand descending slowly until, in a slow twinkling, and as deliberately as if she had always known she would come to that moment, she inserted her small, thin finger into the muzzle of Turley's Winchester.

Mom, don't make me! Turley screamed again.

No one moved behind him, yet all of them—like a fist—seemed clenched to move. Mother Dunne's hand that held the finger held it fast down the rifle muzzle, then she turned her face to Soames and Tar and the rest and tossed her head.

Boys, let Mister Farjeon go to work, she said in a clear, quiet voice. And hurry up—before the whole shift gets laid off for being late!

Turley shouted something no one could understand, and in that moment his spell was broken, a half dozen men from the miners

251

behind him falling across him, dragging the rifle from his grasp, and keeling the wailing Bud backward across a snow-topped pile of slag.

By God, Mother Dunne, we'd not let Turley nor no one else ever hurt you! cried one of the miners, helping the old woman to her feet.

She glared about her, then at him.

And will you let Jack Farjeon through to the pit mouth?

The big man stared at the others still ranked, uneasily, behind the crumpled, sobbing Turley. He shot his big arm into the air, the bright pick glistening in the light.

Mom, if you believe in him this much—I say yes!

Twenty men moved toward Soames and Tar and the others, who parted now to let Farjeon through. Half hung back, silent, unchoosing, uncommitted, until a moment later. Then presently a dozen more broke from them, ambling sheepishly forward, their bright pails glinting by their sides, their picks on their shoulders, as they moved to join the others. Torches were quenched, hissing out in the snow.

Turley sat, sprawled and spent, against the slag pile, his pail and pick on the snow beside him. He did not look at the silent, shivering child who stood a few feet off, watching.

Go home, Bud! sobbed the big man.

Still the child did not move, his eyes fixed wide and dry on the shape of the man on the snow.

I said go home, Bud! Turley cried, scrambling to his feet and glaring at Bud's small, forlorn shape against the snow.

Well, don't stare at me thataway, boy! cried Turley. This ain't done yet!

Still the child did not move—his moon face fixed and staring, its lower half a mass of snot and tears. Turley said something under his breath and caught up a chunk of snow the size of a melon. He stood a moment, his feet apart, glaring at the child.

Go home, Bud! Get home, I tell you! There's more to it! It ain't done yet! He'll get his yet!

252

The child faltered and half turned and when he still did not move to go up the hill Turley flung the chunk of snow at him, striking him in the shoulder. Bud fell, got up, stared at his father a moment more, then trudged up the slope toward the shacks. Turley stood a moment, watching him, then turned and saw the figures of Jessie and the old woman a few yards off. He stared at them a moment, raised his hand as if to speak, then dropped it as if he had forgotten what it was he meant to say. He caught up his pick and pail and moved off down the narrow railroad track which led to the arc of electric lights round the mine portal. In a moment he was gone. The two women stood alone in the hastening wind, staring at the soaring tipple, twinkling and black against the pallor of the morning star. A few fresh flakes of snow struck like blowing, cold sand across the old woman's mouth. She stirred, grasping Jessie's hand, and led her a few yards back up the cold slope toward the road. Halfway there she turned and looked at the girl, smiling faintly.

After all that, she said, softly, bitterly.

She turned her head, staring back down at the shapes and lights the mine made in the pool of the valley below the slaty dusk.

After all that foolishness, she said. And now the real terror begins.

She stared at the pale oval of Jessie's face.

Forgive me, child, she said, shaking free of Jessie's hand. I'm sorry, Jess—but for a spell I just want to be alone.

She turned and left Jessie alone on the white, scarred slope and moved off in that high-stepping, mincing gait up the rutted, snow-clogged land toward the distant shacks among which now—poor solace—some few lamplit windows shone in pantries where women and their children set about to face the long, fearsome vigil till noontime when the deadman's shift, they prayed, would come trudging and spent up the narrow, lonely road.

Part Three

F ARJEON, Soames, Tar and a dozen other of the miners worked now in a corridor of the mine's deepest drifts, some twelve hundred feet below and a few hundred feet west of the hill upon which the tipple soared. Turley and a half dozen of his staunch supporters against Farjeon worked high up in a top drift—an opening into the mine's poorest stratum—and so the war between them was, for the time, in Farjeon's thoughts at least, an abstraction. He had anxiously discovered the loss of his pistol while the crude elevator was descending into the drifts where he and the other fifteen men were to work. The loss struck him with a kind of swift, choking terror at first, as if the weapon had not been intended for its original purpose at all, but rather as if its loss left him somehow more than ever defenseless against other and more intangible threats which in the corridored, glittering strangeness of the place seemed gathering now around him. He fancied how some miner would find the gun in the snow later that day and would take it home and hide it against the time of another strike—for weapons were coveted in that poor, besieged place.

Farjeon listened abstractedly as Soames who, with shy friendliness, had appointed himself his partner or "butty," spent the early hours of the day instructing him briefly in the details of his work. They worked in a vast room ranked with mine posts supporting a low ceiling of coal some forty or fifty feet in width—a chamber in which the surprising warmth of the air and the bright glitter of lights some twenty feet back in the monkey drift to their left gave a curious, spurious atmosphere of coziness and safety. Soames explained that they had been working in this fairly thick seam for some two months now, hewing ever deeper and deeper into this vast, black room in a process known as "robbing pillars." This was a means by which they strove and blasted and undercut more and more into the earth—enlarging the room every day—and thus, beneath that million-tonned weight of coal ceiling above them, increased each hour the danger that it might suddenly collapse. They worked now into a pillar of black bituminous some twenty feet in diameter and, as it was carted back in the wagons, more ceiling would be left working and whispering strangely above them, to be propped with locust posts, behind which, in the ambiguous light, rats perched and watched against the graven, satiny walls, waiting for dinnertime with its crumbs—great gray creatures who stared with eyes black and glittering as the eyes of glass hatpins or who prowled nearby, fearless and even heedless of the men, squealing and stuttering in the clutter and stench of the gob.

Farjeon fairly grieved the loss of his pistol, even after he had grown easier in that new strangeness, for even though he still had a hundred dollars left of his old money, he could not fancy going through the awful business of buying a fresh gun. Still, after a while he grew resigned even to this, and knew how resolutely he would go on with his goal of vengeance, even if chance should leave him with no other weapon but his pick. While Soames was explaining how he should hang a metal check with his number on it upon each car when he had finished loading it so that the check-weighman should credit his pay with the load, Farjeon kept on thinking about the lost pistol. Still, he knew that even if he had had the gun with him that morning he would not have shot Kitto with it—or even Paul; there was still that wanting factor of ultimate guilt—the name he stood a good chance of finding out that afternoon to come—the name of the mine's final owner. He knew that he would then have to act quickly—killing them all within the space of a few hours—and he knew that this would take all the wit and contrivance and luck in the world. He thought of the two great men who were coming to the mine town that afternoon of this his first day under the hill—the UMW head and Senator Hood. He stared at Soames who worked a dozen feet away, striving with a hand augur some five feet long, drilling a thin hole into the black coal, in preparation for a shot. Farjeon leaned his shovel against the half-loaded car and sleeved the gritty sweat from his eyes.

Soames sought around him for his squibs and black powder. He glanced at the black, low, glittering roof and smiled.

Listen, he said.

Farjeon looked puzzled.

Listen, Soames said again. Hear that roof aworking?

He lowered his eyes to stare at a great gray rat who stood upright on its haunches, like a pup, some dozen feet of litter down the gob beyond them. Farjeon fetched up a lump of coal and flung it. The coal struck a few feet away; the rat did not move.

Jack, he's a friend, Soames said.

He cocked his head again, his face smiling, rich with a fatalism Farjeon had not yet learned to feel.

Listen, he said. Christ, she's working fast this morning. Worse than yesterday.

He stared at the small forest of support posts which ranked the black room behind them.

Them props, he said. Pray they hold, mister. And don't chunk no more coal at them rats, Jack. A rat, he's a miner's friend. When the rats start running—it's time to get out. A rat like that one yonder, he can hear a fall coming before it's hardly commenced. There's many a miner owes his life to rats, mister.

Farjeon picked up his shovel and threw the first load clattering into the bottom of the empty wagon. In the interval of stillness afterward he glanced at Soames who still watched him, the match in his hand. And now Farjeon could hear it—the working of the ceiling above them—and yet it was a sound so secret, so imperceptible, that it was more that he sensed it than heard it, and he glanced anxiously round him for some sign of the rats. Soames laughed. He struck the match.

Get back yonder, he said, into yonder monkey drift. I'm going to fire this shot.

Farjeon crept into the low-ceilinged passage of the monkey drift—a narrow corridor paralleling the main course and cut there for cross ventilation. He watched Soames coming running, at a crouch, toward him. The shot blew—a faint thud in the warm stillness—then a cascading, small thunder of falling coal. Farjeon started back till Soames's hand stayed him.

Wait a while, he said, the roof may be working worse.

Farjeon crouched behind the big man in the dark of the passage. He felt him staring at him again presently. Soames chuckled again and stared out. Then he crept back, motioning Farjeon to follow. He stared at the black, whispering ceiling for a moment.

She'll hold, he said presently. For a spell, at least. But keep watching them rats, mister.

Farjeon stared at the small mountain of coal beneath the place where the shot had fired. It looked so hard, so intractable.

He shoveled, thinking again about the lost pistol.

I hear tell it's a dangerous mine, he said.

Soames swung the pick in a quickening rhythm.

But if you knowed how dangerous, he said, you'd not be here. If you knowed what we know—you'd rather be standing in a breadline in the streets of Wheeling or Glory. If you knowed what a deathtrap this place is, mister, you'd not be here.

He stopped breaking coal and leaned on his pick, looking at Farjeon dourly.

But you're here, he said, so I'll tell you. I don't like to talk about it. Most of us—we try half the time not even to think about it. We pray—at the end of the shift we pray for sleep so's we can stop thinking about it—and even then there's dreams! And there's still men who writes letters—still a few—six months ago there was

260

dozens—till they knowed at last they wouldn't do no good. But there's still a half dozen or so letters goes out of this town every week to Governor Kump, to the U. S. Mine Inspectors, to John L.—even some letters to the senator himself.

Letters? Farjeon said.

Letters, Soames went on. Letters of men pleading for their lives. Men like us who work in a mine that most of us figure to go up any shift now. Between gas and the dust—it's a tossup which goes first. And it'll be worse than Benwood or Monongah—except that Breedlove's a smaller mine—there won't be as many dead to seal up.

He studied this statement, sorrowfully.

Maybe it won't even be in the papers, he said. Except in Glory and Wheeling.

He shook his head.

I wonder if we'll be in the papers, he said.

He stared at Farjeon, a small, queer smile on his face.

It's bad to die, he said, when nobody knows you're dead.

He bent suddenly and, after a search, came up with a small piece of coal which he placed reflectively in his mouth, sucking on it thoughtfully. Farjeon watched him.

Try it, Soames said.

Try what?

Sucking on a piece of coal, Soames said.

He shrugged and went back to his pick.

You won't be able to afford 'baccy on these wages, Soames said. Sucking on a piece of coal helps. All the boys do it. Especially the ones that ever had the smoking habit. I used to smoke like a chimbley in the old days when I was making good money in the steel mills. Do you smoke, Jack?

Farjeon fished into his shirt pocket and came up with an old, stale pack of Camels he had had on him the night he and Jean had come there.

Two months old, he said, holding out the pack. Want one?

Soames shook his head, sucking on his coal.

No thanks, he said. No sense starting up nothing I can't afford.

Three hundred feet to the left of them, in a chamber like the one in which the two now worked, Tar and a half dozen other miners had worked for an hour on a disabled cutting machine, trying to get it back in running order. Now the stillness of the mine was filled with the sudden roar of its motor and presently the shrill, igneous scream as the cutting chain bit into the rib of coal they were working. Soames shook his head, gesturing toward the doghole through which the sound came.

I don't trust them cutters, he said.

Why aren't we using one? Farjeon said.

Because we're working a section that's pretty well played out, Soames said.

He shook his head again.

I hate them bastard cutting machines, he said.

Why? What's wrong with them? Farjeon said.

They're what makes a dry mine like this dusty, Soames said. And dust is what causes a windy—that's when the dust blows up. Man, it's like black powder when it goes. It's bad enough in here anyways. This is one of the gassiest mines in the state. Even the inspectors said that when they was last here. There's another thing about them cutters—

Farjeon shoveled on, listening.

When that cutting chain cuts through the rib of coal it's okay, Soames said. But supposing you come up against a vein of slate—back of the coal.

What happens?

What happens? Soames sighed. That whole eight- or nine-ton machine—she bucks sideways like a spooky horse, and pins everything alive under it.

He stopped swinging his pick, took the piece of coal out of his mouth, studied it, then threw it into the gob. He grinned at Farjeon.

Maybe, he said, maybe I will try one of them coffin nails, Jack.

Farjeon gave him the cigarette, lighted it for him, lighted one of

262

his own. Soames inhaled deep and blew the smoke out with a sigh.

Man, that brings back a memory or two, he said, of better days.

Maybe they'll come again, Farjeon murmured.

Soames stared at the cigarette.

Not in this place, Jack, he said. Not here. You better learn that. Learn it good—and get out if you can.

Why don't you, Soames? said Farjeon.

Soames smiled.

Six kids, he said. Does that answer you? Did you ever see man, woman and six kids standing on a breadline? Naw, things is different for a single man like you.

He shot Farjeon a glance.

Or are you figuring to wed Cal's widow Jessie?

Farjeon said nothing, shoveling coal into the half-full wagon.

I'm sorry, Soames said. I didn't mean to get personal.

It's all right, Farjeon said. A man never knows what he'll do these times. It's all right, Soames.

Afterward neither man knew who was the first to see them, the dozen rats that suddenly poured squealing out of the far chamber where Tar and the six others worked with the cutting machine— gray, skittering ghosts that came pouring through the monkey drift that separated the two groups. Soames was the first to react.

Fall! he shouted, flinging down his pick and diving for the gob.

Farjeon did not move, standing frozen, while Soames shouted and motioned to him to follow, and together they heard the explosion of snapping timbers and the thunder of the cascading bituminous in the farther room. Farjeon crouched on his knees till the sound had subsided and watched the vast, thick cloud of dust vomit slowly forth, like smoke from a cannon, from the monkey-drift portal. Belatedly he crept down beside Soames in the stinking puddle of the gob and crouched silent until the sound was over. In the stillness afterward they could hear, above the whisper of the rats, the voice of one man screaming like a woman, the shouts of some others, and the sound of a deathly, muffled groaning. Soames blanched and crept, childlike, on all fours to the monkey-drift opening. At the portal he turned, motioning Farjeon to follow. They crept, huddling, through and stood up in the space of the farther chamber, trying to peer through the immensity of black dust which swam in the glittering air.

Four men stood round the cutting machine staring across it at the section of ceiling which had collapsed, splintering locust posts so that they stood broken at the roots and feathered up from the black debris like used paint brushes. Link lay somewhere under the tons of bituminous; Weathers and three other miners made their way to the side of Tar who lay with a three-hundred-pound piece of coal pressed down into the space of what had been his chest. Tar was alive, his face, black with coal dust, was filled with a kind of puzzled, astonished tranquillity. A fallen post had kept the mass of coal from crushing life entirely from him, his spine was intact, his ruined lungs beneath the smashed rib cage were, incredibly to the others, still able to sustain breath enough for whispers. His eyes wandered from face to face of the men above him, his gaze filled with that curious and graceful candor of some men who come to that condition and do not despise it. He stared at them with those child eyes, his mouth making whispers which none of them could yet understand. They strove now, tenderly, gingerly, with the vast lump of glittering, blue coal, seven men straining to lift it from him without quenching his last lights utterly, and when they had got it off him and laid it down three feet away, Soames and Weathers were kneeling by his side, ears close, to make out his words. Soames, certain that these would be some last words for his lady and her eight children, lifted his blackened face and stared at the others, his expression one of uncertain astonishment.

What's he say, Bill?

Soames stared at Tar's mouth again, then bent his ear again close, as he slowly shaped the word again. Soames looked up again.

He wants a cigarette, he said.

Soames stared longer at them, his face wide with amazement.

Now don't that beat all? he whispered.

Weathers and the others looked at one another with sorrowful dismay until Farjeon fetched out his old pack and fetched one out. He handed it to Soames who stared at it a moment, as if wondering what its use might be, then looked down, forlornly, and laid the tip of it between Tar's thin, blackened lips. The dying man lay there with the cigarette sticking up from his face, while his stricken eyes searched them again, waiting for the light. Soames fetched out a match with care, struck it on the floor; his hand shook slightly as he held the flame. Tar shut his eyes, there was a struggle beneath his flesh, then an expression of ineffable relief crossed the masklike features and, with one, vast rallying effort, he inhaled. And they stood watching while the blue, vivid smoke curled up in dim, wandering tendrils through the stained cloth of his work shirt, smoke crawling from out the splintered pudding of his chest to sift, dissolving like some visible soul of him, through the air. Then with a sigh like a broken accordion he was gone, his eyes seeming still to watch them there, to pity them there, and also—in some haunting, curious way—to reassure them of something. Soames stared a moment, shuddered, then took the cigarette carefully from between Tar's parted lips and ground it out on the floor. He lifted his face to stare, grinning queerly, at Farjeon.

And it won't even be in the papers, he said bitterly. Ain't that hell? And when it happens to us—by Christ, even to all of us—I bet it won't even be in the papers!

Tenderly, as if some untoward roughness might further wound him, four of them lifted Tar's body and laid it atop the heaped coal of a full car and trundled it, striving and grunting, back toward the passage leading to the lift. Weathers caught up his shovel and stared at the mountain of broken coal and splintered posts and motioned to the others. Farjeon went back to the space where he and Soames had been working and presently crawled back through the doghole bringing the two shovels. For a spell all of them stood staring at the black, glittering mound of debris under which, gone beyond hope or caprice of prayer, lay their other dead comrade, Link. Most of the chunks of coal were too big to be shoveled; they set upon them with picks, swinging them with an air of bunched, smouldering fury—not fast, for there was no life-saving hurry to it—but with a slow, swinging savageness full of something smelted in the furnace of years of suppressed outrage and now near to exploding loose out of that hangdog indolence. None of them spoke. And yet each grunt as the pick struck blue coal was like some subtle curse; they broke the murderous, hard blackness of it as if it were itself the enemy—and they shoveled the broken stuff away with the air of men digging their own graves.

Behind them, having escaped the catastrophe by a bare yard of floor—bright and glittering and miraculously undulled by dust—stood Tar's dinner pail, as fresh and tidy as it had been when his wife had filled and blessed it in their shack the night before. As they broke coal and shoveled, the men stepped carefully, circuitously, around the pail; none of them moved it. It seemed as if, indeed, each of them strove, as he moved round or over it, not to look at the thing at all. They had already looked with nothing more than grief and terror on the broken ruins of Tar's body—some of their fingers were still stained and sticky from its sorrowful, seeped-out mortality. But the dinner pail: it seemed a glimpse into some ultimate extravagance of feeling presently unendurable to any man there. It might have stood there among them as some ikon to the slaughtered godhead of human life. They glanced at it sidelong, in frightened flashes, as if it were unendurable and dangerous—like a basilisk—to look upon it full. Perhaps it was because it looked so believable—and there had been something, mercifully, unbelievable about the look of what death had done to Tar's brokenness. The dinner pail: they moved round it, over it, not jostling it, not letting so much as a trouser cuff touch it, working carefully so as not to let any coal dust sift down from their shovels to soil it, picking up and laying down their great, broken boots cautiously as they shuffled and scraped about the floor where this thing—still immaculate from the kitchen in Tar's shack on the hill, above the road, on the living earth a thousand feet above them —that place where, close overhead, stood the tall and limpidly candid infinity of a winter's sky—however bitter with cold—and not here where they strove, like fish imprisoned in the plumbless, bleak fathoms of some vast ocean of stone, and for their roof this whispering imminence of fragilely timbered blackness.

Farjeon sensed what they were all feeling and knew the strangeness of it. And he knew the anguished authenticity of those sentiments. He knew that men can look upon any wreckage of a human body—however it may be disfigured beyond any fantasy of nightmare—that they may stare down at it and feel mere pity or the mere empathy of terror or nothing more, perhaps, than a mild niceness of nausea. Men can pick up any dead mortal thing —however unspeakable its ruin—can handle it, cart it away, bury it, plant above it a flag or a flower, and remember what they have seen and endure that vision. But there are symbols of flesh more unendurably human than the face of death itself: a face of fled life more immutably mortal than mortality. For what is to be done with such emblems? How are they to be reckoned with? If it were imaginable that a man could, at last, steel himself to touch them at all—what should he do with them then? Each of these men who now grunted and strove, breaking coal and shoveling it away, drawing closer each moment to a thing disfigured and smashed even more than Tar had been—each of them dreaded the sight of Link's unimaginable ruin which their labors would presently uncover, yet dreaded it less than they held in awe the sight of Tar's dinner pail. That they had had such feelings before was no comfort nor any precedent of behavior which would help or comfort them now.

For what *should* they do with that pail which Tar's wife had packed and blessed the night before? Should they cart it off and bury it the way they would, as a matter of course, do with Tar's body itself? Should they finally open the pail and take out Tar's austere and pathetic dinner and eat it themselves—Christ, this was a fantasy as unthinkable to them as cannibalism. Perhaps one of them would clench his aching teeth and go, at last, to fetch the thing a kick—to send it spilling out and clattering off into the littered gob. But then the rats would eat the food—an idea as unholy as the thought of their feeding on Tar's dead meat itself. Perhaps they should take the dinner in its pail back to the fingers of the woman who had put it there—that meager meal of two sandwiches of lard and corn bread, the Mason jar of tepid sassafras tea. But would she not find it more unendurable than they did, would it not remind her more of Tar than the thing that was left of Tar? No—the woman, too, was captive within that mystery. And so the pail stood there in the midst of their sweating, noisy hubbub, glistening and undusty in the center of all that dusty commotion. They stepped still round it, over it, casting it from time to time those sidelong, flashing glances as if it were a time bomb. At last, of course—at the end of the shift—they would go away and leave it standing there. And not a man among them, remembering such dinner pails before, could ever after tell himself or anyone what, in the end, became of them.

Each of them thought as well—and shamefully—that he would lose a day's pay in that shift's labors, most of which would be spent in uncovering Link's remains and sending it after Tar's body to the tipple. When they were done even with that awful chore the cutting machine would have to be unearthed and its damages discovered—Soames and Farjeon would help with that, they agreed—and the already dangerous and sibilantly whispering remnant of the chamber's unfallen roof must be set with fresh timbers. So there would be no pay for that shift—except for the couple of cars each of them earlier had loaded—a few pennies for that on the checkweighman's tally. It was a lost day—two friends lost and a day's pay lost, and each man, in his soul, was ashamed to be holding these two facts in equal sum. For in that place the loss of a day's pay was the loss of a little life itself—a small day's death—to be chronicled, black-lettered, in the company book. And in final, crushing ambiguity, there was something in each of them which knew that Tar and Link were, at least and at last, beyond the degradation of such estimations—scribbled mental sums which would make the loss of two comrades and the few pennies of a day's pay equal to each other in stunning and humiliating equation.

Toward the end of the shift Soames and Farjeon were done helping the other miners in the workings where the accident had happened and so they went back to where they had begun the morning. Dispiritedly Soames loaded half a car and then stopped and went to lean against the rib and watch Farjeon. Farjeon slacked off as well; both knew the day was lost. Still, the impact of the accident had not—as sometimes happens—proved any emotional catharsis to the stifling sense of oppression, of imminent threat, which had pressed down upon them early that day. Indeed, the roof fall in the workings next to them seemed like the drum roll preluding a fuller symphony of catastrophe still to come. Soames felt it more strongly for he was the veteran; Farjeon could sense it in his ironic regard. Perhaps that was why neither man was surprised at the thudding, urgent footfalls which echoed distantly toward them down the tunnel leading out from their chamber. Neither of them felt surprise to see the fearful expression on the face of the miner who appeared presently, running toward them between the narrow-gauge rails. When he came abreast they could see that he was clutching something small under his coat. He looked from one to the other of them, then recognized Soames and looked back at Farjeon.

You Jack?

Farjeon nodded.

Jack Farjeon?

Yes.

The miner stood a moment, catching his breath.

Cal Dunne's widow—that fool woman—, he went on in a

hushed voice, as if, curiously, the towering earth above them might somehow overhear.

What about her? Farjeon whispered.

She come in the mine—that's what, said the miner in a still lower voice, waiting and staring, as if that were bad news enough.

Farjeon waited, his face furrowed in concern.

Whatever for? he said presently.

She said to give you this, said the miner.

He glanced at Soames, then back to Farjeon, shrugged, then took the revolver slowly out from under his coat. He looked at it, then back to Farjeon.

She was trying to bring it to you herself, he said. Till Bonar and some others stopped her. On the way back out I run into her. She give this to me. Told me to get it to you—life or death.

Where is she now? Farjeon asked quietly.

The miner glanced swiftly at the shadowy roof, working and whispering faintly a few feet above.

Cal Dunne's widow, he whispered, smiling nervously. That fool woman—coming down in the mine.

Where is she now?

Home, I reckon, said the miner. They caught her on the lift, halfway down to the third-level workings. They sent her back. She come up against me. She was crying. She give that thing to me. Made me swear to bring it to you, Farjeon—life or death, she said.

Soames watched as Farjeon stared briefly at the gun, then put it inside his shirt, under the pressure of his belt.

Did anybody hurt her? Farjeon said.

The miner shook his head.

Nobody couldn't hardly believe it at first, he said. The sight of her. To see a woman in here, in the mine. Nobody touched her. It was like they was afraid to go near her.

Why? Was she pointing it at them?

It wasn't that, said the miner with another nervous smile.

270

What then?

The man shrugged, sleeving black sweat from the tip of his nose.

You know what they say, he said sheepishly, when a woman comes down in a mine. You know what the old-timers all say.

Soames nodded, looked at Farjeon, then looked away.

It means an accident, the man said, shivering there amid the covetous, warm air of the whispering chamber.

Soames nodded.

We done had an accident, he said. But it happened early in the shift. It happened long before she come down, I reckon. So's they can't blame her.

Yes, they can, whispered the miner.

Soames and Farjeon stared at him.

They can blame her, the man went on. And they do. I don't know nothing about no accident down here.

Was there another one?

The miner nodded.

There was a windy up in the workings just beyond the twelfth portal, he said. And it come not twenty minutes after she had gone.

Soames stared.

A bad one?

Bad enough.

Any deaths? Soames said.

Three.

Farjeon seemed heedless of them. He could feel the pressure of the gun again, like the fullness of some recovered meaning, against his belly, under his shirt.

Who died? Soames said softly.

The Polack name of Luchek, said the boy. But that ain't the worst of it.

Who else?

Farjeon's gaze was fixed now on a great, sleek rat who sat on a

271

lump in the gob, below the rib, watching them silently. The sight
of the rat made him think of the justice of the thing he had sworn
to do, and he knew that what the men were talking about, here
deep in the prison of this black place,—that this strengthened the
feeling of that justice even more.

Who else died? Soames said again.

The miner stared at him, smiling crookedly as if he knew not
whether to be sorry or glad.

Mister Kitto and Mister Paul, he said presently. Both of them
blowed clean to kingdom come!

Farjeon stood on the frozen road, his face against the wind,
watching a stooped, old-looking child pushing an old baby carriage full of coal up the broken ruts toward the row of shacks. The
carriage had only three wheels and the coal was heavy, so that the
child had to hold up one end of it as he pushed. The tipple was
behind him, down the icy slope a hundred yards behind, and as
he had passed from under it Farjeon had paid no mind to the
mass of miners clustered there—some of them with shivering
wives and children—staring and listening to the tall, white-haired
man addressing them from the running board of a glistening
black Packard which had drawn up on the rise below the drift
mouth. Two black-faced miners—fresh from home where they had
not even taken time to wash up—came running down the road
toward Farjeon. One of them grabbed his sleeve, pointing toward the tipple.

Ain't you coming?

Where? Farjeon said absently.

Down by the tipple! cried the man. John L., he's down there.
Can't you see him? He's in the car. Him and Senator Hood. That's
him yonder. He's talking now!

He gestured with his finger in the wind; Farjeon could hear the
faint rise and fall of a man's voice addressing the assembled men.
He shook his sleeve free from the miner's hand and turned into

the wind again, up road, toward the shacks. The two men ran off down the road toward the others. Farjeon paused, his eyes seeking out the bleak shape of home, then moved on, a light fall of fresh snow stinging his sweating face. He could hear the senator's voice, ebbing and rising, drifting faintly in the wind but he could make out none of the words and they would not have mattered to him if he had heard them. Farjeon's whole body ached with an ineffable weariness, as if in the aftermath of some enormous effort far beyond the limit of the actual physical work he had done that day. He knew that Mother Dunne was down by the tipple with the others—he had glimpsed the top of her frayed black bonnet above the helmets of the miners; Jessie would be alone up in the house. He walked toward the porch, up the empty, frozen yard, in a kind of daze. When he pushed the door open he saw Jessie standing by the pump, holding a cup of water to her lips. Farjeon looked at her, then looked away as if he could not face her. He leaned his pick against the wall by the door and put the dinner pail beside it. He stood a spell, then went slowly into the bedroom, sat on the straight-backed chair and took off the heavy boots. Jessie came in the doorway, stood watching as he stripped out of his shirt and trousers—black with dust and grime—and heaped them on the floor in a pile. Then he stretched out on the bed, staring at the ceiling. Jessie sat quietly on the chair, watching him.

You shouldn't have come after me, Jess, Farjeon said after a while.

She said nothing.

You know well and good you done wrong, don't you, Jess?

Still she waited.

I kept thinking about you down there with Turley, she said presently. With no defense.

Turley wasn't nowhere near me all day, he said.

He looked at her.

Was that why you brought me the gun? he said.

She looked away.

I know the way you always keep it near, she said. I knowed you'd miss it. I wanted you to have it.

Farjeon turned his head on the bolster, looking at the revolver laid carefully atop the blackened pile of his work clothes.

Jess, he said, it's like I said the night I come home from Wheeling.

I know, she whispered.

It's like God, He keeps moving things round in the dark, Farjeon said.

I know, Jack.

He looked at her.

Kitto, he said. And Paul.

I heard tell, she said.

She came suddenly and sat on the edge of the bed, her hand shyly resting on his arm. He felt her fingers press.

Jack, maybe it was never meant to be, she said, your getting those men.

She watched his head turning from side to side on the bolster.

There's still one, he said.

Jack, nobody on earth, she said, knows the name of the man who owns Breedlove Mine. Mom, she don't know. John L. himself don't know.

He's down yonder now, Farjeon said. In a big black car.

I know.

John L., I mean.

I know. He's going to speak. Mom, she went down to hear him.

She lifted her eyes, watching him.

Jack, maybe you can give it up now, she said.

He stared a long, silent moment.

No, he said presently.

They're all dead, Jack.

All but one.

Jack, you'll never find him, she said, and her heart was suddenly full again of her old fears for him. Jack, give it up. Don't go back

274

to work in the mine tomorrow. We'll go away, you and me **and** Mom.

He looked at her.

Sometimes I believe you mean it when you ask me that, he said softly.

You can believe me, she said. Jack, this time I mean it.

No, he said. I'll keep on working here. I'll find out who he is.

She put her face back on his chest, hearing his slow, thoughtful breath.

There's a man down there now, Farjeon said. He was talking when I went past. On the running board. Lewis was in the car.

Senator Hood?

Farjeon nodded. He half rose on one elbow, looking at her.

Mom said he was staying here in Breedlove till tomorrow, she said.

In this place? Farjeon said. Where's he sleeping?

He's staying up in the manager's big house, Jessie said.

In Paul's house? Paul's dead.

Jessie shrugged.

There's a new manager, she said. They hired him this morning.

Already?

He's up there in Paul's house now, Jessie said.

Farjeon pondered.

Why is he staying two days?

Him and John L., they come here to investigate the violence, Jessie said. The senator wants to look into conditions in the mine.

Farjeon chuckled.

Who'll tell him about that? he said. The new manager?

No, Jessie said. He's going in tomorrow morning.

In where?

Into the mine, she said.

Farjeon sighed.

Lord, you mean he's going down in that hellhole tomorrow?

That's what Mom said she heard.

I wonder why, Farjeon said quietly.

Jessie shrugged.

There's a spring election coming up, she said. Maybe he wants the mine vote.

No, Farjeon said. He's not that kind of vote chaser. No, Jess. There must be another reason. A man like him—he wouldn't go in a place like that just to get votes.

He thought about it.

So he'll be around, he said. So there's a chance.

Chance of what, Jack?

A chance that I'll get to talk to him, Farjeon said. Get him aside for a minute. Maybe even go up to the manager's house tonight. Talk to him.

Talk about what?

Farjeon bit his lip.

If any man knows who owns this mine, he said, Senator Hood would know.

Jessie ran her fingers through his hair.

Jack, she said, Jack, it's finished. Give it up.

It's not finished, he said. And I'm not finished, Jess.

He lowered his gaze to her.

Jessie, I swore that five men weren't fit to live because of something that happened to me, he said softly. Today in that mine I saw things happen to other men that make me even more certain of the rightness of what I swore to do.

There was an accident today, she said quietly.

There was two accidents, he said. Tar was killed. So was Link.

There was another one, she said. And they blame it on me.

That's foolishness, he said.

Just the same, she said, they do.

Who does?

Turley does, she said. And Bonar. And a lot of others.

That's superstition, he said.

Jessie nodded, her lips colorless in the gray light.

There's another superstition too, she said. And maybe it's true.

What's the other one? he said.

That accidents come in threes, she said.

Farjeon thought about it.

You weren't even in the mine when Tar and Link got caught in the fall, he said.

Still, they claim I caused it, she said. They claim it happened after.

And they believe there'll be another one?

Jessie looked away, toward the pale light of the window.

Yes, she said. And Bonar was up here an hour before you come in from the shift.

What for?

To tell me that Turley swore that if there's another accident, she said, and if he survives it—

That what?

That he'll kill me, she said, smiling.

Turley swears lots of things, Farjeon said. He swore I'd never live to work in the mine this morning.

Jack, she whispered, you almost didn't.

She reached up to take his face in her hands, pulling his gaze round to look at her.

Jack, I have this awful feeling.

What kind?

A feeling that there *will* be another one, she whispered. A bad one. The real bad one we've all been so scared of for so long.

You mean a blast?

Yes.

He sighed.

I know, he said. I've seen the place—been in it. I don't know much about blasts but I reckon I saw enough to know there'll be a blast.

He paused, turning his gaze from her.

I reckon there will be, he said. Sooner or later.

Jack, maybe soon, she said.

He shrugged.

Maybe late, he said. After I'm through working down there.

After I've found out what I've got to find out—done what I've sworn to do.

Jack, maybe tomorrow, she whispered.

He looked at her.

Jess, that's plain superstition.

She shook her head.

It's got nothing to do with its being the third, she said. Nor with its being caused by me being in the mine. Jack, it's not superstition at all.

What then, Jess?

She shuddered and squeezed his shoulder with her fingers.

Jack, I have this—this vision.

Of a blast?

She nodded, biting her lip.

He touched her face with his hand.

Jess, he said, it's all going to be all right.

She pulled away from his touch, bowing her face, her eyes closed.

Jess, he said, maybe I won't have to work in that mine tomorrow at all.

She looked at him questioningly.

Maybe, he said, I'll find out what I have to find out tonight— find out and do it and get it all over.

Maybe you'll not, she said. And tomorrow you'll go down there again—

By tomorrow, he said, maybe I'll know. And get it done. Maybe then we'll be ready to take Mom and go.

Jack, they're all dead now, she said.

All but one.

She got up from the bed, went to the chair by the door, sat down to watch him.

Jack, you may never know who that one is.

He looked at her, smiling.

You said you had your premonition, Jess, he said. Well, I've got a sort of one of my own.

Of what?

Of a feeling that I'm mighty close to knowing who the fifth man is.

Based on what?

He shrugged.

Just a feeling, he said. I don't know why.

He looked at her again.

Who knows? I may find out tonight.

Her eyes softened as she stared at him.

Does it still mean that much to you? she said. Do you still love *them* that much?

He looked away from her.

It's funny, he said. Sometimes it's almost like I'd forgotten about them—Jean and the baby. There's been so much to happen since then.

So why go on with it? she whispered.

He stared at her thoughtfully.

I don't hardly know how to explain it, he said. It was an atrocity —a crime done against ones I loved. And in the beginning at least it was only them that wanted avenging. That's all it was—a crime done against the only things I had on earth. And I swore to avenge that. Yes, that's still part of it, Jess.

But it's not all?

He shook his head. He waved his hand in the still air in an encompassing gesture.

This whole place, he said. It's a crime. This town—the mine. They're a crime.

Jack, there's places like this all over the land.

He shook his head.

I don't care about them, he said. I know this place—the crime that *this* place is.

The place that caused the deaths of the ones you loved, she said. Yes, I—

No, he said, it's not only them. It's like I told you the other night. At first it was only them, and I swore to even it all—just for them. Then things—went moving round in the dark. Like God was moving them. I was shooting into a blackness—not even knowing who would die.

He shot her a look.

And then I come to see the crime that's been done—a bigger crime than the killing of Jean and the baby.

He looked at his hands, freshly scuffed and darkened from the coal.

Soames today, he said, I saw him clear. I saw a man who'll live and die in this place. And die because of it likely. Murdered as sure as ever was Jean and our child.

He got up from the bed and went to the window, staring thoughtfully at the blind.

Even Turley, he said.

He turned and looked at her.

A victim, he said.

He sat on the edge of the bed, still staring at the window.

It's queer, he said. Today two men died I'd sworn to kill.

Kitto, she said.

And Paul.

He buried his face in his hands, speaking now into his fingers.

It's almost as if—

As if what? she whispered.

It's almost as if none of the other four mattered, he said. Not even Cotter—not even the man who actually did the killing. Not even Shaloo. Nor Paul, nor Kitto—who only followed orders.

Ain't they just as bad?

In a way they aren't, he said. In a way they're just like checkers moved hither and yon on a board. Heedless. Not like the hand that moved them.

He shook his head.

No, he said. Four men are dead, Jess—and one still lives. And in some queer way he's the only one that matters.

He paused.

Maybe, he said, he's the only one that ever mattered. From the first. Maybe I should have forgotten about Cotter and Shaloo—or Kitto or Paul—and just gone hunting headlong for the only one who really matters. The one man—like the hand that moved all the others.

She stared at him.

And if—by some chance—you find out tonight?

I'll go after him, Jess.

It'll probably be someone far from here, she said. Maybe at Pittsburgh or New York.

Then I'll go there, he said.

Her face was full of trouble.

And if you don't find out tonight?

Then I'll go back into the mine tomorrow, he said, and I'll work. And I'll ask round. And I'll listen. And pry.

He sighed.

And wait, he said.

He looked at her.

Sooner or later, he said, somebody will know, Jess.

In a month, she said. Or a year. And every minute of it you'll be living in that danger.

He shook his head.

Jess, I think it's destined that I'll find out, he said. And sooner than either one of us thinks.

She flung her face suddenly into her hands, keeping it there.

Jack, Jack, I have this feeling about tomorrow, she said.

Tomorrow, he said, it may be all over.

But, Jack, you don't have to, she said softly.

Yes, I do.

You don't, Jack.

She came round the bed and stood staring down at him.

Jack, it's like some kind of madness, she said.

It's a thing I swore, he said.

Still it's that—like a madness.

He stared up at her.

And it was a madness you loved, Jess.

281

She stared down at him, wide-eyed and silent.

I know, she said. Something inside me still does. But not as much.

What *do* you want, Jess?

She knelt by his knee, beside the chair, looking up at him.

I want us to take Mom and go away.

He searched her face with his eyes, smiling faintly.

You have that same look, he said.

What look, hon?

The look Jean had, he said.

The night she died? Jessie whispered.

No, he said. Before that. The look she had all those weeks.

What weeks?

The weeks she was carrying the baby, he said. That same rosy look. Kind of—transparent.

Jessie stared at him a moment, then turned away.

If I was, she said suddenly, you'd never know it.

Jess, are you?

No, she said. No, I ain't. And if I was—well, I'd go away. I'd never make you marry me. I'd get rid of it somehow.

He pulled her round, staring up.

Jess, you're sure?

Sure of what?

Sure you're not carrying a baby?

I reckon I'd know, she said. No. I'm not.

He smiled.

If you was, he said, I'd take you into Glory tonight. Jess, I'd marry you tonight.

She stared at him through brimming tears.

Would you? she whispered.

Yes.

And would you give it all up then? she said. Would you take me and Mom and forget all about the rest of it, Jack?

He smiled at her.

No, Jess, he said, I'm afraid I couldn't do that.

But then! she cried. If I was—if it was true—then it'd be just like with you and her, Jack.

Nothing's the same, Jess.

But it would be like you started the whole thing afresh, she cried. With a wife and baby—and nothing awful to revenge. And we'd all of us be far away from all this blackness and death and visions of fire!

I still have to do it, Jess.

She glared at him, gnawing her lip

Yes, I suppose so, she said. I reckon it's not the same with me.

He followed her to the bed with his eyes.

Are you sore at me, Jess?

She shook her head.

Jess, you *are* sore, he said. Honey, listen—

Not sore, she said. Maybe a little crazy. Yes, I reckon that's it.

Crazy how?

She stared at him.

Crazy enough, she said, to fancy that if I was carrying your baby it would be the same as it was with her.

He watched her.

Jess, you was lying to me, he said softly. I can tell by looking at you.

I'm not lying, she said. I'm not carrying your baby.

She stared at him then.

And if I was, she said, you'd never know. I'd never make you marry me for that.

He saw the tears standing on her flushed, smooth cheeks.

Still and all, she said, it was pure crazy of me—to think that if I was, it would ever be like her. Christ, I mind the way your face looked when you looked down at her in your arms that night! You'd never look at me like that, I know.

He went to her and put his arm across her shoulder.

Jess, I feel a thing about you stronger than ever it was with Jean.

She flung loose and strode through the door into the front room.

283

I misdoubt all that, she said simply.

Jess, why? I swear to you—

She turned and glared at him.

I done things to you, she said, such as she'd never done. Never would. No, Jack. I know what you mean when you say it's different with us.

It's better, I reckon, he said.

Do you? she said. Or are you so sure you didn't just find something with me you could've found in Glory—in a real fancy Baltimore Street whorehouse. I know what you mean when you say it's different all right.

She began to weep then, unchecked, her sobs filling the stillness. Farjeon went to her then, held her in his hands a moment till she struggled and then lay her head back and began to scream in the silence, till he slapped her. He stared at the red his fingers had left on her cheek, then pulled her against him.

I love you, Jessie.

Christ, Jack, she sobbed into his breast. Christ, then give it up.

He pressed her head against him with his hands, stroking her dark hair.

And you, he said. You was the one who always wanted me to go on with it.

I know! she breathed in a fainting voice against him. And it's a thing God's punishing me for now. It's a thing—Christ, Jack, it's a thing I ask Him to forgive me for.

Why, Jess?

Because I'm more to blame for it than you are! she sobbed. At the first—when you first swore it—Jack, I could have talked you out of it.

No, Jess, he said. No, you couldn't have.

Yes! she sobbed. Christ, you was like a child, Jack. You was like some sick, feverish child. And when the black oath you swore— that oath of vengeance—when it began, Jack, it was so small— like a fire just starting. Jack, I could have talked you out of it. But I didn't. Christ, I didn't. I fed that little flame like I was spilling coal oil on a fire. I told you it was a smell on you that made me want you!

She flung back her face, torn with grief and tear-stained.

Jack, Jack, I was lying. It was you I loved. Without all that other. I know that now.

Jess, you couldn't have changed me.

Christ, sure I could. Jack, I can do anything with you.

She pushed away from him, her dark eyes flashing.

Anything, I reckon, she said, but make you love me the way you loved her. And I'm a fool to fancy that could ever be. I know that.

He put his fingers under her chin, tilting her face back to his gaze.

Jessie, I love you more than I loved Jean.

She tossed her face loose from his hand.

But she was carrying your baby. That's the big difference.

Jess, you and me—we might have a baby someday.

She turned and wandered off disconsolately toward the bench by the fire.

No, she said. I'd never want your child.

Why?

She turned and looked at him.

Because you'd think I was trying to hold you with it, she said. You'd pity me.

I didn't pity her, he said.

Yes, but you'd pity me, she cried. I know that. It's different with me.

She sat on the bench, staring into the fire; she wiped her stained cheeks with a corner of her skirt.

No, Jack, she said. I'm not your Jean. Nor nothing even close.

She nodded slowly.

I know what I am to you, she said.

What are you, Jess? he whispered gently, smiling.

She flung her face round, glaring at him.

What am I? Why, I reckon I'm just your whore, Jack.

She sought for the fire with her eyes again.

And a bad whore at that, she whispered. A whore who's led you into all this.

You never led me, Jess. It was me from the first.

I encouraged you!

I'd have still sworn to do it, he cried. I'd have had to do it.

He walked over behind the bench and put his hand on her shoulder.

Jess, I'm trying to tell you I love you more than ever I loved Jean.

She waited, breathing slowly.

Or the baby? she whispered.

Her or the baby, he said.

Then I'll have to call you a liar, Jack, she whispered.

He pulled her head back against him.

How can I make you believe me, Jess?

She turned her head suddenly, looking up at him.

Shall I tell you? she said.

Yes.

Take me and Mom away, she cried passionately. And do it to-night! And leave Breedlove Mine to all the hell and ruin and disaster which my soul tells me is on its way. Ah, Christ, Jack, do!

He said nothing, though still she looked at him, and the fire blew and hissed in the stillness between them.

Please, she breathed again presently.

At that moment the door pushed open and Mother Dunne hurried in, dragged off the heavy army coat and hat and hung them on the peg. She looked at neither of them but went, almost wearily, and sat in her rocker. She sat motionless for a spell and then turned to stare gently at Farjeon. She smiled.

You're a miner now, Mister Farjeon, she said. You should have been down there this afternoon.

I passed by on my way home, Farjeon said. I seen them.

But did you hear the speeches? said the old woman. Lord, you missed some might fancy speeches.

She rocked a little, remembering it.

John L., she said, he made one of his usual talks.

Is he still down there? Farjeon said.

No.

Where is he?

He got back in his car and went back to Fairmont.

And what about Senator Hood?

Mother Dunne rocked a little faster.

Him? He made a speech too, she said.

Where is he now? Farjeon said.

The old woman looked at him.

Up at the manager's house, she said.

He didn't go away, then?

No.

Farjeon went back to the bench, sat down, leaned into the fire glow.

I've got to meet that man, he said.

He paused.

There's a thing, he went on, that maybe only he could tell me.

Mother Dunne sniffed.

And you mean to walk up to him plain-faced and ask him, Jack?

He might know.

And knowing, said the old woman, you're so sure he'd tell you?

Farjeon was silent, brooding.

Just walk up to him, the old woman went on, and say, "Senator Hood, would you kindly tell me who owns Breedlove Mine?" Is that it, Mister Farjeon?

Still Farjeon said nothing, his eyes turned with dejection toward the bright glow of coals.

Maybe, the old woman said, maybe he'll want to know why you want to know such a thing. And what then? Will you tell him then, Mister Farjeon, that it's someone you're after—to kill?

Far off on the wind a train whistle blew, somewhere to the north, beyond Glory.

And tell me this, said the old woman finally, what makes you so sure that Senator Hood would even know the name of the man?

A sneaking idea, Farjeon said.

Is that all?

He knows things, Farjeon said, many things. And he's on the side of people like us.

Farjeon looked at her.

Once in Clarksburg, he said, me and Jean, we heard him make a speech on the courthouse steps.

What did he say—I mean, to make you think he'd know? asked the old woman.

Farjeon looked back into the fire, the glowing coal.

He said he knew the name of every owner of every mill and mine in the state of West Virginia, Farjeon said. And he said he pitied them all.

Pitied the workers is more like it, said the old woman.

Farjeon cracked his knuckles slowly in the stillness.

And so, he said, I'm almost sure he knows. And I have a feeling he's going to tell me who.

Mother Dunne sighed and looked at Jessie.

And so it goes on, she said softly. Even with that only one left alive. Even with Mister Kitto and Mister Paul both dead in that black pit of hell today—still he's not satisfied.

Jessie lowered her gaze to her lap.

Mom, I tried, she whispered.

Did you, Jess? I wonder, said the old woman.

I did try, Mom, the girl said in a choked voice.

Still, you went into the mine this morning, said the old woman scornfully, to fetch him that gun. So he could go on with it.

Mom, I know! Jessie cried gently. But I'm through with all that now, Mom—all that craziness. Mom, I've been trying to talk him out of it—till you come in just now—

You went in the mine, though, said the old woman, rocking faster, and roused up fools like Bonar and Turley—who was stirred up bad enough as it was. And now there's talk that them two accidents today was caused by that, Jess. And worse talk still

—that some third accident's acoming—more dreadful than the rest. And Turley—he's sworn to kill you, Jess, if it does—and if he survives it.

She stared sorrowfully at the girl, shaking her head.

All the rage and hate he felt for Mister Farjeon, she said, now it's turned on you, poor Jess. And if such a disaster should come to pass—

You don't believe that, Mom! Jessie cried.

That there'll be another accident? said the old woman. Yes, it so happens I do. That it was caused by your going in the mine today? No, of course I don't.

She stared at Farjeon.

That windy this morning, she said, it caused a small fire that's still burning. And in a mine as gassy as Breedlove—Christ, yes, I believe there'll be a disaster.

She looked toward the window, now darkening with the sundown.

I'll say one thing for Mister Hood, she said softly, he's got sand in his craw—walking through that drift-mouth portal—going down in that place.

Why is he doing it, Mom? Jessie said.

Mother Dunne smiled.

He said he was going to do it, she said, to give the miners courage—to help them hang on till he could get legislation passed.

Farjeon got up, went into the bedroom, was gone a spell, then came out presently, dressed in his work clothes from the morning shift. Jessie stared a moment sadly, then nodded gravely to herself. Mother Dunne glanced at her.

He's off about his madness, she sighed, rocking fast. I reckon that's so, ain't it, Mister Farjeon?

Farjeon looked at her.

Time's running out, he said.

For what?

For the thing I've got to finish, he said.

He looked toward the door.

289

I've got to get to him, he said. I've got to ask him the question. Tonight.

Mother Dunne fisted one hand into the palm of the other, cracking her knuckles like a man. She raised her gaze tolerantly to Farjeon's face. After a moment she smiled wryly.

You're set on it? she said.

Farjeon glanced away, nodded.

Then, said the old woman, you'd best have me along.

Farjeon shook his head.

You've done enough already, Mom.

The old woman rose.

At least let me come along, she said, so's them two state troopers up there at the manager's house don't stop you at the threshold At least they know me. Hear me, Mister Farjeon.

Farjeon moved toward the door, not glancing round.

All right, he said.

And Jessie sat alone in the lampshine as they moved through the door and closed it behind them—Jessie musing to herself at the secret thing within herself, the unborn child within her flesh— and pondered gravely to herself, smiling, if it would change things any, even if Farjeon knew.

The bitterness of the night had softened, the air was almost warm, and snow broke and trickled in the gullies—the harshness of winter ameliorated for a spell. The old woman, trudging behind Farjeon up the road toward the house, said nothing till they were in sight of it—a hulking, Gothic shadow against the slaty, starless sky, two windows shining on the trellised porch.

Yonder, she said then, halting by the brink of an icy puddle; she pointed. Yonder on the porch.

Farjeon stared.

I see, he said.

Two of them, said Mother Dunne. And you fancy you'd have gotten past them two troopers without me along?

He sighed.

I reckon not.

She looked at his shadowy figure beside her.

Now mind, she said. It'll not do at all for you to press him for the knowledge you're seeking.

I know that, Mom.

It'll not do at all, she said, for the new manager—whoever he may be—he'll likely be setting there all along. And he'll be harking to it all. Every word. And he might suspicion your motives—

She chuckled bitterly.

—as well he might, she concluded, picking her feet mincingly across the puddle. Come along, Mister Farjeon.

He followed her then, as they approached the house, past the black silhouette of a motionless garden glider. At the sound of their footfalls in the snow of the path to the porch the troopers aroused, one swung a beam of light down upon them; a pale finger of light wiping them up and down.

Who are you?

Mother Dunne stepped brightly forward into the beam. She sheltered her eyes with her fingers, smiling.

We've come to pay our respects to the senator, she said. And to the new manager of Breedlove Mines.

One of the troopers chuckled; the light winked out. The old woman stood in the impudence of that darkness, her fingers wound round Farjeon's hand. Presently she cleared her throat.

I reckon, she said, you might have the good manners to cast that light down here so's we can find our way onto the porch.

A stillness then, and the persistence of dark, as the men pondered. Mother Dunne stepped cautiously another pace forward in the blackness; she studied the shape of one of the troopers against the curtained yellow of the window by the door.

He'll be glad to see me, she said. The senator, I mean.

She paused.

We've been friends for many's the year. 'Deed, I reckon he'd be hurt if I didn't come like this.

Something stirred within the black shadows the porch made—the faintest cry of a hinge, the whisper of a latch, and, remotely, the susurration of breathing. Mother Dunne set the tip of her shoe on the first step and flung her fingers loose from Farjeon's hand, folding her arms and glaring at the shape of the trooper by the window.

You're a large man, she observed, that's plain. You may be as big of a fool as you are a man. That remains to be seen.

She paused.

I tell you, I'm an old friend of that man inside the house, she said. Now, if you'll have the common courtesy to shine that light down here so that me and my friend—

The porch light flared on then suddenly, a single frosted globe, flyspecked and dusty with grit, beside the door. It illumined the face of the man in the doorway—a bald, flat birthmarked face set loosely upon a neck that rose thickly from a striped, white-collared shirt. He stared humorlessly at the old woman and Farjeon and pursed his lips. He nodded.

You'd be Roseanna Dunne, he said.

I am her, said the old woman. And this here—

The bald man interrupted with a trumpeting cough.

I've heard tell of you, he said then. I've only been manager of this mine a little under six hours now but I've heard tell plenty about you.

Mother Dunne met his stare levelly, impishly.

I'll bet you have, she said.

The bald man laughed then—a sound as emotionless as his cough. He fetched up a pair of steel-rimmed spectacles, fitted them over his ears and nose and stared at Mother Dunne with that same cold, unquizzical air that his tone of voice had bespoken.

My name is Janders, he said then, advancing casually to the edge of the porch. He stood at the top, staring down at first one then the other of them, then finally settling his gaze on the old woman.

Martin Janders, he said. I'm the new manager of Breedlove. I replaced Mister Paul, who—as you doubtless heard—met with an accident today.

He moved his hand at his side as if, for an instant, he had intended to advance it in a greeting, then withheld it.

And you are Roseanna Dunne, he said then. And I suppose since you're the leading agitator in this mine town I'm obliged to get to know you.

He chuckled.

You're small, he said candidly, almost childishly. You're really quite small.

Mother Dunne did not blink, waited.

And I overheard you say to these two gentlemen here, Janders went on, that you came to pay your respects to Senator Hood.

We both did, said the old woman. This here feller with me. He's Mister Farjeon. We come—

Janders waved his hand like a lawyer.

And did I hear you make the preposterous statement that you knowed the senator personally? If that's so—

I did, said the old woman, I knowed him well. I did.

And her quick blue eyes moved then, brightening, sparkling, as the white head of the senator appeared suddenly behind Janders, over his shoulder.

Roseanna, he said simply, and then edged courteously past Janders into the light. He was a tall man, stooped a little in a way that was almost scholarly, with a great wave of white hair and eyes that were as blue as ice, yet pleasantly warm. He stopped in the middle of the porch and looked down at the old woman. He turned then, abruptly, and looked at Janders by the door.

Do you have any notion how long it's been since I laid eyes on this lady, Mister Janders? Thirty years—if it's a day!

Janders watched him a twinkling, then nodded and half turned toward the door. He waved his hand at the two troopers.

293

It's all right, boys, he said.

The big man was halfway down the steps then and flung his arms round Mother Dunne, hugging her against him.

Lord, he murmured. Thirty years!

He flung a glance back at Janders.

Thirty years! he said again.

Now he held her out at arm's length, his grave eyes twinkling. Mother Dunne stared up at him, smiling.

Yes, it's been a long time, Mister Hood.

It has that, Roseanna, cried the senator, drawing her by the hand up the steps. And if Mister Janders will afford us the hospitality of his parlor, you must tell me everything that's happened to you in that space.

The old woman smiled.

Mines, she said. Sir, I could tell you in a word. Mines has happened to me.

And we'll talk about that! cried the senator. We'll talk especially about that! For it's the subject of this particular mine that brought me to this place. Come along inside, my dear. Mister Janders, you'll let me be rejoined with this old friend in your home, I trust?

Janders nodded laconically and smiled offhandedly and then gestured toward Farjeon who stood still, waiting in the snow of the path at the foot of the porch steps.

How about him?

Mother Dunne ran back and seized Farjeon's hand, pulling him up the steps, into the light. She looked up to the senator.

Mister Farjeon, Mister Hood.

The big man sized up Farjeon swiftly and then seized his hand, shaking it. Mother Dunne intervened.

He's not my son, she said. Yet for all that, he's closer than one.

She squinted a little, pursing her lips.

He has good strong reasons for wanting to meet you, sir, she said.

Then come along, come along! cried the big man. The cold snap seems over and there's a hint of spring in the air tonight but it's still too chilly to stand palavering out here. Come along inside, my friends!

The house was a large one, an old and rococo one, and the rooms were vast and somehow sprawling—it was a place of yellow light and shadows, as if the corners were spun with webs of gold and dusk. The walls of the parlor were hung with—literally clustered with—the mounted heads of creatures fallen before the ubiquitous guns of the late Manager Paul: deer and bear and moose and an elk—a somehow dilapidated and crestfallen elk, with dusty glass eyes and a cracked, varnished nose. This moth-eaten creature surveyed the room as the senator pulled chairs round the fire, at the ends of the couch, and held one of them for the old woman to seat herself. He cast one swift, uncomfortable glance at Janders who furtively tarried in the doorway to the hall, not choosing to join them, yet not letting himself get too far out of earshot. Janders stared at them then for a moment, and in that instant, as the light fell across his face, the old woman had the chance for one shy moment to study its features. She could see the birthmark plainly now: it was large—covering about half of the man's face—a stain the color of a blueprint, calicoing the flesh of one side from brow to chin. She fancied that it looked rather like a map or a chart of some sort, perhaps the definition of some island or continent upon which—judging from the harsh, sullen eyes that flanked it—some soul of this man had wandered and gone, at last, on the beach. Janders looked away, fetched a stump of stogie from his vest, scratched a match, lit it, and wandered off into the hallway. Still she could see the shadow of him; he was listening, marking well every word that might pass between the three of them there.

What can be done about this mine, Roseanna?

The old woman looked at the senator.

It could be closed, she said, till it's made safe. Or till the government decides it never can be made so—and closes it—seals it—forever.

The senator glanced swiftly at Farjeon who sat watching, listening, his own uneasy question somewhere biding in the back of his mind.

Your name is—Farshaw, sir? said the senator.

Farjeon, sir—Jack Farjeon.

Mister Farjeon, said Mother Dunne. It was he who came here the night of the company killings. It was he—

The senator held up his hand.

I know, he said.

He shook his head and stared at his folded fingers.

It was he whose wife was murdered along with the others.

He glanced at Farjeon. His gaze fixed and held, musingly.

How can you endure such a thing, Mister Farjeon? How can you survive it yourself?

Farjeon flushed and turned his gaze quickly toward the blowing fire. He said nothing.

The senator nodded, glaring at phantoms in the blaze which so held Farjeon's eyes.

Hard, he said. I'll wager it was hard. And I'll wager it was enough to make a man want to strike back.

He nodded again.

Were I in your shoes, he said presently, his voice raised a little as if somehow he did not want the company man to miss his meaning, were I in your shoes, sir, I think I'd almost be pushed toward thoughts of—

Of what? whispered Mother Dunne suddenly.

The senator looked at her gravely.

Why, of vengeance, he said. I'll grant you I'm not vengeful by nature, but a crime like this—against people not really even involved in the mine dispute itself—it would almost drive me to that.

He glanced at Farjeon.

But I suppose—instead of that—you'll organize, Mister Far-jeon.

Farjeon still did not look at him.

I have some plans, he said. I have some notions I'm working out, sir.

To organize?

No, Farjeon said, letting it go at that.

He scowled faintly, remotely, as if moving his mind and will toward a moment he had long attended. Presently he cleared his throat and swung his gaze quickly to the older man.

My plans, he said, they involve you, Senator Hood, sir.

They do?

Yes sir.

How can I help? Name it.

Perhaps, Farjeon said, *you* could name it for me.

The old man tilted his face, thoughtful, puzzled.

Name what, sir?

Perhaps, Farjeon said, you could name me the one who owns this mine.

Nobody spoke for a spell then. The wind, already tempered with the first softness of winter's death and spring's oncoming, set itself against the carved Gothic lace upon the eaves; the fire blew and guttered in the grate, and in the hallway the shadow of the company man halted in the middle of a gesture and held its breath, listening.

Tut, said the old woman, suddenly uneasy, what would make you fancy, Jack, that Mister Hood would know such a thing?

The warm blue eyes of the old man held Farjeon's face in a long instant of thoughtful regard. Presently he smiled and glanced toward the long, hushed shadow of the company man which fell across the width of old, arabesqued carpet in the doorway. He looked back at Farjeon again.

Perhaps, he said, this is not the time or place for such a question, Mister Farjeon.

Farjeon nodded and looked back into the fire.

Perhaps, said the senator, this is not the occasion for such exchanges.

He bent suddenly and gestured with one long pale finger toward the shadow of Janders. And Farjeon and the old woman looked and saw it and a sudden chill of uneasiness seemed suddenly to have fallen between them. Mother Dunne laughed an abrupt, soft sound and glanced toward the shadow again. Then she bent suddenly and touched the old man's knee.

The years, she said, they have dealt gently with you, Mister Hood.

He nodded, glaring now into the blaze, absorbed, and suddenly angered as if at something he had said or done, angered perhaps at some circumstance of events in which he now found himself. And he seemed not to have heard her friendly comment. Yet presently he nodded, acknowledging her.

And yet, he said suddenly, softly, they sometimes—the years—find me in the presence of people not altogether friendly, Roseanna.

Recklessly Farjeon turned his eyes again to the old man.

Would you tell me if you knew? he said softly.

The old man pondered a moment, then closed his eyes and nodded.

You're an honest man, he said. I sense that plainly in you. And I know you'd not be close to Roseanna if you weren't, Mister Farjeon.

Farjeon waited.

But you'd not tell me, he said, despite that.

The old man sighed and bowed his face.

Not here, he whispered, his face suddenly grave and sorrowful.

He glanced suddenly at Mother Dunne.

Roseanna, he said.

Yes sir.

Roseanna, perhaps you'd like to show me where you live, he said softly, carefully.

Mother Dunne glanced at the shadow again, then back at the senator, her eyes bright with acknowledgment of whatever it was he was trying to tell her. But it was not merely a shadow now, it was the figure of the company man in the doorway, his scarred, wet eyes fixed on Farjeon.

Don't go, he said quietly, smiling.

I reckon we'd better, said the old woman, rising. The both of us. Mister Hood he's got a big day tomorrow.

No, said Janders, moving into the light. It's such an interesting question.

Not really, said the old woman, restlessly gesturing for Farjeon to join her. Mister Farjeon here—he was just making small talk.

Janders took the chewed stogie out of his mouth and stared at its wetness.

No miner, he said thoughtfully, who has suffered such a loss as that man yonder makes small talk.

He looked at the senator.

You're here, sir, he said, to investigate this mine town. Maybe the first lesson you ought to learn is the breed and shape of the class of people who live and work here.

What do you mean? said the senator.

I mean what I say, Janders went on, his flat eyes fixed on Farjeon. For a man such as that miner yonder—who has a grudge to settle. For him to ask such a question.

The senator closed his eyes carefully and clasped his knees.

You're making a supposition, Mister Janders, he said. Mister Farjeon merely asked me—

He asked you who owned the mine, Janders said suddenly. It's not hard to figure why he'd like to know such a thing. A man who fancies some hurt against those he loves—a thing that happened accidentally one night, with no malice against him or his woman. Senator, you were a lawyer once. It shouldn't take no diagrams to tell you what a man of this class would want to know such a thing for. If—

That's your own fancy, Mister Janders, said the old man quietly.

299

Fancy, is it? said Janders, walking toward Farjeon by the fireside. It's not fancy to someone who's lived amongst men of this class for thirty-two years.

The senator suddenly stood and faced Janders, his blue eyes bright with anger.

Mister Janders, I am your guest in this house, he said, and these are my friends.

Janders nodded.

Acknowledged, he said. My guest. A guest, I might add, unbidden. A guest who has come here, too, with prejudice in his mind ahead of time to make a so-called investigation of conditions. A guest from Washington who—like most of the people there these days—is prejudiced against management.

The senator nodded.

And do you fancy your attitude here is improving that image, sir?

Janders shut his eyes, shook his head.

I've got a job to do, he said. Part of my job is to manage this mine. The other part is to keep my eyes and ears open. To the schemings and plottings of men like that one yonder.

He opened his eyes, staring at Farjeon.

I've worked in mine towns as manager, he said, places where a question such as that man yonder asked would be enough to get him arrested and jailed.

For merely asking? That's absurd.

Janders shook his head.

You've got to consider the circumstances, he said. This man fancies some wrong has been done against him. To the mind of men like that—

Some wrong? interjected the senator hotly. Merely the murder of his wife. And because he asks a question like that you presuppose that he plots vengeance.

A manager, Janders said, he's got to be careful. Especially in times like these. Especially—with all due respect, sir, to your position—in times when Washington is full of radicals and communists.

Are you calling me a communist, Mister Janders?

And at that the flat, dark eyes in the stained face softened and retreated a pace.

I meant no such innuendo, he said. I mean that you're just not real sympathetic to the prosperity of mines such as this one here at Breedlove.

The senator nodded quickly and sat back in the chair.

Mister Janders, I've come to this mine seeking the truth, he said. That is all. I want to know what provoked the massacre of five people one night last month in this place—including the murder of the wife of Mister Farjeon here. I speak frankly now. The guards seem to be down between us. I've made no secret of legislation I plan in Congress to enact fresh mine-safety laws—to close down mines that are beyond help, if need be. Including this one. I propose to press for the prosecution of men who are responsible for massacres like the one in which Mister Farjeon's wife was killed.

But him, said Janders a little more gently, he wants to take the law into his own hands. That's plain enough. If—

Plain to whom? Because he asked me who owns Breedlove Mine you presuppose a plot in that man's mind. Not that I would entirely blame him.

Well, one thing, it's plain to see whose side you're on, Senator Hood. Before you even investigate anything. You hardly set foot in this place before—

I'm on no side, sir, said the old man quietly. I'm a lawyer, one who's seeking a role of guilt in this place. I do not abide violence of any sort. Not from Mister Farjeon, who's given no real evidence of any. Not from this company—or any company like it. And I assure you, sir, there are many. Yes, there are many. That, sir, is why I am here.

Janders smiled at Farjeon.

I'm deputized, you know, he said, by the sheriff of this county. I could make an arrest right now if—

On what charge?

On suspicion of conspiracy, Janders said. I've done it a lot of times.

That's interesting news, said the senator. That shall go into my report.

It don't matter, Janders said. You—you're already prejudiced. In his favor. The mere fact of him coming here to see you. With her—a known radical, an agitator for at least thirty years or more. Him—a man whose wife was killed. Accidentally. But that don't matter to the minds of his sort. Accidentally. I repeat it. On a night when company property was being lawfully protected against the depredations of—

Then arrest him, said the senator softly. Arrest and arraign him. And my law firm in Washington will defend him. Free of charge. And the result of that trial—which should be a short one, even in this rigged county—will go into my report to Congress on the management of this mine.

Janders face flushed so dark that the birthmark almost disappeared. He stared again at Farjeon.

You people in Washington, he said, you don't have no idea how tough a job like mine can be.

The senator kept his gaze on the manager's face.

Even if you so much as fire him, he went on. That, too, will go into the report.

Janders faltered and stared at the rug.

It was only, he said, a suspicion. When a man like that asks such a question— You boys in Washington, you ain't got no idea what it means to manage a mine. If you'd worked in a few, the way I have for more than thirty years—

My report, said the senator, already includes the history of a few mines you've managed, Mister Janders.

Janders gestured weakly toward Mother Dunne.

Maybe if he wasn't with her I wouldn't have suspicioned the

302

way I done, he said. Her, a known troublemaker for more than thirty years—

My friend, said the senator, for longer than that.

He gestured toward the old woman.

Come along, Roseanna—Mister Farjeon, he said. I want to visit your home. I want to see the kind of place you live in. I want to see a little more of the truth of this place than the truth I've seen tonight. And I want to speak to you—

He glanced suddenly at Janders who stood again now by the doorway.

I want to speak to you, Roseanna, he said, with an edge to his voice. I want to talk with you—a little more privately.

He laid his hand on the old woman's shoulder.

Come show me your home, he said.

Farjeon, shaken by the encounter with Janders, was silent now, feeling afresh his sense of outrage at the web which seemed to wrap itself inexorably round himself, round all of them, in that stricken village. He stared a moment longer at the senator, then at Janders, and then with a bitter smile moved past them all and, closing the door behind him, set off down the porch steps toward the road. Janders was standing on the porch staring after Farjeon's retreating figure as Mother Dunne and the senator came out. The old man turned to the two state troopers.

You boys can wait here. I'll be all right, he said. I'm going to take this lady home.

We've got orders, sir, said the older of the two.

It'll be all right, said the old man.

He turned to the old woman who stood watching him with a furrow of curiosity on her brow.

How far is it, Roseanna?

A quarter of a mile, she said.

The senator turned to the men again, smiled, and shrugged.

Follow if you want to, he said, but stay a piece behind us. This lady and I wish to speak privately.

Janders watched them, his face in the curious light of the porch lamp like a stained kerchief set with two malignant jewels. He smiled.

Be careful, he said.

Of whom? said the old man.

Janders shrugged.

A man never knows, he said. Not even an important man like you.

He pitched the dead stogie into the darkness and set his hard gaze on the senator again.

A place like this, I mean, he said teeming with men set on violence.

The old man reflected, then smiled and looked at Mother Dunne.

I think, he said, I know the face of my enemies.

Janders shrugged and turned to the door again, pushing it open. He looked back at them.

I'll leave the porch lights on, he said, in case you have any trouble finding your way back, Senator Hood.

Thank you, Mister Janders. I appreciate your thoughtfulness.

For a moment they were all still, poised, as if in some set tableau. Then Janders closed the door, his shadow diminishing against the curtained glass, and the senator took Mother Dunne's hand.

Come along, Roseanna, he said. Show me the way.

Mother Dunne was silent for a long spell as they made their way down the thawing, snow-scarred slope to the road, hearing in their wake the stolid trudge of the two state troopers. At last Mother Dunne could hold her curiosity no longer. She paused and turned to look at the shadowy shapes of the two officers, then she turned her gaze to the old man. She laughed uncomfortably.

Are you so afraid of us? she said softly.

There was a wisp of moon, a silvered blade that shone at the edge of ragged winter clouds as if it had cut them aside. The senator smiled, seized her hand and moved off down the slope, urging her along. A mild wind stirred against their faces.

I was afraid you'd think that, he said.

The old woman shrugged.

What else should I think? she said softly. You come among us here with two policeman guarding you.

The old man shook his head.

I'm not afraid of you, he said. I told that man back there that I knew the face of my enemies. Well, I know the face of my friends too.

Still she reflected, puzzled and vaguely aware of some new, fresh fear. Her gaze sought his face, faintly lit by the dusk of new moonshine.

I figured, she said, that maybe you'd caught the fear from the rest of them, like a fever—all the talk of us in this poor place—of all the violent, dangerous radicals like they call us. The terrible things we do.

She paused and stared down at the silhouette of the tipple to the east of them, below the hill.

I figured maybe you'd heard, she said, what some of us did to a man down there. That night. Caught him and crucified him on those timbers.

The senator laughed softly.

Myself and a few others, he said, we may be crucified ourselves. Before we're done with this investigation. That and the legislation that it may set in motion.

He chuckled again.

Crucified, he said. Perhaps not so literally. But crucified just as effectively. Still, my dear friend, I do not fear it at the hands of one of you.

Then them two policemen you brought along—?

He turned, paused, and laid his hands on the old woman's shoulders.

Roseanna, he said, there have been two attempts on my life already. One in Fairmont last week. Another a few blocks from the mine union office in Charleston a week before that.

He shook his head.

Roseanna, it was not miners who tried to kill me.

The old woman felt the wind against her face, a wind faintly warm with the promise of winter's end. And yet she shivered and the fear in her heart was close to sadness.

They're after you too, she said.

The old man squeezed her hand.

Roseanna, listen to me, he said. You live in this black pit of a place. You feel that your grief and fear and danger are somehow isolated, unique. You think that this place—this Breedlove Mine and its town—is something that exists nowhere else in the state— in the land. You forget that there are perhaps hundreds of places like this set in misery and desolation throughout these Appalachians.

Christ, said the old woman. I know we're not so different—

Do you? said the old man gently. I wonder. You've lived and suffered here so many years. You forget that the company that owns this mine owns twenty-four more like it—and worse. And that other companies own other mines. And they are all united together like one vast, dark brotherhood—united to keep things as they are—profits as they are—conditions as they are—forever.

He shook his head, smiling down at her.

Do you fancy they will stand by and let an old man like me come meddling amidst that black empire?—perhaps to set it tottering and threatening it with the specter of social change?

Mother Dunne flung angrily loose from his hand, glaring about her at the moonlit hills, scarred with dark slag piles.

They wouldn't dare! she whispered furiously.

The old man shook his head.

They have dared, he said. They have dared twice.

She turned and stared up at him.

To kill a man of your importance? she whispered.

He said nothing; he stood looking sorrowfully at the string of shacks scattered along the hillside which they now approached.

You live up yonder? he said softly.

But still she could not shake her mind loose from the fresh outrage he had wakened in her. Then she flung herself round to face him, all that rage drowned now in sudden fear for him.

You shouldn't have come here! she gasped softly.

He smiled and squeezed her shoulders in his big hands.

Roseanna, he said, I have to *see*. I have to know the face of what I'm fighting. I have to witness it—firsthand.

She shook her head, cold with fear for him.

I could tell you, she said. Me and others like me—

Roseanna, I know of no one like you, he said gently.

But there are! she cried. I know there are! You could call us to Washington. Or even Wheeling. And we could tell you!

He shook his head, urging her on up the road toward the dark necklace of glittering shacks.

I want to know, he said. I want to feel and smell and see. I want to know how you live. I want to walk in the corridors where your men have to work. I want the whole sense of it.

You're more brave, she said in a wave of fresh anger, than you are sensible.

It's more than that, he said.

She waited, listening, dreading, feeling more hopeless somehow than she had felt in years.

Yes, it's more than that, he said. You see, Roseanna, the President is about to push through a bill called the NIRA. This spring. Once it's passed, the gates to the miner's union will be wide open. And that means the companies will begin a more subtle campaign of terror. More subtle—but perhaps more violent. And men like these men here in Breedlove—they'll want the feeling that they are not alone.

She turned and looked at him sorrowfully.

And you mean to go into that mine tomorrow morning? she asked.

He squeezed her arm.

It'll be all right, Roseanna, he said.

She flung her arm free.

But it's not all right! she cried softly. That mine—it's a death-trap, Mister Hood!

I've heard tell, he said.

And you risk your life tomorrow morning by going down there?

Men do it every day, he said quietly. You know that better than I.

But you!

I'm an example, he said. I'm someone who shows those miners they aren't alone. And believe me, Roseanna, in the months that lie ahead they don't dare stand alone. They need proof that they have a friend. They'll want to remember my example.

But you risk everything!

All life's a risk, he said.

He shook his head stubbornly.

And besides, he said, I want to see. To smell. To feel. All of it. Before my fight begins. And I want the miners to know I'm really with them.

Mother Dunne shivered, trying to stifle fresh fancies in her mind.

They might—, she said.

Might what, my dear?

They might even arrange an accident, she said in a whisper. The company might. An accident to you, to put an end to all of this—

And then, before he could answer, they saw the shape of Far-jeon on the road, below the shack, alone and desolate in the warm wind, watching them approach.

Yonder is your friend, Roseanna, said the old man.

And it was then that she turned again, seizing him by the hands and drawing him close to her.

Yes, she said. And hark to me! He's going to ask you again.

Ask me what?

What he asked you back there at the company man's house, she whispered. He's going to ask you—

Who owns Breedlove Mine, said the senator smiling faintly. I know he will.

Then listen to me! she cried softly. And do this thing for me.

What, Roseanna?

Don't tell him.

He smiled, his grave blue eyes searching her face.

All right, he said.

She held his eyes a moment more.

Ain't you going to ask why? she whispered.

He shook his head, drawing her closer to Farjeon who stood behind the warm wind in the puddling snow of the road below the shacks.

No, he said, I'm not going to ask you why. Because I think I already know.

Yet Farjeon did not wait; when he saw them he ran toward them, pulling up pale and breathless before them on the road.

Mind now, whispered the old woman, you promised.

Farjeon seemed heedless of her. He stared at the senator, and in that instant both of them saw the glint of the gun in his hand.

I have a question to ask you, sir, he whispered.

Yes, Mister Farjeon.

Farjeon gestured toward the figures of the two state troopers some twenty feet behind them down the road.

Can you trust those two? he whispered.

What do you mean?

I mean what I say, Farjeon said. Are you sure them two cops ain't in the company hire?

Sure, said the senator. Yes, I'm sure.

Good, said Farjeon. Then you'll need them.

Mother Dunne stepped round to face him.

Jack, what are you trying to say?

Farjeon's face was furious.

Coming down the road a while back, he said. Ahead of you.

309

Before the moon come out. It was dark. They never seen me coming. The ground is thawing and my feet made no sound. I heard them. Then I seen their shadows.

Who? said the senator softly.

Two men, Farjeon said. Not miners.

Where?

Hiding down yonder behind that tool shack you come past not a minute ago. Two of them. Not miners, I tell you. And I could hear them talking.

He glanced anxiously toward the two state troopers who were coming closer now.

Are you sure? he whispered. Can you count on them two? Maybe the company—it owns them too.

The senator smiled and shook his head gently.

I'm sure, he said. Yes, I'm sure of them.

He glanced thoughtfully, sadly, toward the shadows the moon shaped in patterns of darkness and light among the hills and slopes that stretched below the road, above the tipple.

You overheard these men speaking? he asked softly.

Yes.

What were they saying?

Farjeon glanced down at the revolver in his hand, stared at it a moment as if trying to remember its original purpose.

What did they say, Jack? whispered the old woman.

Farjeon looked at her with a queer smile on his face.

They said something about a night in Charleston, he said, and another in Fairmont.

Go on, said the old man quietly.

They said this time it would be different, said Farjeon, because this time it was going to look like an accident. And they said this time it wouldn't miss.

When? whispered the old woman.

Tomorrow morning, Farjeon whispered. But I never heard them say where. Or how.

The two troopers drew close then, saw the gun in Farjeon's

hand and sprang toward him, drawing their own revolvers. The senator swiftly intervened.

Wait, boys, he said, it's all right. These are my friends.

He sighed and turned his gaze gently toward Mother Dunne.

Perhaps, Roseanna, he said slowly, perhaps I'll have to look at your home another time.

He looked with a weary smile at the officers.

These men and I have to be getting back to Mister Janders' house.

Mother Dunne stared up into his face in futile, anguished silence. He smiled gently at her. Then he glanced at his watch, still smiling.

I mean we'd all better try to get a couple of hours of sleep, the old man said before he led the way back up the road again. It's only four hours till I take my tour of Breedlove Mine with the deadman's shift.

In a moment his tall figure, flanked by the two officers, had disappeared up the road. Jessie came down aways, then stood alone, staring after Farjeon who had gone off now too—gone the other way, on the road toward Mexico. Farjeon had no words for either Jessie or the old woman now—he was too full of the memory of the voices he had heard in the shadows, and he was full, too, of a whispering sense that one of those voices was a voice he had thought long dead. And so he was going to that one place where, if it was who he thought, the man would, most likely, show his face that night.

Cotter stared through the dust of moonlight at the sallow-faced dynamiter named Jim Pullman. He frowned, shaking his head.

Listen, Cotter said, quit your complaining. I know we come here early—

He glared at the dynamiter.

This ain't no penny-ante game tonight, he said. This time it's got to work. And it's got to look right.

Pullman glared at his nickel-plated watch in the dim light.

It's nigh seven hours, he said. That's a long time to hang around like this.

Listen, Cotter snapped, what kind of job did you two guys ever have before that paid two hundred dollars apiece? Answer me that? I tell you this job, it ain't no penny-ante game. This is the big time. This ain't no contract to bust open a few Hunkie heads. This is a U. S. senator.

Pullman spat into the shadows.

We could have shot him on the road there an hour back, he said. He was a pigeon. I don't see why this contract has to be so complicated.

Janders and the others, Cotter snapped. He already explained you that. What do you reckon we hired *you* for—a specialist? It's got to be an accident.

Pullman shivered, staring at the wisp of moon.

I don't like it, he said. I never done a job in a coal mine before. I never even *been* in a coal mine before.

That, said Cotter, is why we begin early—get into the mine early—get the lay of things—find the right place—the perfect place.

He glared at Pullman.

What do you think you're getting two hundred dollars for? he whispered. All that money. You never seen that much money before. Not for a job. Any job. And you're complaining about a little cold. Besides, it ain't cold.

He turned his face to the gentle wind.

Hell, I can smell spring in the air, he said. It ain't cold.

I only wish, Pullman said suddenly, Mister Janders, he'd done what he promised us he'd do when first we laid all this out, when he give us our deposit.

You mean get us a miner who'd help? Cotter said.

Pullman nodded bitterly.

You mind he promised us, he said, when we first laid all this out.

Cotter shook his head.

312

I done asked him about that, he said, last night at the hotel. He said he couldn't find a one. Not a one that he'd even dare whisper to about a thing this big. He said if he'd been manager a while longer he might have. But not for this. It was too late for this. He said he hadn't been around here long enough to know who's who amongst the miners.

Pullman grumbled.

I never believed him anyway, he said. The miners is all behind that damned Jew Bolshevik a hundred percent anyways.

Cotter grunted.

I know what you mean, he said. Though Hood—he ain't no Jew. He might as well be one, though. I know what you mean.

He shivered a little. He glanced toward the far, moonlit brow of the hill where the road rose suddenly and disappeared.

Wonder how late that nigger keeps open?

The saloonkeeper, you mean?

Yes.

Not late, I'll wager. These miners likely keeps early hours.

Cotter stirred languidly.

I could use a little sniff, he said. A snort. Maybe two.

He reflected.

Maybe, he said, he'll sell us a bottle. I'm a man who likes a little snort or two before a job.

Pullman spat again.

We could be setting up there, he said. We could be waiting up in that place the nigger runs. The saloon. Not hunkering down here in the shadows.

Cotter shook his head.

Janders—he told us to be careful, he said. He'd be sore if he knowed we'd even been there for as short a spell as we was.

He looked at the dynamiter.

Remember, he said, this ain't my first job in this place. I been here before. I've got to be careful no one recognizes me.

He eased his scarred arm, still aching faintly in the damp air, shifting the sling gently round it. He stared up the hill again.

A bottle, he said. Maybe he'll sell me a bottle. Then we can get past the watchman and into the mine. And do our seven hours wait in style.

Pullman scraped his shoes in the thawing earth.

I only wish, he said, I only wish we had one of them along with us. A miner. A fink miner.

He glared sullenly up at the faint dark string of shacks along the hillside.

Surely, he said, somewhere amongst all them stiffs there's one that Janders could have got us. One amongst them all. I only wish Janders had kept his word. We could sure use a man who knows his way around that mine.

He kicked a piece of coal loose from the thawing earth.

I'd feel a lot easier, he said. For I ain't never done a job in a mine before. Not this mine nor any other. I tell you, I'd feel a lot easier with one of them stiffs along.

Cotter moved resolutely, shifting his arm painfully, and glancing up and down both ways along the deserted road, before he beckoned the man to follow him.

Come on, he said.

Where to?

Up to the nigger's place, Cotter said. Ten dollars ought to get us a bottle. Sure. That's all we need right now. Then we can get past that watchman and start figuring things out. In the mine. In the place where the job's to take place.

He turned his face into the faint wind again, smiling.

I can smell it, he said. I can fairly smell it.

Smell what? Pullman asked glumly.

Spring acoming, Cotter said pleasantly. I can fairly smell it in the night air.

He suddenly forgot about his wounded arm, striding briskly ahead of the dynamiter up the sodden road.

It's the kind of weather, he observed more to himself than to them, when it's really a pleasure to set out on a job. Spring acoming. You know what I mean? Really a pleasure.

314

Along the road to Mexico, against the hill, in that checkered and fragmentary darkness and moonlight, the dogwood blossoms, awakened in that past day's respite, shone like shy, white chards of cheap, shattered china. The single window of the Negro Toby's bar glowed ruddy as a scarlet stain against the black cutout of the stark façade of the frame building. At the threshold, lugging the scarred, brown valise of his trade, the dynamiter paused, rested his burden on the ground and looked at Cotter again, still uneasy. He shuffled his feet, shook his head.

Cotter, I tell you I don't like this, he said.

Don't like what?

Why, I don't like showing ourselves in yonder, Pullman said.

Why? What can happen?

Well, what if one of them miners in there yonder—supposin he was to suspicion something?

Cotter snorted disdainfully.

And what? he breathed. I'm asking you, what will he do? Go down and report us to Janders?

Well, I know all about that but—

Report us to Janders? Cotter said again. And what do you reckon would happen to him then?

Cotter turned, spat cynically, and let his gaze range the huddled miserable valley that stretched outward from the distant black tipple.

Tonight, he said, we're safe from the law in this place. Because this place—it *is* the law. The Breedlove Company—it owns the Glory law. And what it don't own is owned by the Mine Syndicate itself.

Pullman tugged at his thin nose and followed Cotter's stare.

Just the same, he observed, I somehow wisht it was all over and done with.

Cotter lowered his good hand and fetched from his shirt a nickel-plated watch. He studied it in the faint moonlight.

Two-forty, he said softly. The old man goes in the mine with the morning shift at four. That's less than two hours.

He put his watch back and struck Pullman lightly on the shoulder, chuckling.

By four-thirty, he said, we'll be on our way into Glory. To the hotel. To collect the rest of our money. The job will be long over. Then we rest easy till daylight—and catch the sunrise milk train on our way west.

Pullman grunted, staring at the door against which Cotter's hand rested.

Another thing, he said.

What?

It's just that I wisht Mister Janders had kept his word, Pullman said.

About what?

About giving us one of the Breedlove miners we could trust, Pullman said. One who'd help us.

Cotter nodded.

The night ain't over, he said. There's two hours yet.

He shook his head.

Still, I'd not count on that, he said presently. I misdoubt that he will.

He said he would.

I know, Cotter said. But these here miners is a bunch that hangs together like snakes in winter. You don't often find a sellout. Still, the night ain't over—

He grinned at the dynamiter, chucking him on the shoulder again.

And supposing he don't? he said softly. We'll get along. There's complications to this job, I'll grant ye. Still and all, it's simple. Really.

Pullman shook his head silently, his face downcast. Cotter scowled.

Pull yourself together, Jimmy, he said softly. What do you reckon they're paying you two hundred bucks for?—a simple factory job? Christamighty! This is big business, Jimmy. A U.S. senator. You don't appear to understand that. A U. S. senator. Not the penny-ante, half-assed shop steward of some goddamned steel workers' local. This is the big time, Jimmy. And more jobs— maybe bigger jobs—if this one goes smooth.

He opened the door an inch and breathed in a wisp of close air laced with raw liquor fumes.

Come on, he said, I need some reenforcement.

He pushed ahead of the dynamiter through the doorway, into the dusky room. He glanced casually around. The scarred brass lamp shone on its chain from the ceiling, dragging shadows from the chamber's dark corners like a web. The place was deserted— or was it? The sprawl of shadows to the rear, where the few tables were, was a checkering of darknesses and inference of shapes. Cotter swept his gaze arrogantly away from that uncertainty and looked at the bar. He licked his thin lips and eased the hurting arm gently in its sling. He stared at the Negro, dozing in his rickety chair atilt against the frame back wall, and strode to the bar, striking it sharply with the flat of his good hand. Toby started and stared at the two men, then eased painfully to his feet. Cotter stared at his white, watching eyes.

How much is a bottle, nigger?

Toby stared a moment, his face furrowed suddenly.

I ain't never sold no bottle, he said presently. Not a whole bottle. Nobody round this place never had no money for no bottle.

He studied Cotter's face a while longer.

A whole bottle?

That's what I said.

Toby smiled, shook his head.

Drinks, he said, they sells for twenty cents. Scrip money.

I'll pay cash, Cotter said. Green money. Not scrip.

Toby struggled to suppress a yawn, he blinked sleepily.

I never stayed open this late since I been working here, he said. Never once. Mister Janders, he said to stay open all night tonight. He say certain strangers was acoming—

How much Cotter said, for that fresh bottle yonder on the shelf?

317

Toby turned, his eyes agleam with possibilities. He stared at the fresh bottle of clear, pale moonshine on the shelf.

I don't rightly know, he said. Mister Janders never told me nothing about no whole bottle. He say certain strangers was acoming. Strangers who likes to drink. He say stay open all night. Even payday night we never stays open past ten.

Green money, Cotter said again irritably. How much?

And still Toby hesitated, his face struggling with the vain effort to comprehend such extravagance. Cotter walked suddenly round the bar, grasped the fresh bottle by the neck, held it up, shook it, eyeing the bead in the neck, then thrust it into the pocket of his army coat. Then he fetched a roll of bills from his clothes, lifted it, peeled off a ragged five-dollar bill with his teeth and turned, staring at Toby, the green money dangling from his smile. He stood a moment, dangling the money teasingly, close to the Negro's face. Then suddenly his jaws began to work, he gathered the banknote into his mouth, chewing it into a moist wad. After a moment he seized the Negro by the wrist, pulled out his hand and spat the wad into his palm.

That's more green money than you'll ever see again in this place, nigger, he said.

He grinned, fetching the bottle back out of his coat and setting it sharply on the bar.

Now fetch us two glasses, he said.

Toby pocketed the money, wiped his hand on his sleeve and got the glasses from the shelf, setting them before Cotter and the dynamiter.

Toby smiled uneasily, watching the two men.

Mister Janders, he said again, he say never mind the miners tonight. He say keep open late. For certain strangers.

Cotter nodded, pulled the cork with his teeth.

Well, we're them certain strangers, he said.

He poured two drinks, then turned, a brimming shot glass in his fingers, and set his gaze again into the web of shadows in the room's recesses. He could not be certain—it might be the shape of a man—a witness who might one day say he had seen them there. But what did it matter? In the morning—in less than two hours—it would be over. By sunrise he and the dynamiter would be on the milk train on their way to Cincinnati, and from there on west to fresh jobs for his new employer, in the rich strikebreaking fields of the Minnesota iron ranges. Besides, he reckoned, he had been to this place of fools before—he had done his work—he had come back—he would leave it safely again. He turned back arrogantly to the bar and stared round at the dynamiter who stood staring down glumly at his untouched drink.

Whatsawrong with you, Jimmy?

Pullman shook his head, held out his hand, stared at it till it was steady, then seized the shot and tossed it down. Cotter nudged him.

That's the ticket, he said.

Pullman gasped, then shook his head again. He looked round at Cotter with watering eyes.

I'll be all right directly, he said.

Well, why shouldn't you be, Jimmy?

Pullman braced himself, grasped the bottle, poured himself half a shot. He looked at Cotter with a rueful grin.

It's just that I ain't never been in a coal mine before, he said suddenly again. I tell you, it's got me a mite uneasy, Cotter. I always done my job in streets—in factories. I never even seen the inside of a coal mine. Ifn we just had one of them with us—to show us around—to get the lay of it—Mister Janders, he promised us yesterday in the hotel room in Wheeling—

I explained you that, Cotter said irritably. Maybe he will and maybe he won't. The night ain't over.

He pondered it.

I say it's better if he don't, he went on. The fewer of us involved in this contract the better. Meanwhile Mister Janders and them other five gentlemen from the Syndicate—they explained us about where it's to happen—how it's to happen—the way it will look afterwards.

He patted his army coat, feeling his chest with his good hand.

In here, he said, I got the map they give us. The map of the mine. It shows us the place we'll go in—the place we'll make it happen from. It's a setup, I tell you. We don't even have to get past no night watchman. Nothing. It's a setup. I tell you, Jimmy, it's the easiest two hundred bucks you ever earned.

Pullman stared at the half drink he had poured, seized it suddenly and downed it. He shivered and knuckled the tears away from his eyes. He looked at Cotter and grinned.

I feel better, he said. Somewhat better.

You should, Cotter said. I tell you, this is the easiest job you ever signed up for, Jimmy.

Pullman shook his head violently.

I signed nothing, he said. I'd not put my name to no piece of paper. Not even a check. Not for this—a contract to hit a man as big as this. I mean, a U.S. senator—

Cotter shook his head, grinning.

I was speaking figuratively, he said. The easiest job you ever shook hands over. And for the big money—

Pullman shrugged his shoulders.

I got as much as a hundred once, he said. Last fall it was. For that truck we blowed up outside Monongah Heat and Light. At Fairmont. That Hunkie shop steward. What was his name? I disremember. Still and all, a U. S. of A. senator—

Twice a hundred dollars, Cotter said cheerfully. And half the danger. Because there's no law here. Not in this place. No law that ain't the company—or the Mine Syndicate. And that job in Fairmont last fall—it was the law of a labor administration. One hundred percent. You was lucky you got away with a penny of that hundred, Jimmy. Whereas here—in this goddamned place—who's to bother you? Around about four this morning—when we blow that charge—when that ceiling comes down on this party

we've signed up to hit —and afterwards we head out of here—
He grinned.

Who's to get in our way? Who's to stop us? By noon we'll be on
that high iron riding a coach west to—

He paused then, half turning, fancying that he had heard the
scrape of a chair behind him, a sound of faint whispering
movement from somewhere amid that checkering of shadows
where the tables were. He smiled to himself. No, it had been his
fancy. And what if it was—? Then he heard it again, plainer now,
and stared and saw the vague, tall shape behind the darkness,
beyond the circle of yellow from the scarred, gleaming lamp on its
chain above the floor.

Hello there, Cotter, Farjeon said.

And still Cotter stared, and Pullman held his breath as Cotter
fumbled with his good right hand, freeing the revolver from his
clothes and aiming it steadily at the man in the shadows. Then
Farjeon moved, striding easily, familiarly, into the circle of lampshine. He stood in the spotlight it cast, staring pleasantly at the
two at the bar.

Hello, Cotter, he said again softly. Maybe you don't remember
me.

Cotter stared a moment, his jaw fell, then he uttered one
pleased choke of laughter and stuffed the gun back into his
clothes.

Big Boy! he cried. Christamighty, it's Big Boy—the man from
Wheeling!

He turned and hammered Pullman's shoulder with his good
arm.

Jimmy, feast your eyes on who stands yonder! he cried. It's Big
Boy!

He shot his face forward, staring again, reaffirming it.

Christ—ain't it? Christ, it *is!*

He stared with mute delight for a moment. And then—for a
twinkling—his face clouded as an instant of suspicion crossed it;

he considered this, dismissed it as swiftly as it had come and then —with a twist of a smile—he strode forward into the circle of lampshine.

It is! It is! he cried again, his right hand on Farjeon's shoulder. Big Boy—it's Big Boy, Jimmy—the noble I hired on that day in Wheeling—the very one! Sure it is! It's Big Boy—the one who saved my life outside the mill in Benwood. Big Boy, meet Jimmy Pullman—

He turned suddenly and studied Farjeon's face again with that cloud of caution shadowing his gaze, his mouth still twisted in a faint grin.

Who sent you to find us? he said softly.

Farjeon smiled quickly.

Mister Janders, he said quickly. He told me—

What's the job? Cotter whispered.

Why, to get the old man, Farjeon said and then paused, gambling swiftly in his head. In the mine, he added then. In the morning.

Cotter studied him quietly for another instant, then smiled broadly and clapped him again on the shoulder. He glanced round at Pullman who was watching Farjeon's face in silence.

See, Jimmy? Cotter said. I told you Mister Janders was all right. See? He sent us a man. And he couldn't have picked a better one!

He stared suddenly at Farjeon's face.

I mind how close it was, he said, when they come through the window that day in Wheeling. They almost got you too, Big Boy.

He laughed.

Christ, I never seen a man move so fast, he went on. Jimmy, you should have seen it. I was just about to introduce this feller to Mister Shaloo when these two stiffs come through the window— commenced firing—killed Mister Shaloo dead on the spot— winged me in this blamed shoulder of mine—and then took out after Big Boy yonder.

He searched Farjeon's face admiringly.

It was close, wasn't it, Big Boy?

Farjeon grinned.

Too close, he said.

He fixed Cotter's eyes in a steady gaze.

Lucky for me, he said, I was able to kill one of them.

I read about it! Cotter said. Mister, you're all right. You shot one of them through the head in that empty store. And then got away.

He studied Farjeon again, smiling thoughtfully.

I can't tell you how many times I thought about you, he said, since then. Wondering where you was—what you was doing—how I could meet up with you again. Big Boy, I sized you up pretty good that morning in the gutter outside the mill.

He turned and looked at Pullman who still watched in silence.

Jimmy, he cried softly, Mister Shaloo, he used to say there never was a man like me—aside from himself—who could size up a good man quicker! A born noble!—I knowed that about this feller the minute I seen him in action! And now we got him on this job.

He searched Farjeon's face with pleasure.

Whatcha been doin since then, Big Boy?

Farjeon glanced casually aside.

Working, he said, amongst these stiffs. Here in the mine.

What else?

Farjeon met his stare again.

Making my reports, he said, to Kitto and Paul—till they was killed today. Keeping track of any new union stir. Keeping an eye on things. Watching out for any new, radical moves—talk—

He smiled.

And now, he said, now I work for Mister Janders. Still keeping my ears open. Till tonight.

He looked at Pullman who still watched him, unsmiling, cautious. He turned back to Cotter.

No heavy work, he said. Not like that day in Benwood. And now, tonight. I'm glad for a chance at a little fresh heavy work.

Cotter nodded.

It's heavy enough, he said. The big time. No Hunkie heads to bust open tonight, Big Boy. No—this job this morning—it's the big time. Ain't that right, Jimmy?

Pullman stirred faintly, still staring at Farjeon, then nodded, turned away. Cotter drew him back round to face him.

Whatsawrong, Jimmy? he said.

Pullman looked at him, then spat on the floor, still silent.

Jimmy, whatsawrong? Cotter said softly. You don't think Big Boy here—?

I think nothing, Pullman said. I only got your word for it that he's—

Jimmy, you're suspicioning that Big Boy here—

I'm suspicioning nothing, Pullman said soberly. We come to this place. For a job—a big job. And suddenly he shows up—a miner—

Well, what of it? Janders he promised us a miner—a fink who'd help us.

I know that, Pullman said. He did. I heard him. But how do we know that this one here—?

Jimmy, I know this man, Cotter said. I been with him. On a job before. I hired him on. I seen him in action. He done saved my life, I tell you. And that day in Wheeling he killed his man. That's a matter of record. Now, how can you suspicion—?

I suspicion nothing, Pullman said. Nor no one. I'm just saying that on a job this big we gotta be sure. Take no chances.

Cotter looked at Farjeon.

Don't mind, Big Boy, he said. Don't pay no mind to Jimmy here. He just ain't used to the big time yet. I reckon that's it. Come on now, Jimmy. Mister Janders, he promised us a miner. Now here he is. What could be simpler than that?

Pullman nodded.

Maybe that's it, he said. Maybe it's too simple.

Cotter frowned.

Well, what do you want to do, Jimmy? he said sourly. Go back up to Mister Janders' house with Big Boy here—rouse him up out of sleep and ask him if this is our man? Maybe take a chance of—

I say that ain't such of a bad idee, Pullman said.

—maybe take a chance, Cotter went on swiftly, of waking the old man up. He's nervous already—or should be. Maybe make him even more nervous—make him call off the trip into the mine at four A.M.—spoil the whole scheme? Christ, it's less than two hours! Jimmy, listen, what—?

Pullman eyed the scuffed valise which stood by the bar where he had left it. Cotter pulled him round to face him, smiling, sharing in the fantasy for a moment.

Jimmy, listen, he went on. What could Big Boy here do if he wasn't all right? Which he is. I'll swear to it. I tell you I know him already. But still—just supposing your suspicion was right—supposing he was a wrongo—what would he do? Make a citizen's arrest? Haul us up to them two state troopers? How far do you reckon that would go? What else could he maybe do?

He eyed Farjeon lightly, with that same queer smile on his face.

What else could he do? he said. Maybe kill us?

Farjeon met his stare steadily. Cotter still smiled.

Maybe, he said presently, if it'll make Jimmy here a little bit easier—

What? Farjeon said softly.

Cotter shrugged.

I know you got a gun, he said. I can see the weight of it in your pocket yonder. Besides—

He nodded.

I helped you get that gun, he said softly. Remember, Big Boy?

Farjeon nodded, struggling to keep his face from showing anything he was feeling. Cotter still watched him.

Now, supposing Jimmy here was right, he said. Supposing you was a wrongo. Supposing—

He nodded.

—supposing you was to pull out that gun, he said, and kill us right here at the nigger's bar.

325

He cocked his head, his face alive with the fantasy.

What would that change? he said, smiling at the joke of it, the gun from his own coat now held idly, pointing at Farjeon's stomach. What would that change? he said again. The nigger would run tell Mister Janders. Unless you killed him too. What would be different? It would just change the time the old man got hit, that's all. It wouldn't be in the mine—an hour or so from now. It would be up at Janders' house—in fifteen minutes. That way, of course, wouldn't be as good—it wouldn't be no accident. But still—

He smiled.

Maybe, Big Boy, he said softly, if it will make Jimmy here a little easier in his mind—

Farjeon stared down a bare moment at the gun held so idly, so jokingly, with its muzzle toward his stomach. Presently he glanced up, feeling Cotter's gaze on him, grave now, the gun held steadier. And then, without a quiver of emotion, Farjeon fetched the revolver from his pocket and tossed it on the bar by Cotter's elbow. Cotter pocketed both guns, smiled, and slapped Farjeon on the shoulder.

Mind now! he exclaimed brightly. It wasn't me, Big Boy! I *know* you. I trust you too. It's Jimmy here. Jimmy, he was nervous about you. Jimmy's a dynamiter, Big Boy. And we can't have no nervous dynamiter on a job this big.

Farjeon forced a smile. He stared at Pullman who still eyed him uneasily. A moment passed. Then Farjeon turned his smile round to Cotter.

Now why don't you do the rest of it, Cotter? he said easily.

Cotter smiled.

Like what?

Farjeon shrugged, keeping his gaze steady.

Why don't you do like Jimmy here said? he whispered.

What's that, Big Boy?

Take me up to Mister Janders' house, Farjeon said easily. Rouse him out of bed, face me with him, and find out for sure.

I'm sure, Cotter said. Big Boy, I'm sure—

326

You pulled a gun on me, Farjeon said. You took mine from me.

Cotter chuckled.

That wasn't for me, he said lightly, that was for Jimmy here. Jimmy was nervous. He suspicioned that you—

It's like you said, Farjeon interrupted. On a job this big it don't pay to have nobody nervous—suspicious.

Cotter did not move.

Take me up to Janders, Farjeon said again. Why don't you, Cotter?

Still Cotter did not move. For a long spell—like he was studying a poker hand—he stared at Farjeon in the crooked light.

If you was a wrongo, he said softly after a while, you'd not have gambled on that, would you, Big Boy? The chance that maybe I'd call your bluff?

He stared a moment longer, his wits still toying with the fantasy, then he shook his head and struck Farjeon amiably on the shoulder.

Well, I'm a gambler too, Big Boy, he said, and I'm betting on you. Jimmy, get shut of them notions, will you? It's late. We only got about an hour before we hit. And we've got to get into the mine and set things up.

He fumbled inside his jacket and presently fetched out the Breedlove Mine chart, staring over it at Farjeon.

Mister Janders, he said, he didn't go into de-tails with you, did he, Big Boy?

Farjeon stared at him feeling the vast, aching emptiness of the pocket where the gun had been. He shook his head.

There wasn't time, he said. Mister Janders said you'd be here at the saloon. He said to come here and wait for you. He said you'd show up—the way you did.

He shook his head again.

There wasn't time to explain much, he said. Mister Janders said you'd explain it—the de-tails—and I'd help—inside the mine.

Cotter nodded.

Come yonder into the light at the bar, he said, with the chart in his good hand. Come yonder and I'll show you how we make our move. Come along, Jimmy. Stop standing back there in the lamp-shine with your face hanging down.

Cotter wrapped his arm round Farjeon's shoulder and hugged him. He stared close into Farjeon's face.

Don't pay no mind to what I done, he said. The gun and all that shit. That was for Jimmy's sake.

He shook his head, close to Farjeon's face.

Don't pay no mind to Jimmy, he said softly into Farjeon's cheek, his mouth so close that Farjeon could smell the rich reek of the raw booze on his breath. Cotter hugged him again, almost sensually now. He stared at Farjeon's profile.

Besides, he said again, besides—even if Jimmy yonder hadda been right—which he surely ain't!—what if you *was* a wrongo, Big Boy?

He chuckled, his breath still rich in Farjeon's nose.

Supposing you'd come here to kill us, he went on, his wits playing once more with the rich fantasy of it. Which you *didn't!* But supposing you had. And then went running to save the old man. Running where? To the law? What law could you run to in this place, where all the law is us? Eh, Big Boy?

He stood back and stared fondly, almost sorrowfully, at Farjeon.

But that's all bullshit, he said. I know that. Even Jimmy yonder —he knows that.

He laughed, staring back at Pullman.

Pulling that gun off you, Big Boy, he said, that was just for Jimmy's sake. I know who you are. You done proved yourself to me. All that gun bullshit—that was purely for Jimmy yonder. Now—let's get down to it, Big Boy.

His yellow fingers spread the company chart on the bar before them and he pointed with the cracked nail of one long, stained finger.

Here, he said, through the place that's marked here. The old mine portal—a mile and a quarter south of the tipple. Here's where we go in—

He glanced round, half irritably, at Pullman who had come up softly and now stood grinning sheepishly at Farjeon's back. Pullman snuffled and stared down at his valise.

I'm real sorry, he said. I never meant nothing wrong, Cotter—nor nothing to you neither, stranger.

Cotter reached round with his good arm and dragged Pullman close against himself and Farjeon before the chart on the bar.

It's okay, Jimmy, he said. It's all okay now. Everything is gonna be fine. Let's go over it now. Once more. It's little more than an hour till we hit. Let's go over it for Big Boy here. It's gonna be fine, I tell you. How can it help being fine with Big Boy here to help!

The night was warm now, and on the road, as he walked behind them, Farjeon could hear the thaw and trickle of winter in the gullies. Without the gun it seemed to him now as if his hand was played out; he was as much a captive of them now as the senator himself. There was less than an hour now. And yet it seemed to him that time itself might be his ally. Yes, even though there was less than an hour before the thing was set to happen, it seemed to him that somehow—even this late—chance might still intervene. Even with the vision of the hated man in the army coat trudging up the wet road ahead of him, the old dream of vengeance seemed far from his thoughts. He could think now only of saving the old man's life. It was as if, by surviving that night's conspiracy, the senator might—through law—bring about a vengeance more perfect than any Farjeon could have wrought—a full accounting brought about on the highest levels. He let his thoughts wander back to the moments in the saloon when he still had the gun. What should he have done? No, Cotter was right. Even if he had gunned them both down, there was still the Negro

329

Toby; and if he had killed him too, the conspiracy would know of that and change their plan—the conspiracy that seemed to wrap itself round that whole, dark place like a web.

Yonder, Cotter whispered sharply in the moonlight, pointing to a dark brace of timbers surrounding the abandoned mine portal, from which rusting tracks stretched for a few hundred feet onto the crumbling structure of the old tipple. He strode forward, the chart in his hand.

Sure, he said softly. This is it. Come on, boys.

The plan that Cotter had outlined in the saloon was now clear in Farjeon's mind—deathly and vivid in its simplicity. He followed the two men to the mine portal, his mind suddenly racing with the possibility that he might somehow yet forestall them and that plan by frightening them of the plan's danger to themselves. Cotter turned in the moonlight, gesturing toward Farjeon.

Come on, Big Boy, he said softly. Here's where you come in. Lead the way.

Farjeon stared at him.

You know the danger, he said. An old mine like that—

Cotter nodded.

Mister Janders, he said, he done told us about that. Sure. There's risks to every job. That's what you're along for.

Farjeon looked at Pullman who was staring now uneasily at Cotter. Farjeon shrugged.

What good is it having me along? he said. I can't guarantee there'll not be a cave-in.

Cotter shook his head.

Mister Janders, he said, he told us he'd had men from the Mine Syndicate in yonder yesterday afternoon. He swore it was safe.

Janders, said Farjeon, is a fool.

Pullman put his valise on the rough, melting earth and shook his head. He looked at Cotter.

Cotter, I don't like this, he said. The more I think about it the less I like it.

Cotter scowled.

Two hundred dollars, he said, for a simple job like this. A big job—but a simple one. That's what you're getting paid for this, Jimmy. Two hundred. And you start whimpering now about risks. I know there's risks but—

Pullman shook his head, staring at the dark portal.

I ain't never done a job, he said, in no mine before.

Cotter nodded.

That's what we got Big Boy here for, he said, to show us our way around. Come on, Jimmy.

He stuffed his watch back in his pocket after a brief glance at it in the moonlight.

Come on now. In half an hour it'll be all over and done with. We'll be out of here and on our way to Glory.

Farjeon's wits still played with the game of frightening them, of delaying the plan somehow till he could think of something better. And now it seemed to him as if he should ease up on that game some and let them fol'ow the mine into the place marked on the chart and set the charge and hope that in that interim chance or his own wit would intervene. He watched as Pullman opened the valise, squatting above it in the moonlight's dusky shine, and fetched out the miner's caps with their carbide lamps. He looked up at Cotter.

There's only two, he said. We wasn't sure there'd be no third man.

Cotter waved his hand.

You take one, Jimmy, he said. Big Boy he'll be leading the way —give him the other one. I can see enough by the light of both of you.

Pullman shook his head, glancing round uneasily. Cotter cocked his head, listening a moment, then laughed softly, fetching matches from his coat pocket to light the lamps. In the windy distances a dog commenced a far frenetic barking—a drifting, lonely sound in the mild air. Farjeon moved on into the black recesses of the passageway, following the beam of light from his heavy cap. Before his feet he could hear the hiss and skitter of rats scattering before the sound of approaching steps. He saw his own shadow before him, cast by the lamp in Pullman's cap a few yards behind him. Cotter hummed a soft, tuneless chant under his breath. Farjeon's jaws ached, his teeth bitten hard together, his chest aching with the effort to suppress a sob of sheer frustration as he led the way into the hushed, black passageway.

It shouldn't be far now, Cotter said somewhere in the echoing passage behind him. The chart, it shows we're to come in about a quarter of a mile.

It's near, Farjeon said glumly.

He glanced round him for side passages, thinking somehow that he could mislead them, divert the plan for a spell. Until what? The inevitability of what was coming lay heavy on his mind. The passage led straight to the end of the old tunnel, to the spot in an abandoned room where already a glimmer of light shone out from the room beyond—the room where, the morning before, Link and Tar had died in the fall. In the musty, shadowed chamber Farjeon stopped and watched the weaving pattern which Pullman's light made on the ribs and floor behind him. With a sigh of pleasure Cotter fell to his knees and set his eye to the break in the rib. He squinted a spell, breathing softly, chuckling vaguely to himself, then turned in the shadows and motioned for Pullman, his voice a whisper.

Yonder, he said. Neat as we could ask for.

Farjeon stood, the sweat on his face mingling with sudden tears of frustration. Pullman grumbled and knelt beside Cotter, the beam of his cap light falling on the large hole.

Yonder, Cotter whispered, is the place where them two miners was killed yesterday. It's a place the old man will ask to see. Looky, Jimmy. Put your eye here and look round. Be careful that cap-light beam don't shine through. There's a shift working somewhere in there yonder.

Farjeon remembered now, the morning before, they had broken through into the old mine in which they now were. He remembered, too, the remainder of the ceiling in that room—the coal and slate roof that had not yet fallen, still hanging by a hair above the frail posts near the spot where Tar and Link had died. Yes, it was so—it was a place the old man would ask to see. He stared blindly at the beam of light his cap light cast on the rib before him, hoping it would not illumine the tears on his cheeks. He choked back a sob and listened as Cotter knelt by Pullman; Farjeon watched as they took out the single thin, yellow stick of dynamite, the short length of wire, the detonator. Cotter stared at the single stick and laughed softly again.

Not much more than a firecracker, he said. Jimmy, I bet you never done a job before with just one stick.

Pullman had set his eye to the break and was surveying the job quietly, professionally. He nodded, his light weaving.

The hole, he said, it's big enough for one of us to crawl through. And set that one stick where it will do the job.

He nodded.

I figure, he said, if we set it under that one big post yonder— that's the one that seems to be holding up most of the ceiling.

He turned his head, the beam of light weaving.

One stick, he said presently. Still I judge it's enough.

He grinned.

I can see the dust sifting from that ceiling, he said. It's hanging there by a hair—the way Mister Janders and them other gentlemen said it was. One stick under that post. Hell, yes. It'll bring the whole thing down on him.

He glanced round at the ceiling, at the posts that braced the old passage they were in.

Looks safe enough for us in here, he said.

Cotter uncorked the bottle, and Farjeon could hear him swallowing in the shadows. He coughed.

Remotely—a sound so faint as to seem but a whisper—they

333

could hear the distant cry of the whistle from the Breedlove tipple. Cotter coughed again and fumbled his watch out into the shadows.

Turn your cap light down here, Jimmy, he said. I want to check the time.

He studied the face of the watch in the beam of light from the dynamiter's safety hat.

Four A.M., he said. Right on the button. That means he should be entering the mine now. That gives us—

He stuffed the watch back in his pocket.

—that gives us just enough time, he said, for you, Jimmy, to crawl through that hole yonder, into the room, and set the charge.

Pullman sighed. He stared through the hole again at the light bulbs which lit the black room beyond, the shifting dust from the dark ceiling, the glittering ribs, the post which was his objective. He sighed again and put his face to the hole, searching for any sign of human life, of any straggling miner from the departing night shift who might be there to glimpse him as he came through. He paused a moment, then thrust himself through, crawling swiftly through the yellow light beyond, with the dynamite and the wire in his hand.

And Farjeon said nothing, thinking to himself, At least they may die with him, if the charge—as it may—brings the roof down on us in here. That would be, at least, a justice. We may all die in this—and he smiled sadly, thinking that perhaps he deserved that death in some strange way even more than they did. For he had tried—and he had failed—and that failure lay heavy on his mind and soul. Yet still, his wits told him as they raced on with the burden of this reflection, still, maybe, somehow, at the moment before Pullman pressed down on the detonator Farjeon might fling himself through the hole, shouting some warning to the senator, crying out that warning in time for the old man to recognize the danger and not enter the room. The bleak possibilities of what might happen if he failed in his timing of this move—even the prospect of what might then be done to the old man—these fairly sickened him with misgivings. Pullman and Cotter both squatted by the gleaming aperture, watching the deserted room beyond. Pullman sniffed and pulled his nose. He chuckled, glancing at Cotter.

'Deed, Cotter, he said softly, this whole job looks a lot easier than I figured.

Cotter said nothing.

All we need do now, he said, is wait. Watch and wait.

He glanced back at the detonator under Pullman's hands.

You sure everything is set? he whispered.

The dynamiter nodded, and spat nervously.

All set, he said, and ready to go.

He glanced at Cotter again, his profile illumined by the yellow shine from the hole beside which they crouched.

In a way, he said, we could have done this whole job alone.

Cotter chuckled again.

I know that, he said. I knowed that all along.

He glanced round at Farjeon's figure, huddled back against the rib, his face shadowed beneath the bar of light from his cap.

No hard feelings, Big Boy, he said softly.

Pullman nudged Cotter. That's what I mean, he said softly. We could have done without him all along. Your friend yonder.

Cotter nodded.

I know that, he said. But then, in another way, we couldn't.

The dynamiter stared at Cotter's amused face. He shook his head.

What'd we bring him along for, Cotter? he said.

In the hush that followed Farjeon heard, remotely, the faint hubbub of approaching voices. He tensed as Cotter walked slowly toward him, his shadow made long along the black floor by the light from the open hole.

There was just something too easy about all of it, Big Boy, Cotter said softly, pleasantly. Mind you—

335

He paused.

Mind you, he went on, I ain't accusing you. Still and all—

He shook his head.

Something too easy, he said. The way you showed up tonight in that nigger's saloon.

He nodded.

That's why I made sure, he said, you didn't have that gun on you.

What are you accusing me of? Farjeon said softly.

Cotter chuckled.

Nothing, he said, nothing I can really put my finger on. Just a feeling maybe. A place like this. A far place from that hotel in Wheeling—a long time from that morning. And the way you showed up in that saloon—tonight.

He shook his head again.

Are we still friends? he said pleasantly. I sure hope so. I owe you a lot. I know that. You saved my life that day in the Benwood gutter—outside the mill—no denying that. No denying it at all. Still and all—

Farjeon laughed, tensing, keeping his eye on the aperture, the stark yellow glare beyond the hole. The voices beyond the room ebbed and went, like a faint flow of wind song from somewhere above them, beyond them, beyond the wall.

Then why? Farjeon said. Why—if you suspicioned me—if you thought I'd come along to try and stop you—why didn't you take me up to Mister Janders?

Cotter was silent, smiling, weighing it all.

There might be something Mister Janders don't know, he said. He might think you're his man—and maybe you are—I'm not saying different. I'm not accusing you.

You could have taken me to Janders, Farjeon said again stubbornly.

The voices were more distinct now: the murmur of admiring miners following somewhere in the senator's wake and, clear and

336

distinct, the ring of the troopers' footfalls on the black floor of the far passageway. Cotter shook his head again.

There wasn't no time to check you out with Janders, he said. And I wasn't sure—

He shook his head at Farjeon, smiling oddly.

I still ain't sure, he said. It's a feeling—a hunch in my bones. The way you showed up at the nigger's tonight—so neat and timely. So I taken away your gun. Just to be sure. A job this big—a man has to be sure.

Farjeon nodded.

If you suspicioned me, he said, why didn't you just kill me back there on the road?

Cotter tilted his head, still smiling.

I don't suspicion you, he said. But I don't know neither. Besides —you saved my life once. I owe you for that. And so—

He hesitated.

—so I brung you along with us, he said. I figured you couldn't do no harm if you was along with us. And when it's all done and over with—

He nodded.

—when it's all over and done with, he went on, and I'm positive about you—the way I was that day in Wheeling—I'll give you back your gun, Big Boy.

He chuckled.

I mind what a fuss you went through to get that gun. And maybe—afterwards—I'll shake your hand again.

He wiped his mouth nervously with his hand, glancing at Pullman, poised by the hole with the detonator.

I'll even tell you I'm sorry, he said, for what I'm about to do—

A stir now in the passage beyond the room where the charge was set, and the dynamiter turned and motioned for silence, his other hand on the detonator.

Hush, he whispered sharply. I think that's them yonder—acoming towards the room!

337

Cotter strode quickly to Farjeon's side, the gun in his fist, held by the barrel. He stooped. Then, with a single gesture, he rested the gun in his sling, snatched off Farjeon's safety hat, flung it aside into the gob, seized the gun again and swung it at Farjeon's head. The blow caught Farjeon a glancing impact on the neck as he swung aside, grappling for Cotter's legs, spilling him backward across the old rails and scrambling desperately across the ties toward the crouched figure of Pullman, squatting ready above the detonator, his hands on the plunger.

Hood, go back! Farjeon shouted in one full-throated cry, and in that instant his vision printed sharp as silver upon his mind the double image of Pullman's downthrust upon the plunger and, in the portal to the room beyond, in the brilliant flash of the blast, the tall man standing in the archway, his high face startled and searching, his blue eyes flashing beneath the shock of rich, white hair. In the cinematic flicker and flash of images after that sharp-etched double vision Farjeon would never be certain afterward, in times of remembering it, which of them came first. The senator stood a few paces into the doomed, creaking chamber at the instant of the blast of Pullman's dynamite. Beyond him, in the portal to the passage, Farjeon could see the two state troopers and, behind them, shone the stunned, startled faces of a dozen miners. The dynamite blast had made a small coughing sound in the stillness, and in the moment after, the post tottered and fell. Yet still, incredibly, capricious as the earth itself, the ceiling held. Cotter cursed somewhere behind him as Farjeon scrambled through the aperture and into the room, stood up in the rain of coal dust from the groaning ceiling and flung himself forward toward the old man. In a corner of his eye he could see that the blast had ignited the coal dust which lay, thick as fur, on the floor beneath his feet —it flashed and flickered now, spreading in a swift ring of fire toward the portal. Cotter cursed again and fired a single shot over Farjeon's shoulder as he staggered swiftly through the falling dust toward the senator. In the haze of glittering black dust the light bulbs were haloed, and Farjeon could see the two troopers who had their own guns out now, each firing a single shot through the obscurity of smoke and dust at the stumbling figure of the old man.

This way! Farjeon screamed, dragging the senator across the burning floor toward the place from which he had come. He thought of Cotter behind him in that place, armed and deadly, and yet it seemed somehow the only place where any chance was left. Yet what chance was there! He saw the burn of the troopers' revolvers again through the dust, though the sounds of their shots were obscured by the rumble of the working, rippling ceiling. He turned in the choking dust, his grip firmly on the old man's jacket, dragging him toward and through the portal. Over his shoulder, in a flickering glimpse, he saw vaguely the shape of the two troopers, fixed and frozen and doomed, as the chamber itself seemed suddenly to breathe out in one swift, hot exhalation and the ceiling buckled and fell upon them with a long, thunderous roar. Now Farjeon faced Cotter in the dim, cloudy confusion beyond the portal. Cotter fired aimlessly at a shadow amid the swirling dust and cried out something indistinguishable. Distantly, remotely, in his wake, Farjeon could hear the shouts of the fleeing miners. And then—in the moment after—when the mine itself exploded, ignited at last by the racing rimfire of the burning coal dust, Farjeon fell forward, hurled thither by a stunning impact of hot wind. And for a spell he could not remember, could not think of anything. He lay now in a mist, in a dream darker than the nightmare from which he had fled. In that dream, beyond consciousness, vague thunders ebbed and flowed like the murmur of remote oceans. He lay as if in a cup of darkness, heeding no hint of that tumult in the distance, of the ultimate disaster which had overtaken them all, hunter and the hunted, innocent and murderer alike. And then for a spell he lay as if asleep in the big bed, at home, in the house, where Jessie—murmuring something kind —sat nearby. When he woke, at long last, in the darkness of that chamber of the old mine beyond the disaster, that black, glittering room lit now only by the single finger of light from some dead

339

man's cap, his fingers were still gripped tight and aching round the scruff of the hunted man's jacket. In the mine behind him he could hear the roar of burning, the screams of men, and the thud of fresh explosions of gas and dust. But all that tumult was not so loud that he could not sense—from somewhere in the darkness to the left of him—the whisper of a living voice.

Yet Farjeon's first instinct was toward escape. It was a feeling that overwhelmed any other feeling. He could sense, from the closeness of the air, that a good deal of the ceiling of the old tunnel they had entered by had been collapsed by the earth-shaking disaster in the new mine beyond them. Farjeon clambered through the dusty rubble toward that single finger of light from the lamp of the dead man's cap—or was it his own, still lying where Cotter had flung it aside before he attacked him? Farjeon reached down and fetched the cap up and then, feeling stickiness on his fingers, turned the light down and saw what was left of the dead Pullman's head, caught beneath the fall of one of the old beams. The metal hat was dented but the cap light shone on, as if in curious immortality, and Farjeon cast its beam swiftly round the chamber, searching for some possible channel of escape. Again he heard the sharp sibilance of that human whisper, and now it seemed suddenly like two voices, not one, yet Farjeon still paid no heed to the sound, casting the beam of light desperately up and down through the dusty, smoking air toward the collapsed debris in the tunnel through which they had come. For a moment he could scarely breathe for terror that there was now no escape left, and the sudden thought came to him that the disaster in the new mine—those fires which glowed now, like an open furnace door through the aperture through which he had rescued the old man—this inferno beyond that wall, would burn its way through presently, to consume him at last, even in this brief chamber of safety.

Flinging aside the lighted cap, Farjeon fell forward, digging his fingers into the heaped debris in the tunnel, clawing into it until he could feel his nails begin to break against it. He turned at last, breathing hard, sensing in his nose now the curling, nauseating reek of the burning coal from the mine beyond, and reached for the lamp again. He knew, somewhere among his scrambled senses, that panic now would only more certainly condemn him to death in that place: it was a fix that wanted wit and thought and cautious reasoning. He held the beam of the cap light aimlessly against a shattered rib for a moment, seeing nothing, feeling nothing but his fear, all thoughts of the senator or of Cotter—all fantasies of Jessie or the lost Jean, all these and all notions of his squandered dreams of vengeance—all far from his thoughts. He lay back against the sharp mound of litter and he could feel nothing but the small, insect trickle of cold sweat down the small of his back; the chamber was already warming from the heat of the fires beyond the aperture.

Farjeon shut his eyes against the ruddy shimmer of that lighted break in the wall. He choked back a sob. And for an instant, in the prison of his lidded eyes, he could see the sky. For a spell the image, the very notion of the sky absorbed him completely. Christ, had he ever loved the sky enough? He clenched his eyes still tighter shut as if he feared that image might escape from between his squinting lids, and his heart grew faint as his fancy dreamed its way upward through the tons of earth and coal and slate that lay between him and his sky. Yes, it was personal now—it was *his* sky, a very private possession, as his mind and fancy schemed upward like an uncaged bird through that vast and wombing weight of earth. The sky: its concept filled his brain. He thought shamefully of mornings of his life when he had looked up and cursed that sky—merely because it was hot, or cloudy, or dark, or cold—or perhaps only because it mirrored somehow his smallness there on the earth beneath it. Farjeon knew suddenly— he swore an oath on it—that if ever he were to see that sky again —any sort of sky—he would never disdain it. He would look upward, he knew, forever now, with utter worship at any sort of bird, even the plainest sparrow. He felt thirsty suddenly, and suddenly in that parched, dusty chamber his mind seized upon the sensation of snowflakes melting on his mouth, and together now rain and snow seemed to him among earth's most treasured things. And suddenly, almost with peace, there came across his mind that he would still, somehow, survive this trap he was in, that he would escape. And with that thought there flooded back into his thoughts the memory of some responsibility he had undertaken somewhere back in the maze of time behind him, and he remembered again, at the very instant when he heard that human whisper again, the image of the old man. He snatched up the light, darting its beams swiftly round through the dusty litter of fallen debris. The light beam found a face at last, fixed upon it as Farjeon stared. But it was the face of Cotter—a drained, suffering mask that stared at Farjeon's shadow from beneath a heap of timber and slate. Cotter's mouth struggled, then he grinned.

It ain't no use, Big Boy, he whispered. We're done for. Where's Pullman?

He's dead, Farjeon said.

And he stared at Cotter's pained, silent mouth for a moment and still he heard the whisper again and Cotter was not making the sound. Farjeon swung the light again, up and down the room until the beam found the shape of the old man. He was lying back against a rib, his chest and hips free, but with a beam fallen across his legs above the knees. Farjeon kept the light on the quiet, thoughtful blue eyes as he scrambled toward him. The senator smiled.

Who is that? he whispered.

It's me, Farjeon answered, Jack Farjeon.

The old man laughed softly and tried to reach out to touch Farjeon's face.

Thank you, he said softly.

For what, sir?

342

The old man squinted at his shadow behind the light.

For my life, he said. I reckon I owe you that.

He squinted again, grimacing slightly from the pain in his legs.

It seems they went to great lengths, he said, to kill me in there.

His blue eyes filled suddenly with tears.

I guess, he said, I was a fool. I guess I trusted too many men.
Yes, I guess that's so.

Well, it don't matter now, Cotter laughed. We're all done for
now.

Farjeon said nothing, shook his head to and fro in the smoky
air, his eyes tight shut. Because he felt now that it must not end
here, in this tomb of smoke and flickering shadow.

No, Cotter said again, in a clear, high voice, we're done for
now. All of us.

Farjeon turned in the air which grew momentarily hotter as the
fire beyond burned through the wall between them and the holo-
caust. He crept to the barricade of slate and timbers that blocked
the tunnel they had come through. The smoke stung his eyes as he
pressed his face closer, searching swiftly with the small beam of
light. And now it seemed his heart quickened as a breath of cool
air, small as a ribbon seemed to wind against his face. He began
to tug and pull at the timbers, dragging them away, breaking his
nails on the heavy pieces of coal and slate. A few moments more
and it seemed there would be a way. Cotter laughed fatalistically
in the shadows, a sound that was half a groan.

I'll never know about you, Big Boy, he said. I'll never know the
whole truth of you. That day in Wheeling. This morning in here. I
reckon I'll die never knowing—and yet—

He breathed painfully.

In a way, he said, we're even.

Farjeon listened as he strove and dug his fingers into the gradu-
ally diminishing barrier; he felt the cool air stronger now against
his face.

In a way, Cotter said again, painfully, we're even. You saved my life that day—in the gutter—outside the mill. And tonight—when I suspicioned you—I could have shot you to be safe. And I didn't.

He groaned again.

Funny, he said, I always liked you, Big Boy.

He hesitated, gathering strength.

Now I reckon I'll never know, he said. Maybe it don't matter. We'll just call it even.

No, Farjeon thought, it is not even. For now each of them, each human being of them in that doomed pit of smoke and approaching fire, each of them seemed curiously of special preciousness. He could not name it, he could not set his mind's finger upon just what he felt about them. The fate which wrapped round them there now, all three of them, it was a brothering thing. And now the last of the hate which had so bound his life and action in the past few weeks was fallen away from his spirit. He dug on, listening to Cotter who spoke now as if in a fever of anguish and shock.

Old man? cried the man in the army coat in that high, tormented voice. Old man? Did we miss you tonight?

He chuckled.

Sooner or later, he went on, me—or men like me—we'll win against your kind. You know that, don't you?

He uttered another soft cry, half laugh, half sob.

You and your communist kind, he said, you'll not win—in the end—you know that, don't ye?

And Farjeon strove on, his eyes watching as the smoke in the room was drawn and moved by the freshening, widening current of air which flowed now against him from the break he was making in the barricade. He clenched his eyes and gritted his teeth, setting every ounce of his energy against the final, great slab of slate which blocked the way. Fresh heat pressed against the air behind him now as flames licked through the aperture, igniting in small places the wall of old coal in the rib around it. And he felt somehow as if he were removing things which had pressed down long upon his own soul and mind. The commonness of what had happened to the three of them in that place, the brothering threat to them, made him strive and heave more savagely against that last great door of all. Cotter had fallen silent for a spell, now he raved in shrill, keening patches of delirium.

Big Boy! he chanted. Big Boy, look yonder—they done killed Mister Shaloo. And they got me now too, Big Boy. Lord, I'm done for. Big Boy, run for the window—run!

Now the way was open and Farjeon scrambled back quickly to the old man's side, setting his strength now against the timber which lay heavily across his legs.

Easy now, he whispered, half choking in the thickening smoke, easy now—we'll be out in a minute.

The old man made no sound as Farjeon gathered him up at last into his arms and bore him slowly, crouching as he carried him in his careful, cradling grip, toward the break he had made in the collapsed rubble of the tunnel to safety.

And even in the stillness of the fresh air beyond the old mine's portal, as he laid him down in the grass he threw back his own head, filling his parched lungs with blessed air, seeing as he opened his eyes then, the sky—the infinity of sharp, spring stars he thought he would never see again, and framed within them, a spray of dogwood flowering up from the coal-strewn earth. The senator studied Farjeon's face in the dim light.

That man in yonder, he said presently, he's one of the ones—

Who tried to kill you? Yes, Farjeon said, gathering his fainting strength for the one last effort of all.

What else is he? said the old man.

What do you mean?

Something I sensed, said the senator, in what he said—that he'd known you before.

Farjeon nodded.

Did you save his life once?

Yes.

But he seems to think of you in riddles, smiled the old man. What's the rest of it?

345

I saved his life, Farjeon said, in order to be able to take it.

Why? smiled the old man.

Farjeon said nothing.

Does it have to do with what you asked me last night—about who owned the mine? asked the old man.

Farjeon looked away, silent. The senator watched him with a faint smile.

Do you still want to know? he asked then. Who owns the mine? Perhaps you even fancied that I own it? I do not. Do you still want to know who does?

Farjeon looked back at him, the most wistful of smiles on his lips. He shook his head.

No.

Why not?

Because, Farjeon said, it don't matter to me anymore.

The senator gently, thoughtfully, closed his eyes.

Farjeon turned his face now toward the old mine portal, from which fresh smoke now drifted. And mingled with the sound of fresh blasts from somewhere beneath the earth, in the deeps of the new mine, came now the sound of Cotter's high, anguished voice ribboning out its words in fearful, indistinguishable delirium. The senator nodded as Farjeon eased his shoulders back against the dried winter grass. He watched as Farjeon stripped out of his coat and laid it across him. The old man nodded again.

You're going to save that man's life again, he said quietly. That's so—isn't it? You're going back there?

Farjeon turned his face away, silent.

That's so, isn't it?

Farjeon shook his face, as if to free it from the last strands of some ancient doubt which had long shrouded his mind.

Yes, I am, he said.

The old man smiled.

Are you saving his life for the same reason now? he said. So you can take it again?

Farjeon stared at the old man's face, then looked away at the sky again, then back at the smoking portal.

No, he said.

Then why? smiled the senator.

Farjeon stared at him, scowling, studying the question,—some part of him, perhaps, still wondering why himself. Then he was half sobbing, seeing the old man's face in a blur of quick tears.

Because he's in the mine! he cried out then, on his way, his legs aching from his recent struggle to escape, yet finding in his body fresh strength as he staggered toward the portal. Because he's in the mine! he shouted again. In the mine—the way *we* was! Because he's a man in a mine!

And then he was gone into the thickening smoke, leaving the old man alone, staring now at the sky and the cheap, bright chards of dogwood against it, pondering human questions far vaster than that sky or that blossom, and smiling to himself as he lay there staring and knowing that he was left with the fragments of that riddle whose answer he was never meant to know.

In the stillness of the hour when dawn paled at last in the windows Jessie sat on the edge of the bed looking down at Farjeon's smoke-stained face. He was insatiable with questions, his eyes still fevered with anxiety.

But the senator—? he whispered.

Safe, Jessie said softly. They taken him off to Glendale Hospital. The state police, they come—just a spell after the explosion—

Farjeon started up from the pillow.

But the state police, he whispered anxiously, they was in on the whole thing.

Jessie shook her head.

Only them two, she said, the ones that was killed in the blast. Jack, listen to me—

She pressed him back into the bolster, gently, so as not to touch his bandaged forearms, burned in the rescue of Cotter.

347

Listen to me, Jack, she went on. The nightmare—it's done—it's finished now, Jack.

She smiled, nodding.

Janders was arrested. The whole thing's exposed. Jack, it's done.

He stared at the window, not blinking, thoughtful.

And Cotter? he whispered.

Jessie shook her head.

He died, she said, while they was getting him to the ambulance.

And what about Turley? Farjeon said anxiously. He threatened you.

Jessie shook her head. Dead too, she said. In the blast.

Farjeon turned his head slowly, looking at her. He thought a moment, then nodded. He glanced down at his bandages.

When I get these off, he said, there's a thing I've got to do.

What thing, Jack?

I've got to go to Wheeling, he said.

She studied him, the smile fading from her mouth.

Why, I've got to buy something, he said gravely. A thing—

His gray eyes narrowed.

—a thing I swore once, he said, and never got around to—

Jessie stared at his face, her heart chilled in that moment.

Jack, no, she whispered. Jack, it's ended.

No, he said solemnly. It's a thing I swore. And somehow I never got around to it. A thing I have to buy, Jess—in that Wheeling store.

Jessie turned away from him, rose and went to the window.

It was a thing you wanted, Jess, he said quietly, gravely, his gaze following her. And I promised it to you that night.

She turned and glared at him now, her violet eyes blazing.

Jack, I don't want it now, she whispered. That's done with.

He pressed his lips tight, struggling against a smile.

The store was closed that night, he said. It was too late that night, Jess. I hope it's still there—

He grinned at her now.

348

—that hat, he said. With the flower. Jess, it was the prettiest flower.

Now she flung herself upon him, pressing him back into the bolster, heedless of him lying there with his bandaged arms stretched to either side of her.

The prettiest flower, he murmured into her hair. Mind, Jess, you asked me when I left that winter morning—you asked me to bring you that—a pretty flower. Jess, I hope that hat with that flower—I hope it's still there—in that window—

The old woman stood on the threshold of the small, stark house in which they had all so striven and sought and suffered in the weeks of that strange winter's month. She could hear the voices of Farjeon and the girl in the bedroom beyond. She smiled at the murmur of them. Surely there was still an edge of contention in their voices, she could tell that they were still fretting themselves one against the other, moving toward their total answer. Yet there was fresh hope and love and joy in their murmurings, a sound fresh as the redbird's April cry which fled upward now on the bright spring wind blowing up the smoky road now against the old woman's face. She turned from the threshold of the shack then, took a few steps, then paused, pondering over whether there was anything she might still do for them. After that moment's reflection she shook herself crossly and turned toward the road.

They're together now, she said. And Christ be thanked, all of the madness in his eyes, in his voice, in his soul—it's all of it gone now. Clean gone.

She smiled.

And Jessie, she said, I reckon now she'll find a way. A way to let herself be loved! I pray God she will.

She shook her shoulders in the bright morning sunlight and glanced at the far-off throngs round the portal of the smoking, ruined mine. Turley, Bonar, Soames—all dead now—dead with thirty others. She fought back the trembling of her mouth and moved off up the thawing ruts of the road.

Pray for the dead, she whispered. And fight like hell for the living!

And then she moved on, her pace quickening, her mind racing with the fresh, bright instinct of work still to be done in that place, unknown, to which her feet would surely find a way.